The Bear, the and the Wolf

Volume One of the Dark Age Chronicles

Chris Flynn

First published in 2016
ISBN: 978-1-326-58537-2

Copyright © C. Flynn 2016

C. Flynn exerts the moral right to be identified as the author of this work

All rights reserved. No part of this publication may be reproduced, stored in a retrieval system or transmitted in any form or by any means, electronic, mechanical, photocopying, recording or otherwise without the prior permission of the publishers

PublishNation
www.publishnation.co.uk

Acknowledgements

To Lynn Bowden and Margaret Ellis, thanks for the diligent editing, support and encouragement. Thanks to Anita Skinner for the excellent cover design and to Sheila Broun for some of the ritual incantations. A heartfelt acknowledgement goes to the team at 'Bland on the Run Books,' **www.botrbooks.com** for the opportunity to break with tradition and portray Arthur in a different light. Thanks also to Publish Nation for their preparation and marketing services.

Chris Flynn

Dedication

**For Doug Greenwood.
Full sails and calm seas
Chris Flynn, April 2016**

Preface

There is an Arthurian genre, which perpetuates a literary legacy of the myth of Athur in Romance, stories, poetry, prose and film. This well established genre represents a well trodden minefield for those who wish to re-interpret the mythology. It is also, for the most part, abstracted from the history of the Arthurian era.

This first book in the 'Dark Age Chronicles' recounts events of Dark Age history and draws upon research of Britain post 410 AD.

I can remember seeing the film 'Excalibur' when it was first released, and how mortified I was at the liberties of those who sought to visualise the mythology of Arthur.

I have maintained the mythology of the era, counter-posed against historical events and the coming of age of the first in a line of Arthurian figures, rooted in the genealogy of the period.

There is also the sense of redressing an historical error in that the English have made the most capital from Arthur's story. Yet, there is now little doubt from the evidence that this Celtic hero was a significant part of the histories of the Scots, Welsh and Irish, at a time when the English were the enemy. This work is an honest attempt to restore Arthur to his own people.

Chris Flynn

Glossary

In keeping with my quest to historicise the Arthurian age, I have used names from research texts.

The British are the Romano-British, a population of mixed Roman and British blood, blending the various peoples who made up Roman armies of occupation until they withdrew from British shores in 410 AD with the indigenous tribes that populated Britain before the Roman invasion.

The Romans ventured into a vast territory north of Hadrian's Wall to subdue the Pictish tribes. Despite military success, they never fully brought the region into the empire. The Votadini Tribe acted as a buffer between the Roman administration south of the wall and the Pictish tribes to the north of it. Thus, the Votadini were never considered British by those living south of the wall.

The Irish were known at that time as the Scotti. Their kings were called Ri's. A Ri Coiced was a king of a fifth of the current Irish landmass. In this era, Ireland was divided into the fifths of Muma, Mide, Laigin, Connachta and Ulaid. A Ri Feinnidh was a commander of an army.

The Saxons were a loose alliance of raiders. The term is used collectively to include Angles, Frisians and Jutes, all of whom took advantage of the weakness of the Romano-British to raid in the mid 400's AD. A collective name for these peoples was Sais.

Military Classifications

Romano-British forces were divided into regular trained troops, Comitatus (infantry) and Commanipulares (cavalry). Additionally, local untrained militias were used, plus warriors from the wilder regions who might have been infantry or cavalry.

Weapons were varied among the different peoples. The Saxons used the 'scaramaseax' a long single edged blade with a bound horn or wooden handle. The 'seax' was a shortened version and used as a dagger. The six foot infantry spear was called a 'gar.'

Votadini tactics were different from most of the Romano-British. They were predominantly cavalrymen who had blended Roman, Sarmatian and tribal tactics. Horsemen were armed with javelins, swords and shields. Select troops carried the eastern kontos, a long two-handed spear. This allowed them to approach enemy foot troops and stab at them.

The Draco was a form of banner, used by cavalry to terrify the enemy. It took the form of a hollow material balloon in the form of an elongated dragon. Some researchers suggest that a whistle device was fitted inside the Draco, which rose to a crescendo as the wind rushed through it when the cavalry charged.

Characters

The Votadini

Cunedda - King of the Votadini & Gwawl, his wife
Enniaun Girt - Cunedda's eldest son & Ceri, his wife
Cunorix - Cunneda's son
Owain - son of Enniaun and Ceri
Elen - Owain's sister
Ewain White Tooth - Owain's brother
Cadwallon - Owain's brother

Map territories: Guotodin (Traprain Law) and Gwynedd (Dinas Ffynon)

The Romans

Ambrosius Aurelianus/Emrys Wledig
Leontinus - Companion to Ambrosius
Theoderic - Ambrosius's friend and second in command
Seconius - cavalry troop leader

Map territories: Brittany

The Vortigerns

Vitalus the Vortigern - High King of Britain
Servilla - wife to Vitalus, sister to Ambrosius
Brittu - the Vortimer, eldest son
Pascent - younger son
Lucilla - daughter

Map territories; Powys

The Essylwg

Tendubric - The Pendragon of Gwent and Siluria
Bronwen - his wife
Meurig - eldest son
Creiddylad/Creiddy - daughter
Artwerys - Creiddy's son
Cynvelyn - Governor of Gwynedd & Tendubric's brother

Map territories: Gwent, Gwynedd and Siluria

The Barbarians

Hengist - leader of Frisian mercenaries
Hrosa - his brother
Rhonwen - Hengist's daughter
Octha - Hengist's eldest son
Ebissa - Hengist's youngest son
Albric - Hengist's Wyrdman/seer

Map territories: Ruchin/Thanet & Ceint

The Scotti

Loegaire - Ri Coiced of Connachta
Callum McGrall - Ri Feinnidh of Connachta
Finian - Loegaire's servant
Faustus - Loegaire's stepson
Lugid - Loegaire's son

Map territories: Connachta & Laigin

Bishops & Spiritual Characters

Bishop Agricola - Vitalus' main adviser
Bishop Germanus - Papl Envoy & Bishop of Auxerre
Filan - Druid to the Votadini family
Lailoken - Owain's first tutor
Cullorn - a Pictish Druid
Crenda - his apprentice
The Lady of the Forest - Owain's second tutor
Father Jerome - Priest to Traprain Law

Owain's Companions

Edern - a Pictish warrior and closest friend
Gwalchma
Gilvaethwy
Cust
Maelwas
Gweveyel

Others

Gwyrangon - Governor of Anderida
Coel the Young - King of Rheged
Germanianus of the Cornovii - ally to Enniaun Girt
Drust - High King of the Picts
Marcellus Plautius - Governor of Dumnonia
Marcellus Plautinus - Governor of Calleva
Mark - King of Kernow
Moriutned - friend to Vitalus

Part One

Child of the Bear

1. The Shifters
2. The Wild Man
3. Ceri's Grief
4. The Oracle of the Wise
5. The Way of the Warrior – Edern's Lesson
6. The Sword of the Ninth
7. Magus Making
8. Owain's Totem
9. Arth-Ursus
10. The Staff of Owain the Bear
11. The Exile
12. Unwanted Allies
13. Conspiracy
14. The Scotti King
15. Lucilla's Fear
16. The Wolf and the Staff

Part Two

The Saxon Menace

17. **The Sickening Land**
18. **Servilla's Revenge**
19. **Homecoming**
20. **Summer Bride and Forest Lady**
21. **Pious Treachery**
22. **Artwerys**
23. **Egelsprep/Rhyd Ar Afael**
24. **Wicked Peace**
25. **When Kings Make War**
26. **The Bear, the Dragon and the Cross**
27. **Glevum**
28. **Rome's Star**

Britain & Ireland 425AD

Part 1

Child of the Bear

'This is that Arthur of whom modern Welsh fancy raves. Yet he plainly deserves to be remembered in genuine history rather than in the oblivion of silly fairy tales; for he long preserved his dying country.'

William of Malmesbury

1. The Shifters

428 AD - North Guotodin

In the pre-dawn, warriors of the Votadini waited in the grey silence before the first birdsong. The slightest sound would lose them the element of surprise: a spear shaft catching a shield's edge; a snapped twig; a cleared throat; all these were their enemies along with the Picts who approached through the swirling mist.

The Votadini lined the stream bank; a deep cut in the earth the gully's gurgling water was a spear-length wide ally that surged to join the river. The Picts must cross to carry out their raid and here the stream was at its narrowest.

Several paces behind them, where the alder and birch gave way to feathery green bracken fronds, a squirming figure crawled slowly through the undergrowth. A mop of tousled brown hair bobbed above the leaves that hid Owain Ddantgwyn. He wore a tunic that hung loosely on his body. His mellow hazel eyes fought against the swirls of mist to catch sight of a cloak or a helmet; anything to pinpoint his father's warriors.

His russet cloak was belted on the outside to prevent it from disturbing the foliage, a trick he'd learned from flushing small game with the village boys. Ceri, his mother, scolded him for the time he spent with them, but his tutor, Filan counselled that men of standing achieved their position by learning from all who had knowledge to offer. Running wild was preferable to being bullied by his older brothers, Ewein and Cadwallon, who resented Ceri's affection for him.

Enniaun Girt, his father rarely interfered in domestic routines. He was away campaigning much of the time. On this occasion, however, Owain knew he could expect a serious thrashing if he were seen.

Enniaun's instructions had been clear; when the warriors left the village, Owain was to stay behind with Filan.

A shiver ran through him, a mixture of anticipation at seeing his first real skirmish and the knowledge that his disobedience had passed its former limits. Still, how much could a budding warrior learn from the exercise yard? He was sick of being battered to the ground by his older brothers' wooden swords. He'd tasted enough summer dust and winter mud to last a life time. He ran a grimy finger across his swollen lips. Yesterday's training had proved no exception. The lure of real battle drew him now, moth to candle, with no thought of the flame.

The crawl left him sweating, despite the pre-dawn chill. His keen eyes missed their mark. No maroon parade cloaks to help him here; the men wore faded grey, green and madder to blend with willows, alder, bracken and the argent dawn light. The mist thinned, but hung in whorls nearest to the brook. An inner doubt fought his obstinacy, but he quelled it, wriggling closer. A spider crawled across his hand, tickling as it skittered into the brown crushed leaves.

Somewhere ahead thirty of his father's warriors crouched, awaiting the Picts. Those of his own people who held to the old ways called them 'shifters,' swearing that they weren't human at all, but woodland spirits who took on manly shapes to steal cattle, sheep and horses before disappearing back into the otherworld. The Picts appeared and vanished like ghosts. Black and green checked cloaks made them all but invisible in dense forest and their bodies, painted in dark blue tattoos of eagle, snake and deer; swirls, circles and spirals, held the wisdom of nature known only to their wise ones.

The Votadini respected the Picts as wily adversaries because their larch and pine clad lands led them to favour ambush, skirmish and raids. Owain's people favoured warring from the back of a horse, a form of combat learned from alliance with the legions, until they left British shores eighteen years previously. A warrior should look his enemy in the eye; so his father said. Of all their adversaries, Enniaun hated facing Picts more than the Scotti or the Romano-British. He'd asked Filan how a bard could sing of victory when fighting painted men meant that you spent most of the time sitting on your arse or chasing shadows. The wise druid had kept his counsel.

Owain paused where the pale bracken fronds gave way to open ground. Forty paces beyond, the bark of silver birches glistened in the eerie light. He dare advance no further across the emerald shoots of spring grass. He half rose, to secure a better view. A slight movement to his right rewarded his persistence; a Votadini cloak. Elation was quickly tempered by the recognition that he'd moved too far to the left, the direction from which any 'shifter' flank attack would come. Triumph gave way to a flicker of concern. A grey cloak loomed towards him out of the mist like a wraith from his dreams. Other eyes looked on; Morgana, goddess of the dark, in her guise as the black crow, perched silently in a great oak to his right. Owain's heart went stone cold. Despite Filan's warnings about the dangers of superstition, Morgana never augured advantage. He ducked back into the bracken, fighting the urge to run.

Firm hands gripped his cloak. He struggled vainly, but was hauled to his feet. Never in all his years had he seen such anger in the steely gaze of his father. At that instant a thrashing seemed the lightest punishment he might expect. What reckoning might his father wreak, fuelled by such rage? Wordlessly, Enniaun pointed firmly in the direction of the village, reinforcing the gesture with a hefty push from his linden shield. Owain turned, head low, his face suffused in a rising red tide. The worst that his father might impose was nothing to the ridicule that his brothers would inflict. He'd not dare to eat at table for weeks.

The puppy look that oft countered his mother's anger had never worked on his father. He wasn't about to try it now. Yet some acknowledgement of his foolishness was merited. He turned to offer some gesture and stood transfixed, his mouth open, eyes wide and staring. Behind his father Pictish warriors dashed into view, splashes of green and black against the foliage. The Votadini flank guard was lost to the shifters' forest craft. Seeing the terror on Owain's face, Enniaun turned; the crafted steel of his Roman sword slid easily from its goose-greased scabbard. He strained for a solution that would safeguard his disobedient son and his warband. Owain jolted from his trance, turned to run, looking over his shoulder as he bolted.

The foremost enemy ran with their short bows drawn. Owain heard his father yelling for his warriors to retreat from the stream bank. Enniaun veered towards the advancing Picts on an angle to thwart their aim.

Owain's heart beat faster than the pace of his reluctant legs. His tongue clove to the roof of his mouth; his stomach twisted and he felt his gorge rise. Disturbed by the running men, the crow leapt from its perch, flapping away in ungainly flight. His folly might cost the life of his father and the whole warrior band. He couldn't tear his eyes from the scene behind him. The swift footfalls of his father's hearth troops flayed through the bracken as they rushed to his aid. Arrows flew; one pierced Enniaun's shield and Owain ducked as though the barb had flown at him. Another hissed narrowly past Enniaun's shoulder, sheering bark from a birch behind him. He lanced into the Picts, his mail byrnie too robust for their light spears. Two fell to deft sword strokes past their flimsy wicker shields. His headlong rush carried him into three more, too slow to avoid him. They backed off warily; scowling tattooed faces peering from behind their square latticed shields. Owain heard warriors shouting that more shifters had crossed the stream. Enniaun would soon be isolated. Six of his warriors reached him, walling their shields. A flurry of arrows forced them back, rattling like rain on thatch.

Owain breathed more easily. In a disciplined knot the warriors retreated, Enniaun at their centre, his polished helmet a head taller than those of his guardians. Arrows thudded into the shield wall or clattered into the bracken, but step by step the Votadini withdrew to safety.

The Picts yelled insults and curses, yet Owain could see that only three Votadini sported bloody gashes from arrows. A disaster had been averted; his father was safe. A sigh escaped his tense lips; his thoughts turned once again to the punishment that awaited him. He forced his gaze away from the skirmish. While turning, his ankle caught in the root of a gnarled oak. He pitched forwards, striking his head against the unyielding bark of the trunk. Darkness rescued him from thoughts of his father's anger.

***

A stiff breeze rustled the topmost branches of mature oaks, hissing like surf. Owain roused from unconsciousness; his head throbbed. Shaky fingers traced the jagged cut across his brow. The blood was dry. He was irked by the thought that his first scar had been inflicted by an innocent oak.

Groggy from the blow and sick with fear, he sensed his danger. Steadying himself, he crept cautiously towards the village. His absence would have been noticed and he cursed himself for the risks that his stupidity had brought.

Silver stars pierced the forest gloom. Now he needed warrior skills to see him safely home. Squinting into the deep-purple darkness, he whispered promised offerings to Arawn, Lord of the Underworld and Protector of the Lost for a safe passage. The forest suddenly cast moving shadows all around him. He turned to flee, but the circle of painted warriors tightened, trapping him at its centre. Grinning tattooed faces loomed over him. The prick of steel at Owain's throat banished Filan's words on how a young lord should disport himself in the face of the enemy. Fear tasted like metal on his tongue.

***

Edern had but thirteen summers when in his first raid he came across the boy who would mark his life so heavily. No fires were set; the Votadini village was too close. The warriors dragged the crumpled youngster into the Pictish camp. This was no village lad. A torc of gold graced his throat and his cloak was of the finest weave, though smudged with earth and trailing bracken leaves.

Edern watched the elder warriors quarrel. Some were keen to press home the attack, for Drust, the king, had urged them to take what they could to swell his war chest. They squabbled until Baran went off in the dark with the two wise ones. Edern heard later that Cullorn had cast the stones and talked earnestly with Baran for a good while. Whatever was said did not pass to the lesser warriors. Baran did not even wait for the sky to pale before ordering a retreat. The boy was of royal standing and would fetch more in ransom than any plunder.

Ranesh led the discontented. 'Have we not come from our highlands to raid this Manaw of the Guotodin,' he railed? 'Is this not the bull time, the season for war? Will our spears return unblooded? Are we children to ignore our battle skills?' Some younger warriors, roused by his words, brandished their spears and clamoured to resume the attack.

When Ranesh raged further, Cullorn calmed him with whispered secrets of the stones. Baran set Ranesh and the twenty strongest objectors to guard the rear to distract any pursuers. They could keep any booty they took. His wise decision pacified the more reckless. To stay with the rearguard was Edern's best hope for a trinket to start his warrior hoard. But he saw the look on Cullorn's face when he and Baran returned to speak to the men and some kindly spirit led him to believe that an advantage might be had from being near the captive. So he turned with the main body back towards Caledonii lands.

It was not long before Edern received his reward. Baran himself sought the young warrior out as the sky paled into a new day. They were resting, well in advance of any pursuit.

'Well, Edern, long miles for young feet and little gain, eh?'

'There will be other raids, lord,' he answered, awed by the leader's presence.

'Cheer yourself, Edern. All's not lost. This Votadini lord is not far off your age and I'd have you bide by him until we return. Keep an eye on him and I'll see the king knows about it.'

'I'll mind him well, lord,' he stammered, inwardly celebrating his good fortune.

Baran gestured with a thumb over his shoulder.

The boy was slumped in a sorry, damp state, resting with his back to a small boulder. His eyes flared defiance at Edern's approach, yet there was naught but desperation in it. The dampness of his cloak and the dried blood across his face told the tale, though there was still fight in him and Edern admired him for it.

Owain was wretched after a sleepless night. For the first time the real consequences of his disobedience replaced thoughts of his father's wrath. He was damp to the skin with dew; the pleasures of the warm bath house at the family fortress, Traprain Law, seemed lost forever. His head throbbed, his legs shook when he stood and he struggled to follow Filan's tuition to fight the tears that welled behind his eyes. There was no comfort here. No grandmother Gwawl to nurse him, no Ceri to soothe his hurts with herbal swabs and beakers of warm milk. Not even the rasping tongue of his hound, Balan and the doting look from his faithful brown eyes. Worse, he had no knowledge of what the shifters would do. His mind played tricks, flitting from Filan's teaching about being held for ransom, to the worst his imagination could conjure. The Pictish leader seemed to bear him no ill will; a big bear of a man with a foxskin cape and clinking bands of gold on both thick wrists. But some younger warriors eyed Owain's torc enviously and one particularly tall and fierce looking shifter had shot him regular darts of malice from eyes that flashed resentment. Were it down to him, Owain thought he might well be spitted like a boar and eaten. It was a relief to find that when they rose in the early dawn, this warrior, along with several other youngbloods, were absent. A younger warrior sat next to him with a curious appraising look. He had but one tattoo, a circle, on his left cheek. His plain woollen tunic lacked adornment; he wore no jewellery and might have been a slave or servant by his manner.

Over a frugal breakfast of dried berries, crushed in an oatmeal paste, Owain realised that being among strangers would be no easy matter. The slop, served in a plain wooden bowl, made him gag. His hunger made him force it down, but his wry face showed his mind. It didn't help when his guard burst into laughter. He thought to throw the bowl, but considered his plight was parlous enough.

Despite his reluctance, Owain found himself listening carefully as the young warrior talked, with no recognition that his charge understood not a word. In his lessons Filan always stressed the importance of learning from new experiences. Pictish words sounded similar to Owain's Brythonic, but more complex. On the morning march, Owain traded names with the young warrior for the hills over which they trudged; for the larch and pine that towered over them, for the spring fresh brooks that soaked their feet. By the second day of the trek they had mastered sufficient differences between their tongues to talk. They snaked along secret hunting trails. The sky was bright azure and the sun raised tendrils of mist from their drying cloaks.

'What will become of me, when we reach your lands, Edern?' Owain asked.

'You are high born, lord. A ransom might suit my king's purpose, but I've no insight into his head, Owain.'

Owain nodded sombrely, resigning himself to a long period away from his kin. He saw that Edern watched him suspiciously and knew that even if the young warrior was aware of his fate, it was unlikely that he'd share the knowledge.

'How did you come to be taken so far from your own warriors?'

'I was foolish, Edern. I hid to see the ambush. My father caught me and as I ran away, I stumbled and lost my senses for a while. At least this capture has spared my royal arse a tanning.'

'You'll be well treated, lord. Your people think us Caledonii brutes. We paint our bodies and grow our hair long, but we're no savages.'

'You seem not so far removed from us. If I should be ransomed, then it's no bad thing to have this view of another people while I'm so young. Filan, my tutor, urges me to seek advantage in any setback. Few of my people have ever seen the land of the painted men. I consider this abduction a privilege, Edern, and you shall be my guide in the venture.' He grinned, his spirit uplifted by the conversation.

'I'll be a willing guide, Owain. This is the closest I've been to a high born in my life, and it's an honour for me too,' though inwardly Edern thanked Baran for his favour. His standing in the tribe might rise quickly with the reward from this duty. They marched into the high northlands with the rising sun warming their backs.

***

Enniaun was distressed when the Picts failed to attack the following morning. The village defences were bolstered by a further fifteen spears and riders despatched for help to nearby settlements. What men he could spare had been sent to search for Owain, a perilous quest with the enemy so close. They had returned with grim news. The forest seemed to have swallowed the boy.

They waited until the sun was at its zenith before Enniaun stood his men down. Warriors hung their spears and shields in their dwellings. Horses and cattle were tended; women and children entered the woodland to forage for roots; older boys fished the streams and laid snares for rabbits and smiths pounded on metal. This season of the hawk moon, Giamonios, the time that the shoots show, also heralded the season for war; spears, swords and shields were crafted in the hot forges.

Enniaun was consoled by Filan the druid and the village headman, Brec, a burly former warrior, who carried a scar across his face where an enemy spear had seared his craggy features. Enniaun remembered the crow on the battlefield. Sometimes he wished he did not believe so much in the world that lay behind this one. He remained uneasy. The old spirits of the land lurked yet in the twilight of their grip on men's minds. For all their preaching, the 'hung god's' priests proved poor adversaries against the old ways. The certainty that Rome had bestowed was lost in changes that challenged the Votadini and himself. In the turmoil of unpredictability, Enniaun's strength was maintained by a commitment to his people. It anchored him in a time of doubt.

'Young Owain will be held hostage for ransom. Have no fear for him, all will be well,' Filan said.

'My father's treasury alone can stand the loss if it's to be a ransom. I'll be held to account as usual and I have to face the boy's mother too,' Enniaun replied.

'I'd rather face the King, than Ceri,' Brec said, feigned horror creasing his face. 'Still, better that Owain's taken by the painted men, than dead. What if you'd lost him for good eh, Enniaun? The boy still lives and your father's coin will free him.'

'If that's supposed to make it easier for me to face my wife, it doesn't, Brec, but I thank you for the attempt.'

The old warrior lifted his bulky frame from the bench. 'I must be about some village matters, the last few days have been disruptive and we're at odds with our tasks. Good luck Enniaun, the owl be with you.'

When the headman left, an unusually quiet Filan placed a hand on Enniaun's shoulder.

'Don't be too hard on yourself. No harm will come to the boy. There are mysteries we still see. There's much you should know about your son that I can't divulge. But, forget Morgana the crow - she was merely a sign of misfortune at the skirmish. Owain won't rot in some Pictish village, believe me. He has a life to lead shaped by power. I'll be with you when you meet your father and when you confront Ceri. So, cheer yourself and assemble the men.'

Buoyed by the druid's words, Enniaun's spirit rose. Delaying the inevitable confrontation with Ceri would only make matters worse. If word of Owain did not come soon, he would march for Traprain Law, his father's stronghold.

***

The Pictish warband wound its way slowly northwards. It was the first time Owain had experienced a landscape so different from his own. He had seen nothing like the craggy heights of the Pictish domain, nor the wild beauty of its lakes and glens. The pine forests were dense; river and stream banks turned valley bottoms into marsh and swamp. Yellow gorse snagged at any loose cloak on the high moor land; eagles soared over heather clad hills He could see why Enniaun and his grandfather, Cunedda rarely ventured into the Picts' domain. Here was no terrain for cavalry. Thoughts of Votadini horses heightened his loneliness. Though he missed Filan, Ceri and his grandmother Gwawl, his greatest sense of loss was for Mabon, his dun pony and Balan his hound. Filan's wise tuition on uncertainty was all he had to combat his inner dread. Some days his tutor's words were sovereign, on others his fears tormented him, trapping him in a surly silence.

***

Cullorn, the Pictish seer, and his young apprentice, Crenda, sat apart from the warriors; settled in for another cool, spring night in a sheltered glen. They talked of the spring equinox, when raids were launched against their southern neighbours; the time of the 'crowing cock,' when nature was shocked into germination and growth. It was beyond warriors to know that the equinox also signified illusion, but the seers knew this.

The fire sparked and fizzed, the wood still damp from winter's grasp. Cullorn spoke quietly. Crenda strained against the crackle of the fire to hear his master's words.

'All is not what it seems, Crenda.'

'The boy is not a royal one of his people?'

'You miss the features of the equinox,' said the elder man, leaving the field open for his pupil's interpretation.

'It is the time of the fool and the trickster; all is not what it seems. It follows, therefore that this boy might not be of Votadini blood, despite his outer trappings.'

The elder druid acknowledged the effort with a nod.

'Yes, you see the energies and their formulation, Crenda, well done. But, you misinterpret the boy's position. Perhaps the trickster plays in your own head, eh? Perhaps you are the fool,' he chuckled. 'A lesson for the equinox. Heed the point and be like the fox.'

Crenda paused, a dead branch held halfway to the flames. It had not occurred to him that a druid might also be influenced by the very forces and powers that they interpreted on others' behalf. He committed the insight to his growing store of knowledge.

Cullorn stared into the fire, aged grey eyes glittered brightly as the flames began to dance. 'Suppose the boy was a great deal more than a Votadini royal one?'

'How could that be, master?'

Cullorn tutted at the unsubtle reply.

'Sometimes I think you'd fare better as a priest of the hanged god than as a scholar of the mysteries.'

Crenda's mouth set in a tight line of concentration. Cullorn rarely scolded him. He was missing something very important to receive such a rebuke.

'You are thinking within the confines of the everyday world, pupil. That answer would have been worthy of a warrior, a merchant, or even a pot boy - but not a druid.'

'I shall consider the matter,'

'Think on it that you do. I'm getting old and there are shapes here that concern your own future. The equinox is about more than just the trickster's domain. What else does it signify? There lie clues for your consideration.'

With that the elder druid resumed his staring into the flames. Crenda's thoughts whirled like the wispy smoke from the now established fire.

***

Two days and nights passed in the village with no further sign of the Picts. Enniaun despaired at the loss of his son. He suffered alone, keeping largely to his dwelling. After three days he mustered his hearth troops. Morose and self absorbed, he rode for the Guotodin to share his loss with his father, Cunedda, the king and Owain's mother, Ceri.

2. The Wild Man

428 AD - Pictish Stronghold in Caledonii

A grey drizzle drenched the walking Picts. Clouds hung so low that Owain was amazed that the band found its destination at all. The men became increasingly jovial when they were welcomed into the shelter of the solidly built halls of their kinsmen. Edern confirmed that they were nearing the end of their long march and uncertainty coiled in Owain's gut with the anticipation of his fate.

It was a luxury to sleep indoors, for the further north they marched, the more the cold intensified. Seldom used to being outdoors for long periods, Owain was strengthened by the march. His muscles developed and his skin was ruddied by wind and weather to the texture of soft leather. Meagre rations vanquished his puppy fat. There was little about his appearance to show his standing, except for the gold torc that still graced his neck.

Nearing Drust's settlement, Owain saw a sizeable number of hutments set out on the shore of a huge grey lake, at the foot of a high mountain. A wooden palisade enclosed the dwellings. The band broke up when they reached the gates. Warriors were embraced by their families. There remained only those who lacked local kin, the two druids and Baran. Owain stayed close to Edern.

Drust held court in a stone built, turf-roofed hall, amidst a boisterous chaos of warriors, servants, slaves and hunting dogs, all warmed by a roaring central fire. The clamour lessened slightly when Baran entered.

Owain watched the warband leader bow before the huge man seated at the head of the table. Taller than most of his warriors and well girthed, Baran was still dwarfed by Drust. Black locks flowed down his back, matching a fearsome beard. His hands seemed capable of pulling up trees by the roots. He sat with his companions, his checked tunic held by a monstrous leather belt. His only ornamentation was a gold bracelet that banded the muscles of his left bicep. Tattoos of eagle and deer darkened his face, adding to his ominous appearance.

Owain gulped back bile. Despite Edern's assurance that he would be ransomed, the sheer size of the Pictish king threw his fate into doubt. Remembering his lineage, Owain concentrated furiously on Filan's schooling about breathing deeply and found his courage. Achieving a sense of calm, he listened intently.

Baran was greeted warmly by the king. 'So, my warrior returns to the hearth. Take mead, Baran and tell us of your raid. The men are eager for your tales.'

'No plunder, my lord, but I bring you riches of sorts.'

'You speak in riddles, Baran. Tell us more,' boomed Drust.

'I bring you a rare prize, lord, a fledgling of the royal line of the Votadini, Cunedda's grandson, Owain Ddantgwyn.'

The noise in the hall subsided to whispers; Baran beckoned for Owain to stand before him.

'Is this true, boy?' the king asked, fixing him with ice blue eyes.

Owain thrust his chin forward and drew on his courage.

'I am Owain Ddantgwyn, son of Enniaun Girt, grandson of Cunedda, Lord of the Votadini,' he announced, remembering to raise his voice and pace his words so they carried the impact of his station. Despite the queasy clutch of fear in his gut he forced himself to match the king's gaze.

'Well, Baran; gold indeed,' mused Drust, clapping his war band leader on the back in a gesture that left him gasping for breath. 'No small gain here, eh? You've done well. What will this cost me?'

'My thanks, lord. The men would welcome any compensation for their lack of spoils. As for myself, I ask for command of your first newly built fighting ship.'

'So be it, Baran. You'll have your ship and the men their reward. He's worth more than a few baubles. Will you be our guest, boy; until your grandfather pays for your release?'

Owain paused slightly for effect. Filan had counselled that enemies treated prisoners on the basis of their bearing. Fighting the snake of fear that lurked just below his composure he replied: 'I am shamed, my lord. The fault for my capture was all my own. Were it within my power I'd have my grandfather keep his purse strings tight and dwell with you in this miserable, wet place until you wearied of my mischief and let me go.'

The Pictish warriors thumped on the table with beakers and knives. Drust's raised arm silenced them.

'You speak well for one so young. But, your time here shall be short until your grandfather's silver reaches us,' the Overking replied, but the glee in his eyes mirrored that of his men.

Drust turned to share their jests, when the doors to the hall crashed open. Owain turned to witness the entry of a fearsome creature. The company fell silent. Mist swirled in behind a tall, thin gaunt figure with unkempt grey hair and beard. It wore a plain woollen robe with a long dark grey cloak clasped to its throat by an amber brooch. Sprigs of oak leaves adorned its head and its large owlish eyes had an empty unfocused look; as vacant as the sockets in the skull of the small creature that topped its ash staff

Even Drust faltered when the figure loomed over Owain's left shoulder. The boy glanced up nervously as a reedy voice broke the silence.

'This boy will not be ransomed, lord King. I, Lailoken, lay claim to him.'

Owain saw that Drust was visibly shaken. His rich prize was in jeopardy and yet, for all his kingly bearing, there was a high degree of respect in his voice when he answered.

'The boy's future is agreed 'twixt I and his captor. What madness is this?'

The ancient one turned his head slightly, looking at the rafters above the king's head. His eyes swept the hall, but none would meet his gaze.

'Eight years have ye ruled this land, lord King. Ye'd risk your tenure by denying my request?'

Owain sensed the silent warriors bristle with hostility. The veiled threat further alienated the newcomer from his audience. Drust's answer was statesmanlike, though his brow was still furrowed.

'Test me not to my extremes, holy man. You have my respect, but no man threatens me in my own hall. My people have need of ships; his grandfather has the coin to pay for them. Why should I sacrifice such advantage to an old man's whim?'

The response was a wheezing cackle, difficult to interpret as either a disease of the chest or a laugh.

'Lord King. You know that there are matters to do with the people that have no bearing on coin, or keeping the baying Maelcon from your hall. This is such a matter. Ask your own advisors. I see the remains of the Druid order in the shape of Cullorn there. Ask him if this claim is not just.'

Drust nursed the request just long enough to exert his authority, musing on the old man's words, before beckoning the druid to his side. Owain craned his neck to hear them, but they spoke in whispers too low for even his sharp ears.

'What's he gibbering about, Cullorn? Is there more I should know about this boy? Who is this old owl to preach to me?'

Cullorn replied cautiously, supporting his weight with a hand on the huge chair back.

'Lord King, he is 'Lailoken the Mad,' neither priest, nor druid, yet he's envied by many sages. The stones say that this Owain is of power, lord. Here is no trivial thing. If Lailoken makes such a claim it is made from visions he sees that I cannot.'

Drust heeded the counsel. Cullorn rarely worshipped anyone else's sun. He was a fractious old man, much famed for his denunciation of the Christian priests who boldly ventured north to appeal to Pictish beliefs in the hope of gaining fresh converts to their blessed one God and his son.

'Then we shall make this work to our advantage, Cullorn. The boy shall go with Lailoken. If harm comes to him, Cunedda can't lay the blame at our door, eh? This suits us well.'

Owain watched their faces, struggling to interpret the sense of their speech from their expressions. Earlier feelings of unease were changing to dread. He feared the worst.

Drust turned to his people. 'There is power at work here, beyond the ken of kings and warriors. Cullorn, our Druid confirms it. However, the well-being of the people is my duty. The boy may go with you, Lailoken, until his grandfather responds to my ransom demands. I'll not cede him beyond then. But if it is the way of power, your claim holds until that time.'

Owain's heart sank. Any advantage gained by his spirited words had dissipated. He had anticipated spending time with the Picts, learning their ways, adding to the store of knowledge that would aid his own people when he returned. The grip of a clawed hand on his shoulder only heightened his sense of despair.

'My lord, have I no say in this matter?' he addressed the king. 'I have no wish to be dragged away by a loathsome old man. I submitted to your authority and I request the sanctuary of your household, until my family seek my release.' He stood defiantly with his arms crossed, glaring up at the besieged Drust.

The king sighed and sat down, fondling the ear of a Scotti wolfhound that looked balefully at Owain from amber eyes.

'I would be happy to have you remain here, boy. Your company would be welcome when the summer nights slip into darkness. We would hear tales of your people. But there is something that this druid and this old man see that I cannot. I must bow to their wisdom. I am no man of the gods, but a warrior and a king. Perhaps there is something to gain from going with this Lailoken. I will send Edern with you. Baran tells me you have struck up a friendship on the journey here. That is the best I can do.'

Owain scowled, but held his peace. Edern nodded his assent reluctantly. His own reticence was sovereign to the king's will. The old man made no objection to Drust's concession. Lailoken bowed.

'Your wisdom does you honour, lord King. I accept your judgement. We shall do the best we can in the time we have.' Beckoning with a talon-like finger to the subdued Owain and Edern, the old man retreated from the hall. They followed in resistant silence through the ranks of curious onlookers.

Owain had been looking forward to a full platter of food, a change of clothing and to sleep on a comfortable bed. His weariness grew with the knowledge that he must now tramp behind this unknown man into the hostile northern hills. Edern was unsettled too. He was used to the company of his kin or other fighting men. Old men, especially those touched by the hand of gods or goddesses, were unknown to him and only his king's command stiffened his resolve. He followed the young captive and his new protector with his head down, shoulders hunched, out of the familiar surroundings he had marched so long to reach.

Edern recounted the tale many times in later years to any gathered assembly, when requested to speak of the time he met Owain.

'We left the snug warmth of the hall and followed the wild old man out into the darkness. We had few possessions with us, only the clothes we stood up in. Owain was quiet and said little. He disapproved of our new host and I had few words of comfort for him, struck dumb as I was by the apparition that we followed and my own unease. We walked for what seemed like an age, our downcast hearts made each step seem like a league.

'Eventually we reached the foothills and not too far into them, we saw the old man disappear underneath an overhang. When we reached the spot, there was a faint glow, barely cutting through the darkness. We ducked our heads and found ourselves in a large cave, the apparent dwelling of this strange elder, who now had both our destinies in his scrawny hands. He was bending over a small fire, adding fuel to the wan flame. The new sticks caught, lighting the surrounding walls, sending shivery, spirit-like shadows leaping and dancing.

The cave was dry. There were more scrolls than I had ever seen before in one place; rocks and crystals; trappings of a man of knowledge who walks in places that lesser mortals cannot reach. Warm sheepskins were laid ready, as though he knew that he'd have guests. He beckoned us to sit near the fire and we squatted as near to the heat as we could, for the night was cold.

'We have little time to complete all that needs to be done,' he said, addressing us both, though my recollection was that his words were mostly for Owain.

'Ye, young Owain, are to learn to be a mage. There's no point in denying this, it is a matter of need. Ye will thank me in the future when your time here helps ye to discern great men's concerns.'

This was a blunt beginning, and Owain said nought, but looked mazed at the frankness of the old man's speech. He then turned to me.

'The fates have taken an interest in ye, Edern. There will be advantage for ye here also, though what ye need to learn will differ from Owain. Your life has taken the path it follows because ye agreed to Baran's request to mind this lad. Your own choice has brought ye to this point. Now, ye must see the journey through.'

'I was confused. No sign from the gods showed me as any other than a budding warrior. Yet the old man was so sure of his words, that I felt the power of their persuasion.

'He beckoned us to the bedding, drawn close to the fire. The faraway look returned to his eyes. Though his words were for us, he stared into the distance, into the gap between the worlds. He chanted to us; we would become used to such rhymes in his teachings:

'Bed ye down young men, for the dawn brings ye great challenges:

What tortuous paths ye shall both tread
In wisdom, wit and oft-times dread
What mortal powers ye shall offend, with fashioned wills that will not bend
What tales and songs the bards will sing, but not for coin nor worldly thing
What deeds and quests await the spring, for the worldly warrior and the king not king'

'With his chanting rhyme completed, the old man shuffled in a faltering dance, screeched a laugh that would have chilled the hearts of the dead themselves and disappeared into the night, leaving us alone by the fire.'

3. Ceri's Grief

428 AD - Traprain Law, Capital of the Guotodin

The grief that ran through the Votadini at the news of Owain's loss was nothing compared to Ceri's weeping. Her raving sent the slaves scuttling to all corners of the hall to escape their tormented mistress. All Enniaun's attempts to placate her came to naught. He had to accept Ceri's ire.

She was slight in stature, willowy, with flowing copper tresses and eyes of palest blue. With her powerful blend of beauty and quick intelligence she was a match for her rangy husband.

Enniaun Girt's anticipation of her reaction marred his return. He'd reined in his favourite grey at the fringe of the forest earlier in the day and gazed across the cleared ground to where the mound of Traprain Law rose above the surrounding landscape. The welcoming sight of the Votadini stronghold always evoked a deep sense of contentment in him. Its impregnability was his respite from the sorties that took him to all parts of the Guotodin. His return was blighted by Owain's absence. He would be fortunate if he saw the haven of Ceri's bed. Sharing it was well beyond his expectations.

Traprain Law stared back at him across the open ground, where the Votadini's precious horses were being schooled. The stronghold had withstood the worst that its enemies could inflict on it. It was a legacy of his people's relationship with Rome. The solid stone of its foundations gave way to stout palisades with protective corner towers. The double gates were topped by a twin-towered rampart, which overlooked the approach. Fashioned by Roman engineers, it was a mark of the trust established between the Votadini and their masters. From its secure defences and those of its sister stronghold at Yeavering Bell, the Votadini had risen to prominence as the most affluent and powerful tribes of the territories beyond the wall that defined Rome's most northerly boundary.

A mount behind Enniaun whickered a greeting as the woodland fragrance gave way to the aroma of wood smoke and the tang of sweating horseflesh. He sensed the urgency of his men to be home. His own nose twitched at the familiarity of it. Sighing, he urged Cynrir into a walk, still reluctant to deliver his news.

The atmosphere in Enniaun's hall snared him in the edgy silence of a normally bustling household. Retainers, slaves and warriors avoided Ceri as if she had contracted the plague. He was hugely relieved when a servant brought him word that Cunedda wished to see him.

The Votadini King sat at the head of his huge table in the central hall, where supplicants gathered to hear his judgements. Two sleek hunting dogs at his feet continued to sleep as Enniaun entered. He was as familiar to them as their master; so many times had he hunted with his father.

Cunedda was stockier than his eldest son. His round face belied his steel. He was lounging in his huge chair, a maroon tunic trimmed with wolf fur standing in stark contrast to the hall's wooden furnishings. Rome had penetrated here too. Though no villa, the hall reflected long standing trade with the affluent southern provinces. Pottery, glassware and silver affirmed Votadini wealth. A bust of former Roman emperor Magnus Maximus, a gift to Cunedda's father, watched with a stern gaze from a carved plinth. The floor was flagged stone and the walls still boasted the red pigment and scenes of galloping horses; though they were fading now, like Cunedda's memories of the legions.

'Greetings, son. My heart grieves with yours for the loss of my grandson.' The welcome was ritualised and formal, yet Enniaun knew the sincerity of it. Owain was beloved of his grandfather.

'Greetings, father, he has finally paid for his persistent disobedience.' Enniaun paused and the older man stood and clasped him briefly to his broad chest. 'Sit ye down, Enniaun. Word has gone out to secure silver for the lad's ransom. There's little to be done until then. We have matters to discuss other than Owain. There are concerns for the people and I would know your mind.'

Enniaun drew a second chair next to the king. Cunedda poured wine from a silver ewer into two goblets. Enniaun drank, reflecting on how mellow it tasted compared to the wine he drank in the field. His father drained his measure noisily, banging his empty goblet back on the table. Neither servants nor slaves were present. Enniaun leaned forwards, intrigued.

4. The Oracle of the Wise

428 AD - Caledonii Lands

Owain and Edern awoke in snug comfort under their sheepskins at the rattling of the old man's staff on the stone floor. Wherever Lailoken had been during the deep black night was known to no-one but him.

'If ye would stay warm, young sirs, the fire needs tending and if ye would sup and eat, there's the goat to milk and barley cakes to bake.'

'Such tasks are not for a high-born, old man. I'm of royal blood and I'll not be pressed into service like a kitchen slavey,' Owain countered, turning his back to their host.

'Suit yourselves. Fire's more difficult to light than to keep in. Ye can eat and sup when ye please, but there are no servants here,' was the brusque reply. He left again. They contemplated the dying fire.

'He's right,' Edern began, 'Most of the wood outside is wet and we've no kindling.'

'What are you saying, Edern? That we should give in to an old grunt? To the shades with the fire - I'll do without; it's got to get warmer soon, even in your land of the lost sun.'

'You do as you will, lord. I'll fetch wood. Caves are cold places, even in summer. We need that fire.'

Owain snuggled back into his bedding. The young Pict dressed hurriedly and went in search of dry wood. No sooner had he departed than Owain sensed Lailoken's return, though even his sharp ears failed to hear an actual footfall.

'So, Edern goes to his chores leaving ye abed, royal one. Is this a friendship to be shared, or will he play your servant instead?'

'I'll not bandy words with you, old man. You've no rights over me. Edern does what he wants. Now leave me be.'

'That I shall, young one; that I shall. No one receives Lailoken's gifts unless they're ready. But think on this, royal one; ye have a perilous life to face. A wise young man would avail himself of any aid he could to meet such a future. A tiny morsel of knowledge could be the difference between survival and death. Think on that while Edern gathers wood to keep ye warm, young one. Think on that.'

The voice chanted; a hypnotic rhythm that slipped past Owain's pride into the depths of his being. The words seemed to repeat themselves like the rhymes his grandmother had taught him. They went to the heart of him. He thrust the furs aside with an angry kick. Shivering in the cooling cave, he pulled on his boots and set out to find Edern. Lailoken was nowhere to be seen.

The fire was all but out when they returned, carrying sufficient wood to restore the blaze. Edern dropped quickly to one knee, snapping the driest of the twigs he'd managed to find. He coaxed the embers back into life, wafting at the low flame with his hands and blowing gently. Owain followed behind with bigger logs. They would need to dry out near the fire or the cave would be filled with billowing smoke. Owain considered this as revenge on the old man, but thought better of it.

With the fire glowing healthily, they realised their hunger. Their attempt to milk the goat, proved frustrating for all. Neither had experience of milking and the goat responded to their fumbling attempts by kicking Edern firmly in the chest. They finally acquired sufficient milk for a beaker each, leaving the goat glowering in indignation, bleating its annoyance at their retreating backs. They had to make do with the goat's reluctant gift; neither could bake oat cakes. Their only skills lay in snaring rabbits and other small game that they could spit over an open fire, but this took time and they had not eaten since the morning of the previous day. Some time later, with their stomachs rebelling against the lack of food, Lailoken returned.

'I shall eat now. Watchful eyes might well glean enough to repeat my efforts. The slower ye learn to bake, the less time there'll be to acquire knowledge of other things,' he said mysteriously.

He busied himself in the cave, mixing flour with water and herb seasonings to form small cakes which he placed on a griddle over the fire. Mesmerised, the boys fought their complaining stomachs. When he was content that the oat cakes had been grilled evenly on both sides, Lailoken took a jar from a shelf in a corner of the cave and rummaged in a cloth bag. He brought honey and nuts to accompany his cakes, which he ate enthusiastically, ignoring their envious eyes.

Their first attempt at cooking was marginally more satisfying than milking the goat. Spurred by the lingering aroma of their mentor's cakes they shaped their own, sticky-fingered and tunics frosted with flour. Their cakes weren't as appealing, but they guzzled them down. Lailoken nodded permission for them to take a handful of nuts from the bag. They munched in silence.

'I do not eat flesh,' the old man informed them. 'This prohibition does not extend to ye. Ye may lay snares for rabbits. Just down the hill there's a small burn that runs into a pool; fish swim there for the patient catcher.'

The boys thanked him grudgingly. Now that his belly was full, Owain's anger began to melt.

'Tell me, old man, what's your interest in us and what's your purpose in bringing us here?'

Lailoken appeared not to have heard; he gazed into the fire, seeing visions only he could interpret. Just when Owain thought he had been ignored altogether, the old man spoke: 'I am charged to instruct ye in skills that will assist your paths,' he stated cryptically.

'Charged by whom?'

'Ah, royal one, curiosity is one skill ye need not learn. I'm charged by no one. For your peace of mind let us say that I have skills that show the future and your parts in it.'

'You are a seer?' Owain queried, as Edern cautiously made the warding sign.

'That and much more, royal one. Edern, the first lesson ye might learn is that a man's beliefs are both his strengths and his weaknesses. When ye abide by your beliefs too strongly, they make ye their victim. Why do ye make the sign of warding?'

The young Pict was confused. No one questioned the warding sign. He had the right to protect himself against the dark forces of the unknown.

'It was taught to me by my father, it protects against evil,' he said lamely.

'And ye feel evil here?' Lailoken persisted, sweeping his scrawny arms around the cave.

'No sir, but there is a strangeness.'

'Now ye begin to make distinctions, Edern. You're thinking past your beliefs. Stick to that path, it will serve ye much better than the gods.'

Owain and Edern cringed at Lailoken's casual offence of the divinities, half expecting the cave roof to come crashing down on their heads. Lailoken's eyes twinkled mischievously at their fright.

'Rest easy. The gods and I act with mutual understanding. If ye choose fear, then your own limitations are enough to terrify ye for now.'

The fire continued to blaze in the stone hearth. They breathed a little easier.

'What of this Christian God, old man? His priests flood the land with their prayers and hymns. Do you have a pact with him too?' Owain asked.

'I see why your destiny is so important, royal one. Ye have the uncommon habit of cutting to the quick of it, don't ye? Your question has a bearing on your time here. I'll not answer it now. In time ye'll ken the answer. Now, enough banter. There are chores to do. Edern, ye will come with me. Owain, remain here and tend to the fire. I shall speak with ye in a while.'

He hefted his flimsy weight on the staff and rose to his feet. Edern followed him obediently. Owain stared into the fire. Try as he did to create visions, he could see only flames.

5. The Way of the Warrior - Edern's Lesson

428 AD - Caledonii Lands

Edern's first lesson began with the mist still swirling. They walked towards one of the scattered farmsteads. Above the stone-built steading, with its thatch of marsh grass stems and reeds, the old man pulled Edern behind an outcrop of rock. All was quiet, but a wisp of smoke from the roof suggested that someone was awake. Lailoken sniffed the air like a hunting dog and pointed his long staff to the west.

'The royal one will have need of military counsel, Edern. Your task is to learn warriors' ways. He'll have enough cockerels crowing their merry tunes to deafen him. Be ye his sound mind. Your learning starts here.'

Pin-pricks of movement appeared through the rising mist at the point marked by the tip of his staff. Edern gasped when his straining eyes identified Western Picts. They were armed. He moved to warn his kinsmen, but Lailoken gripped his shoulder, sinking talons into his flesh.

'You'll do no learning fluttering around like a mother hen, boy. Watch and have no fear for the steading, all will be well.'

Edern felt his people were being betrayed and wriggled against the old man's grip. But his fingers were like iron bands.

'Watch their approach, boy. Learn to think like a warrior. You'll have need of such knowledge. Learn well now.'

The figures loomed larger, a band some twenty strong, led by a big man with a bearskin cloak. The remainder were check-cloaked, carrying bows and spears.

'Not the best of warriors, Edern. Why so?'

Edern still struggled, unconvinced that the steading was safe. Lailoken shook him savagely.

'There's no time for anger, Edern. Chances like this will be few. Concentrate on what ye might gain. Your ire serves ye ill. Trust me.'

Edern relaxed a little. Lailoken's fingers left painful indentations in his shoulder. He put his mind to the question. Nothing had happened; how could these men be judged? They were now only twenty paces from the dwelling. Their over confident leader urged them on, assured of easy pickings from the nearby penned longhorns, which bellowed mournfully as they picked up the scent of men.

The arrow, fired from inside the dwelling, took him full in the chest above the rim of his casually held wicker shield. His men dropped back in surprise as he crashed to the ground. A flurry of half a dozen arrows flighted after the first, finding four more raiders. They shrieked with pain. The band retreated quickly out of bow shot, leaving their dead leader where he had fallen.

Lailoken chuckled at their plight. His old face creased into a mask of delight. Then he sang in his lilting voice:

'If from the west you do mean
to press your enemy, be ye keen
to tend the wounds, your testament
and o'er your dead your pipes lament
For the sun she rises in the east
and by her light you will be seen.'

He tripped a little jig, his tall stooping frame ill-suited for the dancing. The lesson was a sound one and the first of many Edern committed to memory. The door of the steading opened. Its defenders took advantage of the retreating band by seeking cover among the outbuildings and walls.

'Look at their deployment, Edern. Is it sound or not?'

The young warrior began to take an interest. His mind asked more studied questions now that his anxiety had paled. Two defenders had cut to the right, one into the adjoining barn and one behind a low wall further to the flank. Three others had gone left. The attackers were unaware of how many might still be inside.

'It's cunning, sir. They have a field of fire; they are dispersed to make difficult targets for the attackers who have no cover. The flank defenders can warn of any attempted attack from the rear.'

'Aha, now ye begin to see like a general, Edern; now is the warrior's eye opened. Come, we shall find more for it. If Maelcon's forces are all like this band, Drust has little to fear. They'll do well to defend their own borders against the Strathcluta Scots.'

They left the skirmish. The Picts scurried in retreat. Edern cherished the lesson. Drust's command that he accompany Owain brought strange gifts. He saw the value of Lailoken's wisdom, but kept his own counsel on how to use it. He firmly believed that his own people would have the benefit of such tuition, despite the old man's conviction that his fate was twinned with Owain's.

Lailoken led them back to the cave.

6. The Sword of the Ninth

428 AD - Caledonii Lands

Owain watched them return from beside the fire, which crackled and spat from the dried out logs that he'd stacked in the flames. He'd spent much time staring into them, hypnotised by the dancing yellow swirls. He was aware that the fire soothed him. He felt calm for the first time since his capture.

Lailoken warmed his hands and Edern crouched by the hearth.

'Have you lessons for me?' Owain asked, aware that the comfort and ease gained by Lailoken's absence were ebbing with his return.

'Of a kind. There's a task for ye both, so ye'd best eat now.'

Owain searched Edern's face for clues, but a shrug was all he got in exchange.

'Ye shall both be warriors, though that won't be your only path, Owain. Ye need some practice with weapons, yet we left Drust's company so quickly that ye have none. Not far from here is a band of Maelcon's men in disarray. The challenge I set is that ye shall track them until the chance arises to steal arms. This is not all of it. Edern, ye shall bring back a bow and arrows; Owain, for ye, a sword.'

Owain stood, face redder than the embers in the fire.

'This is folly. We can find arms at Drust's settlement. Why risk our lives to steal from the enemy?'

Lailoken folded his arms and spoke slowly in contrast to Owain's outburst.

'Because ye will learn skills in stealing that ye won't learn begging weapons from Drust.'

Caught up in his own resentment, Owain flared. Who was this ageing tyrant to treat him like a slave? Filan taught with respect for his position. His father and grandfather were the only men he obeyed direct orders from and even those were rarely binding. His grandmother, Gwawl was difficult to refuse a request, but he played Ceri as only an artful younger son could and flouted her authority when it didn't suit his mind.

'I'll not go. This is no challenge for one noble born,' he spat at Lailoken.

He watched the old man move away from the fire and pick up his staff. He moved with an unruffled, but resigned mien. At the cave entrance he paused.

'My art has failed me, I fear. It is never wholly true. The one I foresaw as being schooled for a destiny is not here. A spoiled brat who thinks himself bigger than his years has no space in his heart for lessons. Go back to Drust and await your grandfather's silver. Edern, ye may leave also; my apologies for plucking ye from your family's warmth.'

Owain spluttered. Authority over him was replaced by rejection in one exchange. Speechless, he watched the old man 'tap tap' out of the cave.

'Spoken with the arrogance of a high born,' Edern chastised, stretching out on sheepskins near the fire.

Owain strode to the cave entrance and paced back again. His mind whirled with images of revenge. When his grandfather's men arrived with the ransom, the old man would be hunted down. He'd take personal pleasure in beating the old grunt with a spear shaft and roasting his feet over a fire.

'Don't you speak,' he snapped at Edern

'No need. Your stubbornness walls your ears. You hear only your own council and a pretty petty one it is too.'

'Oh, so your scary old man is the cauldron of all wisdom now is he?' Owain flailed his arms, bringing a smile to Edern's face.

'I learned much from one lesson at dawn, though I almost missed it through my own obstinacy. He teaches strangely, but there's value in it.'

Owain paused. Edern said very little, but when he did it carried weight. And had Filan not wagged a finger under his nose, more than once to reinforce the dangers of a closed mind. The images returned to him; the white robed druid tested to the limits of his considerable patience by his pupil's obduracy, his bald head shaking in frustration.

'So you think this challenge fit for us, then?'

'I didn't say that. I just learned a great deal from one lesson with him.'

Edern swung the lure, but was thrifty with his words. With the rush of blood over, Owain ceased pacing and sat by the fire, staring once again into the flames. He sighed, running his finger round the inside of the torc at his neck.

'You might be in awe of him Edern, but he terrifies me. He sees me as more than I am. I have aspirations for my people, but talk of destiny, that's a different matter. I've no wish to king it on the Gwyddbwyll board. Serving my own is destiny enough for me.'

'I have no counsel on such matters, Owain. I seek the warrior's straight path. But, the elders say that destiny's whole heart is beyond control. If it seeks you out, then you might as well embrace it.'

'Now you're clucking like him. How come everyone has advice for me when there's not a whisper from the gods that I'm aught but a boy seeking to add to his father's lands? Come on. Let's steal the plaguey bow and the sword. With some fortune a Pict will stave my head in. Then I can find some peace.'

Owain ran from the cave, not looking back to see if Edern followed. Outside a hazy sun failed to pierce a grey overcast; the air hung still. Above a patch of heather a plover wheeled. Owain looked around for Lailoken, but saw no one. At the burn, he stopped running, breathing heavily. In his haste, he realised that he'd no sense of which direction to take. Edern loped down the hill a little later at a much easier pace. Frustrated, Owain pointed in two directions.

'Which way?' he asked.

'No sense in running so fast. We need the dark as an ally. Need to track them in daylight.'

Owain followed Edern at a fast walk, watching the Pict scan the horizon. He turned west, settling into comfortable trot. Owain seethed inwardly at Lailoken's rebuff. Still, there was little to be gained by anger, so he set his mind to the task. He'd show the old seer; he'd stick the stolen sword right up that beaky old nose. That'd teach him to respect a son of the Votadini. Nursing his thoughts, he kept pace with Edern, running in the direction of the sun, which lit the grey clouds pearl.

By mid-afternoon, Owain was hungry and tiring. They hadn't eaten and Edern's longer legs ate up the miles effortlessly, while he, more used to riding than running, found the pace difficult. The terrain undulated, moor land cleft by narrow ghylls with fast flowing streams from melting snow on the tops. He slowed to a walk, his legs ached. A flat rock ringed by heather looked inviting, so he sat to rest. Hearing his pace falter, Edern stopped and joined him.

Owain had cause to feel sheepish when Edern offered him smoked trout and an oatcake from the plain deerskin bag he carried. He'd thought about provisions for the trek while Owain, fuelled by only his frustration, had neglected any preparations.

'You sure we're following them?' Owain mumbled through a mouth crammed with fish.

Edern pointed towards the sun.

'Certain. They're up ahead; we'll catch them by dusk.'

'How'd you know?'

'Lots of signs: trampled heather, birds disturbed a few miles ahead. Could only be them retreating.'

Owain chewed the last of the trout. Edern had useful skills. He realised that for all Filan's formal tuition about acting as a young noble, out here in the wild, he knew little of value. Edern's knowledge was similar to that of the village boys, yet more honed. He would observe more closely; there was much to be learned.

They drank from the next stream, brown peaty water, which trickled earthily on the tongue, but it refreshed them.

Edern's estimate was accurate. As the sun dropped to the horizon and the grey twilight settled on the glens, Edern pointed ahead. Peering intently, Owain saw warriors in the distance, strung out across the hill side walking at a slow pace.

They followed until the light faded. Owain was sure they'd lose their quarry with the encroaching darkness, but Edern's steps never faltered and soon a pinprick of light ahead signalled that the warriors had camped beside a fire.

'We should have a plan,' Owain said when they halted to rest.

'You might have thought of that before running off this morning.'

Edern stared at the fire in the near distance. They had closed the gap and the warriors were now within reach. The Pict pointed down at the ground.

'We sleep now. Best go in just before dawn and be stealthy. You can be stealthy can't you? I've no wish to be killed by my western kinsmen if you can't.'

'Look, the old man's barbs are bad enough without you starting as well. I can sneak as well as the best of the village boys. Will that do you?'

In the gloom, Owain saw Edern shake his head. They settled in a patch of heather. Owain's stomach rumbled; there was no more food. Sighing with frustration, he slipped into a fretful sleep.

He started awake and would have cried out, but Edern's hand was clamped firmly across his mouth. It was still dark and the once bright firelight from the warriors' fire glowed to embers. Edern smeared dirt across his face and let him up.

'No talking when we go forward. We get past the sentinels and move slowly straight through and out the other side. Pick a sword up as you go. I'll get a bow and arrows. Then run as if your hounds were chasing you.'

Owain nodded weakly. Now the venture was upon them, the thought of antagonising Lailoken seemed only half as attractive. This was no prank; armed men slept in the darkness before them. The realisation crashed in on him that he was by no means a warrior. But he could not dwell on his thoughts, Edern was already moving in a crouched stance. Not wishing to lose sight of the Pict, he followed quickly, fighting to banish the sleep from his eyes and the cramp from his legs.

Owain stopped when Edern waved him to stoop lower. He could see the fire at the centre of a circle of warriors. They slept with their feet turned towards it, like the spokes of a wagon wheel. The camp site was ill chosen; Edern had used several gorse bushes as cover and had almost reached the fold of ground where they slept. There was a stand of larch opposite the bushes. Perhaps this would work after all. He struggled to breathe silently; panic made him take small quick breaths and he feared they'd be loud enough to wake a warrior. The barest glimmer of pre-dawn grey fringed the blackness, but the birds were quiet; Edern's timing was impeccable. Owain felt Edern patting his leg. He followed the Pict's pointing finger, struggling to make use of the last of the light from the fire, now a dull red. A lookout sat some ten paces from where they hid. His chin was on his chest; his long hair covered his face. He dozed, a spear propped across his body, a shield within reach.

Edern signalled with a wavy hand; they'd move to the left and cut across the camp diagonally, by-passing the watch.

Owain's mind played tricks again; he was sure he was making so much noise he would rouse the camp. An owl hooted nearby, making his heart pound even louder. Far off a wolf howled; the noises were deafening. Someone must surely wake.

Edern stopped. By now it was taking all Owain's discipline not to run. Edern tapped his hand and pointed, mouthing 'slowly'.

As the fire was all but spent they crept towards the warriors. Owain's eyes roved across the sleeping men as they moved between them. His nose wrinkled with the smell of unwashed bodies, greased against insect bites. They lay wrapped in cloaks; snores rose from them like bawling cattle in a byre. He saw spears, with dyed blue markings on the shafts, woven grey and black wicker shields, knives with horn and metal handles, short sinewy bone-strengthened bows and arrows a plenty. He watched Edern deftly lift a bow and a deerskin quiver of white goose fletched arrows. But in their entire traverse of the camp from one perimeter to the other he did not see a sword. They reached the outer edge of the camp. He paused, showing Edern his empty hands. The Pict shook his head and pointed to the east, setting off in his loping run. Owain looked back at the sleeping men. He thought to search again, but across the circle, the sentry sat up, stretched and stood, shaking sleep away like a hound. Owain fled.

Several paces from the camp they paused in the larch copse to check whether they'd been seen. All was quiet. Edern set off at a fast pace, with Owain trailing behind. His stomach rumbled and his mouth was set grimly. When they were well clear of the warriors, he tugged at Edern's tunic. The Pict slowed to a walk.

'Fine plan, Edern; I've stolen so many swords I can hardly carry them,' he whinged.

'You might spend some time thinking on the task instead of bleating like a shorn sheep.'

'If you think I'm going back to look again, forget it. Sneaking I can do, but 'dangerous' twice on an empty stomach is too much.'

'I didn't mean go back. Think more deeply about the old man's task.'

Owain lapsed into silent reflection. They walked briskly, a pace that suited him better than Edern's running. Before them the sun broke the horizon, blood red through the grey haze. The hills shed pearl grey to take on their brown mantle slashed with spring green shoots; their peaks sunlit kissed to golden amber. Edern paused in a steep sided valley and shot a hare with the captured bow. They sought shelter in a ring of waving marsh grass to spit it over a fire, which Edern kindled into life with soft moss from his bag.

Never did a meal taste better to Owain for all the preparation at a Votadini high table. He sucked on the bones to strip the last of the roasted flesh; grease dribbled down his chin.

'If there's a lesson to be learned here, it's invisible to me,' he garbled through the last mouthful of hare.

Edern tossed away the bone he'd been chewing and dampened the fire with roots and earth from the squelchy grass.

'You saw the skirmish between our warriors and your father's men and you walked through the camp last night. What did you not see?'

Owain looked blank. His creased forehead suddenly relaxed and he smiled.

'Picts don't use swords. The old grunt set me up to fail. I'll see him cleaning latrines 'til he goes to his gods, if he has any,' he shouted.

'Crafty old fox. But perhaps too clever this time.'

'How? I've failed. He wants to humble me again.'

'Come, we shall see,' Edern invited, rising to his feet and shading his eyes against the sun drenched horizon.

Owain didn't press him, though curiosity boiled in him. Filan stressed the importance of patience, though he struggled with it.

They walked in the direction of Drust's settlement. The bow was a boon; Edern shot a plump pheasant later in the day and they rested and ate it, now safely within Drust's territory. They drank from passing streams and as dusk fell, Edern led them towards a steading.

'This is where Lailoken brought me yesterday. There is one sword among the Picts. Their leader was waving one before an arrow killed him. It should be with whoever holds this steading. You can bargain for it or borrow it to fulfil the challenge.'

Owain's heart leaped at the chance to thwart the old man. Edern rose higher in his estimation; when his ransom arrived he promised he'd reward the Pict for his friendship.

They passed penned shaggy long horned cattle and sheep showing healthy fleeces from winter growth. The steading was wealthy by the looks of the well fed beasts. A hound, tall and hairy, like those used by the Scotti to hunt wolves, stood at their approach and howled a warning to those indoors. Blue smoke drifted from the roof. Edern rapped on the sun bleached planked door.

A boy near Owain's age eyed them warily through the gap of the part opened door. It was difficult for Owain to make out more than his height in the gloom of the interior.

'The gods' blessings on your hearth,' Edern greeted him.

The door widened; they were beckoned in.

Owain followed Edern into the circle of light cast by a central fire on which a large cauldron bubbled with a thick stew that set his mouth to watering. The floor was beaten earth; stone sided beds hugged one wall, blue woollen blankets topped springy heather. Owain could have collapsed into one and slept. Three wicker shields and a sheaf of spears hung on another wall. He realised that he was being appraised by a wiry man seated at a table big enough to seat a tribe. Destiny or no Owain felt that the gods had truly deserted him when he caught the man's eye.

'Greetings to you, Ranesh,' Edern began.

'Greetings. You are welcome in my steading, Edern. He is not,' was the blunt reply.

'Drust grants him the hospitality of the people, Ranesh. Would you ignore your king's commands?'

Owain rubbed one foot behind the calf of his other leg. Of all the steadings in the Pictish domain, his prize had to be in this one.

'Nice try young 'un. My hospitality extends to letting him leave with his head still atop his shoulders. Now unless you have serious matters to discuss, we're about to eat.'

Owain tugged at Edern's tunic, eager to be away. There was more chance of ending up in the stew than savouring it. Ranesh's tone mocked Edern's youth gently, but the coldness in his gaze was still there for Owain as it had been on the eve of his capture.

'We do have a serious matter to discuss; perhaps some compensation for your lack of raiding,' Edern stated calmly.

Ranesh laughed, shaking his long red hair across his naked shoulders. The laugh brought his facial tattoos to life; Owain swore that the hawk on his left cheek flapped its wings and the spirals on his right spun.

'And what do you offer from your warrior hoard, Edern? You took nought to bargain with from your first raid. Were it not for him,' he pointed with a silver circled finger at Owain, 'we'd be the richer, you and I.'

'It is not I who wish to bargain,' Edern said, stepping aside and pulling Owain forward.

'This is better entertainment than a bard,' Ranesh said, but then more curtly, 'I'm hungry and there's nothing a Votadini whelp might own that I wish to trade for.'

Owain made to retreat, there was no hope of gain here, but Edern blocked his path.

'Strange, this steading's wealth looks to have been gained by a shrewd and wise head of hearth; your wife perhaps, or an elder brother?' Edern said. 'Such a person would at least show courtesy and curiosity about a possible trade.'

He had gone too far; Owain could see the best they might expect would be to find themselves dropped in the pig sty. The smile vanished from Ranesh's flushed face. He glowered at Edern. A woman emerged from the inner dwelling to stand at his shoulder. She wore plain deerskin, which failed to hide her shapeliness. Dark raven hair fell to her waist; a strand of amber beads worth many sheep and cattle graced her throat.

'You know Ranesh to be head of this steading, Edern. Goading him won't help.'

'My apologies; the matter was important to us, yet we are dealt with as boys.'

'If I treated you as a warrior, your head would be on a fence post by now,' Ranesh flared. 'But I'd prefer to eat than fight you for the insult and perhaps my own pride stands in the way of some gain. State your purpose, at least. You can't say that Ranesh failed to take you seriously.'

Edern stood aside again, allowing Owain to address the warrior. He rummaged through Filan's teaching, seeking some lesson on dealing with such hostility. There was none he could bring to mind, but Filan did stress the importance of holding to the truth, even when it seemed that deception might bring better reward.

'I was charged by Lailoken to steal a sword from the western Picts who attacked your steading. We raided their camp last night, but there was no such weapon. Edern says their leader was carrying a sword when your men killed him. I wish to barter for it.'

Owain paused. Ranesh looked no angrier and the woman smiled encouragingly. The silence hung, but he resisted the temptation to fill it. Many a man created error by saying too much, Filan counselled.

'And were I to have this sword, what do you have to barter with?' Ranesh asked in a tone that showed nothing of his intention.

'When my grandfather's men arrive with my ransom there will be silver enough.'

Owain watched for the impact of his offer. Ranesh waved for the woman to heap a flatbread platter with stew.

'The first rule of barter is to offer what you have; not what you might have,' he lectured, digging a slender Hawthorn handled knife into a tender gobbet of beef.

Owain baulked at more lessons. He'd had enough of Lailoken's wisdom, now a Pictish warrior stood as tutor. He felt the blood rise to his face again. One more humiliation from these shifters: Drust had kicked him into the wilderness with a crazy old man, now a mere warrior taught him how to barter.

'Then I thank you for listening at least and for your hospitality,' he said.

He wheeled to push Edern towards the door. The laughter behind him made him want to punch someone hard. Edern made silent appeals for calm, but Owain felt his patience was at the edge.

'Had you a sword and your tongue's skill to wield it, you'd be a worthy enemy, whelp. Is this what you're after?'

Curiosity bested his anger; he turned to see Ranesh lay a battered scabbard on the table. The leather was black, scuffed and faded and the belt lacked a buckle. When Ranesh drew the sword it rasped harshly. Though neglected the scabbard sheathed a fine Roman gladius; the short sword of the old legions. Its blade shone pink in the firelight; the edge was true, without dents and the point well honed. The hilt needed work; the leather binding was old and brittle, but the blade was sound.

'We Votadini fight from horseback; this is no spatha and it's old,' Owain sniffed.

'Then I need a foot soldier to barter with,' Ranesh replied, stuffing his mouth with more meat, 'and one who brings something of value to bargain with.'

Owain nodded resignedly, the sword was valuable for its craftsmanship. Even the mass produced swords of the ancient legions were better forged than all but the best Votadini smiths could achieve.

'How did a western Pict come by such a weapon?' he mused.

'Taken from the Ninth when they took such a hiding that the Romans struck their name from the lists and drafted them to the east,' Ranesh was quick to recount the Picts' one major success against the legions.

'A blade from the lost Ninth,' Owain murmured, the sword was almost mythical; it would carry authority for the bearer amongst the Votadini.

'The only things the Ninth lost were its way and two thirds of its men,' Ranesh gloated.

'Thank you for hearing me out,' Owain said, turning once more to leave. This time Edern didn't block his retreat. The prize was beyond him; Lailoken would have his victory. He thought ahead to how he might deal with the humiliation. Whatever the provocation, this time he swore he'd not lose his temper.

'Of course if the sword was of some use to a Votadini, there's one item of barter that might secure it.'

Owain paused; his heart beat faster.

'And what might that be?' he asked, turning to face the warrior.

'That torc of yours is worth the gladius. I'd accept it in barter.'

'For this torc I could arm a warband,' Owain countered, aware that Edern's eyes rose to the thatch in despair. Yet the offer came as little surprise. Ranesh had eyed the torc covetously on the night of his capture. No amount of humiliation by Lailoken was worth the trade. The torc had been given to him by Cunedda his grandfather, a kin gift whose value exceeded the silver that purchased it. The offer confirmed Ranesh's interest, however. Owain's mind flitted quickly to fashion some advantage. The sword was not wholly beyond his grasp.

'My torc is too small for your bull neck, Ranesh, even if I were to barter it. Here's my trade. I'll leave my torc with you in exchange for the sword. When my ransom arrives I'll commission a gold torc to fit you from the same craftsman. You'll return mine when you receive it.'

Owain held his breath. Edern's face was impassive, betraying no judgement on the trade. Ranesh carved a section of the platter, dripping with broth and chewed on it. The woman moved the cauldron to the side stones to prevent it from boiling over. In the shadows, Owain sensed other members of the steading watching him.

'Your head's quicker than your mouth sometimes, stripling. You ransomed to Drust and your torc ransomed to me? A fair trade for a sword I'd never use. Done.'

Owain resisted the urge to hug Edern in celebration. He removed the torc from his neck and laid it on the table. Reaching out he took the sword in its scabbard and grasped it in both hands.

'Now I'm obliged by the rules of trade to offer hospitality. Will you eat with us?' Ranesh invited.

Owain set the sword back on the table and sat down.

'What does his name mean in your people's tongue?' he whispered to Edern over a steaming platter of stew, nodding at their host.

'Man of stone.'

'Mmm, very apt.'

'I don't want to king it on the Gwyddbwyll board - really' Edern mocked quietly as they ate.

7. Magus Making

Owain was seated by the fire, staring intently into the flames when Lailoken returned. The sword lay on the hearth. Already Owain's mind ran to thoughts of a new scabbard and belt and how he'd change the hilt to make it more fitting for his small hands.

The seer leaned his staff against the cave wall and settled his bird thin frame by the fire. He registered neither surprise at Owain's presence, nor at the sword.

'The quest was a success I see.'

'Thanks to Edern.'

Owain anticipated a lengthy interrogation during which he'd find an opportunity to boast. He'd rehearsed the conversation and wished to let the seer know that he'd been bested. He was disappointed by the old man's next question.

'What do ye see?' Lailoken asked, nodding at the fire.

'I know there's much there, yet I see only flames.'

'Many's the apprentice who'd invent images.'

'We Votadini do not lie. Is there a way to see in the fire? I sense it, but it flits away from me like a bat.'

Lailoken's high-pitched squeaking laugh, echoed from the cave walls.

'Yes, ye have the sense of it, but you're trying too hard. Ye need to be still; in the mind. There's no time for much of my knowledge, Owain. Already your grandfather's warriors prepare to ride to find ye. Still, if ye can see past your anger better than ye see in the flames, I can be of use. How say ye?'

Owain pondered the question. Edern was right to say that valuable knowledge was theirs for the asking. Filan too stressed the value of knowledge gifts. In short sharp lessons his own weaknesses had been cleverly exposed. If he had found the patience to learn from Edern, how much more valuable might Lailoken's knowledge be?

'I'd be foolish to refuse. You stoke my anger so I might learn from it. Yet, you act with a strange kindness. I'll accept your gift. Filan will scold me if I don't.'

'Ye see nothing in the flames, but there's more to knowledge than simple scrying. Look inside yourself, royal one. Can't ye sense your destiny?'

'Sometimes, at night, listening to the owls hunt, I do have some sense of purpose. It hovers at the edge of my dreams. Thoughts of destiny disturb me, old man. I am a Votadini, son of Enniaun Girt and grandson of the great Cunedda. My family is my life's concern. Perhaps this is my destiny.'

Lailoken sighed.

'Destiny's a heavier burden than most men carry, Owain. Such understanding won't come easy. But for now, when ye look into the heavens and see a flying star, think on it and what ye have just said. For the brief time that it traverses the sky, it is the brightest star. It illuminates all as it shoots swiftly across the firmament. Such are men of destiny, Owain. Ye deny it at your peril. It'll not be deterred. For now, what do ye know of people, little one?'

'That's a strange question. I know those close to me love me. I know there is good and evil in all men. Are these the answers you seek?'

Lailoken scratched the top of his head, his ancient face wrinkled in perplexity. He prodded at the embers with a branch of hawthorn.

'Nay, these are from the hearth, lad. It's people in the world that ye must know. And soon, for it's a man ye must be well afore your time. Know this, Owain. This is the matter I can aid ye with and it has to do with people, for all things really do.'

Rummaging in the depths of the bag, which contained his herbs and scrolls, he pulled out five small dice, carved from bone, such as the warriors used for gambling. Catching Owain's eye to ensure his attention, he rolled them across the stone floor where they danced. Four of the five slowed and settled. One continued to spin.

'You'll find yourself like that one when the others come to rest from the throw,' Lailoken said when the last die stopped. 'Most men are like fallen dice. They hide the faces on which they have settled, showing five possible others to the world. The topmost face is the easiest to see. Is this familiar?'

'Yes. I think I see.'

'Mind it well, Owain. Remember that what shows is not necessarily what's in any man's mind or heart. That which is hidden is the most valuable knowledge ye can have about anyone.'

'But you cannot know the die's hidden face, surely?'

'Ah, there lies the knack of knowing people, royal one. There are ways. Ye must study the faces ye can see, and by doing so the hidden one becomes plain. If ye can't tell from what ye know of the five, then look at the sixth with your heart and spirit. Let it know your strength, your benevolence. By such means ye can see what men would hide. '

Owain pondered the lesson, brow furrowed in concentration.

'Why is this useful to me, old man?' Owain asked.

Lailoken's casually seated pose changed; his back stiffened. The vacant look, which stared into the very depths of the universe's mysteries, glazed his eyes. For a while, Owain thought his mentor had gone into a trance, but the voice spoke from the depths of his vision:

'More than any, ye must know yourself and those who believe they have power in this land. You've barely set out to open the way and there are six more paths beyond that for ye to tread. The Pretani are on a perilous course. The fabric of the land is to be rent. Father will fight son; cousin will fight uncle; families will be split like the lightning tree. These shores will be plagued by invaders. Strange customs will take a hold. Ye will be cast into this cauldron as a key that might unlock a secret door. Know your own heart and those of these men, Owain. Know their many faces; know their ambitions; their beliefs, what is dear to them. Only by such knowledge will ye prevail.'

And then, the riddling, rhyming lesson, keened in his shrill, warbling voice:

'If bards are to sing of the king not king
his fame and deeds performed
Of battles won and foes undone
Dangers and obstacles scorned
Then must his skills be adorned
to invade their hearts and minds

To play them at will
With the mage's skill
While to their eyes staying blind.

He stopped abruptly, a tremor running through his whole body. When he resumed his normal state, he blinked like a big, old grey owl.

'Do ye ken?' he asked.

'If I read you aright, I'm to know men if my destiny is to guide them?'

'Hmm. Near enough for now. This is not all of it.'

He retrieved the dice and set them in a circle on the floor between them.

'In the games that men play, there are important pieces and ones less so. On the Gwyddbwyll board the king has the advantage over the soldiers. They must act together and he must be foolish to lose, yes?'

Owain nodded. He was a fair player and was teaching Edern the game.

'Mark these dice as kings on the board; and that board as your life, Owain. I'll tell ye more later, but for now, ye needs know who are kings and who soldiers.'

He took a die between finger and thumb and waved it under Owain's nose.

'Your family; you'll not be as close to them as ye believe. Cunedda and your father have wisdom, as does Filan. Already your grandfather schemes with the Vortigern to secure land in Gwynedd. This will come at a price. Your family will be divided.'

He took up a second dice.

'The Vortigern, High King of the Pretani, or so he sees himself. Cunning, ruthless and self seeking; hardly the qualities needed to protect this land. His family hold a strong position on the board, but he'll play the foolish king.'

Owain watched a third die held before his face.

'The High King's new mercenarie; Hengist and his brother Hrosa. Soldiers with high ambitions. They eye Pretani lands enviously.'

Despite his reticence, Owain felt himself drawn into Lailoken's web. He concentrated hard to follow the information. Such knowledge might off set the punishments his father had no doubt dreamed up for his return. An appeal to Cunedda with this gift might stay his father's hand from its worst.

Lailoken picked up another die.

'The Vortigern's rival for the throne of Britain; Ambrosius Aurelianus; noble Roman and friend to your grandfather. Yet he's not what he seems. You'll need to hone your skills to see his depths.'

And another:

'This one's a stag in the morning mist; I can't see it clearly. Time holds the strands that bind ye, but Tendubric, Pendragon of Gwent and Siluria will cross your path many times. Don't be quick to judge him. Seek what he guards and your own path will be clearer.'

And the last:

'This is a ghost. Not a king, but a wolf that lurks in the shadows of your life. There's no gain for ye here, only danger. Be wary.'

He gathered up the dice and dropped them in the bag.

'Much of your destiny will be to do with God. The new god on the cross is on the march. Make sure that your way is sure; for his priests waylay the people in his name.'

Owain would have thanked the old man for his teaching, but Lailoken waved him to silence. In the flickering flames Owain conjured images of those whom the seer had named. He sought harder for the ghost wolf, but the fire cast only its warm glow and on the wall there was nothing but shadows. His learning routed the last remnants of his childhood. Lailoken's wisdom made for fast growth, but added to his confusion.

8. Owain's Totem

429AD - Caledonii Lands

For all Lailoken's oneness, Owain saw signs of agitation in his mentor. Lailoken's thoughts were troubled by a vision of Votadini horsemen. Samionos, the days of seed fall, were losing out to the dark. His time with the boys was coming to an end. Samhain approached - the onset of winter and the new year.

He had little time for the new religion; a wordy thing, a tool for priestly writing. Writing was a cursed art. Words on parchment were silent killers of those that were spoken. Written words were robbers; thieves of the soul. Its sacraments seduced the people, while his knowledge, though reserved for the few, brought wisdom and benefit. The new religion was fools' gold; its dramatic growth terrified him. Worse still, it created a world of belief that captured the heart and spirit of the people. Among the Picts, the ancient festivals remained secure. Lailoken's knowledge told that as day began with dusk, the new year began with the onset of dark. The seed of the new was enshrined in the decay of the old: thus were death and rebirth linked. No bookish priests would challenge his conviction with their stories for children. The depth of the earth and the flow of the seasons gave his belief its firm roots.

This year he sensed confusion. The rituals were more vital than ever. Fire would burn away those aspects of his being that burdened him. It was a time to focus on his intentions. His work was all but done.

Now was the time for seeing under the salmon moon, the totem of wisdom. The gap between the worlds was at its thinnest. Now he would prepare for communing with those who lived beyond. It was a propitious time to reflect on the past and it reminded him that he too would join his ancestors, one day. At Samhain his most powerful gifts would be fashioned in the new year fires; his most lucid oracles would manifest. He was sad at visions of future Samhain bonfires, lit without the knowledge that marked their importance. He felt the weight of his isolation. Recognising his self-indulgence, he stilled his thoughts and planned what was left to be done.

Edern was solving military problems, using models they had fabricated from carved sticks to represent opposing forces. They were arranged alongside the small stream. Lailoken had impressed upon Edern the importance of using the greatest ally that a military force had, the terrain.

'Will ye walk with me, royal one?' he asked Owain, who was preparing freshly picked mushrooms to go in a broth for their supper. The request was unusual; Lailoken rarely interrupted mundane tasks. Out of such humble duties true power grew, he schooled. Owain swilled his hands in water from a nearby ewer and padded in pursuit of his tutor. Though curious, he had learned that Lailoken rarely dealt with important lessons directly. Such tuition had helped to temper his wilfulness; though patience still challenged him.

Above the cave, they followed the path into a copse, before plunging into dense towering pines. They had sat many times in a glade with the open the sky above them, but Lailoken walked on silently. Owain sensed his strange mood.

'The time's fast approaching when ye must leave my tutelage, Owain. You've learned so little, but there'll be no gainsaying your family's claim on ye. Such is the way of men,' he observed wistfully.

'You can return with us. My father would be pleased to have me taught by someone with your wisdom.'

'Ye think the world revolves around ye, alone? Ye might well have a destiny, but when your kinsmen come for ye, our time will be at an end and that is as it should be. In time ye'll climb the ladder of knowledge. It'll not be my task to hoist ye.'

Owain fell silent, feeling a first taste of loss. He had become fond of the old man and had given little thought lately to returning to his family.

'What of Edern? He's become a friend.'

'He grapples with his future. His fate is bound up with yours now. His head counsels otherwise, but his heart knows his fate.'

'We've not been this way before. Is this another of your lessons?' Owain asked.

'For once I can't give ye an answer. Ye shouldn't believe that men of knowledge know everything. The gods hide their mysteries, even from those who are invited to share some. Ye'd do well to remember that. Never accept that anyone sees all, Owain. Even the best of us only sees a fleeting glimpse of what might be.'

He walked in his usual fashion, the staff tapping with each step; he paused suddenly. The tightly packed pines had not seeded this patch of ground. Irregular shaped rocks circled a perimeter; nature's work. Lailoken sniffed the air curiously. He stiffened, beckoning for Owain to retreat. Owain was no longer beside him. The old man caught his breath when he saw the youngster in the centre of the clearing. He played with a young bear cub that rolled and scampered in delight. It was not cub that Lailoken had scented on the wind. The heavy musk of old bear meant trouble.

The old man waved to attract Owain's attention, lest he scare the cub by shouting. Oblivious to his warning, Owain raced around the clearing with the furry creature that played tag with the familiarity of a human. The trees parted with snapping branches. A monstrous, ancient, brown she-bear erupted into the clearing. Grunting furiously, she pawed the air, her shaggy frame towering over Owain and the cub.

Lailoken watched, bewitched; his everyday mind told him that his lessons with the young Votadini had been fruitless. For once his 'seeing' had been seriously flawed. A deeper voice stilled him. His knowledge ordered him not to interfere. He obeyed.

The young cub slunk guiltily behind its mother. She raged. Men had hunted her and here was one, audacious enough to be near her precious cub. She reared to her full height, paws slicing the air; long claws spread in fists the size of platters. Her thunderous roars signalled her intention to wipe this man cub from the forest floor. Owain stood transfixed.

Lailoken's mind engaged in the thrust and parry of the battle between his rational senses, which called for action, and the deeper knowledge that held him back.

He watched the furious she-bear begin a downward swipe that would have ripped Owain's head from his shoulders. Some inner sense caused her to halt. The massive paws came to a dead stop as though pierced for crucifixion; huge arms splayed out on either side of her body.

Owain blinked, looking directly into her amber eyes. A covert communication passed between them that neither understood. The bear's eyes mellowed. Anger faded, replaced by puzzlement. The two stood silently, staring at each other in mutual awe. Neither knew the reason for it, nor if indeed there was one. The curious cub snuggled into the fur of its mother's hind leg. She looked down briefly and then back at Owain.

Lailoken watched one huge paw arc down to scoop up the cub to her broad, shaggy chest. Hesitating, the other paw gently reached down for Owain, plucking him from the forest floor in kindred complicity.

The seer dared not breathe.

The bear raised Owain to eye level. She peered at him, as though close inspection would provide answers. Pulling him inwards she cradled him with the cub as though they were siblings. Lowering him gently to the ground, she thrust her head back and roared a paean across the treetops. She looked at him once more, bemused, shambled through the gap in the splintered trees and disappeared into the forest, her cub scuttling behind her.

Lailoken waited, smiling at his wariness. He should have trusted his intuition, but he crept from his hiding place cautiously. Owain sat on the ground in a patch of pine needles. His face was angelic. A beatific smile shaped his lips. His eyes shone like moonlight dancing from a leaping salmon's scales.

Lailoken paused. He'd seen the look many times on the faces of apprentices. It was not to be interrupted. The silent pines sheltered them. The old man crouched before the boy; the power touched him slightly, creating a brief, subtle empathy between them.

Owain's unblinking stare, focused on some distant horizon, finally broke. A twitch in his right cheek signalled the return of his faculties.

'Did you see that, teacher? Did you feel the power?' he asked, brushing pine needles from his tunic as he made to stand on wobbly legs.

'Aye, I saw, royal one. You have this day received a gift of power far greater than my teaching.'

'What does it mean?'

'It didn't happen to me, boy. Power has spoken to ye directly. If ye have no clue to the meaning, we must prepare ye for dreaming. By such means will ye see the message in this. Your destiny starts here. Do ye doubt it now?'

Owain hung on to the old man's staff as they walked. His legs needed support; his whole body felt drained.

Edern had still not returned when they reached the cave. Lailoken lowered the spent Owain to his bed and placed extra logs on the fire. If his silence was from exhaustion or reflection, Lailoken could not tell. The seer busied himself concocting a potion, adding hawthorn, mistletoe and hyssop to a pot of spring water. When he was satisfied with the blend, he set the pot to boil on the fire. The cave filled with a pungent, tangy aroma that made the nose of the returning Edern wrinkle.

'Whew! What are you brewing? Some new drink to keep the winter chills from us?'

'This would do more than that, Edern. Your friend has had a most unusual lesson today. He needs to sleep and dream. This will help him on his journey.'

He added dried powder from a small leather pouch to the pot.

'This will sharpen his dreaming,' he said.

Edern moved to Owain's side. The boy's eyes were barely open. He managed only a weak smile of recognition.

'Explanations later, Edern. Get some of the draught down him. I must also drink. Today was propitious, so near the gap between the worlds. We must dream. Sit by us while we sleep, Edern? Watch carefully - keep your wits about ye, understood?'

Edern nodded, confused by the change of routine. He'd expected to be eating, drinking and discussing the day's lessons. He blew on the potion to cool it and held the beaker to Owain's lips. His friend drank half the draught before disapproving with a grimace as the bitter liquid trickled over his tongue. Edern cradled Owain's head to the furs where he fell asleep. Lailoken poured the remains of the potion down his own throat in one gulp and took to his own furs. Edern stoked the fire and munched a left over oat cake from their morning meal. He looked around for more food, but a small piece of goat's cheese was all he could find. He chewed the hard cheese thoughtfully. The salty taste did little to assuage his hunger. Though he was tired, he knew there would be little sleep for him.

To keep himself alert he went over his exercises. Lailoken had stressed the advantage to be gained by using small forces to oppose larger ones. They had moved from military strategy to logistics. At this stage the terrain became even more important. He was musing upon the best advantage to be gained against superior numbers of foot, a point his tutor had laboured repeatedly, when he was aware that his charges were dreaming.

Lailoken bore the discipline of his calling. His mouth uttered unintelligible words, though his body remained still. The same could not be said for Owain. He became animated, as though all the awestruck immobility of his encounter with the bear was being re-enacted in his sleep.

Edern watched as Owain threw his arms and legs about frenetically. Edern tucked the furs around Owain's body several times, only to watch his contortions throw them off. It was a long night for the Pict. The gloom lightened before his head began to nod. He was dozing when Lailoken opened his eyes and sat up.

'Ye have watched all night?'

'As you asked. Though I could make no sense of it,' he said through a stifled yawn. 'You muttered in your sleep, but there was nary a word I could tell. He's thrashed and fought as though beset by demons. I could make no sense of his ranting either.'

Lailoken took pity on the boy. 'Rest now, Edern. Your work is done. There'll be no lessons today. I'll tend him when he awakens. Come, quickly to your furs. Ye look dead on your feet, boy.'

Edern was asleep before his body had fully stretched into his bedding. The old seer rose and busied himself. He mixed a fresh potion, dipping into jars of milk thistle, cloves and lavender from his storage jars. He took a swig of the mixture and set the remainder aside in a beaker.

The autumnal sun was well into the sky before the boy finally awoke with a start.

'Ah, ye return to us, royal one. What news from the spirit lands?' Lailoken said, handing the drink to Owain.

'A jumble of a dream, old man,' Owain struggled to clear the fog of sleep from his head. 'Different scenes as at a festival. I was in the clearing. The she-bear watched her cub and I play tag. When we tired of the game, the cub and I marched like parading warriors.

Men gathered from all over Britain. I knew some of them from your lesson with the dice. The bear appeared again when they waved their swords in the air. I saw battles, men falling wounded and dying. The screams of the fallen mingled with cawing rooks and crows. The birds rent at the dead. I saw battle honours - a red dragon a bear, and a boar.

I saw the bear's standard, tattered, fluttering weakly before falling in the mud. I saw a wolf take the banner in its mouth and slink into the forest. If this is meaningful, teacher, it's beyond me.'

'What colour were the crows?' Lailoken asked, abruptly. 'Think hard, boy, it's important.'

Owain's brow furrowed in concentration. 'Red, old man. They were red, I'm sure,' he replied.

Lailoken nodded, emitting a long sigh. 'That is good, Owain. That is good. My heart is easier for that.'

9. Arth-Ursus

429AD - Caledonii Lands

Cunedda showed his strength. A hundred warriors, astride the finest Votadini-bred horses, clattered into the Pictish settlement.

The second of Gwawl's sons, Owain's uncle Cunorix had been a warrior from the time he could remember picking up his first shield. He sat proudly at the head of the lavish troop. A third wore mail over Votadini maroon tunics and metal helmets. Their swords were of Roman design. Javelins protruded from behind shields sporting Cunedda's galloping white horse. The remainder wore tunics, with leather hauberks, their heads bare. The troop was an awesome sight to the Picts who had horses of their own, but neither as impressive nor as great in number. Drust's people clamoured fearing a raid, until they saw the disciplined pace of the approaching column.

'You must have brought a goodly ransom to need so many men to protect it,' Drust said in perfect Brythonic as the horses fretted to a halt.

Cunorix replied with solemn formality: 'I am Cunorix, son of Cunedda. I greet Drust, Overking of the Picts from Cunedda, King of the Votadini. Our business is the abduction of Owain Ddantgwyn, son of Enniaun Girt, grandson of Cunedda.'

Drust matched the Votadini's formality. 'You are welcome, Cunorix, son of Cunedda. Have your men dismount and enter the halls of the Picts. No man will raise a weapon against you. Join us for the feast of Samhain.'

'It's been a long ride, lord King. We'll sup with you and talk. I can't speak for those Christians of my band, but I'll join you for your feast with much thanks,' Cunorix responded, dismounting wearily from his horse.

In Drust's hall, Cunorix tucked into bread, beer, roast boar and fish, pleased at the relief from rations. Next to fighting, Cunorix's second love was to eat and drink. His excesses were plain to see in his bulk. The wiry, sinewy vigour of the Votadini menfolk was replaced in Cunorix by the sheer strength of the heavy-loined bull.

'Where's Owain? I thought he'd be here,' Cunorix asked, wiping grease from a boar haunch from his fleshy chin.

The king beckoned for Cullorn the Druid to join them. 'Would you tell the Votadini what you know about Owain. The mystery is beyond a mere king.'

The old druid nodded his head, sagely, expressing distaste at the remains of so much dead animal flesh littered across the table.

'Owain has power, Cunorix. Lailoken, a mage of some standing, claimed Owain because he wished to tutor your nephew. Owain is no ordinary boy and his abduction was no accident.'

'I'm sure his mother, Ceri, will be ecstatic to know that,' Cunorix mouthed. 'When can I see him?'

'You can see him at once,' a voice spoke from the doorway.

The guards shrank in respectful homage to the fragile figure of Lailoken as he tapped his way, unbidden, into the king's hall. He supported himself by leaning on his ever-present staff with his scrawny right arm. His left was draped casually round Owain's shoulder. Edern followed the pair, a pace behind.

'Uncle,' Owain shouted, hurling himself into Cunorix's lap.

'Steady, lad. Owain, is it really you? By Arawn's hand, boy, you've lost weight. You look like a common farm boy.' His uncle enveloped him in his burly arms.

'Appearance is no mark of nobility,' Lailoken observed loftily, though Cunorix missed the barb.

'As you're here, old man, be seated and eat with us,' Drust weclomed the mage. 'You too, Cullorn.'

'We'll take beer and bread. There's nothing more here that a holy man could eat,' Cullorn said. Lailoken sniffed in agreement.

Lailoken nibbled at the bread and drank beer copiously from his goblet. Cullorn reversed the process, taking sips of ale to wash down chunks of bread.

'We must talk later about Owain,' Lailoken addressed Cunorix, wiping the beer froth from beneath his nose.

'There's more I should know?'

Lailoken grunted and emptied the goblet in a final gulp. 'I need to see your druids, lord King. I'll need help If I'm to conduct your ritual,' he said.

Drust waved a casual dismissal. 'Cullorn will furnish you with helpers, old man. Attend us later.'

The instruction sparked the elderly mage. 'I'll attend you in my own good time. Don't mistake my generosity for loyalty.' He stamped indignantly from the hall, his skull topped staff tap-tapping loudly.

Drust called for more ale. 'He's a strange one to treat a king like a stable boy. If the people were schooled by him, there'd be no place for the likes of us, Cunorix, eh?'

'I'm no king. Too much thinking. Now, fighting is a different matter.'

'Perhaps, lord, there is just as much use of the mind in battle. Its use is merely different,' Edern observed, shyly.

'Aye, you have it aright, boy. Politicking is one way. Deciding where to skewer an enemy is another. I know which I prefer.'

Owain asked about his pony, his hound and his brothers and sister. Edern excused himself to visit his own family. The king contented himself making inroads into his supply of ale, topping up a giant cattle horn and downing it swiftly. The beer was for the celebrations, but he saw no reason to delay sampling his brewers' skills.

The following day, Cunorix watched a groom tending his horse. A slight tap on his shoulder alerted him to Lailoken's presence. 'Walk with me, the festival is tonight and time is short,' the mage said brusquely.

Cunorix followed, realising Lailoken's infuriating habit of wearing authority so well that even the highest obeyed him before they realised it. They walked past the bustling preparations for the festival.

'There are things ye must know about Owain, so he might not be alone in his destiny,' Lailoken began.

'Am I the person to hear this, old man? Could you not come to the Guotodin and speak with the boy's father?'

'I have more to do than to be travelling the length and breadth of the land after one small boy. Listen well. There will come a time when Owain will be seen as successor to his father, Enniaun, as king of the Votadini. It's crucial that he does not lead the Votadini.'

Cunorix whistled. Succession was no small matter.

'In that case, it's perhaps my mother, Gwawl who needs to know. She keeps the peace among the Votadini. I'll have a hard time convincing her why Owain shouldn't succeed.'

'No ye will not. Ewein is eldest. Even Cadwallon is older than Owain. The danger will be that by the time Owain is of age, Votadini lands will have grown far greater than Cunedda's vision. It will be seen as just that the sons should share the new lands. Ye must impress upon your mother that Owain is excluded. Do ye understand?'

'Never fear. But why should my family abide by your counsel?'

'Cunorix, to fulfil his destiny, this lad must be free of obligations. To mark this, he will carry his own device. He will not bear the white horse.'

Cunorix's eyebrows almost reached his shaggy hair. The Votadini emblem was feared and respected all over the north. How would Owain be recognised without it?

'Don't ask questions when ye'd struggle with the answers. I shall send papers back with ye to Gwawl.'

'As you will, old man. I shall speak your words truly to my mother.'

Lailoken looked him straight in the eye, a piercing soul searching gaze that went chillingly to the heart of the doughty warrior. 'Think on that ye do. There are issues here that run even beyond my ken, let alone yours. But what I have told ye is vital.'

Silence descended as the two walked back to the king's hall. Lailoken's mind was focused on the ensuing ceremony. Cunorix realised that Owain's return would bring complications for the Votadini; far more than Cunedda had forseen.

***

Drust and Cunorix bargained over the ransom. Both needed an agreement. Unbeknown to the Pictish King, the morning's conversation with Lailoken had done little for Cunorix's concentration. The Votadini leader was unaware that Drust felt compelled to settle the matter before the Samhain ritual. It was imprudent to offend the gods by haggling. Neither felt in command when they met in the king's private chambers.

'There are two things,' Cunorix began, following Cunedda's careful schooling. 'The first and most obvious is coin. The second relates to our people. We've fought over our borders for longer than either your grandfather or mine can remember. Times change and there are now more pressing matters for us.'

Drust was suddenly all attention: 'Cunedda wants peace?'

'I'm charged by my father to tell you this as his gift.'

Drust was further taken aback. He listened attentively.

'My father bids you watch your eastern coasts. This Vortigern sends for Frisian sea pirates to war against you. From now on, you'll have to watch for raiders in the east as well as defending the west against your blood kin, Maelcon.'

Drust's face remained impassive.

'Continue, Cunorix, and convey my thanks to your father for this valuable news.'

Pleased with his initial opening, Cunorix seduced the Pictish king with further gems from his father's trove.

'My father is on good terms with Strathcluta. He'll encourage their pressure on Maelcon, if you will cease raiding our manaws. The coin we agree for Owain's release will provide the ships we know you covet. There are richer pickings for you in the south than suffering retaliation every time you raid us. You can repay the Vortigern for his slighting of your people.' Cunorix sat back, rummaging through his mind to confirm that he'd communicated his father's full message.

'Your father is wise, Cunorix. If he's of a mind to aid me, he's a greater plan afoot, no doubt. However, I can't see aught but benefit to us. If we can agree on Owain's price, you have my word that my raids on you will cease. The Vortigern offends us with his claims that we murdered his brother, Constans. He was the killer, but we take the blame.'

They resorted to haggling; a ritual of humour, insult and feigned indignation, culminating in an agreement that could have been arrived at more easily but for the clutter of traditional exchanges. Both were satisfied with the bargain. Drust would build his ships. Cunorix had defended his father's treasury, paying much less than the limit Cunedda had agreed. The negotiations complete, Cunorix sent for the strongbox which had remained under guard in the stables. He counted out the requisite number of leather bags of silver coin. Drust sent for beer.

That night Owain watched Cullorn's apprentices light the Samhain bonfire. Sparks and flames illuminated the pale faces of the celebrants in their orange glow. Silhouettes cast long shadows against the standing stones, monuments to earth and sky. A file of bearers walked past Cullorn carrying sacks of seeds, the following year's wealth. Cullorn blessed the seeds, acknowledging the temporary death that was to be endured before the sun's return.

Following enthusiastic drumming by Cullorn's younger white-robed druids, a mood of expectancy descended. Lailoken ghosted from the shadows into the firelight. His staff was gripped firmly in his right hand, his straggly hair and beard streaked copper by the flames. He took his position between the twin stones as the moon traversed to its lowest point. Earth and sky were joined as it fell between the mighty grey menhirs, a silver back-drop for the dark figure of the mage. Owain shivered; the ritual struck at the depths of him.

The crowd moved forwards, awed, awaiting the words of the black figure. Lailoken stood in silence, framed by the sentinels and the moon. He brought his staff crashing down on a bronze gong. Though physically weak, the power of his art wreathed around him; flames hissed and crackled in the foreground.

A file of druids walked before the old mage, forming a circle around a slightly raised mound at the temple's centre. Pungent smoke rose from pots of burning sage. Those who represented the energy of the east wore feathered bird masks. In the south, the participants held red candles and wore red hoods. The druids in the west held sea shells and carried amphorae of water. In the north their artefacts were stones, crystals and rocks.

From each quarter of the circle Lailoken called for the guardians' protection. He stepped forward to stand on the raised mound, symbolic of spirit, the centre. He rapped once with his staff. The drums pounded a steady rhythm. The people stamped their feet in time. The old man raised his staff again. Silence flooded over the gathering, a silence enhanced ten fold by the sudden cessation of the drums. Lailoken's voice rang out powerfully, with the ritual's opening words:

'Mother of Fire
Lady of the Sacred flame
Who burns away all impurities.
She who is the hearth flame
And the Fire of the Sun.
Lady who brings joy
And Illumination.
Eternal Flame Forever Burning
I salute you.'

The crowd chanted their responses.

'We salute you.'

Stones, moon, fire and drums captivated them. Owain felt himself a thread in a vast web that defied his understanding. Lailoken's words rang clear and strong in the night air, drawing the people in.

'Now is the ritual of Samhain, the time of death, putrefaction and rebirth. Nature now shows us our vulnerability to her benevolence and barrenness.'

'Hear me, people of the old ways. Now is the time to look at your lives; to cut out and burn what ye no longer need; to purify by fire. Be sure of what ye wish to exorcise. Come forth and cast a symbol into the flames; cleanse yourselves of your false hopes. Now is the time to abandon what does not serve ye; to prepare yourself for renewed growth.'

'The veils between the worlds are thin. Think on your ancestors, without whom ye would not be here this night. Thank them for the part they played in your being. Do not forget them, for if ye do, meaning will slip from your lives. Soon, all but the few will forget such festivals as this. Guard the flame of such knowledge in your hearts, for there are those who will snuff it out with no more thought than hooding a candle flame.'

Lailoken fell silent. The crowd stilled in personal meditation. The only sound was the roar of the flames and the whinnying of horses, catching the smoke on the wind in their nostrils. Silently the people detached themselves from the throng to throw pebbles into the greedy fire.

Lailoken stood statuesque, watching them make their pledges. In all the time they ebbed and flowed, he never moved a muscle. Finally, he crashed his staff against the gong.

'There is a weighty matter before this rite concludes. There has been one living near ye, who is not of your people. Yet, his time here has been momentous for himself and for ye also.'

Lailoken beckoned Owain into the circle. He obeyed, flanked by two druids, feeling small and over-awed, but bearing himself proudly. Lailoken threw a protective arm around the boy. He thrust his staff straight up into the air and dropped his head back. Staring at the starry canopy, he sensed the crowd doing the same.

'Look at the sky, people of the Picts. See the stars and know their value. The heavens hold many secrets. Observe the peerless constellation, the Great Bear.'

The crowd rocked on their heels. Here was a new departure. Only portentous events were powerful enough to change traditional rituals. The crowd held its collective breath.

'This grandson of Cunedda, King of the Votadini, has had a sacred encounter of great power. As the Great Bear lords it over all other constellations, so this boy mirrors that celestial order. He has been claimed by the most powerful of the old totems. He will be no earthly king. A beacon in the dark days ahead, kings will use his name for their sons, while his name will be lost to his own. People of the North, remember this night well. Acknowledge one touched by power, Owain Ddantgwyn of the Votadini. His device shall be the bear. His name shall stand above the petty feuds of men - Arth, in Brythonic, Ursus in Latin. He will be Owain Arth-Ursus, the Bear. Know him now and do him only good, for his destiny calls across the void from the ancestors. I curse any who harm him.'

Lailoken stopped. The silence persisted. The moon dipped below the horizon, robbing the temple of its light. The fire's embers cast a muted glow across the circle. From the ruddy eeriness a single voice began to chant, a solitary rain drop joined by others to form rivulets and finally a flood:

'Arth-Ursus, Arth-Ursus, Arth-Ursus,' rang out against the dying flames, as though the name itself would keep the darkness at bay. Shivers descended Owain's spine. The uneasy recognition of his destiny, until now a private thing, blossomed into dread. He was now publicly marked and all the more doubtful for it.

***

It had come to goodbyes. Though delighted to be reconciled with his kin, Owain was mournful on the day of Lailoken's departure.

Edern watched his friend disappear from the village at first light in the direction of the old seer's cave. He had said his farewells the previous day, sensing that Owain wished to see the old mage alone.

Though it was little past daybreak, Owain could hear his mentor as he approached the cave. A sturdy pony was tethered at the mouth, cropping leisurely at the grass.

'It's at times like this, Owain, that I bear the consequences of my art,' the old man's voice floated from the cave.

'And what might those be?' Owain asked, smiling at Lailoken's alertness. He had been scrupulously quiet in attempting to surprise his teacher. He dipped his head into the dwelling to see Lailoken carefully packing scrolls and parchments into weathered leather saddlebags. The volume of papers looked to be far in excess of the space he was packing them in.

'It's like moving the library of Alexandria every time I make a journey. I don't seriously attempt to add to them, yet I seem to acquire more without effort. Hand me those scrolls, Owain, ye can make yourself useful now you're here.'

'Did you think I'd let you go without a farewell?' Owain asked, the fleeting hope hovering in his mind that their parting would not be final.

'I thought ye might not wish to bid me goodbye, Owain. I have changed your life and not all I've had to tell ye has been to your liking.'

Owain paused. 'My resentment is not for you, old man; you've been more than generous with your teaching. It is this destiny that I dislike.'

The seer cackled his wheezing, chesty laugh. 'By the gods, boy, you're more entertaining than any juggler. Who, among all those touched by destiny, has ever liked it?' He shook with laughter.

'As I don't know anyone who has, how would I know the answer to that?'

Lailoken's mood changed. He squeezed several more parchments into the already overstuffed saddlebag. Shuffling several scrolls, he selected one small, ancient text from the pile.

'I have taught ye to seek out the hearts and minds of men, Owain. In our short time, that was my greatest gift to ye. It's not enough for ye to meet the future. Edern has been a good pupil; mark him well in military lore. Listen carefully to Filan, he has much wisdom. Nevertheless, much of your destiny ye will meet yourself. Others can only advise. Remember this when ye seek to slip from under your obligation. And ye will.'

His bony fingers held out the scroll, with some reluctance, Owain sensed.

'This might help. Ask Filan to translate it for ye; consider it a gift. When your destiny comes a-calling you'll find another tutor.'

Owain took the scroll reverently. Lailoken continued, absently shuffling the remaining texts, seeming reluctant to complete his task.

'The Bear is a powerful totem, Owain. This ye know. Your dreams make no sense to ye. I see that ye are in awe of them, even fear sometimes. Look for the obvious. Study the bear, Owain. Why is it powerful? How does it use its strength? Its secrets hold the key to unlocking the resentment ye feel. Waste no time; ye need the bear's knowledge. When you have that, your next teacher will find ye. In the mean time, take this and read it yourself. I've written more about those who'll be important to ye. But remember, a seer's gifts are but a brief glimpse of what might be; not what is.'

He passed a larger scroll to Owain, and fell silent, cramming the remaining texts into another saddlebag. His eyes met Owain's briefly; there was a kindly sadness in his glance. He became brusque again.

'Help me with these to the pony. I wish to make the best of today to put these chilly climes behind me.'

'You go south then?' Owain asked, the lump in his throat defeating Filan's tuition on formal partings.

'Aye, the lands of the Pretani have kept me overlong, Owain. I want to spend some time where the sun warms an old man's bones. Goodbye, Owain Arth-Ursus. Ye can run from it all you like, or hide yourself, yet destiny will seek ye out. There'll be lots of fighting to be done before ye rest, so don't start by fighting yourself.'

He hoisted the saddlebags over his left shoulder, pointing with his staff for Owain to lift the remaining ones. They carried the heavy burdens to the cave mouth and loaded the pony.

'Remember the flying star, Owain. Perhaps it covets a place like the others, but it can't resist when the heavens move it. So it will be for ye. Be well, act honourably. Remember my teachings. Now, have ye a hug?'

Owain threw his arms around the ancient seer; fighting to suppress his tears. 'I shall miss you,' he blurted.

'I am honoured,' Lailoken replied. 'Many will enter your life and leave it. Enshrine them in memory and your heart, Owain. By such means do we hold people close, even though we part from them.'

With great gentleness, he eased the young Votadini from him, shaking his head at Owain's tear stains on his woollen robe. He detached the small skull from his staff and held it out. Owain took it gingerly.

'My last gift. If you find yourself really troubled find a quiet place and stare into its eye sockets. You'll find comfort, but don't use it lightly.'

Taking the pony's lead rein in his left hand, he hefted his staff in his right and started off down the goat trail. Owain watched the man and the pony dwindle in size. The hardest of Lailoken's lessons was learned as the pine trees cloaked them. It was his first loss of someone close. Yet the destiny that Lailoken foresaw lurked in the gap created by his tutor's departure. He had the uneasy feeling that he would know such loss again.

10. The Staff of Owain the Bear

431 AD - Dinas Ffynon, Gwynedd

Owain was aware of the distance that Lailoken's teaching had moved him from his family. Tales of his destiny unsettled his kin; he caught their curious sideways glances. He felt that they were waiting for him to sprout wings, or horns, or both. Edern had accompanied him south, still questioning his own loyalties, and was reluctantly accepted by the household.

Owain had come to Gwynedd. Cunedda had been granted an old hill fort at Dinas Ffynon by the nominal ruler, Cynvelyn. In allying with the Vortigern, Vitalus, Cunedda had solved the problem of the need for more lands for the Votadini. No fool to strategy he could see why the Vortigern wanted Votadini warriors in Gwynedd. It reinforced the separation of Cynvelyn's forces from those of his brother Tendubric in the south. Vitalus' kingdom of Powys already sat between the two and Cunedda's sturdy warriors were a further hindrance to any unification of the brothers' forces. Cynvelyn could not deny the value of Cunedda's aid. The people of Gwynedd were grateful to their long standing brothers, the Votadini, for the help they brought, but it came at the cost of their continued isolation.

Gwawl, Owain's grandmother, kept her blend of firm counsel and spoiling and this reassured him. Ceri was delighted to have him back. She overcompensated by outrageous cosseting. He was too young to be a warrior but old enough to assert his emerging manhood.

'Mother, I'm pleased to be back with my people, but I'm no longer the child you once suckled. I know you love me as a son, but you must stop following me everywhere.'

'You're right, Owain. I must cease being a shepherdess, though it's hard. You're so dear to me.'

He grinned and shook his head. 'The Picts believe me to be touched by the Great Bear, the greatest of their totems. They'd find it strange that I can hardly visit the privy without my mother waiting at the door.'

Their laughter eased the tension.

'Will you go north, son?' she asked. 'Back to the Guotodin? I return there soon, now I know you're safe.'

'I will, mother but not yet. I've learned much from the Picts. I know the north as well as any Votadini. I'd like to continue my travels. Grandfather treats me civilly, but he feels slighted by my bear device. I've much to do, but not here.'

'But where will you go?' Ceri queried, her voice shrill.

'Don't be so fearful. If I'm to fulfil a destiny, I'll not come to harm before I reach full manhood. Will you talk with grandfather; try to make some peace between us? Perhaps he could suggest somewhere to continue my learning.'

Sighing, Ceri rubbed her slender hands together. 'I'll speak for you. You will see your father, won't you? He's delayed. The roads are mired. If he agrees to your request, and Cunedda can suggest a safe haven, you have my blessing. You'll push me to my death bed with the worry of you. Now go, let me practice at having you out of my sight.'

He squeezed her hand affectionately and left the chamber without looking back. Edern, who had witnessed the exchange, rose to follow.

'You'll keep him safe, Edern won't you?' she asked, a tight smile striving to melt the frost of her face.

'We're bound by the fates, lady; it seems I'm his shadow and shield. He's changed in ways that escape a mother's eye. Though he's not yet a man, he knows more than many who are greater in years. He hides it well, lady, but I see the changes.'

'I know you're close to him, Edern. I'm glad his brothers are in Guotodin; they'd resent your friendship. I only want to understand what has happened to Owain so I might help him....' her appeal trailed to silence.

Something in her honesty held Edern. 'You have been kind to me, mistress. I'm a long way from my hearth. If it's hard for me to live in the household of a former enemy, how much more difficult it is for Owain to return home. He wears his destiny like an anvil. He's in a place no man would choose.'

He paused. 'He's troubled, mistress. He dreads a destiny that would have him lead men to their bloody deaths. He fears the responsibility and questions his ability. He is angry. He left here bound to his people. The life he wants has been snatched from him. If you would help him, mistress, free him from your hearth. It pains him here.'

Ceri raised both hands. 'I've been too wrapped up in my own concerns to understand his troubles. Thank you, Edern. You've given me much to think on.'

Edern sighed in relief. With a curt smile to Ceri, he went to seek his friend. Ceri watched him go. Her son had returned from the wilds, a changeling. She fretted in the sure knowledge that he had already outgrown her motherhood. Sighing, she tore her mind away from its ceaseless, unanswered questions. She would have to change her thinking, for the Owain she knew as a boy was no more.

***

Owain and Edern returned from a hawking foray to find horses whinnying and voices raised in joyful celebration. Enniaun Girt had come to Gwynedd. In later years, Edern would count the day of Owain's reunion with his father as the second most important for him. Meeting his friend's sister, Elen, meant that thereafter his heart was never quite his own. One glimpse of her resolved the turmoil he felt between his continued friendship with Owain and the lure of home.

Owain raced into the waiting outstretched arms of Enniaun Girt as the whole family watched their reunion. Even Cunedda beamed a smile. But all Edern could see as he slowed his horse to a walk, was the red-haired beauty of Elen. She stood proudly between Gwawl and Ceri in a russet and green riding tunic, mud-spattered from the road. Edern handed the hooded birds to a waiting servant, pulling his glove off with his teeth. He watched Owain greet his sister with a warm hug. It was one of the few times in the Pict's life that he wished to exchange places with his friend. He hovered, inconspicuously. Over Owain's left shoulder, Edern's eyes were met by the coolest, most shameless shards of grey crystal that pinned his soul to his back bone with a frank, inquisitive stare.

Weak-kneed, Edern turned his own eyes away; he couldn't match such boldness.

Enniaun clapped him vigorously on the shoulder. 'So, you're the one I must thank for keeping this wayward son safe in the north. Edern is it? I'm in your debt; you are welcome in my house. Ceri speaks well of you.'

'I..... I thank you for your kind words, lord. I was asked to mind him. He would have done the same for me, I'm sure,' he stuttered. He reddened at Elen's widening smile.

'Kindly spoken, but I think you too modest. It's not fitting for a young companion of a Votadini noble to be without position. We'll arrange something to suit. Now, let's to the hall, I'm starving,' Enniaun urged.

Edern followed the family to a sumptuous banquet. Through the feasting and drinking, he had to force his eyes to his beef lest they swivel in Elen's direction. There was banter all round the hall as the servants and warriors caught the family's good humour.

Although Owain had spoken much of his high-spirited sister, he had in no way described her elfin beauty. He had dwelt upon their japes and adventures so much that Edern had been unable to form a picture of her in his mind's eye. Her appearance was nothing like the one his imagination had conjured. But he was exasperated. Throughout the feast he heard her ask not one question of her brother about him.

Feeling an intruder and subdued by Elen's disregard, Edern excused himself and left the Votadini to their cups.

***

The following morning, Owain followed Lailoken's advice. Study the bear, he had said. He set about the task with a thick head. There was little else to occupy him in the stronghold, still the pursuit of knowledge about his totem seemed odd. Filan the Druid was his starting point. They walked in the crisp morning to the head of the narrow wooded valley, the only approach to the fortress without scaling hard rock. The druid was at ease in the flame red and ochre woodland, despite the autumnal cold, far more so than inside the fortress that spoke to him of man's futile attempts to find security.

'So, you wish to know of bears?' Filan asked as they halted near a deep pool, filled by a rushing waterfall. Owain clambered to an outcrop of rock, allowing his feet to dangle as he perched atop it.

'I must confess ignorance about both bears and the bear people, Owain. We druids know of them. Their lore precedes ours and we respect it. But, they don't share their secrets with us. I am more use translating the scroll you gave me.'

Owain's curiosity re-awakened. He had all but forgotten Lailoken's gift in the excitement of his homecoming. 'What does the parchment say, teacher?'

'All in good time; such work cannot be rushed. It's in Greek and I've not used it for a while. You'll know the contents when I'm satisfied I have a worthy translation. And when I sense that you're ready to read it. You might count such time in years; it's no easy task.'

Disappointed, Owain sought assistance from his grandfather's woodsmen. They told him where he might find bears a short distance from the fort, though they counselled caution.

With time running out before winter, Owain knew his studies would be short. By the time the rains gave way to snow, the bears would have taken to their caves for the long sleep. This much, at least, he already knew. It was then that he made his first connection between his totem and humans. For a quarter of the year the bear slept through the savage elements, snug and secure in its cave. His people too, remained within their strongholds throughout the winter, inactive until spring greened the land anew. He smiled wryly; if bears had predators, they would be easy victims as they lay in their winter slumber.

He located the domain of a huge male brown bear. His own hunting skills grew as he observed the animal, always upwind. He spent hours huddled in his great cloak, watching the shambling beast build up its fat.

Owain saw the sense in Lailoken's advice. Bears were deliberate in their actions. They didn't hurry. They were resolute. They were patient. He saw the creature stand in a freezing mountain pool, calmly scooping fish to the bank. There were more misses than catches, yet the bear remained undeterred.

Owain learned from his secret observations. As his knowledge grew his own deep anger subsided. Charged with an uncertain destiny, he had far from reconciled himself to it. The insight was sobering.

Several days into his quest, he was drinking with the warriors when his grandmother rose to leave the company.

'Before you seek your bed and while you have the legs to stand, I would speak with you, Owain,' the elderly stateswoman whispered as she passed his chair. Owain sobered immediately. An invitation from Gwawl was a command.

Brigit, his grandmother's personal servant, welcomed him with a smile, waving him into audience with Gwawl, who was sitting in her favourite high-backed oak chair by the fire. She patted the chair opposite her, watching his movements intently as though she could see the truth of him.

'So, you'll leave us, your mother says?' she opened when he had settled himself.

'It's for the best. I need to travel to know more of the world of men' he replied.

'And of women, Owain. No doubt your northern seer omitted to mention our part in the grand scheme?'

'Lailoken's focus was on men, grandmother. Is it not men's hearts and minds that shape the realm?'

'No more so than the gods or women, Owain. Ignore these and your vision limits itself. Do the Votadini thrive because you menfolk engage in politics and war, or because I and your mother bind us together, ever watchful for the cracks and divisions that you create?' She leaned back in her chair, satisfied that this lesson was new to him.

'I'd no cause to consider such,' he admitted, staring thoughtfully into the yellow flames.

'Then I've added to your wisdom, grandson. Now, what of your place in the family? Such a tight weave runs to rents and tears when there's a flaw. Are you a flaw in the cloth of the Votadini, Owain? Your brothers and uncles are wary of you and your grandfather struggles with your departure from tradition. This is the warp of our strength. What am I to make of you?'

'That's why I must travel, grandmother. I pose no threat to my kin. Look into my heart and you'll see I speak truly. Whatever my destiny, I hold no claim to Votadini titles. Lailoken stressed this overmuch.'

Gwawl paused, letting the silence reinforce the solemnity of the occasion. Brigit's shuffling steps could be heard as she prepared Gwawl's bed in the next room. The fire hissed.

'You take this lightly, Owain. While a boy, such matters seem small to you. In manhood, it will be a trial for you to guard against conduct that affects your family. I'll not be here to patch any holes. Your mother will be seamstress by then. Though I'll prepare her for her part, you're too dear to her. I tell you this now, so that you might see it then. She will put you first when the family needs her to be strong.'

'What must I guard against, grandmother? If I'm bound to a fate that sets me apart from you, how can I be a threat to my own?'

'You're young yet, Owain. As a man, you'll be tempted to marry to birth your own kin. At that time your fibres become part of the Votadini weave. Do I speak clearly?' She paused, leaning forward to hold his eyes in the amber of the fireglow.

'Yes, grandmother; I understand. Though my conduct will place me beyond family concerns, my sons' need not. Be assured that I shall never willingly damage this family. Thank you for your guidance; it speaks a different wisdom from my tutor's, yet it's of equal value.'

'Then go with my blessing, Owain. Be open to your destiny but don't forget your roots. Let your conduct be favoured, in the eyes of Nemetona and by this family who love you.'

She leaned forward, grasping his hand with strong fingers. The pressure she exerted lent power to her words, reinforcing the warning she had imparted. He left her chambers deep in thought.

The following morning Owain and Edern were summoned to meet Cunedda and Enniaun. The Votadini leaders looked none the worse for their marathon excesses, though Edern had drunk more than he was used to in frustration at Elen's indifference. His head thumped and his face was whey grey when he met Owain. His friend laughed, but threw a comradely arm around his shoulder.

Cunedda was seated on the Votadini throne, an ancient oak chair, darkened by the years, the seat worn smooth by contact with generations of his predecessors. Enniaun sat to his right. Cunedda beckoned the boys to be seated, an indication that whatever the reason for the summons, they were not to be punished. The ageing king offered them wine or ale. He grinned at Edern's face and his polite refusal.

'Your father shall speak, grandson. Your grandmother, Gwawl, and your mother have discussed this matter also. I am at odds with their counsel. I have the authority to bind you to your kin and meet your responsibilities, but my life would be made more miserable than yours were I to take that course. I find it strange that the words of some ancient northern seer are considered weightier than mine, but kings and sages live in different worlds, so I bow to the family's view, even though I don't share it. As for you, young Pict, Drust has been true to his word; we have had no raids since Owain's return. We are all grateful for the kindness you showed my grandson.'

Cunedda sat back, taking a huge draught of ale from his favourite goblet before wiping his greying whiskers with the back of his hand. He nodded for Enniaun to speak.

'First there is the matter of your standing, Edern. You sit with Owain at table. Being without rank you attract the enmity of our high born. Cunorix says that the pair of you are inseparable. Therefore, in recognition of your loyalty, we have created a new position that binds you to our kin. You may refuse this honour if you feel it cleaves you too much from your own. But you've travelled far already in your allegiance to Owain and we feel it will serve you well to be adopted into our house.'

Edern heard the words, but they failed to register in his ale-soaked head. Enniaun continued. 'As you have been a true friend to our kin, Owain, we hereby appoint you the 'Staff' of Owain the Bear. By this sign others will know that the Votadini have taken you to their own.'

Cunedda grunted. Enniaun continued: 'Your device shall be Owain's Bear with a staff, on the Votadini ox-blood ground. Our kin will acknowledge this Royal dedication of your person and henceforth you shall be as brother to Owain in my household. How say you?'

Edern's fogged mind finally realised that this was no trivial matter. He paused, struggling to find words to match the solemnity of the occasion.

'I'm honoured, my lord. I'd thought to seek advantage for myself and my people by my friendship with your son. The fates and Lailoken's teaching bound me to him. Now, I accept your charge. I will bring no dishonour to your household in this trust that you bestow.'

'Well spoken, lad and honest. He bears himself well for a Pict, eh Enniaun?' Cunedda chortled, banging his goblet on the table and digging his son in the ribs in a manner that undermined the occasion's gravity.

'He does. I seem to have adopted a worthy son. Cunorix tells me you have a military talent, Edern and that needs to be nourished. I'll finalise details of your purse later, but there's another matter.'

He turned to Owain.

'Your mother tells me that you wish to see more of the world, son. I hoped you would return to the north. However, the family has prevailed upon me to support your request. If it satisfies your thirst for knowledge, then the Bear and his Staff will go to our ally, Ambrosius Emrys Wledig in Brittany. Is that far enough away for you?'

Owain gasped. The offer was far in excess of his expectations.

'I thank you. I learned much with the Picts and Ambrosius might teach me more. Thank you for your permission and for the honour bestowed on my friend, Edern.'

'It is settled then. Cunorix will prepare for your leaving. You must travel secretly. It would count ill with us if our enemies knew that the Votadini were lodged with Emrys Wledig. You'd better instruct your servants while your grandfather has letters written to take with you.'

Owain rose and bowed to his elders. Edern managed a rocking attempt at a bow.

Servants packed their clothes in sturdy travelling chests. The household believed them to be returning to the north. They outfitted themselves from Cunedda's armoury, choosing swords and daggers unadorned, lest they betray their status on the road. Edern added a bow and quiver of goose feathered arrows to his weapons.

Enniaun's grooms selected suitable mounts: horses that were durable and sure, not high-spirited for such a long journey. Filan would accompany them. Each had a personal servant. Enniaun reckoned that six warriors would be sufficient as an escort. Any more would arouse suspicion, any less and Ceri would have worried for their safety.

They said their farewells. Owain asked after his sister. He wished to say goodbye. Edern was glad she was absent.

'She's sulking,' Ceri explained.

'She begged to accompany you, but her father forbade it. She's taken to her room in annoyance. Will you wait until morning? The roads are mired, you'll not make good speed at night.'

'We're too eager to be away. We'll make for Dumnonia and the coast. Filan will see us safe. We'll send letters when we arrive.'

Enniaun nodded, remembering the enthusiasm of his own youthful ventures. 'Tell Emrys Wledig we await his coming. Tell him that you are a token of our alliance. Learn from him, both of you. We have need of new ways to wage war. Our warriors are sturdy, but predictable, and that's no security against wise foes. Go safely and with the gods' blessing.'

Ceri turned to brush away a tear. She watched from a window of her rooms, high in the centre of the hill fort, as their small entourage clattered its way across the cobbled paving and out to the open road. The small knot of horsemen dwindled to dark spots against a greying dusk until they wound from her sight behind the lee of the hill.

Owain and Edern were in high spirits; their excitement sufficient to offset the cold. Their eyes sparkled, their cheeks were ruddy from the biting wind. They were buoyed by their journey, trusting in their heavy fur-trimmed travelling cloaks to keep them snug from the worst of the weather. The road was a rutted track, pitted with potholes and puddles. The horses picked their way doggedly, but it was slow going. The small wagon that carried their supplies bounced, sliding alarmingly, as the driver urged his pair to compensate for the mud.

Filan was less enthusiastic about their departure, but as a seasoned traveller he was philosophic about their desire to be away. A few days of such conditions, he knew, would temper their optimism. It was Anagantios, stay at home time, but a druid's discipline could overrule tradition. He wondered how the boys would fare when the real cold of Ogronios, the time of ice, set in.

The men, like the boys' horses, had been hand-picked by Enniaun. They were led by Urien, a grizzled veteran with a wealth of battle honours and more usefully, a much-travelled warrior, who had come late to the Votadini. None questioned the service their lord asked of them, but they shunned winter campaigns and each would have preferred to bide by the fires as the season dictated.

They travelled all night, stopping briefly, illuminating the road with lanterns to avoid the worst hazards. They had put a good distance between themselves and Dinas Ffynon by the time the sky paled into a bleak dawn. The wind blew strongly from the north; clouds scudded across a leaden sky; snow threatened the barren brown fields and skeletal trees bent against the weather, rattling and moaning in their dark sleeping.

'Do you still have the appetite to go on, Owain?' Filan shouted above the whipping wind.

'The journey across Powys is our main obstacle. We should husband our strength between here and the border. Let's push on until noon, then make a halt. We can continue until dark and seek shelter at a shrine to rest the horses. Do you agree?'

'The tavern sounds very welcoming to these ageing bones, Owain. The rest I shall endure.'

Urien judged their arrival at a shrine with the accuracy of an arch astronomer. A walled enclave, the shrine was served by Christian monks and housed a small detachment of militia to deter brigands. It provided shelter for small taverns to cater for passing travellers. Night had fallen again and the whole band was eager for a cooked supper and a thawing of their bones.

Caion the taverner was surprised. Winter trade was rare. He was roused from his fire-side doze by Urien's gruff announcement that he had guests. They stamped into the shelter, pressing Caion's family into action stoking up the fire and preparing food.

'We're not as well-provisioned as we should be,' he informed his guests.'But we'll do the best we can.'

'We're glad to be under a roof, taverner; our servants can aid you and if your stocks are low, we have food. The men have need of a real meal, so be not fearful of asking,' Urien instructed.

From being dormant, the tavern sprang into bustling activity. The travellers gorged themselves on a rich broth, meats and pastries that combined their own and Caion's meagre resources. Urien mulled wine for the men as they sat round a roaring fire, stoked by Caion's younger son. None were late abed. They were stiff-jointed and aching from the cold ride; knowing that the worst of their journey was still to come. They yearned for a bath house where they could ease their pains, but there was none. They took their sleeping-furs to straw palliases laid out in the upstairs rooms.

Owain and Edern bedded down beside each other. Their full bellies lulled them quickly to sleep. A peaceful quiet descended, punctuated by the occasional hissing spit of a wet log on the fire and the snoring of exhausted travellers.

Well into the night, Owain awoke suddenly. It was pitch black. No cock had crowed. A sliver of silver light shafting through the tiny casement was the only light, fading and returning with the clouds' passage across the moon.

What had aroused him? Full wakefulness came quickly, a legacy of his father's warrior training. Something was awry, he could sense it. A hand touched his cheek and dropped to shake his shoulder. He yelped in surprise, bringing Edern awake with a start.

'Ssshhhhh,' a voice urged.

'Don't wake the entire tavern. Gods! I'm freezing, brother. Move over. I need your furs. Now lie down and warm me, I'm chilled to my very bones.'

Owain scrabbled for his flints and tinder, sparking a candle into life. The warm, mellow pool of light battled back more of the darkness, reflecting off Elen's burnished red-gold hair as she shivered, teeth chattering.

'Father will see you in a convent for this; you were forbidden to come. We don't go north to the Guotodin.'

'I know, brother. You go to Emrys Wledig and so do I. There's naught for me at home. Why must I spend my days searching for some distraction, when my brother travels the length and breadth of the land? Now for the sake of all the gods and the new Christ, will you please warm me, before you end up sleeping with a corpse.'

He fell silent. Elen's obstinacy was sovereign. He pulled her close, spooning her body.

'What will Filan will say on the morrow?'

'Leave the druid to me. I will go with you...' her voice tailed off into a gentle snore.

Owain looked at Edern in the glow from the candle. He shrugged, the slight movement bringing a sleepy protest from Elen. Edern pulled his furs closer around him. Rising spirits and despair mingled together in equal parts as sleep took him again to her bosom.

***

A lifetime's training in the ancient arts endowed druids with command. Displays of emotion were rare. However, Filan's art was stretched to its limit when Elen made her appearance the following morning. Gasps of surprise from the men greeted her as they prepared for the day's journey.

'This is folly, Elen. You know your father's wishes. We're come too far to turn back. I can't risk an escort to take you home because we're too few and it will be Gwent before it's safe to hire a messenger to inform your family. But you knew all this, didn't you?'

He fixed her with the practised stare that terrified apprentices. Unflawed, clear, grey eyes stared back, totally fearless.

'If you know my strategy so well, you'll also know that it's pointless debating the issue. I've spent a whole night and day bouncing about in that infernal wagon. My royal backside is bruised black and blue. I nearly froze to death and I stink like a corpse. Against all that, what words do you have to pain me more?'

She almost pierced the shield of his discipline. He caught the beginning of a smile before it blossomed.

'You're beyond hope, Elen. Only one who's goddess blessed could act as you. Who am I to challenge such a will? I'll inform your father from Gwent. Fortunately, we have spare coin for emergencies, so we'll buy you a horse, some clothes and furs before we cross into Powys. Until then, you must travel with the wagoner. You have not long to wash. We're leaving immediately. See the taverner's wife.' He turned away to discuss the day's march with Urien, sensing the mischievous victory smile behind his back.

They fought the roads and the weather for three more days before crossing the border. The challenge became stiffer. They avoided inns, villages and towns, eager to be through the realm of the High King. With cordial relations between Cunedda and Vitalus, a royal invitation to Viroconium would have been difficult to refuse. There was little difference between being a guest at court and a bargaining pawn in the games of kings.

The weather's unkindness reminded them of their rashness. Elen endured the hardships with a determined will. She complained less than the men, even when it came to bedding down on the soaking ground in flimsy tents. Her star rose even higher in Edern's firmament. Although she conversed with him in a comradely fashion, there was naught to suggest that she viewed him as any other than the new brother he had become.

Four days into Powys, wet, bedraggled and dispirited, they left the quagmire of the road to camp for the night. A light sleet had fallen all day, soaking them to the skin. Their supplies had dwindled to frugals. The party was unprepared for a challenge from passing patrols. They had seen several, thus far, but had been ignored by the mounted scouts, who seemed to have their own concerns. As they struggled to erect their tents, a troop of five scouts halted at the road side to witness their sorry plight.

'By the authority of Vitalus, will you not come to the town? This is no night for sleeping in the open,' the young officer called hospitably, steam rising from his lathered horse.

'We thank you for your concern, but these are apprentices from the druidic chapter of Gwent and such trials are part of their training,' Filan replied diplomatically.

'Nay, they're too young in years for such harsh weather. Let us escort you to warmth in the town; you'd be safer too,' the officer persisted.

Filan considered his options. They did not wish to enter the town. Curiosity would trigger an unhealthy interest in their journey, leading to increased surveillance.

'I've no authority to countermand my senior brethren's instructions, sir. I do thank you for your concern, but we must abide by our rules. Please honour these and let us be,' he insisted.

The scout's horse reared and stamped, forcing the warrior to dismount to calm it. He beckoned to his men to do likewise. Curosity creased his face as he caught sight of Elen, her hair not quite concealed beneath the hood of her travelling cloak.

'Have druids taken to recruiting young women as apprentices? I'd not heard of such.'

Filan suppressed an inward sigh. This was not going well. Urien's hand drifted to the hilt of his sword. The scouts were now edgy and suspicious. An incident was brewing which Filan could not afford. They were too close to Viroconium to engage in a skirmish with the scouts. There might be injuries to Elen or Owain and there was no guarantee that they could account for all their opponents.

'A word young man,' Filan beckoned for the troop leader to come closer. Deception was still Filan's favoured course.

The scout walked three strides with the druid, unsure as to how to act.

'Calm yourself and your men. It is as you see; we are not as we announced ourselves, but there is no cause for your suspicion,' Filan soothed.

'We are escorting the cousins of Cynvelin of Gwynedd to see their uncle Tendubric in Gwent. You can allow us the subterfuge; we wished this to be a private journey and had no wish to alert every brigand on the road that the party contained royal personages. Despite the best offices of your patrols, we might well have been robbed or abducted, or worse.'

Filan sensed the tension ease. The scout accepted the plausible tale.

'My apologies. I had no wish to compromise you. But if this is so, then you must come to Viroconium. The weather is evil and my king would have my hide if he knew that valued allies had passed through the realm without his hospitality.'

'It shall be so. Give us time to pack up our tents and we shall ride with you to Viroconium,' Filan conceded. He grimaced inwardly despite his outer calm. Riding into Viroconium would initially challenge them with uncertainty; riding out might well be far more dangerous.

11. The Exile

428 AD - North Brittany

The rain poured, hammering insistently against the windows of the imposing villa. Grey skies matched the mood of the young nobleman who stared out at the drooping elms. Ambrosius Aurelianus chafed to be away. The tall, well built Roman turned from the window and began to pace back and forth. He paused occasionally to glance at the open maps on the low table.

'You will wear away the floor with your pacing,' chided Leontinus, his young companion, lounging with a brimming wine goblet in the white tunic of the ambitious Roman aristocrat, who sought to advance his own military career by furthering Ambrosius's objectives.

Ambrosius paused, a retort on the tip of his tongue. He smiled instead. 'I am like a fish in a midsummer pond, Leo. I should be in Britain standing up to Vitalus.' He started pacing again, a grim expression re-appearing on his clean-shaven face. He flicked his hand through his dark oiled curls in exasperation.

Leontinus's reputation was growing as a commander who took risks to achieve his objectives. He was unpopular with his men as a consequence and the deep amber of his eyes only added to the rumours that he was witched.

'You are making me edgy. Take your hounds and hunt. Call the new Libyan slave girl. Do anything, but please stop your pacing, it's spoiling the quality of my wine.'

Ambrosius halted yet again. 'You're right, Leo. I'm disinclined to hunt in the wet and you know your lecherous leanings are at odds with my beliefs. The girl is yours. I'm going to the chapel to pray for guidance. The Almighty must surely give me some insight, or suffer the consequences of my pacing in his heavenly halls.'

Solemnly, he walked across a paved courtyard to the small chapel. He hardly registered the wind lashing his clothes and his rain soaked tunic. Dripping wet and hardly recognisable as the head of the household, he entered. The candles guttered at the sharp blast of air that accompanied him into the shrine. He knelt, alone, in a damp puddle at the altar. He closed his eyes; his brow furrowed. He mouthed a silent request for guidance. The candles burned with a welcoming steady glow.

Leontinus tired of the wine. Ambrosius's mood had unsettled him. He considered alternatives. Certainly, the girl ranked quite highly, though the wine had dulled his senses. He was about to have her massage him, when he heard a clamour in the courtyard. Peering through the rain splashed window he saw slaves run to hold a sodden horse. Its drenched rider looked sorrowful. His curiosity aroused, Leontinus barely reached the ante-room before the man sloshed through the door. The courier looked as though he'd ridden hard. The cloak was insufficient protection against the rain. His hands were tinged with cold, several tones lighter than the dark blue of his tunic. Sopping boots and a pinched face reflected his misery.

'I have urgent news for Ambrosius Emrys Wledig,' he rasped.

Leontinus nodded. 'I'll inform the young lord that you're here. Meanwhile, the house slaves will assist you out of those clothes, or we'll have your death before your news.' He raised a hand dismissively as the courier made to protest. For all his rashness in battle, Leontinus knew from experience how much the weather and long miles punished a rider.

He hurried quickly to the chapel, cursing the stinging rain. Stooping inside the doorway, he made the warding sign and inwardly asked for protection from the unpredictable God on the cross.

'Your God would appear to have answered your prayers, Aurelianus. A very wet angel awaits you.'

There was a sigh from the dimly lit chapel. 'Perhaps my frustrations are to be answered, Leo. Tell him I will be with him directly. I must offer a prayer of thanks.'

His friend retreated, peering guardedly into the gloom at the crouched figure at the unadorned altar. Leontinus kept a wary eye on the simple cross that hung on the wall. His friendship with Ambrosius was long-standing, but he could never reconcile himself to strange Christian beliefs. A chill accompanied his withdrawal.

A grateful messenger, dutifully rubbed by slaves and clothed in a fresh tunic, greeted his return. Heavy leather despatch bags were draped across his right arm. He held a goblet of mulled wine. The warm clothes and the drink had restored some of his colour.

'Have you been well attended?' Leontinus asked.

'The wine is battling the chill in my bones.'

'What name do you go by?'

'My name is Col, my lord. I greet you from the halls of the Votadini. I've travelled from the northlands of the Pretani.'

Leontinus raised his eyebrows. Perhaps there was something in his friend's joyless god. Aurelianus entered before he could question further.

'Give me time to talk with this messenger; I shall bathe and be tended, but leave me for now,' he said, dismissing his attendants. 'Tell me news from Britain, courier. I starve for a morsel of knowledge in this peaceful boredom.'

'Then here is a feast for you my lord,' Col replied. He handed the saddlebags to Ambrosius. The Roman cleared the maps from the table, deposited the despatches and cut Cunedda's personal seals with a sharp knife. The parchments cascaded across the table.

'Any unwritten messages?' Ambrosius asked.

'Aye, lord, just one. My King, Cunedda, asks you to recognise the strategic importance of his new domain in northern Gwynedd.'

'Gwynedd! He's no longer in the Guotodin?' Ambrosius asked, spreading the letters out.

'It's all there, lord. He wishes you to see how close he is to Powys. With your permission, I would retire. It's been a long ride.'

'Of course, of course. Whatever am I thinking of? I'm too wrapped up in my own head to mind my hospitality.'

Ambrosius shooed Col away with Senta, a young body slave. 'Tend to his needs,' he ordered, turning to the despatches.

'If you're to sink your head in those, I'll take my leave. Of the two, I'd prefer your pacing,' Leontinus announced, wryly.

'Return tonight to dine, I'll have time to digest this feast by then. For once we'll have something important to speak of.'

'As you will, lord. Are we to ride again soon?'

'I don't know. But if Cunedda has moved to Gwynedd, who knows? We might yet be roused.'

Ambrosius immersed himself in the despatches. He didn't summon Senta to help him bathe until the slave's timid arrival to light the evening lamps. When Leontinus returned, a feast was set out with the best wines. Ambrosius was in a jocular mood.

'Come my friend, come. Let us eat and drink. I'll not even take offence at your pagan libations tonight.'

'There's good news, lord?'

'Take your couch, refresh yourself. We'll speak later. Musicians, play a lively tune, to cheer us.' Ambrosius beckoned Leontinus to be seated as the musicians played lyres, harp and pipes. Slaves piled platters of venison, hams in cloves and honey before them and poured Gallic wine from ceramic jugs.

For the burning of two thirds of a candle they ate and drank voraciously. Only when they were stretched out on their couches, so sated that they could hardly move, did Ambrosius change the mood. He dismissed the servants and ordered the music to cease. Leontinus leaned forward and placed his goblet on the table.

'Vitalus's people are disunited. He believes he has secured the aid of Cunedda of the Votadini. He is no blood ally of the usurper, but he was a friend to my father,' Ambrosius began.

Leontinus, stretched out on his couch. His amber eyes glittered over the rim of his goblet. Banished from Rome by his father, Valerius for conduct that flagrantly challenged the authority of one so close to the emperor, his wayward son craved any action to redeem his position. Valerius was old and held extensive estates in Rome and Cisalpine Gaul. Time was a luxury Leontinus could not afford.

'What do you intend, lord?'

'Patience, Leontinus. There will be work for you soon enough. I hope Vitalus has angered more of the British. It is all to our advantage.'

'How so, lord?'

'The Vortigern requested Cunedda's Votadini horsemen to combat the Scotti in exchange for land in Gwynedd. This places our ally on the border of Powys. His son, Enniaun holds the Guotodin. I have despatches from my sister, Servilla, wife to the upstart, Vitalus. She cannot write clearly for fear of her husband's spies, but there's enough to suggest that my brother was not killed by a few drunken Picts. We shall know more when our spies return.'

'Can you trust this Cunedda, my lord? He's willing to deal with the Vortigern. Why won't he betray you to Vitalus, if you ever set foot in Britain?' Leontinus asked.

'I know he's no Pelagian like the Vortigern. Cunedda has always supported Rome, though his family are a strange brood of pagans and Christians. He stood by my father. I see no reason for him to change. His people have much more to gain by supporting us.'

'What will you do, lord?'

'We'll wait on further intelligence, Leo. This can't be rushed or we'll suffer the consequences. I know you're eager, but there's more to being a leader than shouting orders to charge. We have much to do to add to your skills,' Ambrosius said, catching the young officer's mood.

'You're right, lord, as usual. Perhaps I'm fit for nothing more than leading charges?' he observed wistfully.

'Then assisting me will provide you with some answers to your questions, won't it?' Ambrosius replied. He clapped his young friend on the shoulders. Leontinus summoned a stiff smile.

'Don't think you're alone in your disappointment, Leontinus. I'd give much to be going into action myself, but we must hasten preparations here and plan to act when we know we are strong.'

Beside him, the alert amber eyes of the wolf disguised the feelings of the young Leontinus. Patience was a virtue he could not afford if he was to restore his standing in the eyes of his father. He craved to be blessed by the gods of battle. Fine wine and comely slave girls were but distractions.

12. Unwanted Allies

428 AD - Viroconium, Powys

Vitalus the Vortigern had chosen carefully. Word had been sent to the eastern pagans for help. His own allies were untrustworthy and lacked sufficient mobile forces to face the many challenges that beset the kingdom. One company of Frisian Jutes was now sailing to Viroconium, led by Hengist, a Danish free-booter. With only three ships, Hengist presented no threat. The King remained smugly confident in Britain's longstanding peace. Raids were nothing compared with the war across the ocean. Pressure from the eastern barbarians had mounted to threaten Rome, and displaced people now threatened years of stability. The sea was his truest ally.

Bishop Agricola fretted impatiently in his quarters. As senior adviser to the Vortigern, he resented being distanced from the High King's ear. Yet Vitalus often conducted military business personally.

Papers had also arrived from Rome. Bishop Germanus had taken ship for Britain. Agricola was vexed. British bishops would be accused of heresy, despite its contribution to the peace of the realm. Agricola feared that Germanus would also be displeased by the Vortigern's hiring of pagans. His thoughts were disturbed by the approach of a young serving boy, who announced that the High King would finally see him.

Vitalus greeted him jovially. 'Ah, Agricola. Do be seated. Take some wine.'

'My lord, I find little to warrant your high spirits,' Agricola responded, his heron beak of a nose pointing firmly at the ceiling to reinforce his displeasure.

'Is this so? And what should I be so glum about on this fine day?'

'I would have thought it obvious. Germanus and Hengist, here at the same time. A representative of the Papal Legate's Office on his way too. Incursions from all quarters, yet you act like it's the Maying festival and spring blossoms through the land.'

'I'm touched by your concern, Bishop. Have no fear. Matters are in hand.'

'As your chief counsellor, my lord, might I know of these matters?' Agricola sniffed.

'Look, Bishop! Germanus is of no concern. He'll berate the clergy, but they know how close the people are and how far away Rome is. This priest has a reputation as a warrior. I propose to send him on an expedition. Let's see if his duty to God can resist the temptation of resuming his battle honours, eh?'

'Well, there are targets enough. The Picts have long memories. They won't forget how you executed their kinsmen.'

'Can't be helped, Bishop. Any realm is worth forty dead Picts. I could hardly release them after the assassination of our beloved Constans, could I?'

'The murder was at your incitement, lord. God no doubt frowns on the man who beheaded the perpetrators.'

'Don't preach your heresy of moral responsibility to me, Bishop. Find some way of placating those who believe my hands drip with Constans's blood. We're hard pressed and I don't know who I can trust. Servilla's suspicion has frosted us for years. God help me if she ever finds the truth of it.'

Vitalus paced. Agricola sensed he'd opened old wounds. Opportunism had its price: near war with the Picts and divisions among allies. For all his spies' efforts, the picture remained unclear.

'I apologise, my lord. I did not mean to anger you. I must attend to my duties. We need more information about friends and enemies alike. I shall redouble my efforts.'

'Thank you, Bishop. Your duty is acknowledged. Now, I must see Servilla. There is the small matter of my eventual succession and two sons are hardly sufficient in these trying times. Though I doubt there'll be much enjoyment in it.'

'The Lord smile on your endeavours. May you be fruitful,' Agricola blessed the king.

'If he does, then his humour is as strange as yours, Bishop,' Vitalus replied, tartly.

***

Servilla, daughter of the former Roman Emperor Maximus, considered her lot. Her husband was too concerned for her feelings to be sincere. Servilla lacked her peers' classical beauty. Her nose was too large and angular for the rest of her features. Her body was big boned and clumsy. When she walked, she had the rolling gait of a galley in full sail.

Her one satisfaction was the comfort of her husband's court and the honour accorded to her as mother of his heirs. Her abundance was not without problems. Her Christian beliefs were at odds with her opulent lifestyle. Her husband's bed was also objectionable of late. She could not deny the thought that the Vitalus who ploughed into her with the insistent vigour of a king desperate for heirs, was the same man who had instigated her brother's death. Her warmth for Vitalus had dissipated, but she had no evidence for the deed.

She sighed, gazing from the window across a winter bleak forest landscape of naked oaks and beeches. In her mind she saw the tall cypresses and olive trees of her native Rome and caught the pungent tang of herbs on the still hot air of a balmy afternoon. Her reverie was punctured by footfalls in the corridor. She sighed. It was to be another afternoon of wifely duty. This was no way for an emperor's daughter to live; of this she was sure. Though her body was unattractive, there were few whose minds were as sharp. Her husband greeted her with his irritating false bonhomie. She put her mind to the whetstone and spun the wheel.

Her brother, Ambrosius, was the key to her dilemma. Discreet action would benefit both herself and the people. Time and patience; time and patience. She repeated the words in her head as she turned to greet Vitalus. He was already stripping off his tunic. Time and patience ....

She steeled herself for the inevitable physical onslaught. At least it was always over quickly and not a great endurance, which brought a slight smile to her face, which he mistook for affection. Salvation arose from a timid knock at the door to the bedchamber. Cursing, Vitalus threw it open and listened to the whispered message from a cringing servant lad.

'My apologies, lady, it appears we have unexpected guests.'

'No need my lord. The duties of a king outweigh those of a husband' she demurred, curious as to who had saved her from her ordeal.

***

Agricola had anticipated a hectic day, but considered how he had offended God to be at the centre of such chaos. It was one challenge to accommodate the visiting Bishop Germanus, who arrived with a small entourage just after daybreak, and another to host the Frisian sea pirates whom Vitalus saw as necessary additions to his forces. The villa was fortunately large enough to house them, but the bishop's organisational skills were further pressed at mid day by the arrival of Theoderic, from the Papal Legate's Office in Rome and twenty horsemen. To further test the bishop's patience a patrol had returned with a small band of travellers, reported to contain the cousins of Cynvelyn of Gwynedd on their way to visit their uncle Tendubric of Gwent. It was enough to prompt a bishop to consider life as a hermit.

Germanus had proved easy to deflect from his instructions. Frustrated by the Papal charge to strike at a Pelagian heresy that showed little evidence of being undermined, the Bishop was easy game to the High King's hawk. In exchange for permission to preach against the heresy, Germanus donned his battle gear, chose a stout horse from the King's own stables and rode off to fight the Scotti.

Such ingenuity on the High King's part was some relief to the beleaguered Agricola. Hengist and Hrosa proved a sterner test of his patience when they presented themselves to a council of the Vortigern's allies later that afternoon. The combination of their impatience, the arrival of the Papal Legate's delegation and the complication of the bedraggled band of travellers meant that when Agricola came to be seated at the council table, it was the first time his rear had made contact with a chair or stool since he had risen from his bed.

Against the less formal, domestic dress of the British, the Frisian sea pirates came impressively to council in full panoply of war. Hengist, the burlier of the two, strode fearlessly into the chamber. His six foot frame was topped by a burnished metal helmet. He wore a byrnie that any British chieftain would have coveted, over a dark green, silk tunic that puckered into tight fitting sleeves at his forearms.

'Do you come seeking war in my very villa?' the Vortigern asked, seeking to defuse the uncertainty in the room. Hengist looked around at the unarmed councillors, who stared back with cool disdain.

'We come to show our mettle, lord King. You should know who it is that you employ to keep your borders safe,' he replied in faltering Brythonic.

Vitalus nodded, appraising the pair. 'Perhaps you'd like to put up your swords and be seated. We don't bring weapons to our councils.'

'In peace or war our arms are as familiar to us as our shirts and breeches. But, as a concession to your traditions, we will put them up.'

The two divested themselves of their war gear and seated themselves.

'Thank you. Our councillors would be too affeared to speak, had you retained them.' Vitalus made an effort to lighten the mood, but it was lost on his visitors. The Vortigern waved for drinks. When they arrived, the newcomers' goblets remained untouched.

The king put his plans to the Frisians. Hengist listened intently, pausing once in a while to stroke his silky beard between thumb and forefinger. When Vitalus was finished, the huge sea reiver calmly stated the cost of his services, ignoring the contemptuous looks of those around him.

'I have three keels with me, lord King. A hundred and fifty fighting men. Our preferred purpose is to patrol your coasts. We need a base, set aside from your people. I wish to lose neither men, nor cause you affront by risking squabbles between us. We don't wish to live near your priests. Their mischievous tongues respect no others' gods. We need provisions and gold. If these conditions are met, we'll serve you well. Your enemies will know you have a new-found strength.'

'Bluntly said, Hengist. You speak plainly so I will reciprocate. The island we call Ruchin shall be yours. It is well located for your ships. You'll be provided with all that you need to build shelters. You'll be provisioned and paid in accordance with your requests.'

There were some among the council who bit on their tongues at the unsubtle bargaining of their king. Indeed, there was more than one frustrated gesture at Hengist's demands. Who were these 'Yr Eigel,' pagan barbarians from the sea, to insult the sophisticated British in such guttural speech? Yet the Vortigern knew there were no subtle negotiations to be had with these men. Either he must pay their price or decline their assistance. Their employment finalised one part of his strategy.

The business concluded, the council relaxed to drink the Vortigern's wine. Hengist and Hrosa took pork, but their goblets remained empty. As he stabbed his knife into the rich fare, Hengist observed the inherent weakness of his new employers; the confident arrogance arising from their years of assured plenty. These British, with their soft oiled bodies, sat with an ease enjoyed by none of his own. Beneath his tunic, the thin puckered white lines of scar tissue attested to the hard won sovereignty over his own followers. His hands were calloused from long hours of gripping both oar and weapons; his face was ruddied by the weathering effects of sea-salt and wind. His employers' showed little sign of either labour or fighting. He had left behind a land of flooded farms. Pastures had sunk beneath the slurry of rising river levels. If it was not enough that his people stared starvation in the face, their eastern enemies grew more voracious as they in turn were driven from their lands by the dreaded Huns. His people's only salvation was rooted in the skills that he and others like him had crafted. They were hungry and desperate. Hengist had no intentions of failing them.

***

Bishop Agricola cringed inwardly at the feast that followed the council. Vitalus was renowned for his profligacy when it came to entertaining, yet rarely considered the tallies that the bishop so painstakingly kept. The vast table groaned with roast swan, duck, partridge, boar and pheasant. Fresh catches of mackerel and cod fought for space alongside steaming platters of cabbage, parsnips and beans. The High King's opulence was noted by all his guests, small dishes of olives filled the crannies between the larger platters and the wine was imported from Rome and so heady that flagon after flagon disappeared down the gullets of guests that rarely experienced such quality.

Owain was awed. Their arrival at a villa of such proportions had given him the opportunity to revise his notions of kingly status. True, Votadini feasts were indulgent, but so far from the key trade routes the north provided largely local produce. He had never eaten an olive and they proved not too much to his liking neither in taste nor when his teeth crunched on the stone.

They had been met with courtesy by stewards acting for a beaky bishop. Thus far, Filan's fears had not been realised. The story he related was accepted without question. They had not, as yet, received audience with Vitalus, however and the druid carefully rehearsed the deception in his own mind as he crumbled bread and cheese on his platter and held out a plain beaker for beer to a passing serving lad.

Owain observed the other guests as he ate and drank. The Frisians discussed in low murmurs in their own tongue. Their platters were piled high with meats and fowl, but they drank neither beer nor wine. Higher up the table a man of some thirty summers conversed with the bishop with the heron's beak. The High King was short and stocky with an energy that, like his name, exemplified action. He lounged on a padded couch, dressed in a plain woollen tunic that belied his status. He had no need of symbolic support for his authority, as was evident by the respectful entourage.

Filan had warned against conversing with any of the guests, especially those representing the Christians amongst them. Fortunately, they were confined to the lower table and surrounded by lesser lords. Filan and Urien flanked Owain, Edern and Elen, so there was no danger of their being seduced into conversation.

Seated near the head of the table, two guests looked very different from the Frisians in their green silks and the Romano-British in their more muted grey and dark blue tunics. The crisp white linen tunics of the Papal Legate and his companion were edged with the scarlet of the Papal Office and the purple of Rome. Owain's watchful eyes noticed that Theoderic, the Legate, was squat, well-muscled and had a face that creased into smiles, with eyes far more mischievous than his position might have merited. He ate heartily, but watered his wine frequently and waved away servants who made to replenish his cup.

The feast passed without incident. Filan waited for the first entertainment of the evening, a trio of jugglers, to draw the attention of the guests, before signalling that they should withdraw. Owain was relieved; the day had been long and the afternoon, spent in one of the biggest bath houses he had ever visited, had taken its toll. Edern and Elen looked similarly weary. The conversation at table had been stilted.

Owain came awake with a start; no dream of the vibrancy of those he had with Lailoken had awakened him, a more mundane reason in the effect the wine was having on his bladder. Half awake, he pulled on a crumpled tunic and set out down the corridor for a long walk to the latrines. He guessed it was some time before dawn. The villa was silent but for the noisy snores of the guests. Turning a corner, he stumbled into a figure walking in the opposite direction. The two drew apart, Owain mumbling a sleepy apology. His drowsiness was banished by the recognition that he had just collided with Theoderic, the Papal Legate. Initially, he considered that wine might also be the reason for the Legate's nightly excursion, but such an innocent need failed to explain the cowled hood and cloak that all but concealed its wearer's identity.

Theoderic's arm stretched out and held Owain's shoulder firmly. Neither drowsy sleep, nor the bleary effects of wine clouded eyes that bored into his skull.

'No harm done, boy. Get you back to your bed and I'd count it a boon that when you wake in the morning, you remember this as a dream.' The arched eyebrows demanded a response.

'I shall be honoured to have met such a person of your standing in my dreams,' Owain replied.

Theoderic patted his shoulder reassuringly and walked round the shadowy corner. The demands of Owain's bladder suddenly became far less persistent. Pausing for several heartbeats, the young Votadini padded silently in pursuit.

Owain trailed the cloaked figure into a part of the villa that housed the High King's family. Owain recognised the changing status of the decorations; alcoves housed eyeless white marble busts of former family members, gods and goddesses. All seemed to peer at Owain's presence, but he chided himself at his mind's tricks. Hugging the outside wall, where the shadows were cast longer by the flickering candles, Owain watched as Theoderic finally paused briefly outside a room with double doors. He tapped twice and was admitted. Owain marked which room had swallowed the Legate by a figurine of a centaur, which eyed him curiously from its alcove. He paused briefly. Filan had mentioned such creatures in his teachings about a colourful people called Greeks, but this was the first representation of his teacher's descripton he had seen. Considering how useful it would be to blend man and horse into one creature, he retraced his steps to find the latrines.

Filan listened silently to Owain's excited tale of his nocturnal adventure in the morning. They walked in one of the two squares outside the villa's buldings, the perimeter of which formed the long corridors of guest rooms. One quadrangle was ornamented with a large fountain, gushing from the mouth of Poseidon, stone benches and plum trees; the other was a drill square for the High King's commanipulares and several were hard at exercise with javelin, short swords and shields.

'It is no great mystery that such a place as this should be host to intrigue, Owain,' Filan said, scrutinising a badly thrown javelin in the other square.

'Still, you are right to be suspicious. One might expect a degree of discretion from someone as prominent as the Papal Legate. But, men are men for all their titles. We shall see whose room your centaur guarded. That might satisfy your curiosity.'

'What shall we do when we find out?' Owain asked, skipping with enthusiasm.

'We shall do precisely nothing, Owain, and I need your firmest promise on that. Our position here is parlous, if you hadn't remembered. We won't further jeopardise it by being ensnared in political intrigues. It will take all my skill to have us safe out of here and on our way.' He glared to reinforce the message.

Owain grimaced, but nodded his silent assent.

Discreet enquiries disclosed that the room housed no other than Servilla, wife to the High King. Despite his oath to Filan, Owain's imagination ran amok. For his part, Filan ascribed the act as little more than a tryst. Though Owain pressed him again for further investigation, the old druid held him to his oath with a severe scowl that augured ill if he broke it.

Filan's attention was drawn to the short audience that had been granted with Vitalus later in the day. He returned, frustrated and frosty to report that the Vortigern welcomed the cousins of so valued an ally as Cynvelyn and his hospitality was extended to them indefinitely. Filan's most artful pleas to allow their continued journey to Tendubric's domain in Gwent were diplomatically rejected.

'Oily snake. Worst kind of king to deal with,' Filan railed on his return. 'We're all but hostages as I feared. When word comes from Tendubric that contradicts our story, we're in a pickle barrel to be sure.'

Dusk brought them no nearer to a strategy of escape. The villa's fortifications made it impossible to leave. Their horses were stabled inside impregnable walls. Exits to the villa were through guarded gates.

'We have need of allies,' Owain said, when he and Filan were alone. Urien had taken the men to the exercise yard. Edern and Elen had gone to seek for any weaknesses in the villa's perimeter walls. 'Good strategy, Owain, but among this fawning batch of hypocrites no one exactly springs to mind,' Filan countered, though his tone had warmed from their earlier council.

'The Papal Legate is no friend to the Vortigern,' Owain proferred.

'True, but an enemy of the king is not necessarily a friend to us.'

'It's worth a try, teacher. We do know Theoderic is not all he seems.'

'Risky, Owain, very risky. I am charged with your safety by your kin. I'd not wish to face Cunedda, Enniaun and least of all Ceri and Gwawl should harm come to yourself and Elen.'

'Yet you said yourself, when word comes from Tendubric our lie is exposed.'

Filan tutted, exasperated by the simple logic in his student's argument.

'I shall seek Theoderic. Test him out. If there is any gain for us, I'll find a way to employ it. You stay here. Your patience grows, but slowly. We can ill afford the way that your mouth runs like a stream from the mountain of your head with nary a thought for where it gushes.'

Owain's shoulders drooped in disappointment, but he had no counter to Filan's accusation. When his teacher opened the door, Owain resignedly lay on his bed. Sleep was a long way off.

Theoderic was courteous but stiffly formal when Filan sought him out in the exercise quadrangle. He was watching his men go through their paces in matched pairs, with swords and shields. The routine kept their physical fitness, but added little to their skills; they were horsemen and looked clumsy when fighting on foot.

'I rarely have the chance to speak with heretics so far removed from God's presence,' he said, but beckoned for a slave to bring drinking water from the bucket.

'And I rarely seek counsel from one so august in the retinue of the God on the cross,' Filan responded.

The two eyed each other, seeking signs that might proffer advantage.

'And what possible counsel might I give to one so steeped in lore? We are but babes to you're ancient beliefs.'

'Twould be to our gain to dwell upon our beliefs, yet that is not the counsel I seek. The matter is delicate; the same discretion is required that my pupil extended to yourself last night.'

Filan did not miss the impact of his frankness. Theoderic stiffened; formal curiosity gave way to caution.

'He was not so discreet, old man.'

'Discreet enough. His old mentor is the only ear he has sought. Your secret is safe with us.'

'And what secret might that be?'

Filan passed the wooden drinking cup to the Legate.

'The secret that you alone know and which we are content to leave with your conscience.'

'Ah. I believe I see the reason for your counsel. My secret will be safe at a price, is that your intent? What are you after old man, gold or favours?'

'You are not in a king's court now, nor in the corridors of your pope's palace. What need would a man from beyond the world have of gold? You insult us by such a claim.'

'No insult intended, 't'is merely the way of men to seek opportunity from secrets.'

'Then we are at a distance greater than our spiritual beliefs. I have stated that your secret is safe and it is so, whatever the consequences of this meeting. I ask for the same pledge on the matter I wish to discuss with you,' Filan said, hushing his voice to a whisper.

Intrigued, Theoderic lowered his head closer.

'You have it, old man.'

'Then I shall speak plain and hold you to your pledge. We have a secret of our own. I am charged with the welfare of the three young ones in our party. We were apprehended on our way to the coast by the High King's scouts. We are not who we claim to be and the young ones will be in jeopardy once the Vortigern discovers their identity. If you could find it in your way to intercede with Vitalus, we should be pleased to be on our way and count ourselves in your debt.'

'You speak bluntly, Filan. If I held no respect for you and yours, I shall need to review that in the light of this trust. It is true, you are rats in a trap here. I am not unsympathetic to your plight and the lad did well by me in holding his tongue. However, there's little that I can say to the High King that will be of any use to you. His heresy is as far from me as yours. He mistrusts both myself and my office - I hold no sway with him.'

'It is as I believed,' Filan replied. 'Then we are at your mercy also. Would you consider aiding us in our efforts to leave?'

'It grieves me to see young innocents acting as unwilling hostages. The games men play should be for them alone. I leave in two days' time. If your secret holds until then, I'll do what needs to be done to smuggle you out. That's the best I can do.'

'I thank you, Theoderic. We have no strategy, so yours will be our greatest hope. There is some comfort in that. My lord will be grateful to you.'

'Keep your secret as I keep mine, old man. There is some equality of trust in neither of us being what he appears. Two days. With God's grace, we'll have you clear of here.'

'Then for the first time I shall hope your God's influence holds true. Good day to you my lord.'

***

Filan prepared as well as he could. Urien and his men were set to watch the gates for incoming messengers, with attention focused on the gate from which the road wound south towards Gwent. Owain, Elen and Edern were confined to their rooms. Filan's tone left no doubt in their minds that this was no game they played, but the art of high politics.

Whether the God on the cross's hand conjured fresh gales and rain, or Filan's arts manifested the harsh weather, the roads remained mired and travellers were few. A small party rode in from the west, Demetian merchants from the reports brought to Filan and no threat to their identity. Nevertheless, Filan was finding it difficult to maintain his authority, mainly over Elen, who resented being confined more than Owain and Edern. He was thankful when on the evening of the second day one of Theoderic's men delivered a simple message. 'The stables at dawn.'

They slept but lightly until the pale grey of a drizzly dawn barely lit their way to the stable block. Inside, all was preparation as Theoderic's men loaded gear on the backs of their horses. A welcome fug was a brief respite from the damp.

Theoderic greeted them, his Legate's tunic and sandals replaced by a red leather cuirass, heavy purple cloak and well worn riding boots.

'The youngsters in the wagon with yourself Filan. Urien and your men will mingle with mine. Let's hope the sentries are different from when we rode in and that they're too keen on staying dry to pry. '

'We shall not forget this whether the gods prove kind or no,' Filan replied.

'We shall see,' Theoderic grunted, swinging himself up on to a sturdy black; the type favoured by Roman cavalry. He led the awaiting column at a walk into the gloom of the day.

They were challenged at the gate by an alert sentry, who had instructions to oversee their departure. He cast a shrewd eye over the column, taking in the wagon and the four horses tied to its rear.

'You had no wagon when you arrived, Legate,' he observed, rain trickling from his helmet down his forehead.

'This clement weather of yours. My men are used to sun and heat; I've four laid up with snot-filled noses and shakes and shivers. They're too feverish to ride. Talk to the healer, he'll tell you.'

'No need, my lord, safe journey,' he said, waving a spear to open the gate.

The column wound slowly out towards the south, moving turgidly through the cloying mud. A mile from the gate, the wagon dispensed its load. Filan and his charges re-mounted and joined Theoderic.

'We're in your debt, my lord Legate,' Filan said, his face flushed with relief.

'I shall call upon it as and when I need it,' the Legate replied, pulling his hood up to protect his face from the rain. 'We shall set you on the road to Powys from where you can link up with the road to Siluria. You should have sufficient start to keep ahead of any patrols.'

'We thought to be riding with you to the coast,' Filan queried, aware that such an event left them in danger of discovery by the High King's scouts.

'I'd like to escort you, old man. But we swing north once we're out of sight of Vitalus. I need to see an old friend.'

'In the north you say. And which friend might that be?'

'As we're clear of the villa, and there's little intrigue out here, I'm to see Cunedda of the Votadini in Dinas Ffynon.'

'Indeed. Hardly a man of the God on the cross, or so I've been led to believe,' Filan said lightly.

'You are not what you seem and neither am I. It is not God's business I'm on.'

'Then with your permission, we will ride with you to the north, it will be safer for my charges,' Filan said.

'As you wish. To your frozen north it is.'

***

Theoderic was not the only one to leave Viroconium on that cold drab day.

Hengist, Hrosa and their retinue also left the villa to begin their service to the High King. They rode south east to Londinium to rejoin their warriors.

The isle of Ruchin was re-named in a ritual ceremony after the three mercenary ships beached several days later. The flames of a huge bonfire licked into an ink black sky. The newcomers dedicated their new base of Thanet to their gods.

The nomads built solid wood and thatched dwellings; pens for animals and a central hall for their assemblies. Within weeks Thanet gave birth to its first village. Its builders took to their ships to seek cows, sheep, goats and women to breathe life into it. Their prows pointed north. The Picts were their first target.

At the head of the small flotilla, Hengist pulled his cloak round him to off-set the chill wind. The head of one band of misfits and wanderers, he mused over the propitious start he had made to his ambitions for all his people.

13. Conspiracy

429 AD - Dinas Ffynon, Gwynedd

Cunedda's fourth son, Cundig, cleared a way for Theoderic and his aide, Seconius, battling against servants carrying chests and family treasures through the household, which was in turmoil. In a small room, furnished with chairs and a rustic table, Cunedda awaited them. The fire burned brightly, adding to the glow of the candles, fighting the odour of cold and disuse. Neither tapestries nor battle shields graced the walls, which stared bleakly at them.

'Theoderic, I'm told. It does my heart good to see a friend of Ambrosius Emrys Wledig. Sit down and be warm, you must have travelled cold and hard.'

Theoderic clasped the Votadini's offered hand heartily.

'It has been worth the discomfort, Cunedda of the Votadini. We have learned much in Viroconium. We are glad to be among friends.'

The four sat close to the crackling fire. Even swaddled in their best winter cloaks, the visitors' moods were dampened by the weather. It was iron cold; even more so in Cunedda's mountains.

Dinas Fynon was an impregnable fortress, clinging to the crest of a rocky outcrop at the head of a narrow, wooded valley. Roman engineers had seen its strategic value and had strung initial walls between natural crags on three sides. The fourth was a drop so sheer that they had not considered it worth walling. The fortress took its name from the clear, deep well that provided fresh water. Even against a committed besieging army, defenders could mount a lengthy resistance.

Cunedda sensed his guests' discomfort and called for mulled wine, beer and servings of rich broth with barley bread. 'This is neither food nor drink for kings, my friends, but it suits the weather and serves us better for that,' Cunedda grinned as the servants placed the fare before them. 'Eat up, pups. Has Yule's frosts chewed your toes off? It's but Samhain; winter's not settled on us yet.'

They smiled, despite the stiffness in their limbs; taking the steaming broth gratefully. The old king was a ruler with an eye for his people. The broth burned the inside of mouths, but they didn't care; its warmth penetrated straight to the belly. 'I trust, lord King, that our business is conducted well before your winter sets in. I'd be glad to be back in warmer climes by then,' Theoderic grunted, dunking bread into the steaming bowl.

Cunedda chuckled. 'What, you'd miss our winter solstice? There's many a Votadini lass who'd keep you warm, lad. But, if you must return and miss Saturnalia, then it's your loss. Personally, I'd prefer a warm wench in my bed than the sun on my skin. But each to his own.'

The banter continued while they ate and drank.

'We have ridden from Viroconium; returned your grandson safely and got the sense of the land. The Vortigern seems secure in his lair. What can you tell me to cheer Ambrosius?' Theoderic broke the camaraderie at last.

'I'm glad we can talk, Theoderic. Letters are useful, but dangerous. I am grateful for Owain's safe return. He was in danger. Good ploy acting as a Papal Legate. Made me laugh, Filan thinking you were shagging the queen. This viper, Vitalus, is wily. He makes enemies and lacks support, but tell Ambrosius not to underestimate him. He's a worthy opponent. I fear his schemes will ruin us all.'

'We've seen his wiles first hand. Ambrosius insisted that we spoke directly with his sister, Servilla. That's what I was about when your grandson followed me. Tell me more of the High King.'

'He drives wedges among the Britons. We northerners have laughed at the southern tribes since before the Romans. They're a stubborn, uncomradely lot, Theoderic. They squabble and war with each other over a stolen cow or a sheep. They raid each other for sport and cheat their neighbours. Only the hostile land protected their independence for so long. Rome would have conquered all, but for the terrain and the weather.'

'You see clearly, Cunedda, but what shall I tell my lord?'

'Tell him that Vitalus weakens the British. True, he's staunched Pictish and Scotti raids. I've played my part in that. But his Frisian mercenaries worry many. A three way religious schism divides us further. Germanus preaches to restore Rome's dominion, the Vortigern favours Pelagian teachings because it suits his lords' authority and Tendubric? Well, if we knew what he believes we'd be less edgy than we are. Then there's the issue of his accession. The realm fragments like a broken eggshell, Theoderic. He takes advantage by adding to his own power.' Cunedda paused, holding out a deep ceramic dish to Cundig for more ale.

'So, what chance might there be to topple him? Honestly, Cunedda, we may have but one.'

'I'd say it was too early. Traditional families would support Ambrosius, but the real doubt is against Tendubric. Any action might throw him back into Vitalus's arms, despite their differences. It's too risky. Anyway, where would you raise the men? Your troops are having it hard in the east.'

Theoderic and Cunedda plotted well into the early hours. The king himself stoked the fire on occasions and called for regular replenishments of ale and wine. Despite the quantity, neither man showed any sign of drunkenness. Their intrigues were too serious to allow drink to work its magic. Seconius and Cundig succumbed to the beer and warmth of the fire, falling asleep wrapped in their cloaks. Baulked by Vitalus's successes, Cunedda and Theoderic had to be satisfied with their scheming. In the dead of night, the flames from the fire cast huge shadows on the stone wall. Cundig snored loudly, comatose with ale.

'I am glad we have talked, Theoderic. Bid your lord recruit the best men. He'll not find too many ships when the time comes. Now, I'll retire, if Gwawl will stand the farting from this ale. I'll have a servant take you to a bed, though it won't be the most comfortable. We are not yet settled in this Dinas Ffynon.'

Their shadows crawled up the walls and along the ceiling timbers as they stood, bonded by a handclasp that cemented their alliance.

***

430 AD - Gwent

Tendubric, Pendragon of Gwent and Siluria and his brother, Cynvelyn, watched busy carpenters plying their trade, restoring an ancient hill fort as a defensive bastion. Against whom remained to be seen, but Tendubric smelled the times and his nostrils warned him of blood. The Pendragon was convinced that Gwent and Siluria had an obligation to the earliest Christian Church. Neither Rome's orthodoxy nor the Vortigern's Pelagian heresy offered acceptable allies.

'We must protect the Holy Cross, brother. Our ancestor Helen did not journey to the east to retrieve it for naught. Rome envies our secrets. There's no love of us in that unholy city and the greedy Pope covets our sacred relic. And this Vitalus is a trickster and a fraud. A brazen heretic. If that were not enough, he invites paid mercenaries to aid him. You must see my mind on this, brother. We cannot ally. We'd be in error.'

His words were earnest. Their inspection of a chain of hill forts afforded the opportunity to sway Cynvelyn to his vision. The ride was half complete, but he sensed the gulf between them.

Cynvelyn's impassive face masked the irritation he felt at his brother's insistence. He had heard the litany too many times.

'I know your feelings, brother. I'm bound by your counsel. But I fear for us. This Cunedda is no fool. I can't winkle him out of Dinas Ffynon with all my strength. The Vortigern invited him south to aid me, but it's a subtle ploy. I can't march to aid you if necessary. I know you favour independence, but are we strong enough to stand alone?' Cynvelyn mused resignedly.

Tendubric sighed, slowing his bay's trot to a walk. The white cloak, which had billowed out behind him like a sail, covered the horse's flanks.

'You think me inflexible?'

'Your integrity is unequalled. Whereas the Lord may reward you for it one day, you're easy to predict on matters of state. We're isolated as a result,' Cynvelyn observed diplomatically.

'We have spoken out against the High King, but we are distant from his enemies also. What would you have me do?' asked the Pendragon.

Cynvelyn glanced across at his brother. Even on the windswept hill, Tendubric's kingly appearance shone. His body was as straight as a pine in the saddle; his long white hair flowed about him like smoke; his shoulders were square, despite the burdens of the realm.

By comparison, Cynvelyn was more relaxed. His governership of Gwynedd was held at the High King's whim. He was under no illusion that Vitalus considered him a threat to Powys. However, Cynvelyn was a complex schemer, more so than the Dragon, and by far the more dangerous because he looked the more ineffectual.

He smiled at Tendubric; his voice as always was the well-modulated tone of the scholar, schooled, reasonable and considered. He brushed his dark brown hair out of his eyes with a plain leather gauntlet. The dark green tunic he wore, covered by a light fawn woollen cloak, clasped with a single pin at his throat, marked him more as a retainer than a governor.

'Vitalus knows that he can squeeze me between his forces and Cunedda's. I doubt it will come to that. I'm as helpless as a day old pup. If I turn south to threaten him, I must leave spears to guard my back. I don't have the cavalry to match him. He's neutered me, brother. As long as I do his bidding, he'll maintain my position as governor, even though Cunedda carries the real power. If I abandon Gwynedd and bring my forces south to you, he's likely to intercept us somewhere in Powys. We're permanently divided. I'd do the unexpected. I'd conspire with Emrys Wledig, despite his Roman connections. Between us we could defeat the Vortigern for good. Then you could negotiate a peace with Ambrosius. He is at least honourable. Vitalus on the other hand ....'

Tendubric saw Cynvelyn lounging in the saddle, unchallenged by the concentration that had fuelled his strategy. He was so at ease, so content. Tendubric was rarely so, trammelled by the powers of his office and frustrated at his own inability to match Cynvelyn's guile.

'I shall consider your thoughts. It's time I was known by some other title than the stubborn Dragon. I might look like a king, but you have the mind of a general and that best serves us now. I can't share your mind on this. Ambrosius might well be honourable, but he is Roman. He yearns for an imperial government and that means the pope. It's not only the cross that we defend. Joseph's secrets were given to us in trust. Ambrosius is as far from us as the pagans. Do you really believe he'd resist the Pope's desire to crush us if he was so ordered? We have so few options. How I hate this part of being a king. You'd be much more suited.'

'Nay, the people don't see it so. In peace they have a strong ruler who governs fairly. Be mindful of the strength you bring them in your laws. Anyone can wield a sword and lead his people to slaughter. It takes a different strength to keep a peace. You are at one with the principles we are charged to defend; the true faith in our power as men to make of ourselves what we will. Perhaps we should be more open about promoting our secrets.'

'Mayhap, but I am ill at ease. It's a grave burden, yet we'll be prepared when the time comes. It would seem Gwent stands alone. As to our faith, the charge was clear. Only when Rome's power is waning are we to divulge the way. To do so prematurely would bring Rome crashing about our ears. It's a heavy secret we guard. It's not for disclosing now.'

He reined the bay to a halt outside the fort. The outer ditches had been cleared. Four circular, banked mounds created obstacles for any attackers, who would be vulnerable to a field of fire from the ramparts that enclosed the inner, fifth circle. Stout eight foot stakes atop a stone wall enclosed this last inner space, with square, palisaded platforms at the corners providing even higher elevation for archers. It would be a concerted effort by a committed assailant who ousted the defenders. With such defences, Tendubric was confident that his few, highly trained warriors, could deter greater numbers.

'The building goes well, brother; if we're called upon to defend Gwent, then we're well prepared,' Cynvelyn observed, pushing hard against the rampart which remained obstinately resistant to his efforts.

'We are so. But the timing will be all-important. The more of these we restore, the more we have to defend, reducing the number of warriors we can assign to each. It's a matter of numbers, brother.

Too many forts and our numbers will be weakened; insufficient and we fail to halt a committed foe.'

'Spoken like a general! We shall do well enough if we need to. Your decision on alliance is more vital. The people trust your judgement, brother. Consider your options well. The lives of the men who defend these walls rest on where you see Gwent's future.'

'I know, but I'm torn. It's no easy task, I'll share my mind with you immediately it's made up.'

Tendubric drew his white cloak about him, the pale fingers of his left hand fingering the silver ring on his right, where the stamp of the True Cross reminded him daily of his duty to the church. Kingship was no easy burden. Not for the first time he wished he'd been the youngest rather than the eldest of his line.

14. The Scotti King

430 AD - Viroconium

Hengist towered over the diminutive Vitalus, waving his muscled arms to reinforce his displeasure. 'My men will grumble at the extra distance,' he complained.

The Vortigern was deaf to his entreaties. Calmly insistent he repeated his order. 'The Scotti will be raided.'

***

Three Frisian ships approached the Scotti coast through a misty dawn. Hengist knew that such weather would betray their approach easily to any landward ears. So, oars muffled by cloth, they pulled in. The warriors were silent statues in the eerie light. Grim determined men stamped the cramp from their legs and took up shields and spears.

They found the village easily as the mist began to lift. It was big enough for booty. There was a hall fit for a noble, surrounded by a cluster of dwellings, craftsmen's workshops and a church. Hengist gestured for his men to light the torches. Fire was the best greeting.

The villagers found themselves hit hard by wraith-like savages, who erupted in their midst like a spring flash flood; demons from the most fearful of their folk tales. Before they were fully awake, their homes transformed into the hells of their worst nightmares. Thatched roofs roared orange; smoke blinded them from the axes and spears that culled them.

Hengist's men worked systematically. Some torched the buildings, others slew the older and middle aged menfolk. Children, women and livestock were rounded up. There was no rapine.

Additional booty on their return to the ships was at risk if they wasted precious time.

The raid was soon a massacre; the ground slicked with red ooze. The screams of the dying added a discordant wailing to the slaughter. The survivors thought the worst of their banshees was in pursuit, as they ran for the surrounding hills.

In front of the small whitewashed church an elderly priest appealed to God for protection. He waved a silver cross atop a staff to ward off the demons. Hengist watched with satisfaction as one of his young warriors split the old man from shoulder to waist with one clean swing of his axe, catching the staff as the old man fell. Two younger monks' faith failed them. They hitched their robes and took to their heels. Within ten paces, the long single-bladed knives of two warriors reduced them to twitching corpses.

Whorls of dawn mist coiled in the air. Smoke joined the fog, rising sluggishly. The noses of the victims and their butchers filled with acrid fumes. The local lord stood with his own hearth warriors, but they were outnumbered.

Hengist waved to Hrosa. Twenty Scotti defenders faced them, their backs to the burning timbers of their own hall. Hrosa's men fell on them, losing some from thrown javelins as they pressed for the kill. The Scotti's light spears and smaller shields were poor weapons against the Frisians, who favoured throwing axes, which they hurled with practised venom to tear holes in the defenders' ranks. They poured into the gaps, stabbing with their knives and thrusting with short spears.

The Scotti lord made a brave show in a leather harness, with the skillful use of his short sword. His less armoured men fell quickly. Hengist watched from a distance, one eye on the livestock and slaves being herded back to the ships. The cattle bellowed mournfully, skittered by the smoke and fire; their calls blended with the slaves' lamentations.

Hengist admired the surviving eight defiant Scotti defenders. One red-haired giant warrior, splotched with his own blood and that of those he had slain, guarded his lord's un-shielded side. Three Frisians lay dead at his feet. Hengist turned his head to the rising sun, a pale rim of primrose through the shroud of black smoke. He called to one of his men.

'Tell Hrosa to back off. Our paymaster wishes the Scotti King to know that we raid his shores. Let the lord's reward be his life. He'll carry the word right enough.'

Hengist caught the eye of the local leader, dark-haired and helmetless, but proud and stubborn. The Frisian raised his axe in salute. The black eyes of the Scotti chieftain met his, but rejected the gesture. He thrust his blade into the ground in frustration.

The raiders burned five steadings on their return to the coast, adding more cattle, pigs, sheep and chickens to their growing booty. Hengist saw that the slaves were good quality. The younger women showed fiery spirit despite their lost husbands. It had been worth the miles.

***

430 AD - Connachta, the land of the Scotti

Loegaire, Ri Coiced of the fifths of Connachta and Laigin, smiled grimly. He bore himself with regal authority, but eschewed the trappings of rank. He was short in stature, slight in build and so neglectful of his appearance that only his servants' dedication rescued him from being taken for a pauper.

He stood at a window of his Connactha stronghold, a parchment in each hand. In his right was a report from Callum McGrall, describing a ferocious attack on his Laigin lands by Frisians in the employ of Vitalus, the Vortigern of Britain. In his left was a cordial invitation by the same Vitalus to attend him in Powys to discuss 'issues of concern to both our realms.' He was cunning, this Vortigern. Nodding to himself in admiration, Loegaire summoned Finian, his body slave.

***

430 AD - Viroconium, Powys

A buzz of expectancy filled the villa. It was not often that enemies came visiting, but no effort had been spared to prepare for the arrival of Loegaire, Ri Coiced of the Scotti.

Vitalus wanted more time to concern himself with internal matters. It would be no easy negotiation to halt Scotti raiders. His treasury was already stretched to the limit. Despite his talent for diplomacy, Agricola had been unable to suggest a strategy. Little was known of the Scotti King.

Loegaire's bearing fooled friends and foes alike. Dedicated to music and poetry, his sombre visage spoke of tragedy. He looked in need of solace. Beneath this exterior lurked a shrewd, perceptive mind, a clear vision of the realm he wished to build and a powerful grasp of the necessary skills to accomplish it. In most dealings, his vulnerable appearance gave him the edge.

There was little gain for his people in burned villages. The Vortigern's reprisal had moved him. However, his raids on the British added considerable wealth to his own coffers. He must therefore bargain hard to secure a peace.

Loegaire arrived, wearing an emerald cloak of fine material, befitting his royal status. But when his servant removed the cloak, the Ri wore a simple black tunic with no mark of rank. He had no jewellery and little else to distinguish him from the slave who attended him. Even Vitalus started to comment, but caught himself.

'You are welcome, Loegaire of the Scotti. Will you take a goblet of wine to mark our friendship?'

The Ri stared deeply into Vitalus's eyes, relieved the Vortigern of a goblet, raised it to his lips and drained it in one draught. Finian sighed in disapproval. His master often flew in the face of both propriety and good sense.

'Wine is so much the lubricant for music and poetry, do you not agree, cousin? I would hear your minstrels while I'm here. I delight in tunes different from my own.'

'Our bards will honour you. We hope their music soothes the pain between us,' Vitalus replied.

'Well it might, cousin; well it might. For the present, we are tired. Perhaps you would give us leave to see our chambers. We shall be delighted to dine with you later.'

'Of course, my lord. A feast has been prepared to greet you. Until this evening then.' Vitalus bowed deeply.

'Foxy one, this,' Vitalus whispered to the watchful Agricola.

***

Loegaire found it difficult to remain aloof at the banquet. He would normally have sought some weakness in his hosts. But try as he might, his eyes were drawn repeatedly to the Vortigern's only daughter. Finian leaned over his shoulder to pour more wine.

'If I can see that you're under lust's thrall, anyone can. It will do you no good.'

'Thank you, Finian. You execute your duties with true loyalty. I fear I'm distracted,' he replied.

'Then withdraw, lord. There's no gain in this.'

'Be easy, Finian. I'm brideless. What better way to ally with this viper than to marry his daughter?'

'No Ri would consider such with his royal member leading his thoughts, my lord.'

'You're too shrewd, Finian. Perhaps I shall employ your skills better, or behead you for your confounded insolence. Now, desist. We arouse curiosity.'

Loegaire broke away, catching Agricola's smug smile. He raised his goblet. The bishop returned the toast. Servilla and Lucilla rose at the end of a mournful ballad. Loegaire was beguiled. Lucilla was dark-haired and pale of skin, unlike her father. The fates had been kind. She had escaped her mother's angular features. Her face was softer with a pert nose and dark eyes. Her mouth was small and her petite form bore no resemblance to her mother's. It had been impossible to avoid Loegaire's persistent looks. She accorded him a nod before being swept away in a knot of attentive servants.

When negotiations began the following morning, Loegaire knew he was disadvantaged. A smiling Vitalus had the upper hand. Peace at the expense of his daughter was no great cost at all.

'We are at a stand-off, cousin, are we not?' Vitalus opened.

'If you mean that your Frisian raiders are fleas in our pelt, yes,' Loegaire admitted.

'I propose that we cease our raids and that your people on our west coast return to their own land,' Vitalus opened.

'Come cousin; such a proposal does you no honour. Compared to our attacks, your pirates' efforts are thistle pricks. Our communities have been here for generations; they've no wish to return to us. If we're to have peace, it must benefit us both.'

Vitalus tapped the table thoughtfully. His first impressions were accurate. Loegaire was shrewd and far from gullible. Despite his appearance this was a man to respect. 'What do you have in mind, cousin?' Vitalus asked.

'You desire an end to raiding more than we. We can stand the damage you do us, but you cannot say the same. Your forces are stretched and your allies quibble at your taxes. If you wish to see your coasts secure, we need recompense, cousin. That's the only solution.'

Vitalus sucked in his breath. This Ri's intelligence was accurate. He probably knew the state of the treasury too.

'I will be honest, Loegaire. Our purse is all but empty. Can we tempt you with other than coin?' he asked, slyly.

Loegaire smiled his lazy smile. 'You know the answer to that, cousin. Your bishop's eyes see more than people's souls. I'm hounded to marry; my counsellors grow impatient. Your daughter is much to my liking. Lucilla would be acceptable to my people and our nuptials would mark a new peace between us. How say you?'

Vitalus nodded.

'It sounds well, cousin. Neither of us would lose and our peace would be blessed.'

'There is the small matter of the dowry,' Loegaire asserted.

'I'd not secure compensation to prevent your raids, but my allies would be hard pressed to refuse my daughter's dowry, as long as it's reasonable.'

''Twould be a shame to spoil a celebration bickering over the value of the dowry. As long as it's not too frugal,' Loegaire responded, the lazy smile back on his face.

'Then that's settled, cousin. Let's seal the bargain with good wine and have Agricola announce our new peace. Talk of a wedding will boost morale. Our people have had little to celebrate these past few months.'

'Is Lucilla's view of the match not to be considered?' Loegaire asked.

'Nay, cousin. Daughters of British nobility follow their fathers' wishes when it comes to serving the people. Lucilla will assent. I'll inform her later.'

'I'd not wish to transport her to strange lands against her will. We believe a match should be made two ways. I do not care to marry into resentment.'

'You're too romantic, you Scotti. There's danger in your love of songs. What has service to the realm got to do with personal feelings? If she resents you, do you not have women a plenty to bed at your court?'

'I do not, cousin. I take a serious view of holy matrimony, so I ask your forbearance to attend the lady Lucilla and test her feelings for me. I beg your indulgence in this.'

'If it puts your heart at rest, though it's a strange custom. If you consult your womenfolk on marriage, cousin, how long before they begin to interfere elsewhere? You dance with folly by such customs. But, be easy. Your boon is granted.'

'Then I am content, lord,' Loegaire concluded.

15. Lucilla's Fear

430 AD - Auxerre, Brittany

From Bishop Germanus of Auxerre to Pope Celestine
Your Holiness,
Yule marks the sun's turning for the lost souls of Britain. The dark is at its zenith. So it is for us, who strive to have them see the light. As the sun enters Capricorn, Riuros brings the cold time of the eagle moon. Pagans look to their aspirations, the heights they will climb in spring. They dwell on the promises they made during the Samhain fires. The fish is a prominent symbol, signifying the abyss of the dark from which all things emerge - the gate of souls; the deep, cimmerian wisdom of Saturn. Saturnalia is a time of misrule, when the rules are abandoned. Our baptised endure the indulgence of our rustic bretheren.

Feasting for twelve days is an opportunity to consume the last of the autumn harvest. Only the rich can store their stocks, but even for them, the deep winter makes it difficult for trading ships to sail. For the poor, it is the last chance to sustain themselves until spring's new growth.

By the time we observe the birth of our Christ, many followers are benumbed by Yule feasting and drinking. We are 15 days too late. Any reverence has disappeared from all but the most pious by that time. We warn our flocks from the pulpit, but contend with old habits dying hard. The festival marks yet another schism between the British. A people who cannot share the same gods might anticipate the displeasure of our Lord.

Your servant, Germanus.

***

430 AD - Viroconium, Powys

It had taken Loegaire barely the passing of one third of a candle to establish that Lucilla welcomed his attentions. Though filled with an inner dread about marriage, she was smitten by the soft spoken, gentle Ri. Only when he had left Viroconium, to announce his betrothal in Connactha, did Lucilla's deepest fears manifest.

The Vortigern's household was so active, Agricola thought that an invasion was imminent rather than a wedding. Though the coffers of Powys were dangerously low, Vitalus had instructed that no expense was to be spared in preparing the matrimonials and a Yule feast. For days wagons had unloaded all the province had to offer. Cattle and pigs had been slaughtered; the hearth warriors prayed for a raid to distract them from the hunt, so many deer and boar had their hounds flushed for the kill. The brewers sweated over ale and word had been sent to Kernow to secure what olives and best wines were left from summer trade with Rome.

The High King's mood had lightened, improved by Servilla's apparent pleasure at her daughter's betrothal. Her iciness towards him had transformed into an almost civil acceptance.

Yet for all her parents' efforts, Lucilla became observably less enthusiastic about the match. Her servants finally reported her mood to Servilla, who was concerned. The news filtered through to Vitalus. Affairs of state were minimal; the winter months had brought campaigning to an end. The High King took it upon himself to investigate his daughter's melancholy.

Steeling himself for the task, Vitalus knocked on the door to her apartments. Though affairs of state taxed his intellectual cunning, he preferred them to his familial duties, except where Lucilla was concerned. He had found his relationship with his daughter a welcome distraction from his royal power. A shy, deferential maid admitted him, in awe at his rare appearance in her mistress's quarters. He was no less apprehensive than the girl, so concerned with the threat to his stratagem that he failed to register whether he had bedded her. His whole plan for peace with the Scotti rested on

Lucilla's match with Loegaire. He had no contingencies for her refusal.

Lucilla stood at the window, staring out to where dusky shadows were turning the hills a greying purple. The longest night was almost upon them. She was very still, a statue of self absorption, wrapped in a light blue cloak over an indoor shift, her feet in gilded sandals. The room was warm from the under floor heating, but she had the shutters of the window thrown open to the crisp air.

'I'd be less cold with the shutter closed, daughter,' he greeted her casually.

She turned; the dark of the gathering night mirrored in her berry eyes. But the mouth that he'd seen wreathed in the smiles of girlhood was now tightly pursed. Her pallor was milk white.

'Your mother is worried for you. She thought that I might be of service. What ails you child?' Vitalus asked.

She closed the shutter, gesturing with a delicate hand for him to sit on one of the two low couches. She removed the cloak and let it fall to the floor.

'I have a boon to ask, father and I must ask it in keeping with Saturnalia's dominion,' she whispered huskily.

He settled himself before replying. 'We're a Christian household now, daughter. Such rituals invite debauchery. What can you possibly wish to invoke from such self-indulgence?' he asked, though the old celebration's power prompted his imagination into lurid action.

'We're a Christian household when it suits you, father. Don't preach to me of Christian ways when you sacrifice their principles on the altar of your own power.' The words lashed out at him like a scourge. He eased himself back on the couch to avoid their flinty harshness.

'You're too severe, Lucilla. Though I support the heresy, rather than Rome, we hold to the new ways - this is no pagan household. You shouldn't accuse me in such a tone. It ill becomes you.' He fretted with the hem of his robe.

'You asked if you could help, father, and help you can. But you must be honest about your own indiscretions and submit to Saturnalia. If you really believe that cavorting with your concubines, or plotting my uncle Constans' death, is permitted by the new religion, then you're abed with hypocrisy along with lust and murder.'

Vitalus shrank even further. She had struck at the heart of his vulnerability, pitching him headlong into the maw of his guilt.

'And what do you mean by 'orchestrating Constans's death?' he thundered.

'Be easy, father. Submit to my requests and I'll keep my counsel. I overheard you and Agricola as you awaited the Roman bishop. I know of your complicity in my uncle's death. I've told no-one, not even my mother. But should you deign to cover your heinous crime by doing me mischief, there are written instructions lodged with friends who'd testify to your regicide.'

He rose, towering above her, fists clenched as though to strike. Her wide eyes showed no fear. She remained seated, silent. He restored some measure of control. He was defeated, and he knew it. For all her rebellion he could only applaud her scheming. Though lacking formal tuition in the political arts, she carried the family stamp. Yet, her knowledge posed a threat.

'Why are you so persistent about the old rituals, daughter? You can ask all you want of me. Have I ever refused you any reasonable request? What purpose is served by appealing to superstition?'

'You're a victim of your own ambition, father, but I love you still as head of this family. I'll not add to the blackness that you embrace. Before god, this act is mine and mine alone. The festival is your alibi, father. None may accuse you in the future if you act under its protection.'

'You're babbling, daughter. What act? What do you speak of? I'm no nearer grasping what you wish of me. Speak plainly.'

He paused. His eyes sought an answer from hers. She looked away. When she spoke, her decisiveness had deserted her. Her voice rasped as she squeezed out her unwilling request.

'Father, I think that this Scotti Ri is kind and I would make a good marriage with him. But, I can't go to his bed a chaste woman. Despite all the teachings of the one god, there's a fear that gnaws at me about the trials of the marriage bed. This fear is vast, father. It's the reason for my melancholy. I wish you to expunge it, father. You're the only man I can trust in love to take this fear away.'

She looked aside, eyes heavy-lidded, not daring to meet his. Her breathing quickened now her dread secret was shared. Though the wind still moaned outside the shuttered window, silence reigned within the room. The tone of his words broke the spell.

'Daughter, this is folly. All maids are apprehensive on the eve of their nuptials. It's as natural under God's law as the fear men feel when they first march to war. Loegaire is unlike most men I've met. He's gentle for a king. Talk to him of your fear. Conquer it together in your marriage bed and be joyful when your ghosts are put to flight.'

Lucilla's lower lip trembled; a single tear traced a solitary path down her flushed cheek. Her voice was a muted whisper.

'Oh, father. Do you think that I'd be suffering so if this were such a small thing? This fear has been with me since girlhood. Would I stand against God's own laws to ask such a boon of you, if it were not some mighty thing? Only by invoking the old rituals and the love you have cherished between us can I resolve this agony. Now submit, I beg of you, if you wish me to marry.'

She lifted her head and met his gaze. It worked all the magic a daughter can conjure on a father: A concoction of subtle pleading, naked honesty and supreme trust. He was lost, moulded to her will as soft clay in a potter's hands.

He opened his mouth for a final defence, but she silenced his lips with a slender forefinger. Her other hand moved to the gold crafted brooch that pinned her light shift. In one deft movement she freed her sole garment and stood naked, but for her gilded sandals, trembling.

God did not stand high in the Vortigern's scheme of things, a point Lucilla had already anticipated. Though her mind screamed with the agony of her dilemma, her body marched to a different drum. She adopted the most alluring, seductive pose. Her small breasts snatched his eyes away from hers, the tiny pearl nipples stiffening with her body's desire. She half turned, coyly, a shyness that cut through the debate in his mind, straight to his manhood.

He moaned a feeble protest. She freed his tunic, clinging to his nakedness, shivering, but not from the cold. He was gently dutiful, mocked by the laughing Lord of Misrule. Amid the sweat, the heavy tang of spikenard activated by their body heat and the muted cries of their coupling, Lucilla's fear was purged.

***

The wedding was all that the people of Powys could have hoped for. The celebrations slashed through the dark gloom of the Solstice, substituting for the lost sun. The kings and governors of Britain added colour and finery to days of feasting and drinking.

Lucilla and Loegaire were bound in matrimony by Bishop Agricola, before the altar of a newly-completed family church. Never did a bride look more radiant as she stood next to her betrothed. Loegaire had been persuaded by the loyal Finian to abandon his sombre clothes. He added to the gaiety in an otter-fur-trimmed, dark green tunic. He had even acceded to Finian's suggestion to wear jewellery, one finely crafted bronze brooch, engraved with the swirls of his homeland attracted its share of acclaim. If Lucilla lit up the ceremony in her formal Roman ivory gown with silver bracelets and hair seeded with silver bee headed pins, her father appeared less than his ebullient self, somewhat pre-occupied to Agricola and the most observant guests. Though it would be some years before anyone other than father and daughter knew, Faustus, first born of the line of Loegaire, was the last of the Vortigern's sons.

Servilla was caught between joy at the recovered Lucilla's marriage and the sorrow of a mother destined to lose her only daughter. The newlyweds left for Connactha a week after the ceremony. Servilla's mixed feelings were mirrored by those of her husband. Peace with the Scotti had been achieved, but Vitalus was unsure whether he had miscalculated the cost.

16. The Wolf and the Staff

436 AD - Auxerre

From Bishop Germanus of Auxerre to his Holiness, Pope Celestine.

It grieves my heart, Holy Father, to report that little progress is being made in the restoration of the Romano-British to Mother Church.

Ambrosius Emrys Wledig has conspired with the Votadini for eight long years to achieve our aim, but no opportunity has presented itself to test the might of the heretical High King. Despite his transgressions, Vitalus proves himself to be a shrewd leader. His strategies have paid off handsomely, bringing a more settled peace to the realm, with Scotti raids curbed and the Sais more wary now that Hengist's patrols fire their beached ships wherever they are discovered.

In the north the Angles are more active, while Drust's Picts take advantage of their new sea power to raid further south. But the realm is more stable than when Vitalus took the High Kingship The wheatlands of Dumnonia experience a golden revival, adding to the coffers of their masters and to the taxes of the Vortigern. I pray for the Lord's hand to expunge the heresy from this blessed land. I remain the most humble executioner of your will in this matter.

Your obedient servant
Germanus

***

436 AD – Brittany

Seven years on from their arrival in Brittany, safe-guarded on their journey by Theoderic's horsemen, Owain, Edern and Elen flourished in the villa of Ambrosius Emrys Wledig, Cunedda's ally and friend.

Owain proved an adept pupil in learning the skills of a cavalry officer. Edern added the bricks of this new knowledge to the foundations that Lailoken had laid down. He saw how a cavalry arm offered opportunities that foot warriors alone were denied. Elen revelled in the lack of a parental yoke. Despite Ceri's entreaties for her to remain at home, she finally acceded to Enniaun's decision that it was far better to have a distant contented daughter than a petulant one at home. Elen rode, hunted, attended military lessons, and acted the part of a young nobleman. Despite her manly pursuits, she gained a new admirer. Leontinus, the young amber eyed officer on Ambrosius's staff, became Edern's adversary for her affections. Both were denied.

Elen's disregard for both her suitors festered in the wound of unrequited passions. As the months wore on, each blamed the other for her indifference.

'She hardly knows I exist at all,' Edern complained to Owain, repeating a litany that the Bear bore, like fleas in its fur, with immense irritation.

'Edern! This must stop. Elen is a fiery spirit. She'll not be swayed by your acting like a moonstruck farm boy. Have patience. Win her confidence as a friend; she has need of it. This is a new land for her. It's the first time she's been away from kin. What's to be gained by offering the deer fresh corn, if it skips away from you as soon as you approach.'

Edern turned glumly away, realising the fruitless nature of his entreaties. Sensible talk was never a match for a lost heart; the power of his feelings didn't abate. Neither did his attempts to woo Elen improve as time passed. The tension broke like a spring flood tide at the time of the Maying festival. The Beltane heralded the birth of summer, a time for sexual excess under the honey moon.

Ambrosius frowned publicly, but knew better than to prohibit the festival. Too many of his retainers and warriors held to past traditions. Secretly, he envied their licence.

Edern was at his lowest ebb as the festival approached, so disconsolate that even his complaints to Owain ceased. There was to be a celebration in the woods to the north. Word had been passed from warrior to slave, from servant to master, from merchant to courtesan. Christians fought once more to protect their souls against the delights they had once enjoyed; now prohibited by their new faith. The priests' rumbling discontent at their errant flocks reinforced their moral censure. However, the call of the old ways was still loud enough to persuade even some of them to join the dance.

Owain donned a summer tunic, dyed the deep maroon of his grandfather's house, for the first time in the year. He preened before a polished mirror, debating whether to add a cloak. The nights were still chilly. Practicality vanquished his vanity. He cast a light blue cloak across his shoulders, checked the straps on his sandals and prepared to depart. Now a strapping 17 year-old, his tall, well-muscled rangy frame was a legacy of his father's build.

'Are you sure you won't come, Edern? It's unlike you to miss a festival. It's closer to your ways than ours. I thought you'd have been eager to deal with your misery in such a pleasurable way.'

'I've no desire to cavort with slave girls. My heart's lost to your sister. You know this full well, so why do you ask?' He sat on his sleeping couch, his knees pulled under his chin.

'Ah well. The Bear must go forth without his Staff, then. So be it. Though it's strange without you. In all the time since we were with Lailoken, we've never been apart for any great occasion? This will test my independence,' he grinned. But the smile faded at his friend's abject misery.

'I'll just have to go with Elen then. Please don't wake me too soon on the morrow, eh? I hope I'll have cause to lie abed.'

'You mean Elen's going?' Edern cried.

'Of course. Do you think she skulks in her rooms like you? Why should she miss one of the biggest gatherings of the year?'

'Because it's hardly proper for a young woman of royal blood to be out unescorted. Does she know the full implications of the Beltane?'

'You witter like her mother, Edern. Of course she knows. If you know her as well as you claim, you'll see that she keeps a distance from the pleasures of the flesh. But she is curious about the festival.'

'But she may fall prey to someone who doesn't understand. You're not likely to be much use. You'll be given over to wine and lusty thrusting before the sun's fully set if I know you,' Edern accused.

'Calm yourself. She'll have her own servants, plus Seconius, Leontinus and myself. We'll not all be celebrating at the same time. She'll come to no harm.'

'Leontinus! That arrogant bastard! He's the worst lecher in Ambrosius's ranks. You'll not trust her to his care, Owain.'

'I think your view of Leontinus is coloured by your rivalry over Elen. I find him companionable.'

'Yes, but it's not your tunic he'll be seeking to slip his hand up, is it? Why have I had to wait until now to find out about it?'

'You've been so caught up in your own head. Some days ago, you asked for my silence on the Beltane. I've complied.'

Owain walked to the door, pleased to have reminded Edern how tetchy he had been.

'If you're so concerned about Elen, I suggest you bury your misery and come with us. At least that way you'll be satisfied that she's not enjoying herself with someone else. You confuse me, Edern. Are these Christian priests beginning to snare you in their traps? You betray your own beliefs in your concern for her.'

Edern was torn between the sense of duty his feelings demanded and a frustrated desire to be blessed by the goddess with Elen in the manner of his own people. He sat, wringing his hands in the despair created by his inability to choose. Finally, he could stand it no longer. He began to dress. The images in his mind would grow with the night if he stayed. It was the lesser of two evils to attend the festival, but he vowed to maintain a discreet distance. He would keep watch to ensure Elen came to no harm.

It was dark by the time he arrived at the site. Edern had replaced his best sandals with a pair taken from the slave quarters; his tunic was old and faded; a hooded cloak completed his disguise.

The central bonfire cast its tendrils of scarlet and bronze into the night air. Celebrants watched the flames, drinking wine. Merchants and vendors plied their trade.

Edern soon realised the futility of his quest. There were hundreds at the gathering, all dressed to ensure their anonymity. Finding Owain's party was going to be difficult. He worked his way through the crowd, trying to identify people with as much subtlety as he could manage. The task proved fruitless. As the fire died to embers more people drifted away. Some kept pre-arranged assignations, others join the ecstatic orgies that were livening the shelter of the nearby trees. Edern was distraught. He had given no thought to Elen eluding him.

The crowd dwindled to a few who had been too concerned with their cups to join the festivities. Edern realised he had failed. All through the woodland he heard the gasps and cries of those engaged in Beltane pleasures. The walk back to the villa was the most difficult he'd ever made. His own mind was filled with images of a naked Elen, coupling lustily with a triumphant Leontinus, their writhing bodies observed by a ring of approving onlookers. Such images tormented him as he retraced his steps. Jealousy was the brush and his desires the palette; the sounds from the forest etched in the details. He was beside himself when he reached his room.

He dozed fitfully, awaking fully when Owain returned with the silver dawn. Owain threw himself fully clothed on his bed and was asleep before he could be questioned. Edern dressed quickly and walked aimlessly until mid-morning, anguish his solitary companion. On returning, he went to the exercise yard, aflame with jealous misery.

There were a few devout Christian warriors at the training ground. He was met by guarded, curious looks from the men, who knew his beliefs to be alien. Edern threw himself into a rigorous regime. Had he managed to complete the exercises, his anger might well have dissipated, but it was not to be.

He had barely started when Leontinus sauntered casually into the arena with the smug satisfaction of a general who has won a battle against all odds.

The men looked on in horrified amazement at Edern, who wrenched a throwing javelin from its rack and hurled it in the Roman's direction. It was a rash throw. Edern was renowned more for his tactical abilities than his weapon skills, but it was close enough to snap Leontinus out of his swagger. The javelin plunged quivering into the ground, slightly to his left; too close for comfort.

'Either you fail to observe the rules of safety this morning, Edern, or I have offended you in some way,' Leontinus called.

'You know full well how you've offended me these past months, Leontinus. Let it end here. I'll not tolerate your fawning attempts to seduce Elen any longer.'

'How do you know I didn't succeed in the seduction of the fair Elen last night, Edern? After all, it was the propitious time.' He offered the goad with sneering contempt; playing to the warriors for added effect.

Someone more aware of Leontinus's wiles would have recognised the spur, but Edern was too ruled by his anger. He drew a short sword from the weapons rack and bore down on the Roman. Leontinus was unarmed, but seeing the bloodlust in the Pict's eyes, he snatched a sword from one of the nearby men.

Neither was used to fighting on foot. Their skills as cavalrymen were executed from the back of a moving horse, altering the angles at which spear and sword were wielded. Face to face, both were clumsy, but there was no doubting the venom as Edern pressed his attack with two wild swinging blows that clove the air. Leontinus avoided them easily, parrying a third strike as Edern sought to sheer him in half with another clumsy sweep.

Men ran into the arena as word of the fray reached the barracks. Edern's initial rush was thwarted by Leontinus, who now began to gain the upper hand. The Pict retreated stubbornly, taking a slashing cut to his left arm when he was too slow in giving ground.

His anger began to abate with the strenuous effort to anticipate where Leontinus would press the next attack. Edern realised his foolhardiness. He was no match for the Roman. He parried three more attacks, more by luck than skill. He knew, without looking, that a damp patch in his left side was blood. The edge of Leontinus's sword had been deflected by Edern's parry, opening up the Pict's second wound.

Edern realised that the pendulum of anger had swung its fullest arc. Whereas he had been borne on wings of fury, it was now Leontinus who boiled with rage. His attacks were disciplined, reflecting his training, but there was nothing measured about the snarl on his purple face.

The men sensed it too. Leontinus had lost all reason. He slashed and thrust with deadly intent. Edern was all but out of reserves. His body felt sapped of energy, his arm was numb to the shoulder with the jarring blows he had parried. Courage, alone loaned him the will to stand against the ceaseless blows. The blood on his left arm welled and ran in rivulets down his forearm. Each backwards step left a small stain in the sand.

The end came when Leontinus feinted to thrust, then swung back handed into Edern's right side. The Pict stumbled, his sword flailing limply to block, but it was one of the Roman's few subtle strokes. Edern felt the point of impact as it pierced his flesh. He stumbled, staggered a few steps and collapsed.

Seeing Leontinus advance, Edern realised that but for the gods' intervention, his life was forfeit. The look on the Roman's face bespoke neither pity nor compassion. He loomed victoriously, gasping for breath. He raised his sword.

Edern looked him once in the eyes, a soundless appeal to an erstwhile comrade. Against other opponents some respect for an adversary would have shown, but dark jealousy and hatred were all that stared back.

'You puny, pagan peasant. The Votadini might have honoured you, Pict, but you're far less than any Roman citizen. You're unfit to even think of Elen. You've made your own grave, now lie in it.'

He brought the sword back for the fatal thrust. Edern stubbornly raised his wavering blade, knowing the futility of it. The sword hissed downwards with sufficient vigour to cleave his skull. Edern closed his eyes. The blade clanged against metal. Through one opened eye the Pict saw Leontinus's thrust parried by Owain's sword.

Angrily, the Roman turned to face the Votadini; Edern slumped back to the blood-soaked sand, his strength totally sapped.

'I've no quarrel with you, Owain. Back off and let me finish this,' Leontinus spat.

'My friends are few, I'd not welcome losing this one,' Owain replied calmly, left thumb pointing at the prone Edern.

'Then you make me your enemy too,' Leontinus snarled, launching himself into a straight thrust at Owain's throat. He side stepped economically and parried the blade. Fuming, Leontinus attacked again, a flurry of strokes this time, one of which ripped Owain's tunic at the shoulder and opened a cut which welled bood. Grinning at his success, the Roman bunched to press his advantage.

'Hold your hand, Leontinus. What in God's name goes on here?'

Ambrosius, accompanied by Elen and Theoderic, angrily thrust his burly frame through the circle of men.

'They deserve this punishment, lord.'

'They do, do they? If that be so, Leontinus, the law will decide, not you. You know my orders on duels between my men. It bodes ill for the battlefield when comrades can't rely on one another. You are in error, whatever the merits of the case.'

'But Edern attacked me, lord. It was unfounded. Ask any of those present. I merely defended myself.'

Ambrosius looked at Edern's blood-spattered tunic and his forearm, where the wound was congealing.

'You defended yourself? You fight in too much hot blood. It will bring disaster, one day, Leontinus. Friend though you be, these are not the qualities of an officer in my command.'

'Then I'll renounce that position, lord, and our friendship,' Leontinus sneered. 'I'll serve no more with a leader who trains his men to no purpose. You're unworthy to take a kingdom. You sit on your arse while a throne beckons. I'll be bored by your patience no longer.'

He threw the sword to the sand and pushed his way through the throng without a backward look.

Owain took Edern's hand and pulled him gingerly to his feet. They set off for the infirmary, the Pict slumped between his friend and Theoderic. Elen walked with them; she staunched the blood on Owain's shoulder with a strip torn from her tunic and held a wad of cloth against Edern's bloody ribs.

'I'm sorry we have lost you a friend, lord,' Owain said as they passed Ambrosius.

'Think little of it. He lacks patience, that wolf. I've doubted his judgement for some time. Now, see to yourself and your friend and find out what caused this affray. I'm adamant that my men do not duel. That applies equally to you both.'

The three walked away, Edern slumped between them, bleeding profusely from his wounds. It would be a long time before he acted in anger again. The lesson had been harder than those of Lailoken. He would thank his gods that night. Though Elen failed to smile on him, some among the immortals did.

***

Elen visited Edern in the small infirmary, to assist the monks in his recovery. Though he took great pains to avoid her sole company, still as stricken with desire for her as when they had first met, his condition left him little option but to endure her ministrations. He had felt foolish when Owain explained to him that Elen had foregone the Beltane celebrations.

'You're uncomfortable in my company, Edern. Why so?' she asked bluntly, grey eyes fixing him like a snared rabbit.

'You must know my feelings for you by now, Elen. Don't mock my heart. You act the warrior. You talk, ride and fight like a demon, but the first time I saw you outside Dinas Ffynon, all I saw was the beauty of your womanhood. I see it still, though it does me little good. I've been the fool on your account. You've addled my senses.'

She nodded, releasing his captured eyes.

'You think me unkind to ignore your affection?'

'No, you've been a boon companion. My expectations don't run beyond that. My blood boiled when Leontinus fawned around you like a moonstruck puppy. Your affection is yours to bestow and in time I know that you'll give it. We have become as kin. I know that's the limit for us. Knowing your heart will be won by another makes me sad.'

She smiled, running her finger distractedly across the blanket. His heart quickened at the hint of her upturned lips.

'I do have affection for you, Edern. You're kind and gentle. You watch out for my brother's safety. I see you day by day checking his horse's girth, partnering him in weapon skills so that no other might accidentally hurt him. My way is difficult. I'll not sit idly by as our women do. There's fire in my spirit and it needs to burn.'

'You think Gwawl sits idly?' he questioned.

'She does not; she's a great lady. But her way is not mine. Why, just because I am a woman, should I not feel the wind in my hair and a wild horse beneath me? Why should I not ride in battle or scheme into the night? Why should I not hunt and drink 'til the dawn? Have I proved any less able at any challenge we've been set since we arrived here?'

'I cannot answer your questions, Elen. I am a Pict. Our ways are different. Our noble women have more freedom. They take lovers other than their husbands and our gods are not offended. It's not our way to trap them in marriage as your people do. Though we have few battle maidens, there are some who choose the warrior's way.'

'Then to assume that you lack civilisation is arrogant. There's more to the world than what we've learned from our kin, or from these pious priests whose poison turns people into sheep.'

He was surprised at her venom. She had never displayed any sentiments about the church.

'I promise you this for your patience, Edern the Pict. I'll not act the noble woman with any man while I rage for the thrill of battle. I won't be a courtly woman until I've satisfied my desires. Perhaps I might wish to live a quiet life later, though I doubt it. Still, our bodies yearn for warmth on cold campaign nights and I've been too aloof from your affections. Were it not for Owain's sword, I might be mourning your death today instead of listening to you complain about the monks' potions. If it's your wish, I'll lie with you when you're recovered. But a battle maiden I'll be first, so you'll be getting no sons from me. My bedroll you can share, but I'll not conceive.'

His heart skipped two beats. Her statement was as frank as the sale of a beast between two farmers at market, yet the implications of it ran straight to the foundations of his desire.

'I'd not thought you held any feelings for me, Elen. Your offer is accepted and right welcome. I'll not act like some May fool, smitten with love, but I ask you to recognise that I feel like such, even though you'd have me hide it. As to lying like lovers, I'll abide by your wishes in this. I'd not aspired to such joy, even in my wildest dreams.'

'You'll no doubt spend more time binding my wounds than kissing my breasts, Edern. Trouble is brewing at home; we'll be fighting more than wrestling in bed.' She laughed, lightening the mood. The slanting sun rays shone clear and golden through the window, glinting from the red of her hair. Edern sighed and relaxed. A skirmish had been lost and a battle won.

Part Two

The Saxon Menace

17. The Sickening Land

444 AD - Auxerre

From Bishop Germanus of Auxerre to his Holiness, Pope Celestine.

Your Holiness. It would seem that our prayers have been answered. In the old calendar, Lammas arrived in Britain with all the optimism of a sun-drenched summer. A sea of rippling, wheat and barley sways in the fields. Cattle and sheep are fat. Estate owners eye rich returns. Merchants look to autumn gains.

Throughout the realm, pagans celebrate the fire festival of Lammas; a symbolic mourning for the loss of maidenhood, in preparation for the young who will be born during the time of plenty. Despite the best efforts of your bishops, we confront such practices as unsuccessfully as we preach against the heretics. There is much to be done to deliver souls to Mother Church. We overlay our own rites on those of the past to combat superstition. The Loaf Mass festival takes its name from the burying of bread made with summer's first grain. The ancient respect for women remains strong among the people. We teach that the land is a fertile gift from God. They insist that the earth mother is the source of all life, reminding us that we cannot slacken our efforts. Tensions are rife in the rural areas.

People have begun to sicken and die, stricken by a plague, a sure sign of our Lord's distress at the heathen's resistance. Both factions blame each other. Our bishops accuse the population of dereliction in their duty to God; the pagans claim that the Beltane fires were ill prepared and thus the spiritual cleansing of the land has been neglected. The plague adds to the conflict. There is disorder. Death sweeps all optimism away in a black tide of fear.

The rich pack their belongings and make to stay with kin in Brittany or Rome. Estates are given over to managers, who look to their own advancement as their masters and mistresses flee. The stability established by the High King ebbs.

The plague spreads throughout Dumnonia, parts of Gwent and into Powys. The pagan, Hengist, is safe in his bastion of Thanet, which has escaped God's wrath. It is not only estate managers who see the opportunity that the plague offers. If the Lord wills, this is the time to act against the heretics in Powys.

Your obedient servant
Germanus

***

446 AD – Thanet

Hengist's axe almost parted the table.

'This is the time to cast off this British yoke and secure land for ourselves.' He searched the council for dissent and found none.

'We've done well, Hrosa: a growing settlement, wives, children, slaves and wealth. But we don't have enough land to grow further and our paymasters will never grant us more while they're strong. This plague weakens them. We must act on it.'

'If we gamble and fail, we stand to lose what we've built,' Hrosa cautioned.

'I'll not be so unsubtle, brother. Word reaches me that Vitalus suffers bouts of melancholy since the marriage of his daughter to the Scotti king. Neither his priests nor his healers have cured him. We shall see what we can do to restore his health,' he winked broadly, grinning at Hrosa's puzzled expression.

***

446 AD - Viroconium, Powys

The plague brought Angle and Saxon sails in numbers to watchful British coastal towers. Pictish ships struck southwards, dark vultures, picking at a diseased corpse. Although Loegaire kept his father-in-law's peace, there were raids on western Britain from neighbouring Muma. In his anxious state, the Vortigern accused his son-in-law, mistaking the Mumans for Loegaire's warriors, ruining what had been a kin-bound peace. It was a sorry Vitalus who took counsel from Agricola on a hot, sticky afternoon.

'What are we to do, Bishop? My sins are being punished. Families flee every day; our enemies know we're weak. I'm weary, Bishop. All was going so well.'

'It's merely God's test, my son. Endure it. The sickness will end and the realm will be restored.'

'If there's a realm left, Bishop,' Vitalus sighed. 'We're looking at full scale invasion if we weaken further. Your strategic skills would serve us better than your piety.'

A silence, heavy with the heat of the mid-day sun, descended. Neither had answers to their predicament. Their heads turned with only partial interest as a servant handed a letter to Vitalus before withdrawing quickly. It did not pay to be a messenger these days. Vitalus split the seal, which he recognised as Hengist's.

'No doubt our mercenaries plead for extra gold while we suffer.'

The bishop had fallen asleep.

Vitalus read the contents and grunted. He kicked Agricola, none too gently, and thrust the communiqué under his elongated nose.

'Hmm,' the bishop murmured. 'Do you not think this a bit suspicious? In all the time we've employed Hengist's raiders, I've not converted one of the heathen to our Lord Christ. Such men must be considered untrustworthy.'

'Bishop, well over half of those who are baptised are untrustworthy. Hengist has been consistently loyal; bought by coin, I agree. But he's never gone beyond his station and at the moment we need him. I'll accept this invitation.'

'We, lord? I'll not attend a pagan feast; I'd be ridiculed by the brethren,' Agricola replied.

'I thought you'd more courage in your belly, Bishop. No matter, I'll go. You can keep your spiritual purity and your throat uncut too, if there's deceit.'

Vitalus summoned his eldest son, Brittu, a twenty year-old who displayed sufficient skill to suggest that the Vortigern's shaky dynasty would be entrusted to capable hands. He joined them on the shaded terrace, a light tunic and sandals barely cloaking his athletic frame. His father looked on. Envy and pride shaped the smile that came to his face.

'I'm away to Ruchin. They've escaped the plague and wish me to join them in a thanksgiving feast. You'll be in command here. As Vortimer, you need the experience. Let the Bishop counsel you, but follow your own head. Get your brother, Pascent, to aid you. Perhaps he'll listen to you. He seems to bear me ill, though I know not why.'

'I shall, father. Be careful; you place great trust in the pagans.'

'Not so, Brittu. Hengist knows that he'd be destroyed should anything happen to me. He hasn't built up his strength just to crap in his own steading. In case I have him totally wrong your first campaign will be to burn him out. My judgement is not what it was.'

'I shall, father. Take care and God go with you.'

'Thanks for your sentiment, son. I feel God has been giving me something of a wide berth of late.'

***

Servilla had endured a civil peace between herself and her husband since her daughter's wedding. Though he bedded house slaves, this was insufficient conduct to maintain her frosty distance. In seventeen years, Servilla had failed to secure the evidence to prove her husband's part in her brother's death. Indeed, during Lucilla's absence, Vitalus had displayed such melancholy that Servilla took pity on him. Lately, she had considered the guilt of neglecting her wifely duties and the impotence she felt at failing to secure revenge for Constans. The latter occupied her thoughts more frequently than her coldness at Vitalus's attempts to sire sons. Her religion prescribed the joy she should experience at such times, yet she had never been truly fired by passion. Conflict between old and new values unsettled her; she was more comfortable with stability than change. She had engaged in the same discreet liaisons with servants and slaves as her husband. This new Christianity relegated the body from a temple of pleasure to a receptacle for sin. In meeting the conduct of her new beliefs, Servilla had abandoned her former sexual dalliances.

It was a shock for her when she received letters from her daughter.

Lucilla's letter entreated her mother to attach no blame to Vitalus for the events of Saturnalia six years before, pleading that she alone be held responsible for her father's act. But she affirmed Servilla's suspicions about Constans's death by revealing the overheard conversation between Agricola and her father. Servilla ignored Lucilla's pleas. Her anger was directed at her husband.

Vitalus had left with a small escort for Ruchin. This was not an issue to be resolved by her brother, Ambrosius. Family honour could only be defended by her actions. She was close to her husband; Ambrosius still awaited events in Brittany. Servilla soothed the boiling rage that threatened to engulf her; taking refuge in the sharp clear visions that her artful mind began to conjure.

***

446 AD - Thanet

Vitalus was greeted by Hengist and a guard of colourful warriors, who lined the route from the quay to the main hall as the High King and his escort landed.

A feast had been prepared. Cattle had been slaughtered; pigs roasted; fresh breads baked and so much beer and wine had been readied that it seemed Hengist's men would not put to sea for a month.

Vitalus was drawn to enquire from Hrosa the identity of the blond girl who sat next to Hengist. Her hair was drawn into a single plait that ended well below her waist. She was tall, with dazzling blue eyes, a fair open face and a mouth that promised passion. Her silk blouse left little to the imagination, so sheer that the full round of her breasts was visible beneath its thin, red sheen. She wore a long skirt of dark blue dyed linen; she was barefoot.

'It is Rhonwen, Hengist's daughter. She visits us at her father's invitation,' Hrosa informed him.

The opening formalities were short. Hengist thanked Vitalus for attending the celebrations. He professed sorrow at the deaths on the mainland and informed the High King that his wyrdmen would intercede on behalf of the suffering. Vitalus acknowledged his concern; his own God would alleviate the plague as and when he deemed it fitting.

Throughout the feasting, Vitalus could not keep his eyes from Rhonwen's allure. She did little to dissuade him, leaning forwards with brazen looks at his furtive glances. Whenever she did, her full breasts would strain against the red silk, driving all thoughts of eating from Vitalus's mind. Her father pretended ignorance at a plan that was working well beyond his expectations.

Eventually the raucous assembly subsided into drunken snoring. They collapsed across the table, leaving the hunting dogs to scavenge for discarded bones and scraps. The jugglers and musicians saw their audience claimed by strong ale. Hrosa slumped to Vitalus's left. Few remained conscious.

'These men have served us well these last few years,' Vitalus commented to his ale-sotted host.

'They were pirates and now they have families and a home, thanks to your wisdom, lord King,' Hengist slurred.

'Your daughter has great beauty, Hengist. Should she not be wed by now?' Vitalus asked.

'None stand high enough in wealth or manhood,' Hengist replied. 'Our people are hard pressed. Eastern invaders raid us. Our farms are flooded and useless. She's a fiery one that needs taming. It will take a firm stallion to master her.' He drained his drinking horn in one long draught and fell back belching. Sleep took him almost immediately.

Rhonwen did not speak British, but her body announced her intentions well enough as she led Vitalus from the hall to her father's dwelling. There, on a bed, perfumed with oils and essences, she introduced Vitalus to the pleasures of a Frisian coupling. Consorts of kings were compliant to the wishes of their masters. These pagans had their advantages, he considered, as she stripped the flesh from his back with her raking nails and bruised his ribs with the crushing grip of her thighs. By morning the shine of his kingship had dimmed, whilst her wild radiance glowed.

All reason deserted him. Had he brought counsel with him, it would have been ignored. Despite the crises, the objections of his advisers, the wrath of Servilla and anything else, he had to have her.

'Arrangement?' Hengist queried curiously, later that day. 'What kind of arrangement?'

'I would like your daughter as my consort,' Vitalus explained.

'You want to marry her?' Hengist asked.

'Well, not marriage, but I want her with me, Hengist. What can be done?'

'Impossible, Lord King! Family honour is at stake. There'd be keels sailing from our homeland if it were known that a British High King had taken a daughter of ours as a common bedmate, with no recognition of her position in law. You'd be looking at war. No, there's naught can be done.'

'Perhaps there is. Might I suggest a solution?' Hrosa offered.

Hengist looked suitably curious. Vitalus urged him to speak, his mind still occupied by Rhonwen's shameless display.

'Our Frisian marriages are unacknowledged by the British. Any wedding would be ignored by their laws. Your existing lineage, lord King, would be legally protected from any claim by us. But if you wed Rhonwen here, our people would be satisfied. Both parties would be served.'

'Ha, you see the sense of it, Hengist. Is this not a solution?' Vitalus enthused.

'It might well serve,' the Frisian replied, hesitantly.

He need not have been so circumspect. Vitalus was quite lost to his lust. Had the Frisian stratagem been played out by five-year-olds, he would have believed the sincerity of it. He awaited Hengist's ruling with all the pent-up passion of a lovestruck youngster on a first tryst.

'If Rhonwen is happy to leave her people to be with you, lord King, then our honour is satisfied. There's the matter of the bride price, but we can settle that later. You may take my daughter to wed; though you may rue it. I hope your household boasts its share of carpenters, you'll need your bed repaired often with that one.'

Vitalus was ecstatic. Immediately his mind turned to the deceptions he would have to practise to install Rhonwen in his life. There was no way he could introduce her into the villa's routines; a separate household would be needed, somewhere close by. He would have a trusted servant investigate the possibilities. Suddenly, all his crises seemed trivial.

He discussed details with Hengist for the remainder of the afternoon, eager to repeat the previous night's passion. He had seen nothing of Rhonwen all day. He was so intent upon discovering her whereabouts that he failed to realise the costly bride price. Not only would he have to explain Rhonwen to his court, but also that he had ceded a good part of Canturguoralen to Hengist's settlers. However, this was part of the upstart Gwyrangon's lands, so there was merit in it. He could claim it was a pay-back for the young governor's questionable loyalty.

Although his escort was eager to return to Powys, Vitalus remained a further three days, sufficient time for a scout column to appear to check that all was well. The combined company of the new troop, plus his entourage, finally pressured him into leaving. He agreed to return to Ruchin in two weeks time for the official ceremony.

If the men were more silent than usual on the return journey, he was unaware of it. He was oblivious to the signs of plague as they rode north. Smudgy oily smoke from funeral pyres caught their throats and the fear-filled eyes of his subjects looked on forlornly, as they awaited their turn. Vitalus was unconscious of all but the memory of his Rhonwen-inspired nights. The High King was in love, or as near as was possible for a High King to be.

***

446 AD - Viroconium, Powys

Word reached Servilla of her husband's latest paramour by way of court gossip, before she had finalised her plans for action. All the discipline of her Roman background was needed to maintain her composure. It was bad enough realising that her husband's part in her brother's death was compounded by his many indiscretions, while she struggled with the self-denial required by her religion. But the humiliation he created for her by taking a pagan to his bed tested her composure to the utmost. There would be nothing anonymous about his new conquest. In time, all would hear of it and scandal would be her companion.

Patience was vital. A scene would create suspicion and she had no wish to draw attention to herself. In the privacy of her own rooms, now even more private, Servilla brought the strands of her conspiracy together.

She wrote to Ambrosius, confirming the evidence about Constans's death. She wrote to Loegaire, informing him that his first born was of the Vortigern line; Lucilla would have to face the consequences. She wrote to Tendubric, the Dragon of Gwent, warning that Vitalus's bride price brought pagan settlers to within striking distance of his lands. Servilla's pen was quick across the page. Her passion for revenge matched her husband's lust for his new whore.

While Vitalus settled Rhonwen into a small villa on the outskirts of the city, Servilla schemed. For all the spies he had monitoring his enemies, none were turned inwards on his own household. Servilla plotted with impunity.

Brittu adopted many of the Vortigern's daily duties. As Vortimer, he tried to minimise the potential damage his father had inflicted on friends and potential allies alike. He could do little to placate those who actively opposed the High King. Worried about his father's state of mind, he closeted himself with Pascent and Agricola, striving to find some stratagem that would alleviate the crisis. They could find none.

***

446 AD - Brittany

Owain's return home was an unhappy one. His years with Ambrosius had been fruitful. The Bear and his Staff had learned well from Roman tutelage and Elen had blossomed into a woman, despite her rejection of most that was deemed womanly by the times. In all their exercises, horsemanship, discussions of tactics, plus the logistics of war, she had participated to the fullest extent of Ambrosius's authority. This had been pushed and pushed, always to his limits.

They were debating the role of cavalry when a sombre Ambrosius greeted them.

'Owain, Elen, I have letters from your father. The plague has taken your grandfather. Cunedda, my friend, is dead. Enniaun rules the Votadini and requests that you return home. I grieve at your loss. Your grandfather was a great man.'

They fell silent. Owain ran a hand across his mouth, shaking his head in disbelief. All his years, Cunedda had been a larger than life mountain who stood against time itself. He had never associated Cunedda with mortality.

Least affected by the news, Edern broke the silence.

'Thank you, lord. We'll make preparations for our return.'

'Theoderic will accompany you.' Ambrosius turned, leaving them to their grief.

'I'll walk on my own for a while,' Owain said.

He cast back over the years to their departure from Dinas Ffynon. He remembered the harshness of the weather, which contrasted with the afternoon's cloudless sky. The estate's fields and vineyards were lush; the harvest promised a rich yield. Horses and cattle had dropped healthy foals and calves; everywhere symbolised abundance. Yet amongst all this, even in the fullness of summer providence, death stalked the shadowlands. He had felt drawn to home for some time. Cunedda's death reinforced his urgency. Fourteen years had slipped by. His unfulfilled destiny had cemented the wall between himself and his kin, yet he now wished to see them and face whatever fate decreed.

His walk brought him back to the small chapel. His mood drew him inexplicably towards it, though he had avoided religion since Lailoken's teachings. He entered. A single candle burned on the altar, underneath a plain wooden cross. He approached, aware of the silence. For no reason other than that it seemed fitting, he knelt.

His eyes were cast down. Memories of his grandfather flashed across his mind. Curiosity breached his grief. The rectangular altar did not lay square to the wall. It had been moved. Owain pushed against it. It swung back, revealing stone steps leading down in a spiral. A faint glow from below gave light to guide him.

The steps ended in a dimly lit, small cave, carved from the rock. A hooded figure sat in a stone circle, intoning an incantation. It turned to face him.

'Welcome, Owain Arth-Ursus,' said Ambrosius Emrys Wledig. 'We must talk if you are leaving us. Return the altar to its proper place in the chapel, then come and sit.'

Owain dealt with his surprise in the way that Lailoken had taught him. He suspended all judgement. His response was not lost on Ambrosius, who pushed back his hood, to stare deeply into Owain's eyes.

'You thought me a devout Christian?' the exile asked.

'People who build churches usually are, but then my old teacher taught me that people are many things that they hide from public view. In that, you're no different.'

Ambrosius's noble face creased with mirth. He invited Owain to be seated inside the circle. The Bear complied.

'All is never what it seems, Owain. Lailoken taught you that, no doubt. Events in the world are momentous; great changes are afoot. The All-one makes its presence felt in many guises. If I'm to be a serious contender for the throne of Britain, I must demonstrate a commitment to the New God and his crucified son, though the past still resonates within me. There's a power in its links to the land and the Otherworld that the new religion eschews. The two are very different, yet both are necessary if I'm to command authority.'

Owain nodded. Seeing the broad canvas had been one of Lailoken's lessons.

'Lailoken is a great seer; I never met him personally, but I have heard that he's journeyed the furthest of all those who pursue our knowledge. And then, there is the small matter of yourself. Those of our art often wait for years to become worthy of a totem. Yet you were a mere stripling when Ursus, the Bear, claimed you. There is a great mystery here. The spirits of the ancestors mock our understanding.'

'If there is mystery, then it's beyond me. Lailoken had me dream and was content with what I told him. It was as meaningless to me then as it is now. I'm party neither to your knowledge, the God of the Christians, nor that of our forefathers. Lailoken prepared me to see my way beyond such beliefs.'

Ambrosius smiled again, shaking his head at Owain's naivety.

'But in that lies the greatest wisdom. How many men do you know who could so easily free themselves from the safekeeping of their god? You have a rare quality, Owain. Though you make light of it, others can see your power. The bear has sovereignty in the animal kingdom. It has no predators, other than man. It takes the salmon, signifying great wisdom; it eats honey from the bee, a creature sacred to the great goddess herself. It avoids the wolf, the totem of the teacher, because it has nothing to learn; it sleeps long, where its dreams bring it wisdom, and its strength exceeds any other animal. Truly, you have been chosen for a great task. In your dreams, Owain. That's where you'll find your destiny if the bear has taken you for its own.'

'My dreams have ceased. Since that night, years ago, when I lived that vivid dream, I've remembered nothing,' Owain replied.

'Then your time here has been to learn different skills. Believe me, Owain, you will dream your path. You have come to full manhood. You attract warriors because they see you as a leader. It is time to see what Britain holds for you.

'Were you trained in the ways of the seer, you'd realise that you've walked two paths of knowledge: You have opened the way from childhood; you have forged your discipline and accepted your destiny. Now you must learn to pass within, to seek that which fulfils you. You chose to sit in this circle facing the west, the direction of such a path. You will now gain the wisdom to mature your judgement. Only real challenges can provide you with such knowledge. Your time here is ended.'

Owain listened intently. Ambrosius's advice matched his yearning to return to his homeland. Yet, he wished to accompany Ambrosius on his quest for High Kingship.

'And what of your divination? Do you see your path to the kingship? Such arts as these,' he waved a hand around the cave, 'give men power to see what their destiny holds.'

'Would that it were so simple, Owain. True, I can divine. But there's danger in relying on it. Divining provides a glimpse of the possibilities. It's for those with a strong sense of self-belief and a fierce disregard for the gods and fates. I know as little about my fate as you do about yours.'

'Then, you don't know that you'll defeat the Vortigern?'

'No. The picture is cloudy; muddy as at a churned ford. The time's not yet ripe, though we prepare our forces.'

'Then I shall await you in Britain. It's time to see my kin. I have yet to pass the test of real battle. Edern, Elen and the men crave real skulls to split.'

'I'm sure you'll find them in your troubled land. Look for me in your dreams, Owain. I'll come as the blackbird, the creature that transports us to the land of the dreamer. When you hear the blackbird sing, then we'll meet again.'

'Farewell, Ambrosius Emrys Wledig. Come soon and do justice to the land of the Pretani. The people need you. In the meantime I'll do what I can to hold these Saxons. Goodbye.'

The two parted. A stronger bond had formed between them in the tiny cave; two links in a chain that awaited its tempering in a future forge of endeavour.

18. Servilla's Revenge

447 AD - Viroconium, Powys

For a year Servilla had stealthily fashioned the means of her husband's demise. The end move was tantalisingly close.

Initially she saw her intentions hindered when Bishop Germanus arrived on another mission from the Pope, but she soon saw the hidden advantage in it. What better alibi presented itself than being cloistered with the bishop, discussing ethics and theology, while the act she had planned for so long was executed?

She also had allies in the household. Theoderic was once again in Britain, seeking intelligence to aid her brother. Such a trusted man could be used to help rid herself of Vitalus. It was all a matter of timing.

Vitalus was spending less and less time dealing with affairs of state and more and more with his pagan. Servilla had borne the sympathetic looks of the courtiers well; acting with complete disregard for her husband's preoccupation.

The crisis was deepening. Brittu and Pascent lacked their father's vision. The whole architecture of Vitalus's peace, was crumbling into ruin, while he cavorted with his Frisian bed mate. Servilla's spies informed her that the new villa had become a centre for private orgies; another piece of information that she filed in her busy mind with relish.

She made her final preparations, writing a longer letter than was usual to Ambrosius, in the knowledge that it would be borne by his own messenger, Theoderic.

She pulled the strands of her plot together. She had arranged a discussion with Germanus the following night, after the evening meal. Her trusted body slave had hired ruffians from the town to fire Vitalus's villa, on the pretext that its owner was a bad debtor owing much coin to a frustrated merchant. This was the easy part.

Theoderic was summoned to her private apartments.

'You see for yourself, Theoderic. The realm is in crisis. It is the opportunity my brother has been awaiting. You must return at once to Brittany with this letter. I've included all the information necessary for a successful campaign. Do you understand?'

'I do, lady. The plague has robbed the British of much strength. Strong enemies watch enviously and the High King does little to deter them.'

'Then we're agreed. My brother must assemble his army. His allies will be ready. This realm needs a stronger leader than my husband. He needs to be brought to account for his sins along with that hypocrite, Agricola. There is one other service I need you to perform before you leave.'

'Ask it, lady. If it serves my master, I'm at your command.'

'My own intelligence reports that Vitalus is not so enamoured with his new plaything that he ignores all threats to his position. He's wily enough to know that my brother is still his greatest rival. He's hired assassins; five local rogues I'm given to understand. There'll be some diversion at the villa late tonight to allow them to slip away to the coast, unseen. He knows his enemies watch his every move. You must be waiting for them, Theoderic. They must be killed to keep my brother from harm.'

Her earnest conviction persuaded Theoderic that she had uncovered a genuine plot against his lord.

'They'll be dealt with, never fear.'

'You do your lord a great service. I shall tell him of your loyalty.'

Alone, after Theoderic's departure, Servilla added the final touches. Clarissa and Diana, her personal slaves, would be ready in the chaos of the burning villa, to throw the hounds further off the scent by painting the walls with Christian symbols. It would be assumed that religious fanatics had taken action to rid the area of its sexual profligacy, the cause of the plague in their eyes. Such simple thoughts were delightful, Servilla considered; they provided so much fodder for the manipulative mind. Her strategy had a rounded feel to it. She only regretted that she could not witness Vitalus half drunk and spent, attempting to escape from the flames of his bedroom. 'Ah well. No one can have everything,' she thought, then turned her attention to how she would entertain the bishop.

***

Vitalus no longer sat at table into the small hours; so drawn was he to the promises of the bedchamber. He, Rhonwen and two young Egyptian slave girls, staggered into his private upstairs room, while the guests continued to feast. The guards were lax, in keeping with the informality of the villa. Rhonwen had taken one of them to their joint bed the previous week.

It was easy for Servilla's assassins to lure them away to drink wine, enough for the door to be locked from the outside. This accomplished, the arsonists propped a crude ladder against the window of the High King's room and one of their number climbed up to watch.

Despite offers from his fellows to relieve him from his cramped position, he remained steadfastly in place, eyes glued to the cameo before them. Shadowy bodies writhed in shapes and combinations that only someone else's imagination could have conjured.

Eventually, he crept to the bottom of the ladder, flexing his cramped muscles.

'No wonder he owes money; it must cost him a fortune to pay for temple girls like those,' he whispered.

'Stay here,' another instructed.

'Steady the ladder so we can carry the oil.'

Furtively, the three scaled the ladder. A licentious sight met them. The High King sprawled on his back, snoring loudly, a naked slave crooked in his left arm. Rhonwen lay on her side with an arm draped across the dark breasts of the other girl.

The assassins splashed oil liberally down the window side of the room. While two ensured that they had poured sufficient fuel for a fierce burn, the third slipped a leather thong around the Vortigern's outflung hand. He secured it to the pedestal of a heavy marble statue of Bacchus.

They retraced their steps. The last down the ladder took a torch from inside his tunic, lit it with a flint and hurled it into the room.

They ran through the gardens and into the darkness. Inside the bedroom, the flames flared too quickly for the drunken High King to free himself from his bound wrist. He writhed in panic, twisting in confused contortions. Flames licked around his scorching body. Screaming in pain and incomprehension, Vitalus, the High King of Britain was silenced, his body charred to black anonymity, his face a rictus of amazed disbelief. The stench of burning flesh sent the first evidence of his death to his anxious slaves and guests. They milled around the villa's grounds, watching an acrid spume of black oily smoke spiral into the night sky. His bed-mate slave was choked by the fumes, mercifully saved from death by burning.

Rhonwen was better placed to escape. From her place in the bed furthest away from the fire, she launched herself at the door. Aided by fear, she wrestled Bacchus from his plinth, heaving the statue in her powerful arms to smash open the door. Gasping for breath, her hair singed, her shoulders and buttocks reddened by the rapacious fire, she staggered from the conflagration. The second slave girl had sufficient breath left to shield Rhonwen from the worst of the flames. A scorched back was the price she paid for her escape, but it was small sacrifice for the lives of herself and her mistress.

***

The gods saw their opportunity to play a sardonic trick. The assassin who had observed the High King's last excesses was a repository of stories that would have kept him in wine and ale into his dotage. It was an irony that he was the first to run straight on to the sword of one of Theoderic's men, as they waited for the escapees. Those fleeing were no match for trained troops and though two broke through the initial screen, they were pursued by the more athletic warriors, who cut them down. Servilla's plan was complete.

Theoderic gathered his troop. By the time the authorities attempted to make sense of the night's events, they were south of Viroconium, on their way back to Brittany.

Servilla had spent the evening in a sociable discussion with Bishop Germanus. Agricola had politely declined an invitation to join them. Germanus attempted to secure Servilla's aid in returning the realm to the Church of Rome. He was impressed instead by a scholarly discourse on the unique situation in Britain with its three interpretations of the true faith, plus sundry other pre-Roman religious beliefs.

'I'd not thought you so knowledgeable about theology,' the bishop commented, in full recognition that she had more awareness than he.

'It occupies my time, Bishop. It's a solitary life I lead, with only Categan to consider, now that my daughter is the wife of the Scotti High King and my eldest sons follow their father into politics.'

He nodded, wondering why the Pope persisted in sending him to this contrary land. Of all the places he had been, Britain was full of the most obstinate, dogmatic and stubborn people he had ever met. Their beliefs were either barefacedly stated to cover their own self-interest, or so passionately the truth that they were unshakeable. Either way, despite his faith, he was convinced he was wasting his time.

'It's late, lady. I never intended to keep you from your bed until such an hour. I shall retire now. I shall inform his Holiness that you were most valuable in adding to my understanding of the complex affairs of this island.'

She rose to bid him goodnight. A flustered male slave ran into the room, his face smeared black by smoke.

'My lady! My lady, I bring grim news; the master's villa is aflame. It is feared he's dead.' He slumped, choking to the floor.

Servilla dealt with the news with all the aplomb of her position; she slipped gracefully into a swoon with such theatrical poise that the bishop found himself confronted by an unconscious hostess. He bellowed for servants, patting her hand furiously.

***

A sombre Council of the realm's prominent men gathered to consider the succession. The ambitions of High Kingship were stilted by the crisis that pervaded the land. No one wished to take up the challenge. The Vortigern's opponents viewed any long-standing survival of the regime as unlikely. Brittu lacked his father's flair and Pascent seemed similarly unable to generate the creative genius that the situation demanded. The Vortigern's enemies were quite content to let Brittu lift the poisoned chalice of High Kingship.

Servilla kept herself to herself, grieving for her lost husband in the manner expected of a loyal wife, while she quietly organised her departure from Britain. Taking Categan with her, she left to join Ambrosius a month after the fire. Her ruse worked; her revenge went undetected.

It was a mark of his lack of diplomatic experience that Brittu's first desperate act was to request military aid from the governor of Gaul. Aegidius politely refused. The mainland was too unsettled for troops to be spared.

Brittu turned, as his father had before him, to his Frisian mercenaries. Hengist and Hrosa were pleased to promise aid in return for the remainder of the territory that the British named Canturguoralen. They re-named it Ceint. Gwyrangon, the governor, had fled by the time the bargain was struck. Forewarned by Servilla, he had sailed to join Ambrosius.

19. Homecoming

447 AD - Dinas Ffynon, Gwynedd

The ghost of Cunedda pervaded Dinas Ffynon. Owain could feel it when he entered the stronghold.

Cunorix greeted him at the entrance to the main hall, which had acquired the comfortable savour of Votadini residence. It reminded Owain of his boyhood home. His uncle explained that Enniaun was still in the Guotodin. Gwynedd was being governed by Cunorix, a task that taxed his patience.

'It's not like soldiering, Owain. I'll be glad when your father returns. Our battle skills lose their edge with all this sitting about. My arse fits a horse's back better than a throne.'

Owain muted his smile. Cunorix had grown like the fortress in both size and girth. Votadini horsebreeding skills must have been at their limit to find his uncle a mount that would bear him in battle. Yet, Owain observed, that he showed no less a desire to be about his art.

Two days rest at Dinas Ffynon were enough. Eager to see his kin, Owain left for the Guotodin.

***

The first shoots were beginning to show in the month of Giamonios under the hawk moon of spring. There was a freshness to the air and the weather teased them with showers and bright sunshine. The season, so expectant to boys, held no less appeal to men.

The warriors who rode with them were fast becoming companions, creating a fellowship that Owain could not enjoy with his brothers. Closer to him now were Gilvaethwy, Maelwas and Gwalchma, all proud to ride with the Bear device on their linden shields.

As their horses' hooves ate up the leagues, Edern nudged his mount closer to Owain's, glancing at the stern face that had changed from exuberance to concern in the past five miles.

'The men are in good heart, lord. You seemed so yourself a while back.'

Owain's smile, much-loved by his men, was absent.

'We have been away overlong, old friend. I pine for my kin, but I fear there will be no fond greeting from my brothers.'

'Why should they not embrace you, Owain?'

'Would I be so generous were it Ewein or Cadwallon who rode in my place, with every tongue whispering about destiny and great deeds?'

'Perhaps you would, for they are your brothers, destiny or no.'

Their eyes met fleetingly. Owain turned his face to the road ahead.

***

447 AD - Traprain Law, Guotodin

Owain's boyhood memories of Traprain Law flooded back with the first sight of the hill-top stronghold. The troop emerged from the thick woodland that tried vainly to invade the cleared ground surrounding the fortress.

The appearance of the thirteen riders caused grooms tending Votadini warhorses to lead their precious charges towards the walls. Sentries on the ramparts gesticulated to the warriors within. Owain's troop had not covered half the distance between the wood and the gates before twenty mounted Votadini rode to meet them.

'You should have sent a rider ahead as is the custom,' the leader shouted curtly as the horses on both sides came restlessly to a halt. 'Who rides to Traprain Law?'

His eyes were taking in information, registering the quality of their armour and the stout well-bred horses they rode. Their shields were at their backs, which made them difficult to identify. Edern made as if to respond, but Elen was quicker.

'It's a poor brother who fails to recognise his own, Ewein,' she accused, pulling her shield from her shoulder and turning its full face to him.

'Aye, brother. We should have sent a rider ahead, but as we're kin, we thought you'd mark us,' Owain added. 'Perhaps your sister's red hair would have been enough.'

Ewein shook his head in disbelief. He was easy for his kin to place. His large chalk-white teeth protruded from an otherwise easily recognisable Votadini face. His narrow features and slightly hooked nose were flanked by dark brown curly hair that sprouted beneath his helmet.

'We had no word, kinsfolk. We knew you had left Brittany, but that was a while ago. Welcome home sister, your mother will be happy. She has fretted since we heard that you were on your way. You too, brother,' Ewein added; in Owain's eyes, almost as an afterthought.

There was no doubting the genuine warmth that the Bear received from his parents and grandmother. Though Traprain Law had a forlorn air, as though the very fabric of the Votadini capital mourned its lost lord, the flame of Votadini kinship burned more brightly for Owain and Elen's arrival.

Ceri tutted and fussed about them, keen to address her daughter's manly bearing, but wary of Gwawl's ancient bright eyes that urged her to stay her words. Enniaun was overjoyed. Edern observed that Owain's prediction about his brothers was accurate. Neither Ewain nor Cadwallon greeted him heartily. They seemed furtive at their brother's return and uncomfortable with Elen's warrior trappings. Discovering that both brothers had embraced the Roman Church gave Edern an insight into their cool reception.

Owain received confirmation of his suspicions when Filan greeted him. While the welcoming banquet raged in friendly drinking competitions between Owain's Bear companions and the Votadini, the druid pulled his chair close. Ewein looked on distastefully.

'My heart is glad for your return, lord. This ageing druid has missed you mightily. My skills are sought less since your grandfather's death.'

'Know that your advice will always be welcomed, Filan. It's foolish to reject advice from someone who loves us as you do.'

'Thank you for your words, Owain. Your father and grandmother still value me. But I fear your mother and brothers are under the sway of the God on the cross, and falling more under the thrall of yon priest, Jerome, who teaches fear of all but his plaguey scriptures. It's dangerous, lord. Gwawl is too old for combat, and your mother's weakness for the faith blinds her to the damage the Votadini will suffer from such beliefs. Be wary, lord. Though she loves you, her heart is being turned away from any who won't share the faith. She and your grandmother are at their most distant and your father is torn between his duties here and in Gwynedd. In his absence, the canker grows.'

'Then perhaps it's well that we have returned, Filan. A destiny I might have, but it doesn't mean that I can't heal rifts in the family.'

'I hope you will, Owain. But tread warily. Your brothers have ambitions of their own. Have a care.'

He pushed his chair away from the table to talk with Elen; Ewein's eyes followed him. From his place seated to Ceri's left, the portly Father Jerome also gauged the impact of Owain's return from behind a broad jovial smile. His designs had progressed smoothly of late. It had become easier to wrest the family's spiritual direction away from the ageing Gwawl, especially since Cunedda's death. There was no room in his mission for a man of destiny. Such did not sit easily with the views of scripture. Owain's chilling look caused his smile to falter.

***

Enniaun spelled out his plans. They were seated in the old hall, where Owain recalled rolling with his grandfather's hunting dogs. The throne looked smaller than he remembered.

'I have need of your skills, son. We're heading for war and we need to be ready. Will you take our men with your own to Rheged to aid young Coel against the Angles? I know he's a High King's man, but we have nothing but petty raiding in our own domain and we need to do some real fighting.'

Owain paused to consider.

'I had thought to remain a while, but thank you for your trust. We need to fight real enemies too. Yes, I'll go. Do you remain here?'

'For now. I must return to Gwynedd soon. Cundig and Germanianus of the Cornovii will govern here in the Guotodin, with your brothers' help. I can't keep Cunorix cooped up in Dinas Ffynon overlong. War is much more likely in the south than here.'

Owain hesitated, wanting to draw his father's attention to Filan's warnings. He could see that Enniaun's mind was elsewhere. It could wait awhile.

Led by Owain, a mixed troop of Votadini and the Bear's own horsemen rode to aid Coel the Young. They were fast, trained, well-armed Commanipulares, a valued addition to Coel's more vulnerable warrior horse. Owain and Edern trained the two hundred mounted warriors. In contingents of fifty, using flying columns, with beacon fires atop the highest points along the coast from Arbeia to Petuaria, they could often catch the raiders before they escaped to sea.

Laden with booty, animals and slaves, the Angles were caught at their most vulnerable. Owain's horsemen cut them off from their line of retreat; captured or burned their ships and cut them down where they had no cover. The lightning raids dwindled in one spring. The message had been sent; there were no easy targets on this stretch of coast. The Angles replied by sending fewer, but stronger expeditions. Shield walls protected the raiders from being picked off. Owain's tactics were thwarted and his early successes were forgotten.

But the action brought him battle-readiness. It sharpened Edern's tactical skills and Elen was no passive partner in their endeavours, always ready with a shrewd observation. The men grew to respect her as the force honed itself through the time of the bright bear moon and into Equos, the horse time, the early summer months.

Edern continued to watch the growth of his friend from fledgling warrior to leader. He told his stories by many firesides in his later years, persuaded by eager audiences to share his knowledge of the Bear. 'I knew him to be changed far more than I by Lailoken's lessons and his time with Ambrosius. As the years rolled by, I could see the purpose behind the old seer's advice to myself - but not for him until much later.

If he knew exactly, he never divulged it, but it appeared to me that he was laying the foundations for some great deed. I asked him what was on his mind many times, for he'd slump into melancholy. He'd smile his resigned smile, stare at the heavens and keep his silence. I raised his distance from his brothers.

'Family matters will not be for me, Edern, he said. 'Such distractions are dangerous. The Votadini's future lies in the hands of my kin. You'd do well to ensure that I deal with my brothers and uncles cordially, no more.'

And then, with his face set in stone.

'This goes for other concerns of mortal men. If you love me, Edern, see that I keep to my course. From the time I accepted Lailoken's tutelage, my life was not my own.'

Perhaps this was why he kept everyone except myself, Elen and Gwawl at such distance. There was much comment about his aloof bearing. He was more distant from his peers than many kings from their subjects, but no amount of chiding ever made an impression.

He was very different with his men. He cared for them like a father who saw his destiny in a marriage with war, denying him hearth and kin of his own. It seemed as though his followers stood in place of the blessings that ordinary men received that he felt he could not.

He'd ride into the woods whilst we waited anxiously for his return. He often rejected company, as though only solitude, the earth, sky and his study of bears would purge him of his dark moods. Though such interludes seemed to calm him, there was no change in his mien until his second teacher. Then, all but Filan began to think him bewitched and we feared for him all the more.

Before that, there was one incident that had longstanding consequences for all the Votadini, showing that for all the reluctant acceptance of his unknown destiny, he was but a mortal and vulnerable man.'

20. Summer Bride and Forest Lady

447 AD - Gwent borderlands

It was high summer, claim time under the stag moon of Elembios. Owain rode south at Coel the Young's request to escort Creiddylad, daughter of Tendubric, Pendragon of Gwent to her betrothal with the king of Rheged. Though Coel had worthy attributes to woo the Dragon's daughter, his patience was tested by the Gwent King's vehement opposition to their match. Finally, Creiddylad's mother, Bronwen, had interceded. If the British Church was to be a secret to the royal family of Gwent and Siluria, how was it possible to find a paramour for their daughter wedded to its teachings, she had scolded him? Was Creiddy to become a nun? Faced with this conspiracy, the Dragon's stubborn defences crumbled.

Creiddy was more excited by her role of summer flower bride than Coel's advances. At seventeen, she welcomed any excuse to escape from her father's religion. Coel's passion had been fuelled by a miniature portrait of her; a picture that did little to represent the beauty of its subject. Creiddy's dark curls flowed to shoulder length; her robust healthy colouring, bolstered by the energy she used in all her undertakings, was far more vibrant than the pallid looks of her passive portrait. Still, Coel was smitten by the likeness and even more entranced when he had first met her. Her radiance evoked thoughts in him that her stern father would have found unthinkable.

Owain's troop was camped in a clearing, one day's ride away from their rendezvous with Creiddy and the escort from Gwent. The men were at ease after three months campaigning. Escorting a summer bride was a relaxing diversion.

Camp fires crackled brightly. White plumes spiralled skywards. The first aroma of spitted venison blended with the woodsmoke to whet their appetites. They had unpacked their best tunics for the morrow. Camp followers adorned them with brightly coloured ribbons. Summer flowers, woven into circular crowns would replace their helmets. Owain, Edern and Elen sat talking beneath an oak, mature green in its finery. Edern observed that Owain appeared unusually content.

The foam-flecked horse reared to a halt, shattering the men's mood. A broken spear shaft protruded from its rider's shoulder. His head lolled weakly.

Two of Owain's men calmed the panting animal. Others grasped weapons to defend against possible pursuers.

The battered shield with its white cross fell from its owner's outstretched arm. The dying rider was lifted gently to the earth. His purpling lips hardly moved as he gasped out his last report.

'Saxon ambush, half a day's ride. Lady Creiddy taken....'

No order was required from Owain. His men dismantled the camp. Most were mounted before the messenger's grave had been prepared.

Owain turned to them.

'More fighting, my hounds. We hunt Saxons. Ride fast, but tight reins. We need the horses to ride long on the morrow.'

The stag moon shone clearly above them. It half lit the way eerily through deep glades, glinting from spear points and helmets. The ambush had been well set. A monstrous ash blocked the road where it curved. Twenty Saxons lay slain. Tendubric's warriors had fought well. Creiddy's escort lay in a circle, their cloak-shrouded bodies, ghostly in the moon's argent glow.

'They'll be running for their ships. Search for tracks to the east,' Edern rapped.

'It's a fair way to the coast. We'll seek them out,' he judged confidently.

Owain dismounted, his mind re-enacting the ambush.

'Poor Lady Creiddy must be out of her wits with fear; she's but seventeen, brother ...... You don't think...' Elen's thoughts petered out; she bit her lip.

'Best not think on it, sister. They'll be in haste to reach the sea. Turn your head from aught else. There's more value in ransoming her than in ravishing her.'

Elen nodded.

Keen to press on Edern, eagerly awaited discovery of their quarry's tracks. A companion approached.

'There's something wrong here, lord,' the man addressed Owain.

'Gilvaethwy; what is it?' Owain asked.

'It's the slain Sais, lord. They're unlike any I've seen, unless the Angles and their cousins are from different peoples.'

'How? ' Owain pressed.

'There's nary a blond hair among them, lord. Nor a beard, nor a plait. True, their clothes and weapons are Sais, but they're nothing like we've fought on the coast.'

Edern dismounted.

'Show us,' Owain gestured.

Gilvaethwy led to where he had turned the fallen bodies of the ambushers. The dead were mainly dark haired and close cropped under their helmets. In the moonstruck pallor of death, their faces showed no sign of Sais features. Owain was used to fighting big, heavy-boned Angles. The stature of these men was much slighter.

'You're rght, Gilvaethwy. They look much like our own, or Roman,' he said.

'Have the men search in a circle, Edern.'

The black crescent hoofprints of many horses were found in a small copse, trailing northwards.

By dawn Owain's pursuit had taken them to the north of Powys. Two of their fleetest riders, Cust and Gwalchma scouted ahead. Owain was confident that his quarry would travel slowly. The scouts returned to the main column as they approached South Elmet.

'Just ahead, lord. About thirty, all well mounted. They're resting. Sentinels are out. No sign of Lady Creiddy.'

'We outnumber them, but we must use stealth. A direct attack is too risky.' Owain said. 'They've extra mounts. They could outrun us. Agreed?'

The woodland covered Owain's foot patrol to reconnoitre. In the afternoon they laid their plans.

***

Once she had convinced herself that her life was safe in the hands of her audacious dark-haired captor, Creiddy's imagination ran to even wilder fancies. Initial dread at her abduction gave way to a thrilling excitement. She had savoured her journey to join Coel; it was the furthest she had been allowed to travel. But events had surpassed her wildest expectations. Annoyingly, her captor showed little interest in the part she had fashioned for him. He seemed more concerned at his losses and that his band avoided pursuit.

On the following day, Creiddy's mind was jolted from its daydreaming by the effects of the bone-jarring ride. A part of her royal anatomy was more suited to cushions than horseback. Denied the comforts of her regal quarters, her enthusiasm for adventure rapidly ebbed. Her maids were too shocked to provide the succour she expected.

'What do you intend to do with us?' she demanded when they finally halted.

For the first time he seemed to see her. It was hard to ignore the full flush of colour to her throat and her raven tresses. She fired the question with venom, shaking with anger.

'I had thought, lady, to secure ransoms from your father and your betrothed. A neat bargain don't you think? In full daylight, I'm tempted otherwise. Shall I forfeit my reward and seek more pleasurable use of you?'

His lascivious tongue, licking his lips, assured Creiddy their positions were reversed. Girlish aspirations faded.

'Be assured, it would be no pleasure for me. I insist that you provide for my comfort until my father and Coel are informed. Any outrage will be punished.'

'You'll have to make do with your maids' attention. We're on the run, lady. There's little comfort for any of us in that. If I can be of further service, seek me out.'

The deep bow failed to camouflage the mocking twinkle in his amber eyes. Her royal responsibility was aroused. Men had died in her service and her maids were more distressed than she.

'You can be of no service at all, until you escort me to my betrothed,' she spun on an angry foot to rejoin her weeping servants.

***

Creiddy pulled the wolf fur around her, more in hope than in any conviction that it would stave off the cold. She huddled between Megan and Rhia, for their warmth. They slept, but their faces were red with distress. They snuffled, fidgeting in their dreaming. The tent they shared was of skins stretched over lopped tree branches. Their captors slept in the open. She sighed and bit her bottom lip. She had avoided the leader since their confrontation that morning. She hoped that he was more desperate for ransom than to explore her virgin body. His confidence had unnerved her. Her anger seemed to fuel his lust.

They had remained in the rough camp all afternoon while the horses grazed. Night had descended, bringing more misery. They had eaten little and still wore the clothes they been captured in. Creiddy had refused the offer of a spitted rabbit. She had to fight her inner craving for food, heightened by the delicious aroma of the meat as her maids devoured it.

When they lay down, Creiddy's stomach rumbled alarmingly, adding to the difficulty she was having falling asleep. It was so arduous to escape the rigour of her father's teaching. Was this God's punishment for her conduct, she wondered. She had so wanted a distraction to alleviate her boredom. Now her wish had been granted, a generous meal and a bed seemed a hundred times more desirable.

Beyond the shelter the moon battled with patchy cloud, casting the camp into silver half-light and charcoal shadows. Edern worried; the conditions jeopardised their approach. The rescue plan was simple. Cust, whose reputation was for his astute sense of hearing, led half a dozen warriors to stampede the horses. Edern, Elen and Gwalchma were to rescue Lady Creiddy. Owain led the main band, horsed and ready to charge the camp.

Creiddy's captors had allowed her some privacy. The tent was placed some way from the humped smudges of her sleeping abductors. The rescuers made painstaking progress. The moon hindered their approach past alert sentries. They crept to the last cover, unhelpful spiky gorse and twenty paces from the tent. The sentries looked outwards. Edern remained apprehensive.

Elen was less cautious. Reluctantly, Edern gripped his sword. He rose to a crouch, stumbling on cramp-stiffened legs in her wake. Gwalchma followed. Edern's fear of a challenge was unfounded. An owl's night hunting cry pierced the sleepers' snores. Elen reached the tent. She slit the skin and thrust her head through the gap.

A startled Creiddy was about to shriek at what she believed to be a night visit by her captor. Elen clamped a firm gauntleted hand across her mouth, beckoning her to silence. Creiddy bit back her scream.

'I am Elen, sister to the Bear lord, Owain Arth-Ursus. Waken your maids, but quietly.'

Creiddy's heart pounded.

Edern, eager to be away, glanced nervously left and right. They retreated clumsily. They were only half way across the clearing when the moon ghosted from behind a cloud bank, illuminating them as they scurried for cover. Creiddy caught a naked foot in a patch of gorse. Her gasp of pain was stifled too slowly.

'The captives are escaping,' a sentry bellowed gruffly somewhere to their left. Prone bodies became animated shadows, running in the gloaming. With their leader to the fore, they raced in pursuit.

Cust used the noise of the rousing camp to disperse the horses. His men startled them into a panic that took them galloping off towards the east.

Glancing over his shoulder, Edern noticed the slight hesitation among their pursuers; caught between concern for their mounts and their escaping prize. Their uncertainty was enough for the watchful Owain.

'Arth-Ursus, Arth-Ursus,' Owain's companions bellowed, charging into the moonlit clearing. Edern watched them crash into the surprised warriors.

Edern reached the waiting horses in the shelter of the woods. He heaved Creiddy and her maids unceremoniously on to waiting mounts. They skirted the fray, urging the steeds northwards.

Owain judged the rescue complete. The abductors had no means of pursuit.

'To me. To me. Withdraw,' he yelled above the shouts, grunts and screams. They broke off easily, leaving strewn foemen littered across the open ground.

Owain smiled. A knot of enemy warriors, in a protective circle, watched him canter across their front.

A hoarse voice called from the darkness

'That's twice you've baulked my ambitions, Owain. You'll not gainsay me forever.'

'Who hails the Bear?' Owain challenged.

'It is I, Leontinus. Can you not keep to your own lands in Gwynedd and the Guotodin? You've cost me much silver this night; good men too.'

'Leontinus. You think there are richer pickings here in Britain than in the east? I heard you rode against the Huns. It's no easier here for a mercenary is it?'

'Right enough, Owain. I'll not forget your meddling.'

'Thank me for your life, Leontinus. It would be easy to hunt you down.'

'You're welcome to try. These are not all my company. Pursue us if you wish. I'll meet you in daylight, any day of your choosing, Bear man.'

'Have you deserted your military wisdom along with your birthright?' Owain mocked.

'I'll repay you for this night, Owain; by all the gods I will.'

Owain led his men off to the east. Behind him, Leontinus glowered, his scheme dashed to ruin.

***

Owain rode hard to reach Ludenses, the main town of the small civitate of Elmet, Rheged's southern neighbour. The governor was absent, but his household servants greeted the rescued flower bride and her entourage hospitably. The men were billeted with the town garrison and Owain's immediate companions, Creiddy and her maids were entertained in the governor's residence.

Bathed, steamed and pampered into recovery, Creiddy turned her mind to her immediate future. Some of her pains had surrendered to the pummelling her maids gave her in the bath house, but her rump remained impervious to their ministrations. She sat delicately on cushions to ease her saddle sores.

Excitement rose again. Leontinus, had been a channel for her curiosity. Marriage to Coel fulfilled tradition, but Owain was different. Her desires made her shiver with the urge to caress Owain's naked skin. His rescue liberated her from more than her captors. The dungeon door of her father's piety stood open also; her thoughts made her breathless.

She soothed herself with sips of wine. She was tired. The wine made her drowsier, yet she had no wish to sleep. His courage captivated her. As a leader he was without peer, but she could see straight into his forsaken depths. He was alone in a way she had never seen any human. Her love was a compassionate arrow that pierced the cloak of his responsibility. Her body craved to banish his loneliness. The more she dwelt upon it, the more her abduction seemed to have been fated.

Timorously, she padded barefoot along the corridor, a dark green travelling cloak over her night shift. She wondered at her motives, but her body seemed to know her intentions. She had seen Owain only once, in the clearing where he had trotted at the head of his men. His face was flushed with the excitement of the skirmish, his hair wild and long, streaming in the night breeze; his horse, whinnying in celebration of his master's victory. Yet for all that, when he had formally kissed her hand, she saw a man not yet mature. Warrior he might be, but he was a stranger, an aloof mountain peak clouded by his destiny.

'We are glad to be of service, lady. We shall escort you to your betrothed, have no fear,' he had assured her, hollow and matter-of-fact. Yet, his eyes danced from her dishevelled tresses to her bare bloodstained feet.

'Have the lady's maids wash and bind her cuts; we ride for Ludenses,' he had instructed. She watched him bow from the saddle. He wheeled away and didn't look back.

'***

She halted at the door of his room, rubbing one foot hesitantly against her calf, supporting her weight on the door frame with an oustretched arm. Her convictions ebbed. She hovered, caught on the bridge between her desires and the righteous conduct of her father's teaching.

A sound from inside the room startled her; he might be coming to the door. A fleeting image of having to explain why she was running away flashed across her mind, prompting her to knock.

'Enter,' came the response.

Breathing deeply, she walked in. He had stripped himself of his mail. Bathed and oiled, he lounged on the bed in a plain white tunic. His hazel eyes opened wide.

'Is all well, lady?' he asked, moving swiftly to grasp the hilt of his sword in its scabbard at the bed head.

'You don't need your sword, lord. All is well,' she blurted.

'Then what, lady? Do your maids not attend you?'

'I am alone, lord. I wished to thank you for my rescue. We have had no time to talk.'

'You need not creep here in the dead of night to thank me. We would have rescued any lady from your plight.'

She ran her fingers across her lips; discouraged.

'You might think me forward, lord, but I came to comfort you. You lack even a servant. You lead valiantly, yet you keep no company. I thought I might ease your solitude for one night at least.'

She paused, stunned by her own boldness.

'Lady, your ordeal distresses you. You are betrothed to a king. This is folly. I am flattered by your attention. But this does neither of us honour.'

Rebuffed, she part turned. But her stubbornness turned her once more.

'Honour is not my guardian tonight, lord Owain, though it governs my life, true enough. How can you fulfil your destiny so distanced from the lives of others? Your eyes belie your words. Order me to leave and I'll retire. But be honest. Honour is not soiled by this tryst. I'll marry Coel, but Holy Church has not yet sanctified our betrothal. I wish to repay you for my rescue. If God sees ill in such an act, I'll be damned right happily.'

Her passion coloured her cheek deep red. He laughed at her mettle.

'Had I three hundred men like you, lady, neither Picts nor Saxons would trouble us. You read me true. My duty is all to me. You cannot measure how much comfort one night would bring. If I lacked as much in silver as I do in solace, I'd be fighting on foot with a wooden staff.'

She moved closer, taken by his honesty. Her slender hand moved out to caress his hair, still damp from the bath house.

'I know you lack affection, Owain. Hang your honour with your sword. Let me soothe you that you might know a little of what men without a destiny live and die for.'

He gave ground to her soft push. A gentle finger hushed his lips. Slipping artfully from her robe, she joined him on the bed. He took her clumsily in his arms. Laughter bubbled up from deep in her throat.

'This is wrestling of a different kind, lord. Loose your grip, lest you crush me.'

***

447 AD - Rheged

Festooned and garlanded in the flowers and colours of late summer, Coel the Young and Creiddy were married in Rheged under the hound moon of Eorionos. Owain's belief that his destiny protected him from the trials that plagued other men underwent a sharp review. Both Coel and Tendubric insisted that he occupy the place of honour at the high table. He accepted with a degree of discomfort that made the summer bride smile wistfully.

***

447 AD - Dinas Ffynon

He had been day dreaming, lost in a tangle of thoughts. On such occasions, his horse frequently found its own way. This morning, Owain exercised Cobyl, his second mount. When he regained his everyday awareness, he realised that he had left the track to Dinas Ffynon. The terrain was unfamiliar, yet he had been convinced that he knew the whole area for several miles around the fortress.

The horse followed a discernible path. Owain allowed it to continue, curious as to his whereabouts. The trees grew densely: oak, alder and beech overhanging the narrow path. He was contemplating turning around when his mount walked into a small clearing. Mystified, Owain saw a woodsman's cottage set against a giant oak, which stood like a guardian, its branches protectively spread over the dwelling's roof. The horse stopped. Owain shook his head in annoyance.

The cottage door opened. Owain was expecting a woodsman; he was ready to ask directions, but the query died unformed.

A tall willowy woman in a pure white dress stood before him. She was older than he, perhaps Ceri's years. Her long, straight black hair hung to her waist; a sprig of primroses decorated her left temple. Her smile suggested familiarity, though he had never seen her before. Light grey eyes laughed at his open-mouth.

'Will you rest awhile, Owain Arth-Ursus? We have been awaiting you.'

Bemused, Owain slid from the horse. Cobyl cropped contentedly at the lush grass.

'I am disadvantaged, lady. I know these woods well, yet this is strange. Who are you?'

'All in good time, Owain; come, walk with me.'

She took his arm as his mother might have. A path ran from the side of the cottage, beneath the oak into the woods. They walked in the ancient forest, a hemmed-in, secret guarded by stalwart sentinels. The smell of moist vegetation rose from the earth. Sunlight filtered through the leafy canopy.

'What do you wish of me?' he asked.

'To be of service, Owain; that is all.'

'You would serve me? How?'

'Did your tutor, Lailoken, not tell you that you would find another teacher when you needed one?'

'Are you she?'

Laughter creased her milk pale skin. Yet all was not humour. Wisdom, compassion and sadness shaped her face.

'It falls to my lot, lord. You are ready for a great lesson, Owain Arth-Ursus.'

'I had thought most already learned, lady.'

'The folly of manhood, Owain. All that is new in life is the greatest lesson at the time. When boys become men, they believe themselves complete. Such arrogance fails them. Recognise that much as you may know, there is always more that eludes you. There you have learned already.'

'Are you related to Lailoken? What name do you go by? How am I to be tutored by you when I don't know where I am?'

She sighed, as though a fleeting sprite had stolen her smile.

'Nothing in life is unrelated, Owain. I know of Lailoken and Lailoken knows of me. If I were to give you my name, we would be bound in fate, for all gifts have their price. Far better for you that I remain darkling, like the winter nights. When you wish to see me, just ride the horse that brought you here this morning. It knows the way.'

'Then what is the lesson I'm to learn?' he asked, frustrated.

'What is of most value to you, Owain?'

'Perhaps a listener, lady. Of all that commands my thoughts, my destiny still grieves me. I have studied the bear and its gifts have been generous. I have learned patience. I have learned the way of the warrior and I lead a chosen band. Yet, I chafe at my burden. All men know what they carry: the warrior bears his fear of death; the cleric, the weight of his private sins; the lover, his fear of rejection. But me, lady? I know not what I bear. If you have any insight I shall be ever in your debt. My life is a rent tunic. Can you sew it?'

'You have no inkling, Owain?'

'Lailoken said I was to know men in order that I might lead them. It's an obligation; like a salmon in a net. It displeases me. I would have led the Votadini joyfully, alongside my kin, adding to my grandfather's lands. Against such a vision, this destiny lurks in dark shadows. My family stands off from me as though I had the plague.'

They walked into a tiny clearing. The lady seated herself on a fallen stump. She beckoned him to join her. He sat. A startled song thrush burst from a hawthorn bush; its wing beats louder than an eagle's.

She took his hand and placed it in her lap. Her frank gaze emphasised her words:

'Your tutor was shrewd, Owain. He saw your need to move in circles where true power has become jaded; lost to men's foolish scheming. It was not ever thus, but you must know how men act from their lusts and greed; their views of gods and fates.

Never believe that this has any bearing on your destiny. Leading men is a small thing. Any petty king sees himself thus.'

She chuckled at her impish thought.

'Indeed, that's the problem with leaders; they lead. You're more than that, Owain.'

'What then, lady?' he asked.

'You were chosen by the bear because it is the oldest of totems, Owain. Its links with humans go back into the mists of time beyond memory. Though you have learned much from bears, no mere watching can tell you all there is to know. In this matter, let me be your guide. The bear people have guarded secrets for thousands of years. These are amongst the oldest of mysteries, powerful even before the goddess. If it's your destiny that troubles you, the nub of it lies not in leadership, though you'll fare well at that, for what it's worth.'

'Then what, lady?'

'The land calls you, Owain. The earth upon which men perform their follies. While they strut and preen, lust, battle, placate their gods and talk of piety, they ignore the gifts that allow them to fashion their crude designs. Not one of their ideas will endure Owain; not for a breath in the time counted by the stars. Yet they forge kingdoms, build fortresses, defeat their enemies and have the bards sing of their exploits. It is but a play, Arth-Ursus. Now you are chosen to be one of us. To be of the Bear and stand for the land.

The bear's greatest lesson is in what it takes from nature without force. It grows mighty from the fruits that the land gives. Men forget this. The Christians are to the fore. The rituals that bound our forbears to the land are rooted out. The groves have been cut, the stones stand silent. The God on the cross owes no allegiance to the land and a great suffering is brought by the bearers of this new religion.'

'What can I do? You'd have me fight God...?'

'No, Arth-Ursus, but in making your stand against the threats to your people, you'll fashion a legacy for memory; something to vex the minds of those unborn as yet, who'll know when the time comes that you stood true for the land. That's why the bear chose you. You and your kind have a purpose that has rung down the ages, even though the darkness will shroud it to the very pinprick of a candle flame. Still, in that time, the stones will stand; beyond Rome; beyond the God on the cross; beyond the arrogance of men.'

***

I was in the map room when Owain returned from the forest. No one could break his trance. Elen was in her rooms and rushed to the central hall, following the anxious tone in Ceri's voice:

'Edern, Elen, come quickly, something ails Owain.'

On first sight it seemed a strange illness. Owain sat on his father's throne, a look of such wonder on his face that my first thoughts were that he'd been smitten by love. I looked more closely. This was more like someone had witched his faculties.

'Where is Crenda?' Ceri demanded, her voice agitated.

The servants found the druid who was wandering in the woods. Crenda and Gwawl pacified Ceri who was pacing the room, crying.

'He has been attacked by forest spirits,' she wailed, clutching the cross she had taken to wearing on her best silver chain.

'I must pray for him. Take me to the chapel.'

'It might well be the best place to calm her,' Crenda suggested, knowing full well Gwawl's antagonism to her daughter-in-law's convictions.

'I agree, Crenda. She will quieten at her prayers. I'll walk with her as far as the chapel. But it sends shivers down my old spine.'

Crenda walked several times around the throne as soon as they had left, his face a picture of concentration; his eyes remained firmly fixed on Owain's face.

'Go to my dwelling, Elen. Bring me the leather bag you find there. Edern set water to boil on yon fire.'

The water was boiling when Elen returned. Crenda threw herbs and roots into the pot, which he stirred with a wooden spoon. When the potion cooled, he poured a measure into a beaker. He supported Owain's head with one hand and poured the liquid past the glazed smile.

'Is he bewitched?' I asked.

'I cannot say. I have not seen the like of this in all my years.'

'Then what have you given him?' Elen queried.

'Poppy and herbs to make him sleep. We shall see his condition when he awakens. Help me carry him to bed.'

We did, passing curious servants, warriors and household retainers, who all either crossed themselves or made the warding sign as they glimpsed the beatific smile that transfixed his face.

Crenda bade me summon him when Owain awoke. Elen and I settled down beside his bed to keep vigil. I took her hand, partly to comfort her, partly because it pleased my heart to hold it.

Owain awoke in the night, curious as to why we were sitting by his bed.

'Have you no beds of your own?' he asked.

'We were keeping watch,' Elen began.

'So it seems,' he replied: 'But why?'

'Don't you remember returning from your ride?' I asked.

He sat up, pulling the furs to his chin, his face a twisted mask of deliberation.

'I met a lady in the forest. It was strange. She told me my destiny. Yes, I remember now. My fears were groundless; I'm to be no butcher wallowing in bloodied fields. I'm to be a steward of the land. That is the bear's path for me.'

I looked at Elen; she looked back. Something had happened. Owain's destiny was running beyond the ken of those close to him. I watched him smile, staring into the purple blackness. We cloaked our disbelief in soothing words, our silent concern drawing us closer.

21. Pious Treachery

447 AD, Traprain Law, Guotodin

Father Jerome's thick lips curved at the news. Word of Owain's bewitchment sent a fleshy tremor down his heavy jowls. His designs were well advanced by the carefully engineered splits in the Votadini family. The sons were easier to manipulate when their father and their meddlesome grandmother were absent. Enniaun had just returned to the Guotodin; caution was now the watchword.

The priest sat alone, a valuable copy of the Holy Book open before him in the light of a flickering candle. It was not Holy Scripture that he read, but a letter from the Holy Father's office. Father Jerome's appearance epitomised his ambition. Beneath the plain habit of his calling, his corpulence mirrored his aspiration. The outward show of pious poverty disguised a burning desire for power; authority that the letter before him promised for bringing the northern peoples into the fold of Mother Church. Papal authority was not beyond clandestine operations in the wake of the official failure of Germanus to defeat pagans and heretics.

Father Jerome anticipated the promised Bishopric with relish. The first step in his plans for advancement was established. He had the complete trust of Ceri, Ewein and Cadwallon. Overly concerned with political and military matters, Enniaun would succumb to Ceri's entreaties for the family to recognise the orthodox church. Father Jerome's main obstacle was Filan the Druid. His jowls quivered from another grin as he fondled the letter. He glowed with satisfaction. Soon all would be resolved.

***

Filan walked in the woods, drawn to a life of quiet contemplation. It was time for Crenda to take his place in service to the Votadini. Filan wished to pursue his healing arts in solitude. Gleeful at the sight of wild garlic beneath a towering oak, he stooped to pluck it. On his knees, his attention focused firmly on the plant, he failed to see the disturbance in the undergrowth behind him. His senses finally warned him to look up. The foliage was flattened by an enraged male boar. The animal erupted into view a few paces from where he knelt. It hurtled towards him, its tusks curved, red eyes gleaming.

Filan shuffled quickly on his knees, showing a sprightly turn of speed for such an awkward stance. Putting the tree between himself and the boar, he rose to his feet behind the bole. The animal juddered to a frustrated halt, its tusks almost touching the bark. The acrid stench of the boar's urine rose to Filan's nostrils as he looked down at its broad bristly back. Its mouth slavered. Its head shook with rage.

Filan had treated boar wounds which were often more ragged than those inflicted by weapons. Victims either bled to death or died from the prurient decay. He had no desire for either fate.

The boar smelled him. Its black snout twitched. It retreated a few steps, then angled in at the tree in a short bursting run. Filan withdrew further. The boar's left tusk shaved shards of bark from the trunk. It paused briefly before circling the tree.

The druid feared the worst. He had left no instruction as to where he should be cremated or where his ashes were to be scattered. This was a lesson in humility, even for one so steeped in forest lore. Reduced to being chased round the tree, Filan knew that he lacked stamina. Panting heavily, the first waves of panic began to pound on the shore of his discipline as he scuttled just a few paces ahead of the pursuing beast. Snorting and squealing, steam rose from its flanks. The boar closed the gap with every stride. In desperation, Filan stopped and turned, swinging his leather carrying bag downwards in an arc. The bag glanced off the animal's taut shoulders; Filan's last futile defence was exhausted. Sensing his desperation, the beast bunched.

Anger replaced panic. Filan took a deep breath.

The boar launched itself. Its snort transformed to a howl of pain. An arrow took it in the flesh of its haunch. Mesmerised, Filan watched it turn, wriggling to dislodge the barb. A second shaft whistled to embed itself in the creature's chest. Grunting in pain, its front legs collapsed. It careered a faltering two steps and collapsed on its side.

'You'll eat well this night, Druid,' a voice floated from a bowshot away.

Filan slumped to his knees, breathing deeply. He wondered how his spirit had avoided joining his ancestors. The boar's eyes carried death's neutral gaze. Its head was but two paces away.

'I think I've lost my appetite,' he wheezed.

'He'll look different skinned and roasted,' the archer said, walking into view. He retrieved his arrows. He wore a faded woodsman's tunic over dark trousers more akin to the Sais than the men of Traprain Law. His quiver was of plain leather, functional like the short hunting bow he carried. His open generous face was fringed with fair long hair and his fingers long and slender.

'I owe you my life, woodsman,' Filan said, breathing raggedly.

'I live in the forest. I shoot well. My named is Gweveyel.'

'I am Filan, the King's Druid. He will reward you well if you escort me back to the fortress.'

'If you have your breath, there's something you should see, Druid.'

Curious, Filan walked shakily after the retreating woodsman. Gweveyel paused several paces away. He pointed to the undergrowth. Filan saw shattered pieces of wood strewn on the ground. Booted feet had trampled the grass. Flecks of blood spattered the greenery and where the earth was visible there was the unmistakable imprint of boar hooves.

'The beast was goaded to attack you, Druid. You have subtle enemies. The wooden spars were a cage. The boar was an assassin's tool.'

'Aye and I know who would gain most from my death,' Filan muttered.

'Will you do me one more service, Gweveyel?' Filan asked, his mind racing.

'You keep me from my labours, Druid. My family will sleep with empty bellies tonight if I return empty handed,' the woodsman replied, but with dry humour.

'I promise they'll sleep, glutted from the King's own larder, if you aid me further,' Filan pledged. 'But we must work quickly.'

'Then say on, Druid. I care not for such cold attempts on an unarmed man's life. What would you have me do?'

***

Father Jerome's quill raced across the special vellum that he kept for communications with the Pope's Office. Traprain Law was hung with grief for the passing of the druid, Filan. Not as heavy as for Cunedda's departure, but heartfelt, nevertheless. Father Jerome's mind ran to his reward. The letter bolstered his claim. As a bonus, one more pagan had been eliminated. More, the stupid woodsman was unaware of the druidic custom for cremating their dead. He had buried the body in the forest.

Completing his letter, Father Jerome rolled and eased it into the leather tube and affixed the Papal seal. Smiling, he called for the awaiting messenger. He instructed the monk, and then composed himself. He must extend sympathy to his grieving flock and avoid appearing as victorious as he felt.

He sought out the king. Enniaun was sitting alone in the main hall, his dogs at his feet and a goblet of wine before him.

'The Druid is a loss to us all, lord,' the priest intoned; his voice lacking sincerity.

'I would think you'd be glad to be rid of him,' the king answered.

'No my lord; the souls of all God's creatures are precious, even those of sinners and pagans,' Father Jerome responded, eager to promote the faith.

'He was greater than that to this family, priest. He was a friend,' Enniaun snapped.

'I meant no offence, lord. It is difficult to see past my beliefs,' the priest wheedled.

''Tis a strange church that sanctions murder, priest,' came a voice from the doorway.

Father Jerome's jaw trembled in horror. His jowls shuddered in disbelief; his ringed hand flew to his mouth.

Filan blocked the doorway, the woodsman at his side. Appealing against his treatment, the messenger monk was on his knees before them.

'He stands accused by his own hand, lord,' Filan said quietly, handing the scroll to the king.

'That is the Pope's own seal; for no eyes but his,' Father Jerome squealed.

'Not when it carries proof of murder. There is no authority high enough to save you, father,' Enniaun addressed him evenly. He read the letter slowly, one eye on the sweat that beaded the priest's brow.

'I am satisfied, Filan. This man would have taken your life but for this woodsman. You shall pronounce judgement, Filan.'

Filan stared at the deflated priest.

'You have done this family ill, father. You have poisoned the lady of this house with your lies and two of her sons also. I'll not sanction your miserable death. My judgement is this: You will be chained by the ankles and sent out to the villages around Traprain Law where you will preach your faith to the poor as your Church bids you. Should you try to escape, Votadini horsemen will recapture you. Perhaps a life of such service to the people will bring you some understanding of your soul.'

'Take him to the smithy and fashion his chains, Enniaun said coldly. 'You have a light judgement, priest. Thank your god that I was not your judge.'

'What of the monk?' Filan asked.

'He will carry letters to the Pope. I shall write them,' Enniaun commanded.

'Now, woodsman, how can I show my gratitude?' Enniaun asked.

'I hear your youngest son rides against the Angles, lord. My father grows old. If my family were provided for, I would ride with Owain if he would have me.'

'I have no doubt he will, Gweveyel. This Druid is very dear to him. Your family shall receive succour. I will send you to Gwynedd with letters for Owain. Now, Filan, send for those troublesome sons of mine. It's time I put Votadini family affairs above those of the people. I had not thought that this priest could make such mischief, though I was warned frequently enough.'

Ewein and Cadwallon sheepishly received the lash of their father's tongue.

'Whatever that fat priest has been seducing you with is no more. If you wish to follow this Christian faith, that is your affair. But it will not hinder Votadini concerns. We have suffered too long from idleness. You shall be reconciled with your brother, Owain and ride with him and your uncle. In war, you might learn more honourable ways.'

His words carried the conviction of his standing. The priest's deeds were being reported by every scullion throughout Traprain Law. Lacking allies, the brothers sullenly obeyed their father.

22. Artwerys

448 AD - Rheged

Culwyn, the midwife rubbed her perspiring hands together. Neither Father Matthew's holy water, nor Druid, Talian's herbal potions would ease her mistress's suffering. Creiddylad writhed on the bed. Her body glistened with sweat, her raven hair was plastered to her face. She moaned through gritted teeth, biting back on her screams.

'There's nought else we can do, for them,' Talian conceded.

'The child will not feed at his mother's breast. We can save one or the other, but not both.'

Culwyn knew it. Giamonios, the time that the shoots show, was propitious for birth, but her appeals to Rhiannon, the goddess of women's burdens, had not been answered.

'This is a royal heir. Holy Church decrees that the child will be saved,' Father Matthew pronounced.

'Mayhap, but King Coel is sovereign here,' Talian contested.

A pain-filled voice rasped weakly behind them, but the anger in it stilled their debate.

'My wishes will be carried out while I breathe,' Creiddy panted, gripping Megan's hand to fight the searing tremors that wracked her womb.

'This child will be born. It is my desire and you will fulfil it. Now leave me. I will speak to Megan.'

Reluctantly, Talian made his exit. Father Matthew looked more relieved to be out of the dingy room. The smoke of burnt herbs, used to protect the childbed, stung his eyes into watery rivulets.

'Listen, Megan. I have a last errand for you. I have little time. Father Matthew won't stand against my husband's wrath when he hears my wish. The priest will be telling Coel right now what I intend. You must help Culwyn do what is necessary. If I cannot love Coel, I can give him an heir. Now listen, this is what you must do.....'

***

Coel the Young stared hard at the portrait of his beloved. All the discipline of his youth vanished. His joy at the expected announcement of the birth of his heir was dashed when Father Matthew fretfully informed him of Creiddy's intentions. A headlong rush through the villa brought stares of disbelief from the servants. It also brought him too late.

Creiddy lay in quiet death. A bloodstained sheet covered the severed womb from which Megan and Culwyn had wrested her unborn. Her pallor now matched her portrait for the first time. Her ruddy vibrance had departed, along with her pain, entwined in the soul that had fled her butchered body.

Coel was overwrought with grief. Yet he knew in his heart as he gazed at her still form, that his love had not been returned. She had fulfilled her wifely duties, but their marriage lacked passion. Her loss seared him nevertheless.

'You had no right to act, Talian. Mine was the right to judge. Does being a king count for nought in this realm?'

'Your judgement would have haunted you, lord. She knew it. She asked your forgiveness for relieving you of it. The child is a boy. You have an heir.'

If Coel heard, he showed no sign. He twisted a lock of her dark hair in his fingers as it lay across the pillow.

'Did she suffer, Talian?' he asked quietly.

'No, lord. I gave her mandrake. Will you take your son, lord. He has need of his father now.'

Culwyn offered him the tiny bundle. A tiny arm wriggled free of the swaddling cloth, fingers flexed in curiosity.

Distraught, Coel took the child reluctantly, hardly seeing the small round face that peered up at him.

'What will you name him, lord?' Talian asked gently.

'Had his mother not been rescued last year, I might not have enjoyed any time with her. I shall name him Artwerys for the Bear lord, Owain,' he said distractedly.

He looked down at the squirming bundle.

'The cost of an heir was never so great, little one. You had best become the son your father desires and be worthy of the woman who gave herself to let you see the world.'

He handed the child back to Culwyn. Turning his back, he walked away, clutching Creiddy's portrait tightly in his fist. His eyes blurred.

***

448 AD Dinas Ffynon

Owain rode into the familiar clearing. All thoughts of war, destiny and scheming had been banished from his mind by Megan's message.

Robed in spring green, his mentor greeted him warmly. There was a freshness about her. It seemed to Owain that she changed, along with the seasons, reflecting the moving year. Her radiance mirrored the hawk moon; the time of new growth. New growth troubled him.

'Why so sad, lord? Does the season not cheer you?' she asked.

'It does not, lady,' he dismounted wearily.

They sat on furs on the grassy sward.

'Tell me,' she urged.

'Lady Creiddy is dead. Coel, King of Rheged, names his heir, Artwerys, for me. I am disturbed, lady. Her maid assures me that the child is of my blood. If so, I am the instrument of Coel's grief and a father who will never know his son. We spent but one night together, Creiddy and I.'

'And in that night you learned much about men and sired a son. Why so distressed?'

'I should not be so? Have I not killed the mother of my child?'

'Think, Owain. A man of destiny is merely that. Do you walk with the gods now? Though the child be of your blood it does not follow that Creiddy died in childbirth because of that. Had the child been of Coel's line, it might well have been the same. Know the difference between what the gods ordain and what men may know. You are lost in your own sense of self- importance. Will you fail this first real test of manhood?'

Her words were icy water.

'I didn't come to be scolded, lady. Are you saying I should ignore this?'

'You're wholly immersed in it, Owain. I merely ask that you take a different path. Guilt is no shieldsman for a man of destiny.'

He sighed, unable to grasp her lesson. Compared to Lailoken's, her teaching was obscure. She took pity on him.

'There's naught you can do, Owain, but bear the knowledge of your son. Confessing your part in his birth will be more of a burden for Coel than he can carry. You must tread the eighth path of cleansing. This is the end of one cycle for you and the beginning of another. You must seek a deeper truth and justice than your own concerns. If your son is to be yours or no is not for now. Knowing of his life makes you vulnerable, as other men. Consider this a gift. Learn from it.'

She took his hand gently, forcing him to gaze into her eyes. When she was sure he returned her look, she raised her brows slightly, a silent request for his acknowledgement.

'I am self-indulgent, lady. You are right. Coel's loss is the greater. He loved Creiddy dearly.'

'And she, you,' the lady replied.

'Aye, yet honour stood between us.'

'Owain, Owain. Honour never stood between you; only your own stubborn view of your destiny as marking you different from other men. Think on it. Is it not so?'

'But I was charged so by Lailoken. Gwawl warned me of confusing Votadini family loyalty. It condemned me to loneliness. Creiddy was torture; wine and vinegar in one goblet,' he pleaded.

'And you confuse the Houses of Gwent, Rheged and the Votadini. Or you would if they knew of your son? See how your conduct contradicts you, Owain. You are but a man. Your destiny does not demand that you be a god. Your principles have done worse damage than had you openly taken a wife and sired a family.'

For the first time, the enormity of his actions revealed his selfishness.

'Can it be redeemed?' he asked.

'You know my answer to such childish questions. You must deal with the matter in your own way, at a more favourable time. This is the time of new growth. Past deeds must lie fallow for a while. Consider it your penance.'

He sighed, dropping his chin to his chest. Memories of his night with Creiddy flooded back. His mind fashioned a picture of how his son might look.

'If I had thoughts to be other than a man, lady, I know full well this day that they were foolish. Such sadness as I feel for Coel and my son was never felt by a god, I'll warrant.'

'No, but the greater part of such a feeling is borne by women, Owain, every time you who call yourselves men ride to war. The moon will rise many times before you understand that. Now enough of this melancholy. We will look at the violets and primroses. The trees are in their greenery.'

23. Egelsprep/Rhyd Ar Afael

455 AD - Viroconium, Powys

Brittu's nights were sleepless. The realm recovered slowly from the plague. Hengist's promised mercenaries rowed their sleek craft into the narrow channels that cut through the morass of Ceint fenlands, disgorging eager warriors and their kin. Brittu knew that he could not pay them.

Empty seats at the British High Council table marked the seriousness of the crisis. Tendubric, Enniaun Girt and sundry other petty kings were absent. Brittu fumed inwardly at his flouted authority.

He sought for the mood of those who sat in the council hall where his father's ill judgement had brought them. Their presence was no guarantee of their allegiance; he was not so naive to think so. The kings and governors of Elmet, Rheged, Dumnonia, Calleva, Demetia, Ceredigion, Dyffed, Ratae, Londinium and Eboracum were here more from insecurity than loyalty. They sought in him his father's early vigour. He must make a show of it, despite the hollow desperation that lurked where his own strength should be. He stood, hoping for reinforced courage, but no inspiration flowed in his blood as they fell silent.

'Thank you, my lords. You know our position. We can't pay Hengist. I value your thoughts on where to steer our course.'

Silence greeted his opening. Those who believed that some strategem would be announced caught his uncertainty. Honesty might not have been the best first throw, he considered. Some wished to accuse Agricola for the dilemma; still others laid the blame firmly at Vitalus's door, especially for the loss of Cantuorlagen, where wood-built, thatched roof steadings grew so rapidly to house Sais settlers that it seemed a nation had found their shores. Such outbursts were muted; Brittu knew that despite their concealed anger, they would not stoke his displeasure publicly.

He struggled to hold his stance and his words, finding some measure of command in the silence.

Coel the Young rose to speak. Brittu braced himself for the assault. Warring prevented Coel's mind from dwelling on his lost love. His concession to the council was the wearing of a plain cream robe and sandals. If Brittu's reports were accurate, he slept in armour and boots and was rarely seen without wargear.

'The vermin must go,' he all but spat at the assembly.

Brittu framed a reply, but hesitated overlong.

'Easier in words than deeds,' Agricola shouted, raising his grey-robed frame to glare at the roused king of Rheged.

'Aye, as easy as your words that these heathen would be converted once they'd settled,' Coel sneered. 'How big is your flock, bishop?'

Dry-mouthed, Brittu sought to restore his authority, in the full knowledge that ritual respect for his standing was all that prevented his councillors from coming to blows. Again, he delayed too long.

'Had your father not departed from the true faith, God would have been your defence. The plague showed his anger,' Bishop Germanus accused him. He alone of the assembly had the integrity to speak his mind. The Pope's authority shielded him from retribution and there were few favours with which Brittu could buy his peace.

The High King made to respond, but Coel was the quicker.

'You bastard bishops have failed with your holy books and prayers. Now it falls to deeds,' he persisted, bringing grunts of disapproval from around the table.

'If we'd had the strength for deeds, Coel, my father wouldn't have invited the savages here at all,' Brittu finally broke back into the dispute.

Turning his rage from the bishops Coel appealed more coolly to the High King.

'We hired these rat eating sea-farers to keep our coasts secure. But they're building more steadings than our sheep bear lambs. No, our militias wouldn't fight raiders, but they're thinking twice now they see Saxon hearth fires smoking from their own villages. We must fight them now. They can't number more than twelve hundred. We more than match them. Why do you deliberate?' Coel pleaded, 'When their numbers grow by the season?'

Brittu sought to soothe him, yet he sensed a changed mood. Coel's passion was heating some to agreement.

'Numbers in our heads and on the field are different, Coel. We must leave sufficient strength to defend our towns and cities,' he counselled.

'Such thinking got us in this mire,' Coel fired back. 'The Sais can't raid the west; we need only sufficient defenders there to see off a few Mumans. A standing army would push the Sais back into the sea. If we needed them once, we do no more. Delay and they'll be hanging boar and raven banners in your villa and pissing in your privy.'

Brittu heard the laughs.

'A thought I would not wish to hold among such civilised company,' he said, more smoothly than he felt.

Agricola stroked his pate. Brittu realised why he had been in the family's confidence for so long. The bishop's mind was as sharp as his beaked nose.

'We're saying then that there's no alternative to war?' Agricola challenged.

'We're seeing Coel's mind set on it? Do you counsel otherwise?' The king replied, respecting his father's aged adviser.

'We're weakened by the plague. We could cede more territory in lieu of payment. Perhaps Hengist would be satisfied with more land.'

There were gasps round the table. A dull murmur of dissent passed like a wave and was not lost to Brittu's ears.

'What!' Coel raged. 'Have you lost all your wits, Bishop? They're arriving like fleas on a hound; their ships reinforce them, daily. If we cede Dumnonia, we'll starve in the mountains. Will your faith feed us there?'

Brittu's desperation raised his voice to a shrill note. Bickering would avail them nothing. A strategy must be agreed to secure unity. 'Coel's plan might just work. We fool ourselves if we think we can avoid war,' he said, with more conviction than he felt. His palms were sweating and his legs ached to be seated.

Coel pressed his advantage. 'We've sat too long on our arses. The enemy is plainly seen. Strike him now and let's be done with the scavengers.'

A roar built around the table; many stood, raising fists and yelling for a fray.

Agricola sighed; there was to be no avoiding bloodshed. The young were in power and saw war as a solution to any problem. Others in the assembly, who shared his views, remained silent.

Brittu felt the chill creep from his neck down his spine. He had his strategy, but his soul thought of aught but celebration at the realisation of it.

***

455 AD -Thanet

Hengist waved the letter from Brittu in the air.

'He has done it. He demands that we return to our homelands. He wants war.'

'Are we strong enough?' Hrosa asked.

'Never fear, brother. More keels are on their way. The British are in for a lesson. They think us few. Without our ships the coast is open for rich pickings.'

'All the riches in the realm won't atone for the hurt they've done me, father. I was almost killed in that fire,' Rhonwen said.

She was dressed as a Frisian battle maiden, the seductive body cloaked in a heavy linen tunic and gaitered trousers. A broad belt held weapons that male warriors would have envied and her hair was plaited tightly. Looking as much a warrior as her brothers, she quaffed ale from a silver-rimmed drinking horn, which she banged on the table.

Hengist was elated. 'You shall be avenged, Rhonwen, but there are greater prizes to be had than the defence of family honour. We can end this pup's kingship and be reinforced before the other Roman lands to make his claim.'

A craggy blond giant who smelled of oiled leather and the metallic tang of mail, Octha was the elder of Hengist's two sons. Sired on Hengist's first wife, Brunhil, the only visible distraction from his rough-hewn beauty was a wound suffered in his early years' training. Over enthusiasm had deflected an opponent's seax from his shield rim, searing a seven inch cut from his right cheek to his chin. Octha eyed Rhonwen's Egyptian slave girl covetously, tracing a habitual finger along the white scar, but even he would not openly challenge his sister. He might beat her in a fight, but there was no telling what damage he would receive if he tried.

'We've come ready to fight, father. Our islands shed warriors and their families. We must prevail for our people's sake. We need this land to expand and grow; it's fruitful. We can live well here and provide for our children.'

'So be it. We'll await reinforcements and march on Powys. Brittu must meet us. We need a decisive campaign. We'll draw them into battle and finish them at a stroke. We'll have a few surprises for them.'

Ale-filled horns were raised. The fire roared. Slaves brought roast pig and boar. War band leaders and warriors celebrated the coming blood. Rhonwen smiled her wicked smile at Octha, running her hand through the long, dark hair of her rescued slave, whom she kept half naked to incite him. He smiled back, but there was no humour in it.

Ebissa smirked inwardly at their rivalry. He was short, dark-haired, with the slanted eyes of the steppe peoples. His mother was White Hun, a tribe of the tenacious alliance that flooded from the east. Hengist had taken her in a raid on a Saxon village where he had cut down the warrior who owned her. Kurtai was like no other woman he had taken in battle lust. With the bloodied right hand that had struck down her owner, he had held her throat, parting her thighs with his left. While he rutted into her, he awaited her expression of fear or supplication. He saw neither. From the oval face that stared back at him, dark brown eyes flashed a different message; resignation and contempt in equal measure. He couldn't be sure in the fireglow of the burning village, but she matched his stare until his manhood wilted. Another time, another raid would have seen her sent to her gods for such a challenge, but Hengist stayed his hand. Kurtai became his second wife and Ebissa was her first born. He evoked the same ambivalence in his father as his mother did. It failed to prompt any challenge to Hengist's pride in Octha and Rhonwen.

***

Brittu doggedly began to muster south of Viroconium. He laid the foundations with his own trained cavalry, a hundred Commanipulares, and three times their number in trained Comitatus spears. He set the militia to defend the province.

Marcus Plautius led his contingent from Dumnonia and Coel the Young brought warrior cavalry and foot south from Rheged to join him.

The eastern provinces pleaded that they were hard pressed to hold off the new raids. Elmet, Dyfed, Kernow and Ceredigion sent small bands of untrained warriors. Cynvelyn arrived with a personal troop of forty trained horse. The remainder of Gwynedd's strength was obedient to Enniaun Girt. The Votadini did not come. Neither did Tendubric.

Brittu's strength numbered nearly three hundred mixed cavalry, five hundred Comitatus infantry and over two thousand untrained warriors. The king's blood thrilled.

***

466 AD - Ceint

Hengist's promise of rich pastures sharpened the interest of two thousand five hundred seasoned countrymen. When he set out, his host numbered nearly twice Brittu's infantry. Mature, battle-hardened warriors sought to carve a land for themselves in the green pastures of eastern Britain. To the north, the Angles sent raiding forces. The fates took up their dice cups.

***

455 AD - River Darenth, South Gwent

British scouts reported the enemy to the south of the narrow river Darenth. Brittu felt uneasy that the Sais had marched so far, but Tendubric ignored his pleas for help, though the conflict gathered within the Dragon's borders.

Despite his inexperience, Brittu knew that his best position was to defend the river. He deployed along the Darenth's steep bank, challenging Hengist to cross. Cavalry guarded the flanks, the lesser-trained warriors were mixed between his most experienced foot. Warriors ran to their positions in the early morning. They locked shields, spear tips dulled by the mist, awaited the sunrise to spark them. Marcus Plautius led the right wing, Coel the Young, the left. Cynvelyn held his cavalry in reserve behind the centre.

Brittu watched Hrosa lead a small Saxon force to face the British. Against his own swollen ranks, they looked pitifully few. He could not see Hengist's main force, hidden in thick forest a few miles to the rear, where a narrow strip of open ground ran down to a ford the British called Rhyd yr Afael; Egelsprep to Hengist's people.

Hrosa's warriors beat their scarlet painted shields with angons and franciscas; their bass voices adding an unholy anthem to the clatter of metal on wood. The sun burned away the early mist. Another hot, still, cloudless day saw the greedy rooks flail expectantly to their perches in the high trees. Other creatures that did not scavenge crawled away. Death hung on the air.

British priests and monks chanted hymns, but the Saxon cacophony heightened the tension along the British line.

'Why do they stall?' Brittu asked. A trickle of sweat rolled down his cheek from beneath his polished helm; his gauntleted hands twitched at the reins of his bay.

Caranog soothed the king's nervous horse. 'They seek to tempt us, lord. We have the ground. They'll need more than songs to raise the courage to cross.'

They watched the Saxon host drumming itself to frenzy. The din continued all morning. The sun hauled its way to its zenith. It seared both lines. Trained troops quenched their thirst from personal water skins, while dry-throated warriors awaited buckets, transported by slaves, to end their parched misery. The sweat that ran down ranked faces attracted every flying insect. Warriors blinked through the gathering flies.

Brittu sensed waning morale among his untrained warriors. They fidgeted, muttering curses at the enemy's inaction.

'Tell Marcus Plautius to throw cavalry across on the right. It will give the men something to watch,' he ordered. The messenger galloped off.

A column of horse splashed across the river to the cheers of the British. Javelins flew at the Saxon lines. A hail of missiles whirled in return. Casualties were light, but the horsemen withdrew after two attacks, their throwing spears expended.

The sun dropped half way through its lazy descent, threatening further disadvantage to Hengist's forces, when without warning, the Saxon line burst into action. Brittu was frozen by the enemy's speed. He sat dry lipped and sweating watching many of his warriors dozing, propped on their spears.

A barrage of thrown axes woke them. Howling to Tir, god of battle, Brittu cringed as the Saxons plunged across the shallows.

The untrained warriors met the assault poorly. Abandoning their shields, weighted by thrown Saxon axes, they gave ground. The trained troops held more ably, filling the gaps where comrades were struck down. They replaced useless shields with ones passed forwards from their rear ranks.

Jolted from his paralysis, Brittu urged his mount forward, shrieking above the noise.

'Hold them. Hold them.'

He cantered along the line, his face contorted, body shaking with fear and excitement. The power of command intoxicated him.

He watched his warriors crouched behind their shields, thrusting with short spears against the colourful wave of Sais, which tore at their line. To his right he could see Hrosa fronting a wedge of veteran warriors. The air was a thick blanket of screaming voices and relentless heat. The sweat of exertion joined that caused by the sun. Tiring muscles cloyed in desperate limbs.

Brittu bellowed orders. He moved men to plug gaps where the Saxons threatened to break through. Gradually, British numbers began to tell. The Saxon impetus weakened.

Seeing that he had done enough, Hrosa shouted above the din for his men to give ground. The Saxons withdrew over uneven ground, stumbling over the wounded and dying. They waded back across the river, aiding wounded kinsmen. British warriors, flushed with success, turned the water carmine, striking at their backs as they fled.

Coel and Marcus Plautius inflicted the heaviest Saxon losses on the flanks. Volleys of javelins felled the retreating Sais. The Saxon flanks broke simultaneously. The line turned and ran, pursued by the rashest British warriors.

The dying sun hung red.

'Well, lord Bishop; God loves us despite our sins?' Brittu goaded Germanus over the roars of his cheering troops.

Agricola was quick to press the point. 'Perhaps this heresy you so despise has some merit,' he gloated.

Germanus had one eye on the sky, the other on the gleeful warriors. The rooks shuffled agitatedly in the high oaks, eager for the living to depart.

'The day is yours. Tomorrow it begins anew.' He kicked his heels into the grey's flanks, leaving Brittu and Agricola staring at his swirling purple cloak.

'It begins anew? They're beaten. If their ships aren't close by, the fishes will be banqueting along with the ravens,' Brittu hurled at his back.

Coel and Marcus Plautius rejoined the High King, eager to report on the Saxon slain. British losses were three hundred dead or wounded. The Sais had lost seven hundred, half their attacking strength. British warriors were already stripping their bodies of brooches, belts, ornaments and weapons.

Around the British camp fires that burned into the long summer night, Pagan and Christian alike thanked their divinities. Pagans bragged of the power that Goibnu the smith god had invested in their swords and spears, and thanked Llew, the tall warrior god of the skilful hand, who had towered beside them in his shining golden armour. Christians laughed away their comrades' superstitions. They celebrated the value of prayer. Much ale was supped long into the night. Brittu entertained his allies to wine and food. Agricola and Germanus attended the wounded and the dying well beyond dusk. Germanus was in no mood for celebration. He had never left a battlefield with as much blood on him as that which clotted the hem of his robe. He questioned again his choice to follow the church.

Secure in their camp, Brittu congratulated his commanders, exactly as Hengist was praising his brother, Hrosa among the Sais.

'By all the gods, Hrosa, that was brilliantly done. They see us beaten.' He filled Hrosa's drinking horn for the fourth time. His brother drank deeply to ease his parched throat.

'The fates were with us. I thought they'd pursue in more strength, but he's cautious, this High King,' Hrosa gasped, through the froth of his moustache.

He peeled off his mail. A slave was set to rub it with sand and cloths. His undershirt burned on the fire under the panoply of bright stars, ruined by perspiration and the rents of enemy weapons. His body gleamed in the firelight, splotches of blood marking dozens of lacerations. He took huge gulps of ale with mouthfuls of blood, sucked from a jagged wound to his left hand where a British sword had caught it beyond the rim of his shield. Still, he was in high spirits.

'I thought we'd break through; they were half asleep where we charged,' he boasted.

'We'll cheer tomorrow, brother,' Hengist replied. Octha and Ebissa nodded silently. Rhonwen sat by the fire gazing into the starry heavens and then to the pinpricks of light that marked the British fires.

'I'll take British souls. They'll wish they'd burned Rhonwen of the Frisians.'

Her words were soft spoken, but there was steel behind them. The frost of bitter winter sent shivers of disquiet down her brothers' spines. They were glad they were not opposing her when the new sun rose.

Brittu's forces were late to assemble. Ale gave his warriors more sore heads than the Sais had inflicted, but there was heartiness about the British camp that even the sight and smell of carnage could not dispel.

Crossing the Darenth, they disturbed the massed black carrion eaters, sending them cawing in protest to the highest branches. The British had buried their dead, but the slain Sais lay in the river and along the banks. Their stiff, bloodied, half-naked corpses served their leader's purpose, conveying to Brittu that Hengist was too well beaten to attend his fallen. Sightless heads followed the British advance. The eyes that had once filled them proved delicacies for the feathered gluttons. The stench from bodies with opened stomachs and bowels hung sickly on the air.

A jovial High King steadied his frisky horse. His experienced troops led off leisurely in the direction of Rhyd yr Afael. His scouts reported that the remnants of the enemy were encamped just beyond it. They would be overrun by the cavalry if they fled. They had elected to make a final stand under their totem of the Boar at the ford, where the ground was narrow.

'Order the cavalry out on the flanks, beyond those trees,' Brittu commanded. Marcus Plautius and Coel galloped to instruct their men.

'Will you hold me in reserve again, lord?' Cynvelyn enquired, anticipating the answer.

'Yes, when we break their centre, there'll be a task for you, Governor. When we break them, you'll pursue. Fresh horses in this damnable heat will be an advantage. Hold here until we're through them.'

Cynvelyn acknowledged the order. There was to be no honour for his house. The High King was exacting payment for Tendubric's absence and Cynvelyn's dearth of authority over the forces of Gwynedd. Unarmed Saxons backs were as much as he was going to see.

Brittu watched the resigned band of defenders, massed in a packed formation. They were silent, feigning defeat. Their totems, the boar and raven wavered. Tufas, baskets atop poles decked with feathers and plumes of dyed animal hair, drooped dismally.

'Sorry lot, aren't they?' Brittu commented. 'We should be on our way back to Powys soon.'

'It's a poor commander who ignores God's judgement,' Bishop Germanus cautioned.

'Have our standard raised high, Pascent. Have the men attack immediately. I ache for the bath house and a slave girl, not the prating of foreign bishops.' Brittu kicked his horse forward.

The bearer hoisted the White Hart of Powys on its deep blue ground high, but the day lacked air and it hung limply to its staff.

Brittu ordered a charge by his warriors to sap the Saxon strength. There were no theatricals; they were straight to it, calling down blessings from Christ or Llew. The clash of their impact on the defenders' shield wall shuddered in the inert air. All was chaos; shields locked in a melee of darting spears and cleaving swords.

The warriors gave their best, but mail and hard-boiled leather gave the defenders the edge over their unarmoured opponents. The British fell back. The Saxons defended the ford behind a line of their own dead, their numbers reduced even further. In the centre, Hrosa wiped the sweat from under his iron bound leather helmet and leaned on a gar.

'This time, men. This time. Give ground slowly. We don't want those horse at our backs when we run. So, this is it; pass the word.'

He glanced to the edges of the dark woods, reassuring himself that the jaws of Hengist's main strength were about to close from the silent shadows.

'This time.'

Brittu's Comitatus came on more steadily than the warriors' wild rush. Their shields presented a steady line, spears thrust forward in a uniform hedge; their armour, equal to the ford's defenders. The measured tread unsettled the surviving Saxons who knew little of such order. The rhythmic bobbing of their yellow plumes added to their disciplined advance. The British halted a few paces before the clotted, reddened water. Their officers dressed the line. With a roar, *'For the King and Powys,'* they charged.

Though the Saxon plan was to give way, the shock of the assault shunted them backwards. Fatigued defenders struggled desperately to hold the new advance. Hrosa watched the enemy hew viciously into his men. Realising that he couldn't hold, he passed the word to retreat. Saxon warriors turned and fled, leaving a thin line to prevent a rout; then they too turned and ran after their comrades.

The British halted, surprised at the Saxon collapse. They needed no urging to pursue. Quivering with triumph, Brittu threw in his reserve warriors with wild gesticulations of his sword.

Hrosa panted with exertion. The mail that had minimised his wounds now impeded his escape. As he tried to clear a fallen warrior, his leg caught on the shield, bringing him crashing to the ground. Gasping for breath, he willed himself to his knees, searing pain from his left leg telling him that his ankle was broken. He supported his weight with a splintered spear shaft, urging his men to flee. Despite his commands, two turned to assist him.

'Go now. Avenge me on the morrow,' he shouted, waving them away.

They ignored him; a young warrior, his long fair hair plaited beneath a simple iron helmet, rushed to his side. An older warrior, his face crimson with blood from a sword cut, peered from his one good eye and held out a gnarled hand to help him.

'Guard our backs, Tir. Between us, we might yet see our way through this day,' the elder said.

They stumbled in pursuit of their fleeing comrades. Every pace sent spirals of pain up Hrosa's leg. He gritted his teeth and leaned his weight against the older warrior. Tir walked slowly backwards, ready for the onrushing British. His warning cry halted their clumsy three-legged retreat.

Hrosa stared into the warrior's one good eye.

'You're a fool, old man. Tonight we walk in the halls of our gods; Who dies at my side?'

'Fool as maybe, Hrosa, but I'd fare ill as a one-eyed warrior. Ebba is my name. We can take some of these British with us, eh?'

They turned, Tir backing to Hrosa's left, Ebba to the right. The British crashed in on them. Tir downed two with his gar; one to the throat and one to the chest. Hrosa skewered the man to his front. Ebba cleaved a fourth with a deft axe stroke.

The British took stock. They advanced with caution. Tir fell to a spear thrust through the left shoulder, which spun him for a killing stroke from a short sword to the chest. He collapsed to his knees, leaving Hrosa's left side exposed. Hrosa and Ebba exchanged a last kindred look. Hrosa fell to the thrusts of the British warriors, which bled his remaining strength. A red-haired warrior breached his shield with a well-timed lunge. Ebba inflicted more wounds with his dancing axe, until he was downed by the spears of five warriors who surrounded him.

***

Brittu inwardly celebrated his heroic victory. He revelled in the anticipated gratitude his followers would bestow. The Saxons were running; his men swarmed to cut them down. With the speed of a kingfisher plucking a fish from the river, victory was snatched from him.

A horseman on a lathered mount galloped to his position from the rear. No sooner had Brittu turned to see the rider's approach, than the woods began to sprout Saxon warriors on both flanks of his advancing infantry. Germanus alone kept his position, keenly observing Hengist's sprung trap. Brittu's companions yelled at each other in desperation.

The messenger arrived, his weary horse wheezing breathlessly.

'The Scotti. The Scotti. Loegaire invades from the west. There are none to stand against him,' he shouted.

Germanus wheeled his grey. Snatching the reins of Brittu's horse from the dumbfounded king's hands he barked orders. 'Cynvelyn, use your horse to screen our escape. This battle is lost. The rest of you, ride hard for Viroconium and pray we arrive before Loegaire so that the militia have some leadership.'

He kicked his mount into a gallop and thundered off to the north, leading the king's horse. Stricken by despair Brittu gazed back at the slaughter. Moriutned, Pascent and Caranog looked aghast at the scene before their eyes, then followed in the Bishop's dusty wake.

The British Comitatus fought desperately to break through Hrosa's weakened line to link up with their cavalry. The untrained British warriors took the brunt of the Saxon attack, their cries of panic and pain assailed the ears of their fleeing leaders. Caught up in the crush, the trapped warriors were cut down in their hundreds.

Rhonwen, full of demonic bloodlust, whirled and threw her shield, downing a blond haired warrior whose teeth splintered as the rim bloodied his mouth. With a sword in one hand and a seax in the other, she scythed through the packed British ranks. She pierced, slashed and severed them with such frenzy that her men had difficulty in keeping pace. Octha and Ebissa were more methodical. Hengist glowed with battle fever. He hewed and cleaved his way into the bloody melee.

Trembling British villagers watched Saxon fires roaring into the summer heavens that night. The bards sang songs of eighteen hundred British warriors claimed by their gods at Rhyd yr Afael. Only a few Comitatus escaped the field and the crows feasted for days.

Hengist's joy at his victory was countered by the loss of his brother with whom he had pirated and fought from their youth. Octha and Ebissa were still raw to lead warbands. Still, the gods had sent their message; his sons must now share leadership of his forces.

Still in her battle gear, Rhonwen sat in a daze as the others drank their fill round the blazing fires. The rings of her mail were clotted with gore, her tunic spattered dark madder; her hands and face caked with dried blood. Her eyes were dull and lifeless as though the gods had robbed her of the remains of her strength. Even the seasoned warriors who had seen death on the battlefield many times were uneasy in her presence. Never had they witnessed such battle lust. She sat by the fire as they whispered warily; her bones chilled despite the heat from the flames.

She ignored her father's pleas to attend Hrosa's burial. In the dead of night Hrosa's warriors carried him to a grave at the fringe of the wood, under a drooping yew. The warriors were from the Frisian elite, the Brotherhood of the Boar, bound by allegiance to their gods, land and people by their sacred symbol, the seax. Their foremost wyrdman, Albric, led the ritual. He interceded with the gods for Hrosa's spirit to be accepted by his heroic kinfolk. Hrosa's war gear was buried with him, all except his seax. This, Albric brandished in the moonlight, the blade reflecting silver in the dark glade.

'The gods will honour the spirit of Hrosa who ensured the day's victory by his courage. This seax, enshrining his mortal power, will now pass to another brother, marking him as a worthy successor to the war lord who wielded it.'

Albric flipped the seax in a twirling arc, catching it by the keen point. A less practised hand would have been severed by the blade, but the old wyrdman had performed the ceremony too many times to incur injury. The younger brotherhood gasped at his display. Maintaining the serious mood of the ritual, Albric offered the horn handle to Hengist.

'To his eldest brother goes the power to bestow honour on Hrosa's successor,' he intoned.

Hengist grasped the seax, staring solemnly at Hrosa's corpse. He addressed the hushed assembly.

'My brother, your brother, shed his blood for all his people. He has no hearth kin. He was a warrior true to the Boar in all deeds. He has no son to inherit this gift. He was ever a second father to my kin. I bestow this seax on Octha, my son. Acknowledge his entry into the Brotherhood.'

He held Octha's left hand by the wrist, opening the palm with the hilt of the seax. Looking his son squarely in the eye, he drew the blade across the exposed palm, slicing a furrow of blood. He turned the knife, offering it to Octha's keeping. His son took it in his bloodied hand. The Brotherhood bellowed their welcome as the crimson stream wound its way down the knife's length to drip into Hrosa's grave.

***

455 AD - Viroconium, Powys

Brittu's fearful arrival at Viroconium on a lathered, winded horse, found no marauding Scotti. All was calm.

'Timely arrival by a false messenger. Hengist is more vexing than we thought,' Germanus observed, when Brittu's followers assembled.

'It was a dishonourable ploy,' Brittu raged.

'You will learn, lord King, that it's winners of wars who determine what constitutes honour. Right now, Hengist is the more likely.'

'You said yourself, Bishop. One battle does not win a war.'

'I did indeed and you should consider it. I must return to Rome and from there to my flock in Auxerre. You'll lose your only general.'

'Where was your skill at Rhyd ar Afael, Bishop?' the king thundered.

'Why, my lord. Would you have listened to me? I think not.'

Brittu's stomach churned. As if he needed reminding of his error.

'You have me there. I was deaf even to God. I admit it.'

He took a breath and poured wine.

'What would you have advised?'

'The first day's action was vital to an observant commander. I searched the entire Saxon host as it stood offending the Lord with its pagan chanting. Hengist was nowhere to be seen. You didn't think it strange, that their leader was absent? Make as much use of me as possible in the time I have left. I'll await your summons for a private audience, lord King.' Germanus bowed deeply and retired.

'Papal footstool,' Agricola threw in his wake.

'Maybe, but he knows how to fight battles, Agricola. We fared badly,' Moriutned said.

'It was but misfortune,' Coel the Young insisted, exasperated by the defeatism. 'We know our opponents use trickery and deception. Next time we'll be ready for them. We need to re-assemble the army and hit them before they're reinforced. Our mistake was to underestimate their strength. Next time we'll test their numbers.'

'Next time. Do you hear your words, Coel? It took us weeks to assemble. It will take more time to muster an army capable of defeating that horde,' Brittu railed.

'So, a bloody speck cripples us now does it?'

'No, Coel. But we believed that Loegaire had landed in the west; what if he had? We'd be cowering in the hills. We must guard against all threats, not merely Hengist's.'

'Loegaire didn't come, lord. He keeps his bargain as he always has. He married your sister. There must be some honour in that,' Caranog said, attempting to lift the king's crushed spirit.

'Honour. We've just lost two thousand men to a demon's tricks and you speak of honour!' Brittu shouted.

Marcus Plautius tried to soothe them.

'We are confounded. Coel, you're too hasty. Lord, we can't sit and wait. We must buy time to re-assemble the army.'

'Buying a peace would achieve that,' Agricola offered. 'We're still weakened by the plague. What strength we have is elsewhere. The Picts and the Scotti will hear of this defeat. So will Ambrosius. Buy a peace, lord. Turn our forces to defending new borders in depth, so we keep the Sais in their new lands. Peace is what we need.'

'That would suit them also, Bishop. Can we do no better than throwing our lands away to these barbarians?' Pascent shouted, his anger re-fuelled by the bishop's advice of appeasement.

Brittu waved them to silence. The battle had been a bitter blow. It confirmed what he had suspected, that despite his warrior aspirations, he lacked his father's skill. Such a crushing defeat undermined what initial confidence he had mustered. A jaded bleakness descended, clouding his mind. His authority evaporated; he could barely prevent his followers from fighting with each other.

'Peace with the Sais? We can't even speak peacefully with each other. My head spins, my lords. Let's retire to our rooms to calm ourselves,' he commanded, wearily.

They bowed solemnly, leaving Brittu and Pascent alone with their servants. The atmosphere of defeat hung as tangibly as an autumn fog in the same room that Vitalus had lit with such confident energy in the early part of his reign.

'Ours is a troubled realm, brother,' Brittu said. He gazed through the window to the south. The day was hot; heavy with the scents and noises of nature. A songthrush trilled in the Rowan outside the window, but his ears still rang with the anthem of death sung by his butchered men the previous day. Pascent threw an arm around his shoulder.

'It was so for father, yet he forged a path to prosperity. We squabble amongst ourselves over anything. Our disunity costs us, brother, do you not think? Our enemies are strong. How can we prevail?'

'You see the affliction, Pascent,' Brittu replied, glumly. The glorious weather and the view across his domain did little to cheer him. 'I'd best talk to Germanus. I hate his smugness, but we'd be foolish to ignore his advice. Damn the man.'

'You could have offered him overall command of the army, brother. The choice was yours. As he said, there was little anyone else could have done.'

'Yes, yes. I know. Leave me. Inform Germanus that his audience is granted.'

***

Brittu watched an incoming cavalry troop, riding hard. The door opened.

'More grim noise for my ears, no doubt, Bishop. Well, you have your audience. What do you wish of me?'

'God's wishes, not mine.'

Brittu sighed.

'Please, Bishop, stop dressing your master's desires up in theology. I'm a practical man, as was my father. Our conviction about divine matters was ever tepid.'

'Then you are blind to your tragedies. The plague, your father's death, Hengist's successes? Are these not signs that you lack divine favour?'

'So this is His punishment, is it? You use more subtle tactics on the battlefield, Bishop. These are not issues of God, but the scheming of men.'

'Then, you have no use for me. Continue with your denial of the Lord. The next time I visit, I'll come to convert the barbarians. Better that than appealing to a Christian who's turned his back on God.'

Brittu fell silent. A shrew of doubt gnawed at his mind. Might matters improve if he renounced the heresy, bringing Powys back into the fold of mother church? New allies would replace those who deserted him. It would deter Ambrosius for a while. The faithful could hardly rally against the heresy if Powys had already renounced it.

'What if I agreed, Bishop? What then?'

'You'd gain support and Papal authority. Agricola is right. Peace is your best option. Better cut your losses now and garner your strength. Every battle you lose makes Hengist stronger. This is my advice. Look to your defences; seal your borders. I'll talk to the Holy Father as a favour for your renunciation of the heresy. Perhaps his joy will bring you coin. Wealth will buy the men you need to drive Hengist out; the Sais are not the only mercenaries to be had.'

Brittu nodded. The bishop's offer reached to the heart of the matter. 'I'll speak with my brother, Bishop. Thank you for your representation to the Holy Father. I've done little to merit it.'

Germanus made as if to reply, but merely acknowledged the king's words. This was no time for homilies, he thought. If Brittu were to be restored to the faith, the crisis would achieve it far more effectively. He bowed to the king and left. A servant attracted Brittu's attention from the window by clearing his throat.

The High King did not turn. 'Tell me the worst; you'll not suffer. I'd not have a servant left were that so.'

'The cavalry troop leader, who's just arrived, greets you, lord King. He brings word that some Comitatus troops broke Hengist's lines and escaped from Rhyd ar Afael, yesterday. They're returning to Powys.'

'Indeed. You've charmed our ears. I thought we'd lost them all. Give him my thanks and have him attend me when he's been to the bath house, I would know more. Thank you, you may go.'

Alone with his thoughts, Brittu turned from the window. He wanted to discuss the bishop's advice with his brother, but his insecurity pushed him firmly in the direction of the orthodoxy. He needed the certainty that only the Church could provide.

24. Wicked Peace

457 AD - Auxerre

From Germanus, Bishop of Auxerre to his Holiness Pope Celestine.

Disturbing reports from your new bishops talk of two years' skirmishing between British and Saxons. Hengist has consolidated his new Ceint lands. More alarming are the new Saxon settlements which stretch from the south east to the marshes of Lindum in the midlands.

Brittu's allegiance to your authority displeases those who were taxed less heavily under the heresy. He has lost the loyalty of many. They obey him, but do not love him.

The High King strives to pacify his kings and governors. He awaits your promised coin. Explorations of peace have failed. Hengist wishes to see how many settlers he can count on. He is urged to perpetual war by some of his following, but is wary.

Muma raids from the west. The Picts attack Elmet. Only in the north east is the enemy denied. Coel and Owain Ddantgwyn resist the Angles.

Tendubric of Gwent, maintains his own borders, seeking no allies. He proves too strong for the Saxons, who try to rustle his cattle and burn his villages. Britain is in a stalemate.

Your obedient servant, Germanus.

***

457 AD - Dinas Ffynon, Gwynedd

The lady awaited Owain's frequent visits, eager to add to his lore. He pieced together a much less foreboding picture of his future than under Lailoken's tutelage. For all his new-found optimism, his mentor never encouraged him to believe that his task would be easy. Had he not been so preoccupied, he would have seen the despondency in her clear grey eyes. Relief at the direction his destiny would take blinkered his attention, but in his mind, Owain saw the complications in his way.

'Your judgement of the Christians is harsh, lady. If I am charged to defend the land, they are more at fault than the barbarians against whom I am set to war. How can I reconcile this?' he asked one clear morning when slanting rays of sunlight pierced the green canopy.

'Your destiny is your own to interpret, Arth-Ursus. I am not here to resolve contradictions. Consider what you must do to counter the Christians' beliefs. You must be subtle, bear lord; wield your mind as you wield your sword. Their star is rising - you must plan accordingly.'

He smiled ruefully. Her lessons never informed. Always she led him to ask further questions, explore more possibilities. Always he was in command of his own thoughts and actions. Filan had a similar style. Owain recognised how different they were from the priests who demanded obedience to rules and dogmas.

He could see how the church bound the minds of its followers in chains of authority, requiring blind faith rather than integrity; allegiance rather than growth. The trap of the new religion was in its capacity to crush the imagination. Yet he saw how necessary a fertile mind was to the dilemma faced both by his people and, if the lady was to be believed, the land. For all this, he would forge alliances with these Christians to preserve the realm.

He sighed. A knowing smile crossed her lips. She caressed his hand. The lightness of her fingers said far more than her words. 'Don't strain at it. You'll find your way,' said her touch.

***

457 AD - Ceint

His fighting force augmented by seven thousand new settlers, Hengist was, however, disappointed. He could fight pitched battles if the British could be tempted; he could winkle them out of their western strongholds or defend his newly gained territory, but not both.

He had moved to Ceint, the centre of his new heartland and whilst Ebissa and Rhonwen remained with him, Thanet was given to Octha.

'We need some way to break this deadlock,' Hengist addressed his war council. 'We must either defeat them or meet their requests for peace.'

His words fell into a stony silence. A silky seductive voice whispered above the hush.

'There's a way that can marry victory and peace.'

The words flowed into the silence. But, as gentle fingers might tickle a summer trout, they lacked innocence.

Hengist eyed his daughter suspiciously. In the two years since the victory at Egelsprep she'd become more introspective, holding herself apart from the life of the Frisians. She was the first to don mail; she had fought in both encounters with the British. But she was absent at seed time, harvest and the Frisians' festivals. She caused unease. She sat opposite her father at the foot of the long, rough-hewn table. The seat was Octha's by right, but he would not contest it.

'Say on, daughter.'

All eyes turned to her, but she might have been talking to ghosts. Her once clear beauty had faded to an alabastrine sheen. Her clouded gaze fixed on no one.

'Brittu has sued for peace often since Egelsprep. Accept his submission for a council. Gather them here in Ceint, as many as can be persuaded. Then kill them.'

The lack of feeling in her words, struck at the hearts of even the most seasoned warriors. Rhonwen cavorted with dishonourable wickedness as easily as she had once coloured their celebrations with licentious dances. Even the dogs fell silent.

Hengist's eyes roved the table. The wizened, grey-haired Albric spoke first.

'I've never seen you in the Otherworld, Rhonwen. Yet, your spirit flies somewhere among the stars. Demons have claimed you. Some already call you mad. We're loathsome barbarians already to the British. Would you have us seen as worse?'

'I would, old man. I'd be their greatest horror. This land is ripe; we must be strong and take it. Why do we fear to be named heathens by a people who nailed their own god to a tree? The British cling to the shreds of Rome's glory. But Rome's star is fading. They should die with it.'

Some round the table muttered in awe, making the warding sign. Hengist saw that others were less antagonistic.

'Have we become too concerned with honour, to do our gods' bidding? We came here to settle and the omens were with us. How can we win without cunning?' Ebissa challenged.

'Where do your loyalties lie, Albric? You have brothers of your art among the Pretani. Is it honour that you serve, or your own?' a young warrior, Egil, threw at the wyrdman.

The old seer smiled through worn yellow teeth. There was no malice in the twinkle of his eyes. He leaned back in his great chair.

'Before the pup knows how to bark, it yaps. No one here will accuse me of neglecting the people. When I travel between the worlds, it is for them that I fly, not for myself, or others of my kind. My art only works when put to its true purpose; consulting with the ancestors; with the totems, with the gods - to serve the people. You lack the skill to rile me, Egil.'

'Then put this to the test, Albric. Use your art to test the gods' judgement on Rhonwen's wile. Then we'll know how we stand,' Ebissa urged.

Albric turned to Hengist.

'You brought us here, Hengist. Thousands have followed you to this shore. Our people are scattered from here to the fens. What is your wish?'

The Frisian leader weighed the balance around the table. Rhonwen's suggestion had divided them. The numbers were roughly even.

'Rhonwen's plan has the smell of rotten flesh. But fighting alone, with our numbers, won't serve. Brittu's turned to the old church of the sacrificed god; there's much power there. I wish to safeguard our gains. I'll not fight the British with the sea at our backs. Speak now if you can see a way through this, or Albric, put Rhonwen's case to our gods.'

His challenge went unmet. Albric sighed in resignation. This was no journey to anticipate with a joyful heart. Yet, he must comply with the council's wishes. Had he not placed a heavy emphasis on his service to the people?

'It shall be done, Hengist.'

***

457 AD - Dinas Ffynon, Gwynedd

Owain awoke in a sweating terror. He was convinced that he had the plague, until the dream broke. A dream; he had remembered a dream. Not so much remembered, but experienced, like the one years ago in the cave of the old seer, Lailoken. He must not lose it.

He rose from his bed. It was Riuros, the cold time. Campaigning was over. Wind, snow and ice strangled the realm. He placed more logs on the embers and lit a candle. He sat near the fire, staring hard at the glowing wood. The dream was sharp - a white hart struggling to escape from a pool of blood, so thick its legs were mired with gore. At the pool side, a gross male boar barred its flight. Its jaws slavering, its tiny eyes glittering with malice. A black raven, its wings beating the air, screeched as it tore at the hart's eyes.

Owain shuddered. Years of undisturbed sleep heightened the impact. What was it that Ambrosius had said? - 'When I come in your dreams it will be as a blackbird.' No blackbird sang in this nightmare.

Owain dressed. The mountain fortress was like the depths of an icy sea. He pulled on warm, heavy, woollen trousers, and an over-tunic lined with fox fur. He threw a woollen, russet cloak across his shoulders and pulled on fur-lined boots.

He hurried out of his stone walled, thatched house, into the sparkling night, pausing briefly to catch a view of the heavens. A short walk brought him to a small dwelling, where he pushed open the planked door. He moved to the fireplace and stoked the fire.

'Has the Bear never heard of the long winter sleep?' a voice muttered.

'You're supposed to be the one who stays abed the longest through these freezing nights, Owain. Has your totem taught you nothing?'

'I had thought, Crenda, that you had a curious mind,' Owain replied, as the druid hauled himself upright, scratching his tousled hair.

'Indeed, lord, you're right in that. Crenda's too much a creature of contentment to learn his best lessons,' Filan said, coming awake and alert.

'No doubt, there's a good explanation for your visit, so I'll brew us a hot posset of camomile to ward off the cold. Tell us why you wander the night like an owl, Owain.'

He donned his robe over his night-shirt and set water to boil.

'I've had a rare dream; I need an interpretation, I fear it's important,' Owain said.

'Describe it to us. We'll ease your mind,' Filan urged.

Owain recounted the dream. When he stopped, Crenda looked as though he wished to bury himself beneath his furs. Filan was more thoughtful.

'Would you interpret for our guest, Crenda? Some practice will do no harm,' he invited, scalding dried camomile leaves into three beakers. He spooned honey into the drinks and stirred each cup thoughtfully.

Crenda yawned and scratched his ear vigorously. He spoke hesitantly, interrupted by long moments of deliberation.

'The boar is the totem of the Sais.... and.... the Hart is the device of Powys. This much is plain..... I can interpret neither the raven, nor the pool of blood.'

'You have the gist of it, Crenda. Well done. Blood signifies unknown danger, a threat to the lineage itself. Ravens are birds of ill omen, though they're more to do with changing aspects of the goddess. Its appearance is unclear. It seems that the High King is threatened from an unknown quarter,' Filan concluded.

'Thank you both. I thought the dream meant danger to my own. Perhaps the High King will be toppled. When I dream of the blackbird I'll know the time is nigh.'

'It's not so simple, my lord. The threat is to the British, not just the High King. The Hart was alive, wasn't it?' Filan said.

'Yes. The boar gloated and the raven slashed at the hart's eyes, but it had not fallen.'

'Mmm. I shall ponder on this. You haven't remembered a dream since boyhood. Your father must hear of it. Now drink and scald the cold from your bones.'

They sat by the fire, Filan lost in thought. The hypnotic dancing flames carried Owain back to boyhood.

***

Enniaun Girt crept from Ceri's bed in the early hours of a spring morning. Cutios, the time of winds was over. Brooks, streams and rivers, flooded with melted snow, rushed along their courses awakening a new season's growth.

Household morale had risen with the vanquished cold, yet Enniaun's spirit was deflated. Discussions with Filan and Crenda had not reassured him. Owain's dream was taken seriously by the druids. The campaigning season approached. Enniaun alerted his whole family to unforeseen dangers. He sent spies out; he informed Ambrosius of his son's dream; he wrote to Tendubric to entice the Dragon from its cave; he sent despatches to the Scotti High King, Loegaire. Yet nothing appeared other than how it should be.

A messenger arrived with letters from the north informing him that all was well. Drust still raided to the south, but Votadini lands prospered.

There was talk of peace. Hengist had agreed to Brittu's requests for a treaty and a meeting was planned for late spring. Enniaun should have felt optimistic, but the dark foreboding persisted.

***

455 AD - Rheged's East Coast

On Edern's advice, Cunorix ordered mounted spearmen to accompany the cavalry. When the Angles raided, Votadini horse threw a screen between them and their ships. The mounted infantry attacked the Angle ship defenders while their returning comrades were dealt with by the cavalry. Even large raiding forces failed to deal with the modified Votadini tactics and many ships were captured, burnt or sunk. The Sais failed to repeat the successes of their southern allies.

Owain's sense of timing, anticipation and judgement were skills that others envied. His brothers strove to match his exploits, but were less able. Cadwallon was particularly resentful. Cunorix, with some pride, saw Owain as his military successor.

Edern's mind was the Votadini's most precious asset. For all his experience, Cunorix failed to match his guile. Edern set the most elaborate traps for the raiders where the dunes of the east coast met the forest.

He, Owain and Elen discussed their most recent sortie on a spring evening. Two Angle ships burned on the beach, their skeletons charred like dead mythical beasts. One ship was limping to the open sea, carrying the survivors. The beach was littered with Angle dead and wounded. Squealing horses writhed in the dunes.

Cunorix supervised the enslavement of the captured Angles. Warriors had become gravediggers. Flames crackled, surf hissed and the sun dipped low against a scarlet-slashed dusk.

'If we could merge the infantry with the cavalry, we'd do even better,' Edern mused.

He took off his helmet and shook his hair free; perspiration splashed his companions.

'Go and cool down in the sea, if you're so hot,' Elen chided.

'His head heats up with all the thinking he does,' Owain grumbled. He loosened the cheek flaps of his own helm and tugged it free by the eye guard.

'I heard from Ambrosius that the eastern Romans met cavalry that attacked formed infantry,' he added.

'Impossible. They'd be seen off easily. Your best troops would be slaughtered like pigs. He must have been testing your imagination, Owain,' Edern replied.

'No. He was very serious. I remember he called them Persians. He said that the eastern Roman armies equipped some of their horse in the same fashion.'

'Unlikely. How would they stay in the saddle with the shock of a charge? They'd be toppled by the impact,' Edern disputed.

'I don't know. It was just a conversation when he was telling me about how big the world is. Just because we haven't the wit to solve it, doesn't mean that someone else hasn't,' Owain retorted.

'Oh, stop bickering. We've had our fill of battle today. Let's wash the grime away. It's nearly dark and I crave one of yonder sheep on a spit for supper,' Elen silenced their debate.

'Will you have one for yourself, or may we share?' Owain asked mischievously, fending off her helmet, which hurtled towards him for his attempt at wit.

They climbed slowly on to their mounts, fatigued by their labours. The sun dipped to the horizon, throwing the trees into black relief against the purpling sky.

***

In Gwynedd, Enniaun Girt lay beside Ceri, staring at the ceiling. Their love-making had been as sweet as summer clover, but his mind would not settle. It ran like a spring freshet, swollen by melted snow.

***

457 AD - Gwent

'Peace talks; what nonsense. We've not been to war with the Sais, so why should we attend peace talks?' Tendubric ranted at Cynvelyn and Meurig.

'Perhaps to show unity against the Sais,' Bronwen said easily, ignoring the king's sour mood.

'If that upstart, Brittu, hadn't believed himself capable of defeating Hengist's host in one battle, we wouldn't need peace talks,' he raged.

'Bronwen has a point, brother. It's time to demonstrate some loyalty to our kind rather than just to our religion,' Cynvelyn countered.

'Ah yes; our kind. The ones who steal kingdoms from under our noses and give them to northern barbarians more close to the Picts than ourselves. Those kind of 'our kind', brother? And our religion isn't 'just our religion,' remember? We're charged with protecting teachings direct from the Christ. This is no small thing. If 'our kind' supported the British Church, we wouldn't be so isolated.'

'That's an unjust tongue from a king who swears by justice,' Bronwen defended her brother-in-law. 'The Votadini kept our borders for years against the northern Picts. They're unlike the Sais.'

Cynvelyn took Tendubric by the shoulders, staring into his brother's eyes.

'I didn't have a kingdom stolen, brother. I was governor of Gwynedd. I'd no strength to contest it. The Votadini are strong. Vitalus invited them south, not his son. Brittu suffers from inexperience, not the vile habits of his father.'

'You know that for sure do you? Kings have power and power is a thick cloak against prying eyes, Cynvelyn,' the Dragon roared.

'Then what do you hide beneath yours, husband? Are there secrets of your power I should know of?' Bronwen giggled. Tendubric caught himself and calmed.

'You test me mightily, wife. There are men in the realm who would thrash you soundly for scorning your husband's wrath,' he said, but gently.

'Aye, but the King could not mete out such punishment, wedded as he is to the teachings of the true faith,' Bronwen replied.

'Mmm. More's the pity.'

Cynvelyn interrupted. 'So, we don't attend then?'

'We do not. If Hengist wishes to make peace with us, I'll entertain him, but I'll not be party to Brittu's flatterers. Besides, there are urgent letters from Gwynedd. Enniaun Girt might well sit as King where you once governed, brother, but he urges us to be vigilant lest the Sais catch us unawares. Something about a dream his son had, the one they call Arth-Ursus, the Bear. Strange tale that.'

'So you're ruled by boys' dreams now, is it?' Bronwen taunted.

'I'm ruled by nought but God and yourself on a good day, wife. Enniaun is wily. If he warns us, I'll heed him. We stay here. Let Hengist come courting us for peace if he wishes. My mind is set. Now can we attend chapel? Brother Anselm awaits us for evening prayers.'

***

457 AD - Ceint

It was the only dwelling in the settlement that no one entered unbidden. Even Hengist's timbered hall was open to the people, but not Albric's domain.

There was a fire pit, but no cooking took place there. The elderly wyrdman took his meals, by invitation, with his people. There was a simple bed frame with sleeping furs and a shelf for clothing. The remainder of the dwelling was given over to his art. The fire pit was just off centre, within a circle marked out on the earthen floor by pebbles. A central pole, dyed blood-red, rose from the floor, towards the roof. On it was carved all his protective symbols; gods, goddesses, totem creatures, the elements. The peak of the pole, lost in the apex of the straw-thatched dwelling, boasted Albric's personal ally, the wolf, the symbol of the teacher.

His door had been closed to all-comers for two days. Albric was engaged in a major flight between the worlds at the behest of Hengist himself.

Inside he prepared as diligently as for any journey. A day's solid fasting, drinking water drawn from a stream known only to himself and purified by powerful cleansing rituals. Inside a tented lodge fastened to the pole, he sweated the impurities from his body with hot stones doused with water. Clad in his deerskin spirit shirt, he placed his wolfshead over his shoulders for protection against the evil spirits that roamed the Otherworld.

His people gave the dwelling a wide berth. The first sounds of drumming throbbed across the settlement. The people's mood was hushed, tinged with the apprehension that prevailed when important rituals were held.

The hypnotic beat silenced even crying infants. It blended with the cosmic dance, splitting the fabric of corporeal and spiritual realms. The drumming pounded on. Albric focused on his power mantra:

'Wolf who gave me knowledge
Wolf who gave me power
Wolf who gave me strength
Guard me in this hour'
'Deer, fleet of foot
Deer sleek and fast
Deer take me upwards
to high planes and past

He chanted, gathering momentum for the leap into the Otherworld. He had journeyed many times, but never with the doubt that accompanied this flight. Deep in the night, the drumming stopped.

Albric sped lightly across the ground, following his sure-footed deer guide that led him effortlessly into the Otherworld. The terrain was unfamiliar. He turned to watch his wolf companion, taking strength from the ally that walked with him, some three paces behind.

The prancing deer led him up a steep mountain slope, striped with purple, grey shadows on snow. Its peak pierced the heavens. The deer turned abruptly some distance short of the pinnacle and bounded away; dappled quicksilver. He was left to conquer the crest with only the wolf for company.

His first thought on reaching the summit was that the journey had been fruitless. He looked to the wolf for guidance, but saw only wariness in the animal's yellow, baleful eyes.

He half turned to descend, when a flickering in his peripheral vision alerted him to a presence. A black-cloaked, cowled figure appeared. The face was hidden, but from within the hood, a red gimlet gaze of power fixed him. The chill was more than that from the cutting wind on the mountain top.

'You seek an answer to a reluctant question?' the figure said, a rustling dryness in the voice like leaves blown by an autumn breeze.

'I do not take this journey lightly. I am loth to ask,' Albric replied, knowing full well the folly of attempting deceit.

The hood inclined slightly in silent acknowledgement of his honesty.

'What is your enquiry?' intoned the voice, rasping as though its throat was filled with sand.

'You know it well enough. I am sent by Hengist to determine what might befall if he accedes to Rhonwen's plan to massacre the British at the peace council.'

There was the briefest of pauses.

'There would be peace for many, would there not?'

'That is not for me to know,' Albric countered, resisting the impulse to offer a view of his own.

'Astutely said. Peace, nevertheless, or their souls hounded to eternity by their own naive trust, caught in the twilight world, unclaimed by their god. Who can say?'

'You have such power; that is why I made the journey.'

'I do; it is so.'

The figure glared at the wolf, which backed off, cowed by the shadowy visage.

'Will you not answer me?' Albric asked, more boldly than he felt. 'This is your realm. If you would but bandy words, let this be ended. I will tell my master the gods were silent,' he added.

'You're a testy one. You speak truly; the gods are silent. You dread their answer to the question. That is why you're afraid for the first time in many journeys. Gods are fickle beings. Yours are assured of victory, but they tremble at the manner of it. Such propriety - hardly god-like at all.'

The voice snickered and lapsed to silence.

Albric fought down the panic in his throat. In all his journeys he had confronted many creatures. Some were helpful, others mischievous; some steeped in trickery, others in benevolent power.

Never had he come across one of such hidden malevolence. The question lurked behind his lips. He clamped down with his teeth, biting hard to stifle the query. The salty taste of wet warm blood ran across his tongue, hardly registering in a mind that recognised whom he addressed. The silence hung in the clear air, a tangible presence that bound them together across the worlds; Albric, the wolf and the stooped creature.

'You are wise, traveller; bold, despite your fear. You are mistaken about your master. Hengist is but a man. I am master of you; indeed I master all. As the gods are silent, you may tell Hengist that I am the one who shall be served by his daughter's deception.'

Albric nodded grimly.

'I shall inform him; my thanks for your judgement, wise one.'

The hood nodded as though Albric's spirit was open for scrutiny from within the folded depths.

'You show more than a little power yourself, Albric of the Frisians. It is well that you hold your query about me. You know the price you'd pay for my answer?'

'I do, lord.'

'Then go. The gods will come to some arrangement, as always. There'll be a price for Hengist's scheme. In their silence, inform him that I shall intercede to prevent their worst. I am well pleased.'

The creature flickered once more and was gone. The wolf rose, shook itself, looked pleadingly at Albric, then turned and led him swiftly down the mountain.

***

The blinking of his eyes was his only movement, save for the shallow rise and fall of his chest, signs that he still had attachments to the world. The settlement was silent. Albric shuddered awake, with the weight of a weariness so great upon him that he could not stand. His deerskin shirt was stained dark brown where perspiration had run down his body. His eyes were sunken, hollow and dazed. When they re-focused, he caught sight of his flowing hair, a grey-black when he had begun the ritual. It was now bereft of all colour. Snow white strands protruded from beneath the grey wolfshead.

Despite his condition, he gazed to the top of the pole that supported his back and mouthed his thanks to his wolf.

Feeling returned to his cramped legs. Feebly, he pulled off the wolf mask. Using the pole to work his way into an unsteady upright position, he tottered like a creature new born and splashed water over his head from the nearby ceramic jar. He was unaware of time.

He shambled to the door, craving food so badly that his legs barely carried him. The sunlight blazed in his eyes, red hot spear tips that brought his hands across his face. He didn't register the large crowd, gathered to witness his emergence. Some two hundred men, women and children waited, patiently silent outside his door. At their head was Hengist, flanked by Rhonwen and Ebissa.

A woman offered him a beaker of ale, but he refused; food was more vital. The crowd took a collective pace backwards, overawed at the sight of him.

'Your journey has been long, old man,' Hengist said.

'If you say so; for me it was not so,' he mumbled.

'You've been between the worlds for three days and nights. I posted guards at your door. Your neighbours would have had us rouse you,' Hengist informed him.

Albric nodded, leaning his weight on a comrade's shoulder to ease the tremors in his legs.

'That was wise. Had they tried, I'd not have returned.'

'And did the gods support our plan?' Hengist enquired, eager to have the answer in public.

'The gods were silent on the matter, Hengist, as I believed,' Albric answered. He sat on the ground, seeking to regain lost strength from the earth's nurturing energies.

'Such a long journey seems strange for no reward,' Rhonwen interrupted, drawing dark looks from her father.

'I didn't say that I don't have a reply. I said that the gods were silent,' the old wyrdman explained wearily.

'Then what, Albric? What did you hear in the Otherworld? We've waited here for three days for the answer,' Hengist urged.

'You'll not wish to hear it, but since your impatience shows no respect, I shall give it to be rid of you,' Albric answered.

'The reply is from the Otherworld's paramount power, Hengist. Your gods are shamed by your daughter; they'll not pronounce on the matter. But the Otherworld's overlord promises support for your plan.'

'The Otherworld's overlord, Albric? Who is lord over the gods themselves?'

'Death, Hengist. Death declares himself your ally. Now you have your answer. I have kept my promise to visit the Otherworld. I would be free of this undertaking. I only survived by the wisdom of my years and the strength of my teachers' knowledge. Few return from a meeting with Death.'

He signalled to be raised to his feet.

Hengist tried to sense the impact of Albric's message among his people, but he couldn't read the silence.

***

458 AD - Viroconium, Powys

Brittu's court at Viroconium hummed; a multi-coloured beehive. Messengers galloped to the far flung reaches of the realm. Pascent and Brittu wrote letters summoning the foremost leaders. Servants and slaves scurried to meet their masters' orders, packing provisions, and the finest tunics and cloaks. The British gathered to make peace.

The solstice, mid-way through a glorious summer was the appointed time. Wiser sages shook their heads. Symbols of the ancient festival: clarity of wisdom, far-sightedness and quick intelligence, rooted in the eye of the goddess Sul and her sacred bird, the peacock, were lacking. Ancient divinities abandoned the British to the new god. Feelings of disquiet among their womenfolk were ignored. The most orthodox civitates and kingdoms sent their representatives to Viroconium, accompanied by their priests.

The sense of joy, warmth and love of the old festival remained. Early summer had been bountiful; clear, bright and hot. The seed of approaching darkness, acknowledged by their forebears on the longest day, was ignored. The sun's warmth and the celebration of its supreme position in the heavens seemed magnificently propitious.

The British hierarchy flocked to Viroconium like plumed exotic birds.

Horses, wagons, retainers, escorting troops, merchants and entertainers flooded into the city. Brittu set up a camp not far from his villa, where the noise filled the long hot nights. Viroconium's market swelled with traders, vying to entice the multitude.

'This peace fills our coffers, brother. The taxes are rolling in,' Brittu beamed, caught in the benevolent mood of the gathering.

'Our expenditure matches the income. Those merchants are doing just as well providing us with fare as our visitors. The two cancel each other out,' Pascent replied.

'Ah well, it's a pretty sight, nevertheless. After all our trials, it's good to see the people so light-hearted. I begin to think we can see our way through this, brother.'

Pascent remained silent. He had sought intelligence on matters vital to the realm. He was less optimistic about the 'peace' than the High King. Warnings and ill omens bestrode the realm, contrasting vividly with the weather and Brittu's mood.

Pascent would remain in Powys as nominal ruler and commander-in-chief. If anything went awry, Powys would not lose both her sons. Agricola had gone south to Dumnonia, disgusted with Brittu's return to the Roman Church. The heresy still held sway there over the estates of the most affluent landlords.

Brittu led a gaily clad procession to the south. Two hundred kings, governors and administrators marched for peace. A hundred riders preceded them with another hundred in the rearguard. A contingent of a hundred and fifty spears completed the company, swelled further by a motley band of camp followers, entertainers and merchants, eager to profit from trading with the Sais.

Pascent watched them from the courtyard, a riotous swathe of colour, sun glinting from spear tips; banners and dracos fluttering in the light breeze. The horses' steps were sprightly. Followers strutted to the sound of pipes and horns. The colourful noisy throng conquered the darker doubts flitting at the edge of Pascent's mind. How could such a joyful company come to harm?

Several days later the column saw the transformation of their south eastern provinces. The sights became alien; ruined abandoned villas and estates. Settlements of timber-built thatched dwellings had sprung up. Seas of golden green corn and barley testified to the newcomers' farming skills. They were far more than warriors.

The company's light-hearted mood subsided. This was the first they had seen of Saxon domesticity. Visions of raiding warriors were replaced by ones of permanent settlers.

***

458 AD - Ceint

At Hengist's main encampment they were further dispirited by the size of the new town that greeted them. At the centre was a recently built shelter. Strong timbers supported a massive roof of thatch, but the walls were open to the air and the roof protected those in its shade. The British were impressed by its size and grandeur. They were shown to where they could set up their tents. Hengist greeted the High King with an honour guard of unarmed warriors. The mood was easy; summer had pacified the settlers too.

A night of feasting around camp fires preceded the conference. Brittu moved through the throng watching signs of the peace he wished to bring to his people. His warriors wrestled with their enemies. Sweat glinted from their slick bodies. Grunts of exertion were joined by shouts from comrades, who urged them to greater efforts. Many more experienced the newcomers' beer for the first time. The High King smiled to see the many drinking bouts, good humoured quaffing as the champions of both sides matched each other flagon for flagon. In the most earnest contest a huge Saxon, fair hair plastered to his face by sweat and ale, held a small barrel between his brawny arms, drinking in huge gulps from its rim. His opponent, a red-haired warrior from Powys, knees bent in exertion and brow furrowed in concentration, wrestled manfully with his unfamiliar vessel. He spilled waves of beer down his sopping tunic to the jeers of the observers.

Bards and wyrdmen ushered in the night. Saxons narrated sagas of their exploits in language unfamiliar to the British, who caught the drama of the tales nevertheless. Saxon warriors riddled with each other, bringing laughter from their guests, who had the suggestive sexual themes hidden in the puzzles translated for them. British bards recounted poems and songs from their own heritage. In their resonant sing-song tales of a Celtic past, the Saxons caught a glimpse of the spirit that binds all people, though the lilting language was alien. Many of the British had all but forgotten it themselves. The camp went silent in the small hours. Tales of heroes, heroines, myths, gods and goddesses filled their heads as they took to their beds.

Brittu was re-united with Rhonwen, his step-mother. He passed her, walking alone in the early hours. He could see why his father had been besotted. She wore a semi-transparent, summer blue, silk dress. If Brittu harboured half a desire to follow his father to her bed, he was disappointed. She ignored him, despite his attempts to catch her eye. She walked on, staring silently into the drinking horn she carried, ignoring all.

It was mid-afternoon on the solstice by the time the talks began. Both Saxon and British had dulled senses following their celebrations. Kings, governors and administrators sat side by side round the colossal table underneath the thatch, grateful for the shade that kept the sun's glare from their sensitive eyes. Hengist stood at the head, Brittu by his side. The clamour died as the crowd awaited his words.

'This day sees the cementing of a peace with enemies we have fought for the past two years. From this day, new boundaries will be set. There will be an end to warfare between us.'

He paused for the words to take effect; the silence continued.

'I have one weighty matter to raise before we begin.'

The British were absorbed by his words, sluggish from their clash with unfamiliar Saxon ale. Oblivious to the increased tension around the table, they missed their hosts flexed muscles. By the time they realised the changed atmosphere, it was too late.

'*A seax, a seax, a seax,*' Hengist bellowed, drawing his secreted knife from the folds in his robes. He struck left into the throat of the attentive Moriutned. The governor of Dyffed crumpled on the table, blood spewing from a severed artery in his throat. Brittu was restrained by two of Hengist's warriors. All around the table the Sais rose up, stabbing and slashing at the guests seated beside them.

Brittu's hangover disappeared instantly, his mouth dropped in slack-jawed horror at the scene. Despite his shock, he could not close his eyes nor his ears to the sights and sounds of the carnage. He was drawn to watch Rhonwen. She stabbed repeatedly at the unprotected body of Coel the Young. His silver-ringed fingers, lacerated with deep cuts, weakly tried to fend off her frenzied assault. The High King watched the blend of colours. Coel's blood spouted in stark contrast to the saffron yellow of his robe, striping it in scarlet.

The ordeal was long in Brittu's mind, yet the assassination of his retinue was over instantly. The High King retched violently, his stomach a volcano that erupted to add to the blood of his friends and courtiers. The Saxons dragged him away from the scene. Jubilant Sais warriors plundered the still- twitching corpses.

The fire was back in Rhonwen's eyes. Coel the Young's face was torn to a bloody mask, his eyes gouged by the wicked point of her blade. Octha finally gripped Rhonwen's wrist. She turned like a trapped rat, blazing anger.

'Enough,' her brother shouted. He slapped her face.

For an instant, it seemed she would re-direct her lust towards him, but something registered deep in the recesses of her tortured mind. She slumped next to Coel's mutilated body. The glaze descended once more over her eyes. The only movement was the stain of blood soaking her dress, which changed the pale blue to a deep maroon.

No one escaped the attack. A single incisive stroke of inspired, malicious frenzy damaged Brittu's foundations beyond repair. Marcus Plautius of Dumnonia, Marcellus Paulinus of Calleva, Caranog of Demetia and Catellius of Dyfed died in bloody brotherhood with Coel the Young and Moriutned. A host of minor kings, bishops, governors and administrators fell with them.

Spearmen and cavalry, who had marched so jauntily to this hall of death, were butchered. Panic spread among the merchants and camp followers, but they were granted safe passage from Ceint, to spread the horror they had witnessed throughout Britain.

Cities, towns and villages the length and breadth of the land were thrown into terror, their leaders absent, their direction uncertain. Rhonwen's evil ploy was the shattering advantage that Hengist had sought. Only Gwent, Siluria and Gwynedd, and the far northern provinces, escaped the massacre. Britain's glorious summer ended. Winter's chill gripped the minds of the population. Hengist had achieved his peace.

25. When Kings Make War

458 AD - Lindum

The taverner was uneasy. Few strangers passed through the small hamlet, tucked in the marshlands of south Lindum.

All evening, the solitary figure had stared into the fire, as though all the answers of God's universe were to be found there. He looked like the worst of beggars. His clothes were rent and torn, his feet bruised, bloodied and all-but bare. A worn, tattered cloak hung over his shoulders, secured by neither pin nor brooch. His wild look was topped by hair that sprouted in unkempt snow-white tufts. The landlord wanted to move him on; at least away from the fire. But something made him reluctant to exert his authority. Though his patrons muttered in quiet conspiracy, they failed to raise the courage to approach the visitor. Despite his beggarly bearing, some indefinable quality deterred them.

A timid servant approached him, encouraged by the inn-keeper's gestures.

'Will you be wanting supper, sir?' she asked hesitantly.

Something registered behind his eyes. He saw her as if for the first time. His smile was so self-knowing that she shuddered at the thought of the deeds which had brought him to this state of mad poverty.

'I'll not trouble you for supper. Thank your master for asking.'

He rose slowly and stamped several times to get the blood flowing. With a cursory nod in the direction of the men, he walked out into the night. Behind him the mutters of bigotry, reserved for all outsiders, continued.

A little way from the inn, the track met a road that continued to the southlands. The ragged figure paused on a bridge over a sluggish river. He looked to the south. Memories flooded back and his mouth winced in pain. He had asked his men to bury him on the coast when he died; at one of the ports that faced the incoming enemy. His soul would add weight to their valour. He shook his head. If they knew his whereabouts, that wish would go unfulfilled.

This was his last act of contrition. Neither the Pope's god, nor the more humanitarian deity of Pelagius had championed him. There was only one explanation and his mind soothed with its revelation. His downfall was due to his neglect of the old gods. His misfortune resulted from their rejection. Smiling, his spirit at last purged of its guilt, the strands of his madness finally woven together, he used the remains of his fading strength to haul himself up to the timbered rail. No human witnessed his sacrificial plunge, a votive offering of himself as recompense for deserting ancient divinities. But a tawny owl, on its favourite hunting perch at the river side, saw the falling form and heard the splash. It turned its yellow-flecked eyes briefly in his direction, then resumed its nocturnal hunting. Perhaps the old gods did witness the death of Brittu, High King of the British.

The villagers dragged the body from the river on the following day. Brittu would have found himself in an unmarked grave had it not been for the observant eyes of a local priest, who recognised that the last item of any value on the body was the royal hart of Powys, a signet ring on the corpse's right thumb.

Pascent read about the death of his missing brother in a letter from Lindum. The ring accompanied it. He took it with some doubt. He had hoped that Brittu was recovering somewhere in private from the ordeal of the massacre. Sighing, he reluctantly transferred the ring to his own thumb. The curse of his family, the High Kingship of Britain, passed to the last legitimate heir of the Vortigerns.

'Write a letter to the governor of Lindum,' he instructed his scribe.

'A headstone is to be erected on my brother's grave that does him honour. Mention is to be made of the part the Sais played in his death.' Pascent caught the query in the scribe's eye.

'He'll lie where he is; there's no time to bring him to Powys. I have troubles a plenty. I'll pay homage when time allows.'

***

458 AD - Brittany

Ambrosius Emrys Wledig walked with his sister Servilla. His thoughts were muted. Letters from Enniaun Girt had shocked him to his core.

'Who would have thought it, sister? Rome's decline allows the worst conduct. Who would have dared to commit such a crime with the thought of a legion to mete out justice? We're staring at barbarity; who knows where it will end?'

'It will end for the British when you're High King, brother; not before. Nothing prevents your accession now. British families flee from the south. Brittu was inexperienced and Pascent cannot fill the void. Hengist will expand his lands with ease. You must act now.'

'I shall, I shall, and not as some avenging angel either. I have the support of the Holy Father. The coin he intended to strengthen Brittu now buys the men I need. I must unite the British or Hengist will take the whole realm. His conduct contravenes the very basis of kingly rule. I'm sorry for the loss of your son, Servilla. Had I acted sooner perhaps you'd not grieve. It's worse that I must now defeat Pascent.'

'You must do what you must do, brother. My sons never recognised their father's position. He blinded them with his power. It's a dangerous light. I'll pray for your victory and, if God wills, my son will be spared his brother's fate. I still have Categan and Lucilla and must be thankful for that.'

***

Recruits flocked to join the banner of Ambrosius. The war in the east went ill, with successive defeats for Roman armies. Emrys Wledig had coin, plus the added incentive of rich agricultural land where a retired warrior could raise healthy sons. As the days passed, Theoderic, Gwyrangon and Seconius busily trained new recruits and organised supplies.

The force grew rapidly. Not only mercenaries enlisted, but those who had heard of the massacred British; sons and kin of those who had lost families, found their way to Brittany. By the time he was ready to march, Ambrosius had amassed a force of thirteen hundred infantry and two hundred cavalry.

He commandeered ships along the coast.

***

458 AD - Dinas Ffynon

Northern Britain was quiet; Angle raids subsided. Cunorix returned to Gwynedd, his battle sharpness honed to a peak by blunting Angle incursions.

Owain was glad to be home, all the more so when he heard about other families' losses at the massacre. Gwawl was very old, but still able to spoil him; Filan and Crenda were pleased to see him and even the grizzled Urien smiled a greeting as they rode into Dinas Ffynon.

Enniaun raised warriors from the Guotodin, plus support from their ancient allies, the Strathcluta Scots. In the face of Hengist's crime, Enniaun knew that the British must resolve their own affairs. Their council was earnest.

Tendubric remained aloof from the preparations, despite Enniaun's entreaties. He did send courteous letters, thanking Enniaun for the warning about the peace conference. After the massacre, Enniaun detected a gentle thawing. Should the rest of Britain fall, Tendubric would remain one of the last bastions of Christianity in the whole realm. The entire weight of the Saxon, Angle, Jute and Frisian nations would be arrayed against him. Knowing that he must have arrived at a similar observation, Enniaun felt a flush of admiration for the Dragon's faith in his strange God. He could sense the conflicting pressures on the Pendragon of the Cymry. Tendubric was bound between two horses pulling in opposite directions. There was no doubt that he shared British abhorrence of Hengist's conduct, yet he remained steadfastly neutral in the British conflict.

After months of hectic action, Owain, Edern and Elen found the days long and tedious. They supervised their men through strenuous routines, but it was unlike real fighting. The waiting weighed heavily on Owain whose thoughts ran to his absent son, Artwerys, now fully orphaned. The Lady's entreaties to stay his hand were all that prevented him from riding to Gwent to claim him. Artwerys now lived with his grandfather, Tendubric. The Lady urged Owain to consider what impact his declaration of fatherhood might have on the tenuous peace with the Esselywg. When he freed his mind from this dilemma, he was aware that for all their skirmishes with the Angles, he and Edern had found no significant strategy that would help defeat Hengist's growing numbers.

Filan walked with Owain one late afternoon in the wooded slopes beneath Dinas Ffynon. It was nearing twilight, a time when the druid believed that appeals to the Otherworld were more likely to be heard.

'Now that you aren't scuttling about the coast, hunting for raiders, you might wish to see why Lailoken left you this particular text,' he said, handing Owain a scroll from beneath his robe.

'You've not taken all these years to translate this,' Owain accused, remembering his old teacher's gift.

'No, I completed it some years ago. Lailoken concluded that I should judge when the time was most favourable to give it to you. I judge that time is now.'

Owain stared into the Druid's eyes, seeking for some deception, but they laughed back at him in frank denial.

'Your boyhood hardly endeared you to reading, Owain. You were more used to hunting and riding. Now, you're different and so are the times'

Owain reverently took the scroll whose touch reminded him of the last time he had seen the old man.

'Thank you, Filan. How can I reward you? You've spent years on this.'

The old druid smiled.

'I am getting old, Owain. It's time for Crenda to serve the family. A woodsman's hut would suit me, somewhere beneath Dinas Ffynon. I'd complete my own studies.'

Filan had served the Votadini for three generations.

'It's a small reward, Filan. You shall have your shelter. You think Crenda capable to serve in your place?'

'He's still learning, but he can grasp changes that escape an old man's understanding, Owain. His mind is more politic than mine. The old ways grow dimmer with each passing winter. They'll soon reach the long sleep. Many years will pass before the green man walks the earth as consort to the goddess again. But you know this, you don't need me to confirm it.'

'Then I bow to your wishes, Filan. Know you are dear to us. I shall visit you regularly.'

***

Owain closeted himself in his own quarters for several days, absorbed by the ancient text. He ignored Edern and Elen's entreaties to go riding.

Study of the manuscript confirmed that his idea for shock cavalry were not original. Lailoken's Greek text described the tactics of Alexander of Macedon's own cavalry Companions. Owain shook his head in disbelief. All that time ago, Macedon relied on exactly the use of cavalry that he had unsuccessfully urged Edern to consider. Close order, more heavily-armoured riders had attacked and beaten close formation foot by shock charges. A thrill of vindication ran through him. He read avidly for a while longer. Satisfied that he had the evidence he required, he ran to the stables to ready Bran for a ride. He needed to allow his thoughts to coalesce.

Beneath the cool shade of the trees, his mind raced, pulling together the strands of a solution. Excitement, followed by exultation rose in him. The manuscript's contents plus his insights gained from the bear locked in a harmonious answer to the military challenges his people faced.

'You beautiful old man,' he shouted to the treetops. Birds rose from their perches with his cry. Owain dug his heels into Bran's flanks, urging him into a gallop along the narrow twisting paths. Sensing its master's mood, the horse strained its muscles in response and they thundered along the forest lanes.

He could see it clearly now; the advantage they had been seeking. Bran carried him willingly up the climb to Dinas Ffynon. Edern would have no cause to refuse his suggestions now. The Sais were due for a military lesson. For the first time in many months he laughed until tears blurred his vision. His destiny could wait. Now was the time to show both the Sais and the Vortigerns what mounted troops could achieve.

***

I could not ignore Owain's ideas on cavalry the next time he offered them. Wide-eyed, his tangled hair made wilder by the wind, his generous face set in a mask of triumph, he had my attention immediately.

'I have it, Edern. I have it at last.'

He brandished the manuscript, dancing in a circle. His heavy riding boots clattered on the stone floor. He appeared capable of single handedly riding down the whole Saxon nation.

'It would appear that I'm bound to listen, lord,' I said soberly.

'Oh, Edern, you'll not be so dour when you hear my news,' he replied, his eyes brimming with fire behind the wet glaze.

'Then say on, lord,' I invited.

'I've pieced it together, Edern. My bear studies, this manuscript and our Votadini horsemanship give us the solution we've been seeking.'

'I'm all ears, lord.'

His enthusiasm was too intense for him to register my sarcasm.

'This text describes Macedonian cavalry tactics, Edern. They had no better armour than we, neither were their horses too different from ours. Yet, Alexander repeatedly defeated close-order foot with them.'

I queried the source. Though I had added to my book knowledge, largely by studying maps, I had never heard of these Macedonians, nor their leader, Alexander.

'They ruled a vast empire before the Romans, Edern,' Owain explained.

Before Rome, I thought. Such men were kin to the gods themselves to have lived before Rome. I had little time to reflect on the magnitue of such knowledge.

'That's not all, Edern. It isn't just battlefield tactics. We can change our whole strategy. Our people used 'horse' to steal their neighbours' cattle before the Romans. The Romans showed us how to support infantry in battle, but they relied on infantry legions for the bulk of their strength. We learned to attack infantry with horse from the Sarmatian detachments sent to guard the wall. But their two-handed use of the kontos was clumsy. They protected themselves in their own land with mounted archers. We have none. If we attacked like that, we'd be ripped apart by Sais missiles or Pictish arrows. The horses are too valuable to risk.

We're going to change both traditions. Long spears, held single-handed, will allow us to keep our shields. We'll protect the horses with barding. We'll mount long sorties deep into their territory, avoiding pitched battles against large forces. We'll scare them with surprise attacks, like the bear, Edern. It bellows and rears when confronted with danger and the wolf slinks away. We'll destroy crops and villages; pick off their smaller warrior bands and harry them, Edern. If they stand, we'll defeat them using Alexander's tactics. One thing we'll do that the bear does not. We'll campaign in winter, catch them sluggish and drowsy when they least expect us. Can you see it, Edern? Can you see it?'

It was difficult to escape his vision. His words painted a picture in my mind of untried risky ventures, yet the more I considered his ideas, the more I could see sense in them.

I paused, showing serious consideration for the first time. He paced earnestly, while I ran the images through my mind.

'I'm still doubtful, Owain, but you have a point. We could travel faster. Just the advantage we need against the Sais. How will we test this?'

'So, I have your interest at last have I? We must keep this secret. If Hengist gets wind of it, we'll lose the impact of surprise. It's important that Pascent doesn't know of it either. He has cavalry too.'

'If it works,' I cautioned. 'We must train a select troop away from the exercise yard. Too many prying eyes here.'

'I agree. We'll use my companions. We can use them to train up others, if it's successful.'

'Calm yourself, Owain. We need to think long on this. Our javelins are too flimsy. Our two-handed spears won't do either; they'd shatter at the charge.'

Quiet consideration replaced his enthusiasm now that I had been won over. We could take time.

We spent several days in our quarters. When we had anticipated possible pitfalls, we put the idea into practice. Armourers and smiths, busy with the king's preparations, met our requests for the strange nine-foot ash-hafted spears with elongated blades in the way only artisans have for communicating that their time is being wasted; disdainful whistling. Owain's unquestioned status meant that our requirements were met, albeit grudgingly. Owain enrolled other armourers to assemble neck and chest protection for the horses and improved mail for the riders.

Such a project did not pass without arousing curiosity among Owain's peers and elders. Elen was displeased at her exclusion.

'I shall go to father if you don't tell me what's going on,' she complained one afternoon, as our plans swelled.

Owain grinned his disarming smile and I could not repress my mirth at her irate expression.

'And what do you believe father will do? Remember, we supported your claim to become a warrior, Elen. Would you reward us now by appealing to the authority you once rejected?' Owain chided.

'But what have I done to be so ignored? Have I not shared all the perils, trials and dangers of battle with you? Do you believe I can't keep a secret?' she railed.

'We're engaged on a trial of new tactics. Best we spare your disappointment if they don't work. We might need your comfort after all the time we've put into this,' Owain explained.

'I promise I'll comfort you anyway, but please don't leave me out. I'm wearied to distraction. You keep yourselves to yourselves so much. I'm becoming used to Ceri and Gwawl's company, I'll be swapping my armour for a wedding dress soon.'

She spoke slyly; her whimsical comments targeting my insecurity.

'Perhaps she'd be better knowing our intentions, Owain. She's made excellent contributions to our campaigns, thus far,' I persuaded.

'I'll allow you to help, sister. But you must meet one condition without knowing what we're about. I'll not be shaken on this, understood?'

Elen wrinkled her nose, hating to be bound by such an ultimatum. Her curiosity won the day.

'I accept, brother. No doubt I'll rue it.'

'You witnessed that, Edern?' Owain asked.

I nodded solemnly.

'What we're about, sister, is the creation of a new breed of cavalry. One that can attack formed infantry. Such a tactic is most dangerous. If we do succeed, you'll not ride with us. That is my condition.'

I awaited the volcano of Elen's response. It seemed for a heartbeat that Owain would bear the brunt of her explosion. But she saw the steel in his eyes. Her sisterly wiles were useless.

'I accept, brother. I shall ride with the supporting horse. Now, tell me what you have devised.'

***

We refined our designs. Excitement mounted as the day came for testing the tactics. Owain found a field a few miles from the hill fort suitable for our purpose. Farming slaves set up a dense formation of straw stacks at the end of the field. Owain led the chosen band there two days later. We had set out early to avoid curious eyes.

The new equipment was carried in two wagons. The men spent the bulk of the morning modifying their saddles to take chest straps. They grumbled at the task, but Owain had banned grooms from the expedition.

Further time was spent in persuading the horses to accept the new barding. Elen had modified the design, adding protective mail to foreheads and plated casings for the eyes. The horses skittered with anxiety. They were walked until they calmed. Well past mid-day they accepted their riders. The men rode in the dense order that Owain demanded. They walked, trotted and cantered, easing their mounts into the new formation.

Finally, Owain was satisfied. The new long spears were unloaded. The men took their new weapons and re-mounted. Owain demonstrated a couched spear under his right arm. A mailed glove protected his hand against friction. He tucked his shield under his chin. The men donned their gauntlets and took up their positions.

'It's important that we stay together. Sarmatian order, but at the charge. Our success will be due to our united impact, not as single riders. So, keep close and on my command move through walk, trot, canter to gallop. Understood?'

The line fell quiet.

Elen told me later that she wished upon her life that she had not given her promise. Owain instructed her to observe the point of impact.

'Walk on,' Owain ordered.

We moved tentatively forward.

Half-way across the field, we cantered; by the last third we galloped. I could see Elen holding her breath, anticipating the rush that we felt as our horses' gait increased. At the last moment it seemed that we'd pull up. Our whole warrior lives were impregnated with the belief that cavalry were not shock troops. Now, in the time that it took for a heartbeat to dictate the gap between life and death, Owain challenged our faith that such a belief was not divine. With a last yell of fear, exultation and panic, we smashed into the straw barrier.

Though Elen always obeyed Owain's orders, she failed on this occasion. I saw her shut her eyes and turn her head away.

The thunder of our hooves was silenced and Elen opened her eyes. The men laughed in relief. Cust, Gwalchma and Gweveyel were among several unhorsed. A few mounts had jumped at the barriers and were staring at their riders with straw hanging from their ears. Owain and I embraced each other excitedly. Though the charge was poorly co-ordinated, the stacks had been shunted backwards. Shattered spears protruded from them. Others were being retrieved by the men, still whole, but buried two thirds of their length in the compacted straw.

'Did you see it, Elen?' Owain shouted as she cantered towards us.

'I didn't, brother. I couldn't watch,' she confessed, sheepishly.

'If you closed your eyes, imagine what enemy foot troops would be doing,' I chimed.

Owain plucked straw from his mail. His horse was covered in it, as were most of the others. This brought more raillery from the riders, jubilant at their lord's success.

'Now, Edern. Have we something to work with?'

I grinned at his appearance.

'It might work better, lord, if we decked ourselves out like scarecrows. We look so much like village idiots the Sais wouldn't take us seriously. But you seem to have struck upon something, I'll grant you. It'll take time and effort. We need to perfect this. I'll be bored no longer.'

The troopers reclaimed their mounts. They stripped off the barding and stowed their spears back in the wagon. We rode back to Dinas Ffynon in high sprits. The key to open the deadlock with the Sais might not have been cut to perfection, but it had begun its first crafting in the day's labours.

***

458 AD - Ceint

The Saxon gods deferred their judgement on Hengist's treachery. More British abandoned their chaotic land to join their kin in Brittany. Where once there had been certainty, now Britain's fate was unknowable. The new God on the cross seemed to have abandoned the Pretani along with their ancient divinities.

Hengist's successes brought more keels to Britain. Territories north, south and west of Ceint sprouted settlements. Villages grew crops, livestock and warriors; Hengist planned further expansion. His intelligence about the British was poor. Albric refused to 'fly', His last ritual had troubled his spirit and he retired from his service to the people.

'No man should meet death more than twice in a life time,' he claimed.

Other seers were called upon by the Saxon leader, but none had Albric's experience.

Rhonwen continued to worry both her kin and the people. Military inaction plunged her deeper into the abyss of melancholy. She disappeared into the countryside for long periods. She would return hungry, unkempt and jabbering incoherently, her eyes glittered like a starved wolf, her face lacking in all expression. Though he consulted his wise elders and healers, Hengist found no solution to her condition. Secretly, Albric wondered at the response from the spirit world to Hengist's perfidy. Death had offered to influence the gods, but might Rhonwen's deterioration be part of the price for the Saxons' success?

Neither his spies nor his wyrdmen supplied the knowledge that Hengist sought about his enemies. The source that did was unfamiliar and unexpected; so much so that he doubted its credibility.

Alone in his hall, one afternoon, he was disturbed by a lone warrior who burst in on him.

'British horsemen, lord. Perhaps fifty. They ride under the symbol of truce.'

Hengist's immediate thought was that this was a suicidal attempt by Pascent to avenge the massacre. Nervously, he barked out orders. 'Have the troop halted at the palisade gate. Assemble as many warriors here as you can. Quickly, man, I might be cut down while you gawp at their approach.'

He buckled on his broad belt, thrusting his scaramaseax through it. He drew his shield down from the wall behind his great chair and hefted a francisca in his hand for balance.

The cavalry troop met massed warriors at the town's perimeter. Several hundred had thrown down their everyday tools to take up their arms. Hengist started for the western boundary, but his warriors were massed to the south. Curious about the enemy's approach, he walked in the direction of the clamour.

The troop sat easily. Hengist saw they were no ordinary cavalry. Their plumes were white, not yellow; they were mail-clad to a man.

Horse trappings suggested affluence; silver and bronze glinted in the sunlight. Their shield device, a red running wolf on a black ground, was unknown to him.

Their leader sat nonchalantly, his leg crooked across the saddle. His white-plumed helmet rested on his left knee. Droplets of perspiration jewelled his greying black curls. There was no fear in his wide amber eyes, nor in his casual posture.

'Who visits the Sais in truce?' Hengist bellowed from behind his screen of warriors. His fingers strayed uncertainly to the haft of his sword.

'Who asks?' came the even reply.

'You have ridden far, Briton. State your concerns and don't test my patience,' Hengist rapped, unnerved by the man's effrontery.

'As you speak for those here,' the rider gestured lazily at the warriors, 'I take you to be Hengist, the one who leads this invasion. I would speak with you in private.'

'Am I a fool that I'd speak to you in private? Every warrior in Britain craves such a meeting, so he might strike down the treacherous Hengist to avenge his people.'

'You are wrong, Hengist. I'm a Roman, not a Briton. I'm from Brittany and more recently from hard fighting in the east. You may disarm me and keep your weapons if it makes you feel safer. My troop is too few against your warriors, yet their lives would be forfeit, should I strike you down. I didn't pay good coin to equip these men to lose them by a foolish act.'

The Roman's poise added weight to his words.

'You will dismount and be disarmed. If you can keep your nerve, you may attend me in my hall. Your lack of fear makes me curious. The last Britons to come here found it their last act.'

'They did not bring what I bring you, Hengist. That's why I lack fear,' was the measured reply.

He slid gracefully to the ground. He threw the horse's reins to one of his men and handed him his helmet, sword and an ornamental dagger. Two burly Saxon warriors searched him for secreted weapons, but found none. With the casual movements of his wolf device, he walked fearlessly through the throng in Hengist's wake.

Hengist posted two reliable warriors at the door and sat in his high-backed chair, which was on a raised dais at the head of the table, ensuring that any visitor was disadvantaged. Hengist restored his shield to the wall behind him, but retained both sword and seax in his belt. The francisca lay on the table before him, within easy reach.

'Your guilt makes you edgy, Hengist,' the visitor said, smoothly.

'Your impertinence tests my patience, Roman. Who are you and why are you here?'

'You wish to know what the British are about. I can tell you.'

The words were so dear to Hengist's heart that the Saxon leader was immediately suspicious.

'You think I'd accept the word of a Roman about what my enemies are plotting. You are one of them.'

'Roman I may be, but I'm no ally of the British. I'm not your enemy, either, unless you wish it. Listen, Hengist. Hear me out. My name is Leontinus, many years ago a commander in the forces of Ambrosius Aurelianus. My wealth has equipped the force you see out there. I have a hundred and fifty more like them. I'm a soldier of fortune. I'm here to offer you more land, Hengist. The intelligence I have is worth double this year's harvest. Does this not allay your suspicion?'

Despite his reticence, Hengist was drawn. He still doubted the Roman's unruffled words, but there was no harm in hearing what he had to say.

'There's ale in the barrel, or wine in that amphora, if you'd prefer,' he nodded in the direction of the drink.'Hengist has never lacked in hospitality to his guests, Roman. Now say on.'

'I'm sure enough of my position to risk your hospitality, Hengist. I doubt that any Romano-Briton would seek to take salt with you again in your life time. You have sundered the most precious of their kingly principles. You're the greatest threat to their traditions. Truly, you have introduced them to fear.'

Hengist ignored the jibe. The buzz of the flies in the hall merged with the snoring hunting dogs and the measured tones of Leontinus, well into the evening. Hengist's attention remained firmly focused on what his dubious guest had to say.

***

458 AD - Dinas Ffynon, Gwynedd

Owain awoke in the depths of a midsummer night, under the hound moon of Eorionos, the strands of his dream intact. There was no anxiety attached to the images. It was high summer; the corn rippled gold. On the branch of a nearby oak, a blackbird trilled its song. Ambrosius was on the march. Owain smiled.

***

458 AD - Viroconium, Powys

Pascent knew that he could assemble a force sufficient to meet either Hengist or Ambrosius; his dilemma was leadership as he lacked military experience. Both enemies had better tacticians than himself. Appeals to Tendubric proved futile. As the harvest ripened he sought an experienced ally.

He had slipped into a day-dream, staring out across the hills from the window. His thoughts turned to his sister. Lucilla was his only remaining family within reach. It hit him like a spear thrust. His kin links to Loegaire were the answer to his crisis. The bardic king had combined his love of the arts with successful military gains and such a man might well prove the realm's redeemer. Pascent called excitedly for his scribe, formulating the start of the plea he would make to his brother-in-law. He was only half way through the letter when a slave begged admission.

'Quickly, this is urgent,' he rapped, curious at the slave's insistent gestures.

'Riders approach, lord. The scouts report about two hundred, all mailed and in good order. They're unknown to us.'

Pascent reviewed his recent instructions. He had ordered no muster. Visiting dignitaries would be familiar.

He dismissed the scribe. 'Attend me later. Secure the gates; archers to the walls.'

Pascent glanced in a polished metal mirror. Satisfied that he looked kingly enough, he went out to meet his visitors.

Leontinus was used to being greeted from behind solid defensive positions; one of the pitfalls of travelling an over-cautious land with an unknown battle device. Armed defenders observed his approach warily from palisaded walls.

He waited patietly for Pascent to appear. His men were disgruntled by the miles they had ridden. He insisted that they wore mail, despite the summer heat. It enhanced their discipline and suited Leontinus to have his cavalcade reported far and wide. It added mystery to the confused politics of the realm.

'Who rides so boldly into the High King's domain?' the challenge rang out from the walls. A young, dark-haired, summer-robed figure peered down.

'If you are Pascent, High King of the British, I would speak with you. If you are not, seek him out,' Leontinus replied.

'I am he. Who are you and what is your business?'

'I am Leontinus, former commander in the forces of Ambrosius Aurelianus. For a suitable reward, I can provide you with both men and military advice, lord King.'

Pascent was taken aback. The day sprang surprises. He had a strategy to improve his command by petitioning Loegaire, and fully-armoured cavalry on solid horses sat at his gates, led by one who claimed Roman training. Were the fates finally turning?

'If you are who you claim, why offer your services to me?'

'I seek land for my services. You lack kings and governors. I've lost faith with Ambrosius. The Votadini have many sons; it's cold in your northern climes and the old dragon of Gwent has little to offer in the south other than his strange religion. You're my man, my lord, if you'll have me. Otherwise, it's a long ride back to the coast.'

The reply was calculated. Pascent realised that here was a man who knew his art.

'Have your men dismount, Leontinus the Roman. I'll send out slaves with water buckets. You and your senior officers will attend me.'

The head disappeared from the wall. A postern opened in the double gates for Leontinus and three officers to enter. The remainder of the men dismounted, thankful for the opportunity to stretch their legs. The bowmen watched keenly from the walls.

Leontinus was impressed by the villa's grandeur. Information gleaned in Brittany about the plight of the British had been only partially true. The capital of Powys still offered naked opulence to the eyes of a visitor.

He inwardly commended Pascent for his caution. He and his staff officers had retained their swords, but were met by the High King, flanked by the captain of his guard and discreetly positioned bodyguards.

'Now. Tell me what prize you want in exchange for your services, Leontinus. I've no time to waste in subtle negotiations; I prepare for this usurper you once served.'

'I'm of the same mind, my lord. My men rode hard to reach here. I don't want their journey to be fruitless. I pledge you my experience, my men and my knowledge of Ambrosius, in return for the kingship of Dumnonia.'

'A kingship for so few men, Leontinus?'

'Dumnonia's estates are rich, it's true, lord King. But you'd gain a buffer against the Sais were I in command there. They must march against me, before they reached your lands. The price is fair when all's considered.'

Pascent was in no mood to lose any advantage. Dumnonia lacked leadership. The biggest exodus of absent families had fled from there. Haggling was inappropriate. The stakes were too high. This might still be a ruse by his opponent, but from what he knew of Ambrosius, he doubted it. Aurelianus was too honourable for subterfuge.

'My word on it, Leontinus. When we triumph over Ambrosius, you shall have your kingship. Now, have your men billeted in the town; Drusus will show you the way. Join me on your return. You must tell me of your service with Emrys Wledig.'

Alone, Pascent pondered the auspicious benefits of the day. His thoughts returned to the uncompleted letter to his brother-in-law. The odds were shortening.

***

458 AD - Brittany

Ambrosius had stared at the maps so long, his officers were convinced they would never begin the march to the coast.

'We must avoid the Sais; we're too weak to meet them. We have too large a force to ship to Gwynedd, therefore we must approach Powys from the south, with our main allies in the north. It's a dilemma. Your comments?'

'We should land at Anderida,' Gwyrangon offered. 'We can add to our forces before marching straight to Glevum, where the river narrows. Pascent will defend against us there. Enniaun must make a detour round Powys to rendezvous with us. If we're caught unsupported, we're doomed. Pascent's numbers will be too much for us.'

'You've thought this through, Gwyrangon. The Votadini must link up with us. If only that stubborn old Dragon, Tendubric would join us, I'd feel more heartened.'

'We can be too cautious, lord. Outnumbered we might be, but Pascent can't match your skills. The Votadini are the most experienced warriors in Britain. They'll meet us; have no fear,' Theoderic urged.

'You're right, old friend. There's uncertainty with any venture. Assemble the men. We'll see if God be so kind to grant us a realm, divided and distressed though it be. Send word to Enniaun and have him ask for the Dragon's aid one last time. No doubt Pascent will be making his appeals to Gwent. We should do likewise.'

A ripple of excitement ran through his officers. Ambrosius's caution, chained so long by circumstance, was countered by his order. Tomorrow they would march with intent. The next time their men bore arms would be the test of all their endeavours, in real battle. They hurried to rouse the men.

Ambrosius sat long into the night. He pored over the map. One part of him screamed to put his shamanic powers to the test, but he knew that this was an act of selfishness. He folded the map deliberately, resisting the lure of his hidden cave under the chapel. It was time to put his faith not in God, nor spirits, but in the strength of his men and the faith of his allies. He wrapped himself in his cloak and slept, dreamlessly.

***

458 AD - Connachta

Loegaire considered that his pact with Vitalus had bestowed major advantages. Free from the petty raiding engaged in by the lesser kings, he had attacked the fifth of Mide, which lay between his own fifths of Connachta and Laigin.

The Scotti tradition of hostage-taking now extended his authority over several Tuatha. His Fianna were led by Callum McGrall the Ri Feinnidh. Despite his warrior prowess, Loegaire remained more at ease with harp and pen than sword. His mind out-foxed the other Scotti kings, though his warriors were well respected for their battle skills.

Up to this point, he had ignored Britain. Lucilla broke through his indifference to report the massacre of her brothers' followers, but the British seemed a long way off as he schemed to secure the advantages he had gained in his own land. His views were changed by Pascent's letter.

'Your brother is desperate for my support in his coming war with Ambrosius. Shall I join him and forfeit my designs on uniting this land?' The voice was sing-song. Even when discussing serious issues of state, Loegaire never lost his bardic qualities.

Lucilla remained silent. Never close to Pascent, she had no wish to see her husband embroiled in her family's affairs. Connactha was her home and it had been beneficial. Loegaire's prominence had established firm foundations for Faustus, Lugid and herself. He had been a doting, caring husband, unlike the boorish arrogant British, who lorded it over their womenfolk in the Roman fashion. Loegaire discussed his plans with her; he asked her advice; he ensured, despite pressures of state, that her concerns were dealt with. It was challenge enough when he campaigned within the boundaries of Ireland. It would be much worse were he to embark on a risky venture to rescue her brother. Her love for him had ascended to even higher peaks when he had received Servilla's spiteful letter informing him about his first born, Faustus. Loegaire had been withdrawn for days. He announced abruptly that he and Callum would raid against Mide and had thundered out of his settlement as though pursued by hell's hounds. When he returned, he was serious. He showed her the letter with her mother's betraying signature, seeking an explanation from her downcast, guilt-clouded eyes. She had taken a deep breath and told him the truth. He had nodded. A deep sigh escaped from his tight lips. Then he tore the letter into shreds.

'He'll not be told of this, ever. That's all I ask,' he said, taking her weeping and trembling in his arms. Some day, she promised herself, when she was strong enough, she would tell him of her terror. She owed him that.

'You're quiet, Lucilla?' Loegaire enquired.

'What are you offered, husband?' she asked, buying time for thought.

'It's no small gain. All Gwynedd. He cedes Dyfed in the south too. It's tempting. Powys would sit between us. He'll not see a united Scotti presence in the west of Britain. What do you think?'

'Your plans are well advanced at home, husband. You know what you're about. Aiding my brother is risky. He's inexperienced, with powerful enemies. Hengist looks to expand in the south. Why be drawn? Are your own campaigns not enough?'

Loegaire moved across the room, waving Pascent's letter idly. His favourite hawk, on its perch by the door, turned its attention to the lure of the fluttering parchment, but settled back again. It peevishly preened its russet feathers.

'Risky. But one battle will settle it. Hengist would seize the advantage from a long campaign. Two provinces are rich pickings for one battle.'

'If it's won, husband.'

'You advise caution. I'll consult Callum. I'll honour your feelings.'

'You mis-read me, my lord. I do not counsel caution. We've too much at stake here for foolish ventures. I'd have you safe for your sons. You're paramount Ri Coiced of this land. Finish what you have begun, husband. That is my advice.'

'Is there something missing from your entreaty, my love? You'd have me here near you, rather than across the water. True?'

'My feelings don't contradict my advice, husband. I confess that I've no wish to see you march further than Laigin. I'm distressed when you're gone with the Fianna. You shouldn't love me so well if you wish me to wave you off with a joyful heart. But, there's sense to my counsel also. The remaining Ri's would be unleashed like hounds if they knew you'd taken ship for Britain.'

'Never fear, my sweet. I'll think carefully. Perhaps I merely chafe for a fresh challenge. The revenues of Gwynedd and Dyfed are not to be ignored lightly. I'll give you my decision when I know my mind.'

She rose to greet the entrance of the boisterous brothers, Faustus and Lugid, both dark-haired, bright-eyed and far too energetic for their bewildered house servant.

'I shall school the boys in their letters for a while, husband,' she said. 'I might have to carry your memory in the mirror of their eyes if you take ship to join the Cambrogi. Best that I set my mind to their education. It will occupy me should you go.'

The boys scowled resentfully. The hawk looked on smugly at their distress. Loegaire stared out of the open window across the green hills of his domain.

26. The Bear, the Dragon and the Cross

At the song time of Cantlos, the harvest under the Heron moon, Britain's fate hung in the balance. The equinox signified the equal length of night and day. Hengist was the most comforted by the portents when the British chose to contest their leadership. He needed no wyrdman to interpret the meaning for him. Civil war among the British opened the way for his designs. Leontinus's scheming added to his advantage.

In more ways than one, it was the time of the enchantress. Hengist planned homage to Eostre. She would receive libations and ritual honour. The season was sacred to the sow, among the most revered of the Frisians' creatures. Yet, Hengist guarded against over-confidence, for the dark goddess was a shape-shifter in the dusky twilight of the year. She danced in the void to spin the strands of the future; always beyond the reach of men's minds.

For Ambrosius too, on the voyage to Britain, the time was heavy with the symbolism of his hidden craft. The crane, the spirit bird, flew between the worlds, bringing magical artefacts to aid those in need. He smiled ruefully as the ship pitched in a swell, nearing the coast of the land where his destiny would be revealed. Other than the strength of his men, no mystical advantage had presented itself.

So they gathered. Across the realm, the mightiest host left the harvest to its womenfolk, the young, the elderly; those unable to fight. The languorous heat of summer presaged a slow, inexorable conflict. Though men marched slowly, march they did.

***

459 AD - Viroconium, Powys

Pascent looked out across the fields to the south of his villa, as his brother had gazed before him. Tents sprouted like mushrooms; the

Romans had taught much about the discipline necessary to convert a host into an army. The tumult of the assembling warriors sounded across the fields like the rush of an incoming tide. The numbers were far greater than Brittu's army had been. Leaderless kingships had sent their forces, fearful of being isolated. From Dumnonia, Dyfed, Elmet and Rheged they came; from Demetia, Ceredigion and Eboracum; from Calleva, Ratae and Lindum. King Mark of Kernow left the privacy of his southernmost kingdom to serve the cause. Excitement gripped the young Pascent. With such forces, how could he lose?

Tendubric sent ambiguous letters. Pascent sensed the old Dragon would stay in his lair. Despite eloquent letters from Loegaire, Pascent could not say with certainty whether his hoped-for Irish allies would arrive either.

A glance across his new warrior ranks brought his mind back to practicalities. King Mark was a doughty commander and the cavalry had benefited already from the tuition of Leontinus. If it came to it, he would make a strong show with what he had.

In Gwynedd, Enniaun Girt with his three divisions of battle-ready warriors prepared to take to the field. Germanianus had arrived with a sizeable force from the Guotodin, along with spears from Strathcluta. The north was enjoying an unaccustomed peace, because for once the Picts warred amongst themselves: Maelcon battled for supremacy with Drust's heirs.

***

459 AD - Gwent

To the south, Tendubric gathered his strength, intent upon defending Gwent, Siluria and the true religion. Despite Cynvelyn's urging, and pleas from both sides, he refused to deploy the most prized battle-relic of the British, the True Cross.

Cunorix, accompanied by his nephew, Owain, led a troop of Votadini horse into Tendubric's stronghold.

Tendubric greeted them cordially enough, but remained impervious to Cunorix's pleas for assistance. Cynvelyn looked on, frustrated at his brother's intransigence. The Dragon was more interested in Owain for reasons best known to himself. Cunorix was left in Cynvelyn's capable hands when the Dragon lord invited the Bear to a private audience.

'Your father warned us of the massacre because of a dream. I'm intrigued by your powers of prophecy and in your debt. Can you tell me more?' Tendubric asked when they were closeted in his private rooms.

'No, lord King. My dreams are strange. I need interpretations.'

'Unfortunate. I have an interest in such portents,' the Dragon mused, disappointed by the reply.

Owain sought advantage from Tendubric's curiosity.

'My first tutor charged me with understanding the hearts and minds of men, lord king. Yours are well hidden. Your religion isolates you from the British, might I know the reason for it?'

Immediately cautious, Tendubric searched the Votadini's candid face, but found no guile in the hazel eyes. Indeed this Bear bore himself in a strange manner that set him apart. Despite his intuitive trust of Owain, Tendubric's reply was guarded.

'Our religion is no stranger to us, Owain; the Roman and Pelagian beliefs are. They portray a flawed view of our Lord.'

'How is your view so different?' Owain pressed. The Lady had warned of the dangers posed by the new religion.

'Such knowledge is for us who are guardians, Owain, not for outsiders who would ridicule or destroy it,' the Dragon continued.

'But if it's not shared, how can it thrive? Will Gwent forever be a secret garden that none may admire?'

'Only until Rome's mistruths fail. Then will be our sowing time. Until then, we must guard our seed through the long winter.'

'They might accuse you of the same. Who really knows what happened so long ago in a far-flung land? How can we test your claims when you keep them so close to your bosom?'

'I see no deception in you, Owain, so I'll divulge this much. The authority for our belief lies with Paul. He who was close to the true teachings before Roman scholars blighted his message. The church's creed is a monstrous heresy, promising reward for loyalty to the faith. This is not the way.' He paused and studied Owain's face.

'And you keep your forces within your borders because of this, lord King?' Owain challenged. 'It might drown us all in a Sais flood. Is your secret worth the loss of the land and our ancestors' spirits to Hengist? How do you know that your beliefs will survive?'

'Take your reason to Ambrosius and Pascent. Does their bickering not weaken the realm?'

Owain shook his head. Tendubric had cut to the quick of it. The Bear had no more a moral position in asking for the Dragon's aid to promote a civil war than Tendubric had in his isolation from the conflict.

'The realm has been sore troubled for years. This you know. Must we not sort out our own differences before we deal with the Sais?'

'It's a matter of what you mean by 'we'. I would stand against Hengist's pagan hordes, but I hold no allegiance to the High King. Nor to Emrys Wledig.'

'Not even when the True Cross would inspire our men? Can you deny them such a talisman to keep your faith intact?'

'Aye, but their view of it would be falsehood, Owain. No man should go into battle misunderstanding either his religion or his relics. Where do you stand in your beliefs? You question mine.' Tendubric shifted the argument, wearied of Owain's persistence.

'I stand beyond what men hold true, lord King. I'm to guard against all beliefs that threaten this land. Britain is my belief. I'm to defend it, though I know not how. A simple view against the weighty doctrines we face.'

Tendubric caught the sincerity. Powerful conviction mixed with naivety. The casual way Owain dismissed religion sent a shudder down the Dragon's back. For the first time he realised that his faith provided comforting answers to his terrifying questions about death. This Bear faced his destiny free of such fear. His courage was admirable. His love of the land was embedded as deeply as the faith that the Dragon held dear.

'I'll pledge this, Owain. It's folly to hand Hengist any more advantage. I'll be alert to any gain the Sais might seek from the clash between our brothers. Pascent and Emrys Wledig can count on my vigilance. You have my word.'

The king clasped Owain's hands firmly, experiencing the Bear's quiet energy. There was something about this man that matched the prophecies about his destiny. He could sense it from his touch - such power!

'Then I am content. Hengist is more of a threat than any civil strife. He stands against the sacred principles of kingship. If he succeeds, honour will disappear as quickly as the moon at dawn. Yet, there is more you should know before you make your stand, lord King. Those who stand for honour should not act from deceit.'

He sighed, rubbing a hand across his brow, unsure how to proceed. The lady's warnings about raising the issue of Artwerys were sound, but his own lack of integrity vexed him as much as the continued separation of himself from his only close blood kin. Now he had hinted at his own deception, the words would not come. The whole balance of the coming war might hinge on Tendubric's neutrality. If his admission tipped the scales, he stood fair to commit the British to disaster. Yet his destiny deemed the opposite.

'You are troubled, Owain. What deceit?' The Pendragon urged.

'It concerns your grandson, Artwerys, lord.' Owain began, finding the words elusive.

'Ah, the poor stripling. Eleven summers old and both parents dead. Still, Bronwen and I comfort him. He has Cynvelyn and Meurig and is well cared for. How is Artwerys a concern to you, Owain?'

'Both his parents are not dead, lord King. He is more than just named for me; he is Votadini blood. I am his father,' he blurted.

The weight of his confession lifted Owain's spirit. His secret burden burst into fragments.

'You defiled my daughter?' Tendubric exploded. His hand reached for his sword hilt.

Owain made no move.

'Not so, lord. You knew your daughter well and until this admission you thought well of me. Am I a man who would take a maiden against her wishes? Though we do not share a faith, our conduct is bound by honour. Creiddy saw my need for comfort. She promised me one night; one night we had. It was her gift, lord King.

Artwerys is born of love, but her honour was to marry Coel. She kept her promise.'

Naked sword in hand, Tendubric advanced. Owain felt the tip against his throat. The Pendragon's hand trembled. Still Owain made no move.

'If you place your beliefs above your daughter's kindness, then thrust it home. But don't believe that you do it for her. Hot anger compels your sword.'

Tendubric's arm wavered. Finally, with a groan, he flung the sword across the room. It clattered on the tiles. The noise brought white-cloaked sentries running, but the Pendragon dismissed them.

'You try me, Owain. I thought I knew the line between a king's judgement and God's.'

Owain said nothing, relieved that the Dragon had conquered his rage. The trickle of blood down his neck attested to how close he had come to pushing Tendubric past his discipline.

'I'll not speak in hot blood on this, Owain. My daughter's loss caused me much grief. Her mother grieves even now. You shall know our mind when my blood cools. This is a matter of honour between our two houses. I'll not change my position about where Gwent lies in the coming war. I am a King where Gwent is concerned, but a man in the matter of my grandson. We shall speak of this later.'

'I thank you for my life, lord King. I too grieve for her. I'll carry your pledge to Ambrosius. Your God be with you, Tendubric. You are all that stands against the Sais.'

Tendubric grunted. He retrieved and sheathed his sword. Awash with conflicting emotions he left Owain to rouse his warriors.

27 Glevum

459 AD - En Route to Glevum

When Ambrosius landed at Portus Adurni, Pascent ordered his host to march south. The High King, Leontinus and King Mark led six hundred and fifty cavalry; two thirds trained Commanipulares, and over 14,000 infantry.

Enniaun Girt marched out of Gwynedd under cover of darkness, to join forces with Ambrosius. The Votadini's four hundred horse and three thousand foot moved east before turning south to join the Roman at Glevum.

Pascent's dust-shrouded host reached its destination before the allies joined forces. He camped in a defensive position to the north of Glevum where the Severn narrowed. The river reflected the thousands arrayed along its banks. His best trained infantry and militia held the centre, dense formations of warriors on either side. King Mark took the right flank; Leontinus's mailed horse the left. Pickets were posted, scouts were sent out. Preparations complete, he waited.

The allies' strength lay in their experienced troops and the guile of their leaders. But, odds of two to one against, plus Pascent's excellent defensive position, troubled Ambrosius and Enniaun Girt when they met in the town of Glevum two days later.

'Where did he find them?' Enniaun queried. He gazed from the town parapet along the serried ranks of the men across the river. Ambrosius stared intently by his side.

'He's done well. I thought we'd be outnumbered, but not by so many,' the usurper replied.

'We'll have to out-fox him. He has numbers, but no leaders. Mark of Kernow is a pirate. Who holds the left; there's well equipped horse there?' Cunorix asked, shading his eyes against the sun. His query went unanswered.

'Well, he means to stand. We can't meet him head on. What shall we do?' Ambrosius asked. He tipped his helmet to the back of his head and gestured for wine. Ruffled by how much they had underestimated the loyalty of the British to their young king, the senior commanders gazed across the river. Their leader's question remained unanswered.

***

459AD - Ceint

Hengist marched North West with seven thousand warriors. Ambrosius would be taken from his undefended rear. The opportunity had arisen to eliminate the Saxons' real opposition. With the Votadini and Ambrosius defeated, the realm would be all but his. The young high king could not maintain a huge standing army for long. Hengist had great affection for Romans. They showed no tribal loyalty. Thirst for power was a magnificent weakness. Like grey wraiths in the twilight, his men marched to deal a hammer blow.

***

459 AD - South West of Glevum

Loegaire's advance party, five hundred Fianna, landed in a small west-coast village that still retained its link to a Scotti past. Two thousand warriors followed. Moonlight glittered from their spear points as they disembarked. Callum McGrall harboured the hope that his Ri Coiced would pit their forces against the Sais. Many nights' sleep had failed to erase the burning memory of his stand against Hengist's raiders. He had no clue to Loegaire's intentions. The Ri had not confided in him. Lucilla's pleas for assurance had also fallen on deaf ears. Though Loegaire led them into Britain, he had no clear strategy himself. Part of him queried why he was there at all.

Callum sent out patrols. Upon their information, it seemed, Loegaire would fashion his plans.

***

459 AD - South East of Glevum

Tendubric's men swept south east after crossing the Severn on Pascent's right flank. The Dragon wore a troubled frown as he rode his white charger at the head of his column. The red Draco standard of Gwent fluttered in the breeze. His companions were no less edgy.

'We could face the whole Saxon nation alone. Neither Ambrosius nor Pascent will be strong enough to stand against Hengist's hordes after they've torn themselves apart,' Cynvelyn broke the broody silence. He rode next to his brother, on his favourite bay. His serviceable armour and cloak enhanced his brother's magnificence.

'I agree. This is folly. Do we join Pascent and rid ourselves of Ambrosius or do we aid the usurper and scatter the Vortigerns for good? What say you, Meurig?'

Tendubric's son rode to his left. A frisky black stallion was the most inappropriate mount for the campaign, but his father allowed his son to learn from his own errors, except in religious matters.

'My eyes would be on Hengist, father. Not those kinsmen who squabble over a kingship. Were I in command, I'd be watching the Saxons.'

'He knows more about men than horses, doesn't he?' Tendubric laughed, punching his son on his mailed shoulder with a leather gloved fist. The stallion skittered again.

'Aye, brother. So he does. Well done, Meurig. We've crossed the river to do just that. Your father sent out scouts two days ago. If Hengist hopes to prosper from this madness, we're ready for him.'

'We're bold, father. I hope that the True Cross lives up to our faith if we do meet the Sais. They'll outnumber us if Hengist brings all his warriors.'

'He won't. Too near his harvest. And watch your tongue, Meurig. You know better than to doubt our faith. If we face Hengist, we shall do so in good heart. Let's hope that he's decided to let the British mend their differences.'

Behind the white, billowing tented shrine of the True Cross, mounted on a mule-drawn wagon, the trim, disciplined ranks of the Pendragon of Gwent and Siluria marched south east. The sun reflected from their white-crossed shields.

***

459 AD - Glevum

'If we don't deploy, lord, Pascent will gain advantage from our men's faltering morale,' Cunorix appealed. Enniaun and Ambrosius stared fixedly across the river.

'The Staff has the mind to solve this, Emrys, though it's daunting, even for him,' Enniaun said. He gestured Cunorix to be quiet. His brother paced, irked at the rebuke.

'Do you really believe that he can fashion a victory, Enniaun?'

'He lacks warrior skills. But the Angles curse him. You could do worse than consult him. How many of us have fought such numbers?'

The silence deepened. Senior commanders chafed with frustration, displeased by the impasse.

'Bring him. I'll listen to his advice,' Ambrosius ordered, drawing sighs of relief from his entourage.

The senior commanders made way for Edern. Owain, Elen, Ewein White-tooth and Cadwallon were with him, resplendent in battle gear.

'We meet again, Edern the Staff. Enniaun tells me you might unpick this lock for us,' Ambrosius greeted him.

'I've observed their position, lord. It's near impregnable. Even his untrained warriors would defeat an attempt at a river crossing. How many bows do you have, lord?'

'Two hundred. No doubt there are others who can use one. Why?'

'I'd seek them out. Place them on your right flank. We need as many shafts as the people of Glevum can fletch. Put your militia and Comitatus in the centre; token cavalry on each flank. Use peasants and townspeople to swell your numbers. Assure them, they won't fight. Hold the line here. Our advantage is in cavalry. I'd take four hundred horse across the river at night. Skirt their left flank and hit them hard. Your archers will pour volleys into the warriors across the river. It's a simple ruse, lord. Their left will crack and we'll press into the warriors weakened by your bowmen. They'll panic. The rest will be unsettled. Your infantry can then cross in safety.'

Ambrosius stared hard at Enniaun, who raised a grey bushy eyebrow.

'He has a general's eye. This Staff is a bold one, by God. Any questions?' Ambrosius asked.

The commanders looked on. None queried Edern's plan.

'Then we shall deploy as he suggests.'

Ambrosius rapped out commands. Edern and Owain rejoined their men.

'You learned well from the old man,' Owain said, as they mounted.

'It's nought compared to what you learned, Owain. Your knowledge is yet to be revealed. When it is, know that your Staff will stand beside you and not just in battle.'

When their eyes met, fleetingly, Owain was the first to turn away.

The one hundred newly-trained, heavily-mailed cavalry were divided into three squadrons; two of thirty and one of forty companions, led by Owain. They had perfected their tactics. The force was a mailed arrow with Owain's troop, the cutting head and his brothers' flank guards. Elen, Cunorix and Enniaun led traditional warrior cavalry. They sought advantage from the havoc wrought by the shock that their comrades created. Enniaun's initial reluctance to adopt his son's new tactics had been replaced by enthusiasm when he saw the results.

'Come, we have a battle to win,' Owain commanded. The Votadini cavalry, resplendant in gleaming mail, maroon cloaks billowing in the breeze, wheeled to join Ambrosius's yellow-plumed riders.

***

459 AD - South West of Glevum

'They're gathered in thousands on the north bank. Pascent waits for Emrys Wledig to act, but he dallies to the south of Glevum. He's outnumbered two to one by our reckoning.'

Loegaire thanked the scout.

'So, Callum. Pascent has the advantage. Shall we join him and take our prize?'

'Nothing's so easy, lord. We've been outnumbered more than once and prevailed. Numbers count for little in a major battle. You know it.'

A running warrior interrupted them, breathlessly trying to speak.

'Steady man. Kieron is it? Calm yourself,' Callum urged, lowering the exhausted warrior to the ground.

'Men to the west of us, lord.' he gasped.

'They'll be behind Ambrosius by morning. They have horse and trained troops. They're not Sais. Some six thousand in all,' Kieron blurted.

Callum called for water. He glanced at Loegaire.

'As you say, Callum. It's never as simple as it seems. What do you think? Allies for Emrys Wledig or a subterfuge by Pascent?'

'If Pascent had subtlety, he'd have stopped the Votadini and Emrys Wledig joining forces. I sense he's content to stand.'

'Then who marches south and why?'

'We should find out.'

'Are we to spend so much time scouting that we miss a battle, Callum? The lads are ripe for it. They'll fight all the harder over here than with their own back home.'

'You taught me that fighting with one eye shut was stupid, lord. Forgive me if I remind you of that lesson.'

Loegaire considered his commander's words.

'Aye, my spitfire. Lucilla'd not thank me for coming home on my shield for lack of knowledge about my opponent. Get a small patrol together; fastest runners. We'd better see who lurks to the south. We can catch them before dawn. Hurry now.'

***

459 AD - South East of Glevum

Pascent's camp fires pricked the darkness and cascades of sparks rose into the warm night. His men slept in comfort. Some sought solace from guardian angels in their dreams; others twitched fitfully, locked in nightmarish battles.

Loegaire's reconnaissance patrol caught up with Tendubric's slowly moving column well before dawn. They tracked the men of Gwent for a further three miles. It was still too dark to identify them. Finally, Tendubric's force halted.

'If we wait until full light, we'll have little chance of bringing up the warriors,' Callum whispered.

Loegaire panted. Though he trained regularly with his men, swift running had taken its toll.

The clouds lifted again. Silver gleamed briefly. A warrior grabbed Callum's arm and pointed.

'There lord, see. White crosses on their shields.'

Callum saw the crosses briefly before the clouds closed in again.

'It's the Dragon of Gwent, lord. Tendubric heads this force.'

'Tendubric was at my wedding. There's none more honourable. Let's see what he's about. Come, keep your weapons in your belts. We don't want to alarm them,' Loegaire commanded.

His men rose from hiding and followed his confident strides towards the Dragon's column.

The Pendragon of Gwent was suddenly roused from a quiet night march by scouts to his front bringing him news. The Saxons had been sighted, on a course that would bring them into confrontation by mid-morning. Excitement filtered through his ranks. On his right flank his men assembled defensively. He could hear their cries as they hurried to position themselves.

'What's the alarm?' he asked. Meurig spurred the black into a tight turn, galloping down the column to investigate. He returned with a small knot of warriors at his heels. Tendubric peered down from his horse.

'It's the Scotti Overking, father; Loegaire. He says he is known to you,' Meurig reported.

'That he is; that he is. What are you doing so far from your shores?' the Dragon asked of the dark-haired bard king.

'If I knew that, I'd know what God knows,' Loegaire replied. 'I came to aid Pascent against Ambrosius, but he has numbers enough. I wonder if the provinces he promised me are worth the trouble I'll have holding them. I'm here to reconnoitre. What do you intend, lord?'

'To protect Britain against the Saxons. You'd think Hengist a thief to steal what he can from this civil war, wouldn't you? He's on the march. I'll stand against him. My kinsmen are as brainless as those massacred by the Sais. They now seek to kill each other.'

'Why not join Pascent or Ambrosius? Your forces would make the difference.'

'Who would stop Hengist? We fight under the True Cross to bloody these Sais.'

'You march under the True Cross?' Loegaire gasped.

'It's in the shrine on yonder wagon,' Tendubric replied.

'Might we have the privilege of seeing it?'

'You may. It's sacred to all. Meurig, take Loegaire and his men to the shrine,' the Dragon commanded.

The first shards of grey dawn lightened the sky. Loegaire reached the wagon. The guards stepped aside, allowing Meurig to pull aside the curtain. Loegaire's men watched in hushed reverence as the pin-pricks of dawn alighted on the bejewelled cross-piece of the Holy Relic.

'Would you have thought it, Callum? We marched for reward, yet we are blessed with such a sight,' Loegaire gasped.

His men stood in silent awe.

'May we touch it for its blessing?' Loegaire asked, reverently.

'You may,' Meurig replied.

Each in turn approached the relic. They touched its surface, murmuring quiet prayers. Loegaire was the last. He removed his mailed glove and stretched his long musician's fingers in a gentle caress of the cross.

'Of all the tales I'll tell my sons, this will be the best, Callum,' he sighed.

They emerged from the shrine to the full dawn. The birdsong rose to a powerful crescendo as the sun's red rim arced above the horizon. Loegaire shivered. Tendubric witnessed their rapture when they rejoined the head of the column.

'You'll join us to break our fast? We'll eat here, then find a place to meet Hengist,' he said.

'We shall be honoured, Dragon lord. My men are at your service,' Loegaire offered.

'You're welcome, Scotti king. See, Meurig, you believed we'd be outnumbered, but the Lord brings us aid in the form of these good Scotti men.'

Meurig was silent. His father did seem to have God's ear.

'Send runners, Callum. Take this ring as authority for the men to march south east until they reach us. Tell them to make haste, but not enough to tire them. We'll be fighting before the day is out.'

Callum passed the ring to his fastest runner.

'Now, my lord Dragon. Let's find a place to tan these Saxon wolves' hides. I've one who would give much gold to face Hengist,' Loegaire said.

Callum McGrall smiled grimly.

'That I would, lord. That I would.'

***

459 AD - Glevum

Ambrosius's forces deployed in the amber glow of morning sun to the north east of Glevum. Commanded by Gwyrangon and Cundig, they flew the white horse banner of Enniaun Girt and the eagle of Ambrosius alongside the standards of Anderida, Strathcluta and Glevum. Skilled bowmen were swelled by a further two hundred archers, each with two full quivers thanks to the skills of the town's fletchers.

Pascent believed that all his enemies opposed him across the river. But Ambrosius had used night as a curtain to cross upstream stealthily. Secreted in sparse woodland to the north-east of Pascent's left flank, they watched their own men settle into their battle ranks across the river.

'They look a bonny lot,' Enniaun enthused proudly. The Votadini's white horse banner streamed and flapped next to the green Draco of Anderida. His son's Bear standard was raised alongside the town colours of Glevum and the dark blue cross of Strathcluta.

'Now, Edern,' Ambrosius tightened his helmet strap. 'Shall we advance?'

'We may, lord. Their flank scouts have been silenced. With your permission, I'll rejoin Owain.'

'Do so, Staff. You plan well.'

Edern watched the dark mass of flying arrows across the river.

'Quickly, my lord. We must press our advantage.' He turned his mount to Owain's side.

Ambrosius rode at the head of his own troops with Theoderic and Seconius in support. Enniaun, Cunorix, Elen and Owain led the Votadini squadrons at a purposeful canter towards the unsuspecting flank of Pascent's army. The dust swirled about them, cloying mouths and noses.

Pascent panicked at the arrow storm.

'They're just shooting us down,' he screamed. Each time the bowmen bent their elbows, more of his men fell dead or wounded. The archers avoided the better-trained militia. Discipline among the less-ordered warriors was more easily weakened by the stinging missiles. Circular shields were inadequate protection against the persistent volleys. Groans rose from the heaps of wounded.

'What can we do?' Pascent shouted, his face purple.

'Withdraw them out of bow shot, lord,' King Mark advised.

'No. He wants you to do that. He'd gain the space he needs to cross. If you pull back, it must be the whole line,' Leontinus countered.

'Damn it. Can no one deal with this? Our men are being shot to pieces out there,' the High King raged.

A messenger yelled urgently.

'My lord. The left flank reports enemy cavalry.'

Leontinus leaped into action.

'Sound tactics. They have us watching a few bowmen, when our whole flank is threatened. Time to earn my reward, lord. By your command?'

He waited for Pascent's gesture. At the High King's half-hearted wave, he galloped to join his men. This was his whole destiny. The thrill crept from his loins through his whole body. He turned their heads to the east.

***

459 AD - South East of Glevum

At mid-morning Hengist's warriors halted abruptly, their path blocked by the white cloaks of Gwent and Siluria in battle order. He turned to his sons. 'How many?' he asked.

Octha eyed the Pendragon's line.

'About six thousand foot, half trained, half warriors,' he growled, tapping his francisca against his shield.

'Agreed, son. Your eye's improving. Then there's the horse,' Hengist added.

'They have the ground too,' Ebissa observed.

'We can see that,' Hengist thundered.

Ebissa scowled. Rhonwen said nothing. Her soulless eyes stared at the hill.

'We'll not reach Guoloph if we've to cut a path through this lot,' Octha said.

'They're a crafty bunch. One force meets us, while two others prepare to slaughter each other. I'll never understand them,' Hengist replied.

'It's Tendubric of Gwent, father. They're as able as they look; we shouldn't take them lightly,' Octha advised.

'Should we take them at all?' Hengist muttered.

'Well, if we pull the old Dragon's teeth, the entire south west will be open,' Octha gestured with his seax at the silent ranks.

'Assemble the war band leaders, son; we'll take counsel,' Hengist ordered.

Rhonwen stood like a statue; her eyes blazed with battle lust as they took in the white crosses. Ebissa thrust his gar into the earth and leaned on it. He did not smile.

***

'Well, do we fight or not?' Loegaire queried. He watched the Saxon deliberations from the low hill in the centre of Tendubric's line.

'If your men were hidden in that small wood to our right, I doubt they'd attack' Tendubric said.

'They'll be here soon enough, lord King. They run like our wolf-hounds and they'd love to pluck those peacocks.'

'No doubt they would. It's a long way to run half across Britain without a fight, Loegaire. Yet I fear they may be too late.'

The Dragon's prophesy rang true. Saxon warriors ran to their positions. Hengist had taken his son's advice.

'You wished to fight on British soil; choose your place,' Tendubric boomed, urging his horse to join his bodyguard.

Loegaire caught Callum's eye.

'Where do we stand?' he asked.

'Wherever Hengist will be; the centre I'd guess.'

Tendubric's Comitatus dressed sideways to make way for the wild warriors. Callum was helmetless in the Irish fashion. His padded tunic was worn over a silk undershirt, a material which aided the healers in the treatment of injuries. It was pushed into the wound by a sword or spear thrust, protecting the wearer from infection. His purple silk cloak was tied up between his legs to the leather battle harness, his minimal armour. He had a gold torc at his throat and wristbands of boiled leather. His sole weapon was a two-foot short sword in his right hand and he carried a circular buckler, much smaller than the British shields, in his left. Loegaire was similarly dressed, but wore no cloak over the plain black tunic that he favoured in both peace and war.

The Saxon wyrdmen whirled and howled. Their naked figures, striped white in dried clay, hair matted in grease, traversed the warrior lines, inciting their comrades to battle frenzy.

Rhonwen had no need of them. She stood ahead of her own warband of Frisian youngbloods. There was no inspiration more potent than her god-touched madness. They would follow her if she charged stone walls.

'He'll not be subtle about it.' Tendubric said.

He despatched Meurig and Cynvelyn to the flanks.

'Wait for a break somewhere. Then get the cavalry in amongst them,' were his only orders.

'Now, Scotti king, we'll see if our dragon scales shatter these wolves' teeth, eh?' he called. The Ri Coiced raised his sword, his eyes roving across the line of approaching Sais.

The Saxon war bands came on at a gentle trot. Their shamen wheeled and pivoted, casting spells of fear and disquiet on the ranks of the waiting Comitatus.

'Put your faith in the True Cross. Their gibberish is no match for faith in our Lord,' Tendubric hollered over the din of the enemy's approach.

The disciplined, trained infantry, backed by Tendubric's militia, waited their moment. Their yellow plumes danced in the light breeze, the sun reflecting brilliantly from the bold white crosses on their black shields. The Saxons ground relentlessly towards them. Tendubric's officers judged the distance that separated the two forces. When the Saxons reached the incline and prepared their missile storm, the Pendragon dropped his raised sword. His men responded: *'For the cross, Gwent and the Dragon.'* They charged down the slope. Flanked by the select men of his Fianna, Loegaire, Ri Coiced of the Scotti, ran with them.

The Saxons paused briefly. They believed that the British would stand. Seeing the leather-clad line rushing towards them, they hurled franciscas and angons. The missiles tore gaping holes in the Dragon's most experienced men. Limbs were split; heads cleaved. Eyes aflame, Rhonwen urged her men into a frenzied assault. With her hoarse, rasping cry *'A Seax, A Seax,'* she led them to a gap in the British line.

The two forces crashed together, a dancing, weaving tangle of whirling swords, stabbing spears and clashing shields. Cries of fear, pain and exultation reached the ears of those on either side who had not yet engaged.

The momentum of the British halted the Saxon shield wall in most of the affray. Only Rhonwen's impassioned collision with the weak spot in Tendubric's line carried her men into the ranks of the British militia. Here, she whirled in a crazed dance of death, slashing, stabbing and thrusting. Inspired by her assault, her men carved out an alarming space to the watching Tendubric. The Saxon red, ox-hide shields spread like a slow blood stain across the body of the British forces.

Loegaire and his Fianna fought as ably as their trained allies. They were more agile, less inclined to fight as a body, but in the manner of ancient champions, man to man. Their personal skill with arms was more than a compensation for their lack of discipline and their minimal armour. Loegaire and Callum fought side by side, executing moves they had rehearsed many times. Loegaire's movements had the same rhythm as his music. His strokes flowed. His body moved like that of a dancer. The Sais had no time to applaud. With his economic, calculated style Callum was less fluid. As they cleared a space to their front, Saxon warriors gave ground.

Loegaire sensed the uncertainty among Tendubric's warriors as Callum neatly despatched an incautious Saxon, whose gar was deflected by the small round shield and his neck slashed through by a measured swing of the short sword.

'They're making ground to our left, Callum. Pull the men to us. Let's see what we can do.'

Callum rallied the ten Fianna, who still stood. Tendubric oversaw the seething ocean of men from the top of a knoll. His entire flank wavered. The reserve Saxon warbands watched the progress of their battle-maiden with anticipation. When they advanced, Tendubric knew it would be tough to hold his left.

He bellowed to his standard bearer and to the driver of the True Cross's shrine. 'We'll move to stiffen them.'

He kicked his horse into a gallop, his white cloak and hair flowing behind him. Gwent's red Draco standard ballooned above his bodyguard.

In the centre, the press was so closely packed that it was difficult to breathe, let alone fight. Hengist felt the battle was going his way. He could sense British nervousness. Yellow plumes that had been a sea at the first charge were now but ripples. He was into their militia, whose numbers were greater, but whose armour and resolve were less. The multi-coloured silks of his warriors splashed a riot of colour in a patchwork across the throng. Rhonwen's blood shields ground relentlessly on.

Tendubric rallied his militia. Loegaire reached the knot of British who stood against Rhonwen's whirlwind. He would have engaged her, but Callum held his sword across his king's body.

'No lord; God marks this task for me. It was not yourself who saw his villagers slaughtered and enslaved by these heathen. I've waited long for this.'

Loegaire made to countermand his Ri Feinnidh's claim and pushed the sword away. But, he thought better of it when he looked into Callum's eyes. Memories were painted there for anyone with compassion to see.

'Then make amends, Callum. This battle rests on stopping this damned woman. And keep yourself safe. We have three fifths of the land to take at home. I'd only manage two without you.' He grinned broadly. His boyish artist's face, slick with perspiration, beamed out from under a warrior's brow.

Callum smiled dourly.

'I'll do my best, lord. Now Kieran, Barry and Donal. See to it that my lord is well protected, should I fall against this demon.'

He turned to face Rhonwen.

She had paused, breathing deeply to recover from her exertions. The militia had given way before her. Dead, dying and wounded were strewn at her feet like slaughtered chickens. Her men were at her back, eager for victory.

'Who is it that I must send to God to win this day?' Callum's clear tones floated to her ears above her victims' groans.

'I am Rhonwen, daughter of Hengist, soon to be King of Britain,' she rasped defiantly. She wiped a hand across her dried, cracked lips: 'And I'll not be meeting your God today, nor any.'

'Hengist's daughter,' Callum whispered. 'Thank you father, for your justice,' he added, staring to the heavens.

'Your dead God won't help you. If there's aught in your obscene beliefs, it's to your hell you'll be going,' Rhonwen spat. She whirled to attack without warning.

She held the long cutting sword of her people in her right hand, with a shorter seax in her left. She was mailed to her knees in a byrnie, now a dull, red brown with the dried blood of past victims. Her weapons were blurred arcs. It seemed that Callum would be slashed asunder by the human windmill who scythed towards him. His quick judgement allowed him one economic side-step at the last, taking her downward knife arc on his buckler. She wheeled, fuming and screamed at him in rage. Impassively, he returned the black look from her demented eyes. He wrinkled his nose. She smelled of decay.

She slashed again. Once more he moved late. Her flailing sword stung him across his left upper arm. Blood welled crimson through his woollen tunic.

She flashed him a scornful grimace. Bared yellow teeth sneered.

'See, Scotti. Your God really did die on his dead wood. Hell awaits your soul.'

'You fight better than you talk,' Callum replied quietly.

He ignored the burning pain that lanced up his wounded arm. He moved for the first time; quickly for a man of his bulk. The manoeuvre surprised her. She believed him too wounded to attack.

He thrust his shield at her body, forcing her to back away. He swung the short sword against her left hand. The solid thud sent judders up his arm, as the blade connected. She cried with pain. Her seax dropped to the ground. When he backed away to appraise the damage, she clutched her wounded hand to her mouth. Blood flowed from a shattered wrist.

'Your gods desert you too,' he chided.

Anguish drove the demons from her mind. Rhonwen looked around, aware for the first time since she had charged the British line. A dull confused glaze replaced her bright fury. She half turned to her men, her mouth twisted in agony.

Callum struck. His wounded arm bled profusely and his shield would soon weigh too heavily, small though it was. He covered the ground between them in three swift strides and plunged his sword through the mail of her left side. If she saw the warning in her own followers' eyes, she failed to make sense of it. She turned to Callum and gazed in astonished detachment at the protruding sword. Agony forged flimsy spans of reason between her battle lust and the blank, empty madness, which had replaced it.

Her smile was born on fleeting flashes of coherence; a silent thanks for her release. She fell back into the arms of her shocked companions.

Hengist considered the gods' ruling on his prior conduct as victory slipped away from him. He heard the dismayed yells of his own men to his left. Loegaire's two thousand warriors swarmed to support the Dragon's forces. He was now outnumbered here by over two to one. To his centre right, where Rhonwen had carved her bloody path, a sudden exultation exploded from the British. A groan ran through the Saxon ranks.

Hengist ordered a retreat. Though he had eliminated the Dragon's best troops, the advantage had been lost. He sensed his daughter's death. He was now in a perilous position. He had no way of knowing how many Scotti there were. There would be other days, but for now, the challenge was to minimise his losses. The Dragon held the field and the victory. The gods had claimed their debt.

***

459AD - Glevum

Stricken by indecision, the High King panicked. Pascent watched Leontinus deploy his outnumbered cavalry to defend against the onrushing enemy. His warriors sprouted shafts from the archers across the river. Their morale had all but ebbed.

Leontinus resolved to buy time. If he could halt the first charge, he believed that Hengist's arrival would force Ambrosius to retreat. Ecstatic, the running wolf launched his men at the advancing horsemen.

Ambrosius pitted Owain's new cavalry against Pascent's unsettled infantry. When the first wave of enemy cavalry thundered to meet them, Ambrosius galloped to intercept them. Elen and Cunorix charged with him. Skirting the two forces, Enniaun led the remainder towards the awaiting infantry, now distressed by the sight of such strange horsemen.

Leontinus and Ambrosius were re-united in combat. Horses whinnied; dust rose in clouds to choke their riders. Though less in number, the wolf's men gained the initial advantage from their better armour; Ambrosius's men were repelled.

Two snaked lines of cavalry entwined in a bloody melee. Through the dust clouds, Enniaun could not see clearly. He urged his own men into action. Owain, Edern, Ewein and Cadwallon formed the wedge formations they had practised while Enniaun's horsemen supported their flanks.

'Best get on with it, son. There's your target. I'll be right behind you. Now ride.'

He spurred his grey into a canter. His men followed the raised sword and red cloak. The white running horse standard unfurled to whip in the breeze.

Owain glanced at his Staff and his brothers.

'For Britain, for Ambrosius and the Votadini,' he bellowed, and rode hard for Pascent's flank. Behind him the cry went up as the ground quivered.

'Arth-Ursus, Arth-Ursus.'

In a tight wedge, Owain's mailed arrow struck at the heart of Pascent's warriors. Had they had the brvery to stand, they would have been smashed by the shock of the new terror, but their resolve deserted them. The more courageous turned to meet the attack, but most were already breaking ranks to run when the Bear's horsemen reached them. Enniaun followed immediately. Pascent's first lines fell like skittles and the remainder dropped their weapons and fled. Four and a half thousand warriors streamed away in confusion.

Seeing the carnage across the river, Gwyrangon ordered the infantry forward. The allied Comitatus waded the river towards the gap where Pascent's warriors had stood.

A more experienced commander than Pascent would have used his superior numbers to plug the gap. But the sight of his cavalry lost in a dust storm and his warriors racing from the field, broke his resolve. Calling for the retreat, he fled.

The cavalry engagement was a blood-bath. Neither side could see clearly. In the thick of combat, Ambrosius's men barely held Leontinus's wolves.

Elen was embroiled in the mass of twisting horses and desperate men. Owain's insistence that she ride with the supporting horse left her fighting for her life.

She used her sword deftly. Opposing warriors presented few opportunities with their strong shields and mail byrnies. Their metal helmets, made it difficult to find a clear mark. The horses were easier targets. Her men changed their tactics. One by one, the wolves were unhorsed. Leontinus foresaw the consequences. His men would be reduced to fighting on foot.

'Break off. Retreat,' he shouted.

He could not understand what had happened to Hengist. Ambrosius should have left the field. Fuming, he reached down to assist one of his men, and changed his mind when an opponent struck at the neck of his horse.

He parried the stroke, deflecting the blow with his shield. Wheeling his horse away, he met his opponent's eyes. 'Give way, Elen. I've no wish to fight you,' he shouted.

'You've chosen your ground Leontinus; now defend it,' Elen spat. She urged her horse forward.

He met her renewed assault. All round him, his men broke away to rescue unhorsed comrades. Ambrosius attacked with vigour. Leontinus realised that his plans had gone badly wrong.

He had to escape quickly or he would be surrounded. Setting his jaw in a determined line, he reluctantly sized Elen up for a decisive stroke.

He leaned into her attack and pushed his wolf-shield against hers. A sword stroke spliced through her helmet's cheek guard and she moaned in pain as blood exploded from beneath the helm. Swaying in the saddle, clutching her hands to her face, she fell from her horse.

Leontinus spared her one look before racing after his retreating men. Behind him, he heard the victors' cheers. Despite his artful schemes, Ambrosius Emrys Wledig, and not he, had a hand on the High Kingship of Britain.

***

459 AD - Lindum

A solitary rider on a bay mare pulled his cloak hood further forward to shelter his head against the steady autum downpour. The road was already wintry. Mud, puddles and ruts tested the animal's patience as it picked its way delicately.

Smoke from a local inn's fire rose through the roof and hung lazily grey in the damp air. The rider dismounted, tied his horse to a rail and sought sanctuary in the tavern.

He was scrutinised by the locals. In spring and summer travellers used the roads, but when autumn nights drew in, people kept to their own villages after harvest.

The slavey tended to his order. Curious, the proprietor detached himself from the knot of regulars and served wine to the traveller. 'I hope your coin is good to be asking for best wine. We're not used to strangers at this time of year,' he said, mid-way between surliness and cautious welcome.

'My purse is full,' was the reply.

Coins rattled on the table.

'One of royal blood was buried near here last spring. Do you know where?' the stranger asked.

The inn-keeper bit hard on a coin. Satisfied, he replied.

'Aye, the poor soul left from this very inn on the night he died, lord,' he said, bestowing title on the visitor, now his purse conferred it.

'Dori'll show you, lord, when you've supped. Just tell her when you want to go. It's a foul night, lord. If you sit by the fire, I'll feed you a strong mutton broth and bread. There's chicken if you want it. We have one good room spare. You'd be best served leaving in the morning.'

The stranger smiled. Any trade was a bonus to the inn-keeper. Ordinary folks worked hard to live in these marshy Lindum fenlands.

'You're persuasive, inn-keeper. I accept. It will be good to get out of these wet clothes and spend an evening by your fire. Ensure that my food is hot. I need my horse for riding, though I could eat her, I'm so hungry.'

The rain had stopped the following morning. Clouds, splintered by watery sunshine, sped fast in a brisk north-westerly. Dori walked at the mare's head until she stopped at the roadside by the small village church. She pointed towards the graveyard. The rider eased himself from his saddle and hitched his russet cloak above his ankles to avoid the puddles.

Dori waited by the horse and watched the stranger moving among the graves until he stopped, head bowed.

'You made a better job of it than I, brother. But we couldn't walk in his footsteps, could we? Rest easy in this marshy land. I doubt they'll know where I lie either, when my time comes. Sleep well, brother. Farewell.'

He prayed silently, and then retraced his steps to the gate. He handed Dori a bag of silver coins.

'For as long as these last, girl, make sure the grave is kept. I'd like prayers said every year on the anniversary of his death. Will you do this?'

Dori took the bag, feeling the weight. There was enough coin to keep the grave for generations.

'We're honest folk, lord. I'll do your bidding, never fear.'

She thrust the bag out of sight inside her dress.

He hoisted his weight slowly into the saddle. He turned the mare's head to the north and raised his hand in a departing salute. Pascent, the last of the Vortigerns, had kept his pledge to his dead brother.

28. Rome's Star

459 AD - Viroconium, Powys

Messengers had ridden to Gwynedd urging Ceri, Gwawl and other Votadini to hurry south to Powys.

The ride was made with mixed emotions. Victory had been gained with few losses; Edern's plan had worked smoothly. But, they reckoned without Leontinus's stiff resistance.

Elen was carried barely conscious, her head swathed in bloody bandages. The sword cut had opened the left side of her face from her forehead to her neck. Without Filan and Crenda's dedication, the Votadini would have grieved, but Filan would not reassure them about her fate. The druid had given of himself on the return journey from Glevum. Grey lines of fatigue marked his dedication and Crenda too was exhausted. Owain was full of self-recrimination. All his efforts to protect Elen had come to naught.

Ambrosius gave personal instructions for her care when they reached the High King's villa.

In the days that followed, she hovered, a gull, born on updrafts and downward spirals. Gwawl and Ceri joined her attendants. Filan's arts were tested to the full to stave off death's stalking. There were times when her heartbeat sounded as weak as the patter of a spring shower. At such times, Ceri's wailing assailed their ears.

Finally, the druid's skills, coupled with the love of those surrounding her, rescued her from the abyss. She recovered, slowly at first, but then more quickly. Edern was constantly at her bed side, sleeping fitfully on the floor beside her and refusing to leave. Finally, an exasperated Filan assured him that she was out of danger and urged him to seek his own bed.

Roman administration returned to Britain. Emrys Wledig restored the traditions of the imperium to resolve the chaos that Brittu and Pascent had left behind. Time was the watchdog of their efforts as they prepared for further threats from Hengist's hordes. All knew that the storm would gather again.

Ambrosius was summoned to the villa walls several days after their arrival, to witness a tiny cavalcade approaching from the south. He identified the white crosses of the Pendragon of Gwent as the troop rode in.

In the room where he had chastised Vitalus at the beginning of the Vortigerns' reign, Tendubric exchanged tales with Cynvelyn, Meurig and Loegaire.

'I didn't know you battled with Hengist,' Ambrosius told him.

'It seems I am in debt to you as well as my own supporters for this exalted position. And you, Loegaire, you who came to fight against us. My heartfelt thanks.'

'Ah, what's the gain of two provinces in this tortured land, lord King? My grandsons will hear of conquered lands a plenty, but to hear that their grandfather was blessed by touching the holy cross - now there's a thing.'

Tendubric rose.

'We have kept to our lands, Ambrosius. On the first count because of the Vortigerns' perfidy; on the second because of our church. We know the pontiff in Rome supports you. This makes us sad. If Hengist was weaker, you'd be asked to war on us. Rome believes our heresy far more dangerous than the Pelagians.'

'This Roman Christianity is strange, Ambrosius. The Roman god is dangerous. It demands allegiance to rules, pomp and splendour. It serves as a bastion of Roman power. Now that the military can no longer hold the empire, fear will be re-assembled afresh in men's minds. This was not the way. He would have been rid of the Roman yoke, just as he would have been rid of the temple that bound his people to its priests' demands. He wished for an end to external gods so people could find their own way. If you hold the Roman view, Ambrosius, we must be as wary of you, as of Hengist's pagans.'

'Hengist won't settle for the lands he holds. We can defend ourselves now, but that may not always be so. I offer you a treaty of mutual aid. We'll help you in any future campaign against the Sais. If we're attacked, we hope you'll support us. Our only condition is your oath that you'll not take arms against Gwent and Siluria at Rome's behest. How say you? '

'I'm not your enemy. Our religious views mustn't stand in the way of unity against the Sais, Tendubric. I shall honour your treaty. Hengist will meet a united people. What we can do together, we shall, and respect our differences. I'll not use the title, High King, Pendragon. You will be the only dragon among the British. We shall not forget we owe our success to you. Who has true knowledge? I don't, and I don't intend to persecute others.'

The two eyed each other across the table. Tendubric smiled in acceptance. Thankful for his new ally, Ambrosius moved on.

'Now. This realm of Powys is too great a land for myself. I have no wife and no offspring. I propose to cede Powys to the Votadini, in exchange for their northern kingdom of Gwynedd. Dinas Ffynon is a fitting place for my residence; I've had too much luxury. Do you agree?'

Enniaun was taken aback.

'I accept, lord. As long as those Votadini families who are settled in your realm can stay.'

'I'd be pleased to have them. I'll not lack for recruits.'

'Now, there is another to be rewarded. Gwyrangon, who rallied extra spears to our cause at Glevum. Your lands of Anderida are restored and the lands of Dumnonia, the most affluent in the realm are yours. Hengist envies them. I might not be doing you any favours. But...' 'I accept, lord,' Gwyrangon interposed. 'You took me in when I fled in fear of Vitalus. I owe you for your kindness. I shall hold Dumnonia for you.'

Ambrosius nodded.

'Owain Arth-Ursus, our most capable field commander, will you hold the north for me? The Angles are wary of you. The title 'Dux Britannicus' is yours. You have command of the forces of Elmet, Rheged and Eboracum.'

Owain bowed. He kept an eye on Tendubric when Rheged was mentioned. It touched on the unresolved legacy of Artwerys. The Pendragon kept his peace. 'Gladly, lord. My sword is yours.'

'And you, Edern, the Staff, architect of our victory. You, I want at my side. I offer you a position in my personal household.'

Edern stuttered, but composed himself. 'Thank you, lord, but my destiny is twinned with that of Owain Arth-Ursus. Whatever the future holds casts its net over us both. My advice will be ever yours to command, but my place is with Owain. I shall accompany him to the north, if it pleases you.'

'Spoken like a loyal friend, Edern. Go with our thanks and a gift from the treasury of Powys.'

The formalities complete, Ambrosius gestured for them to celebrate the new order of Britain with feasting and song.

***

Owain stood alone as the revels rang out through the central hall of Viroconium. Out here on the town's ramparts, the breeze had blown up. It caught his maroon cloak, exposing the white tunic beneath. Unlike those who feasted inside, he was unadorned. A simple bronze clasp fastened the cloak, a leather belt at his waist boasted no jewelled buckle. He stared into the heavens, lost in the mass of stars.

A shimmer of white, ghostly in the sputtering torches, drew his attention.

'We have matters to settle, Owain Arth-Ursus,' the even voice of Tendubric reached his ears.

He turned to greet the Pendragon. 'I pledged I would abide by your judgement, my lord,' he sighed.

'Rest easy, Owain. My blood is cooler tonight. Bronwen and I agree. Our faith bids us recognise you as the sire of Artwerys. Megan confirms your claim. If it is his wish, we shall not prevent Artwerys joining you. There is the matter of Rheged's succession. Artwerys is Coel's rightful heir.'

'I have no claim to Votadini Kingship; still less that of Rheged. Let Cynvelyn accede. He deserves compensation for my grandfather's usurpation of Gwynedd. I wish only to be father of Artwerys and for you to be his grandparents.'

'Owain, do we not weave an impossible cloth?'

'I hope my son will share my destiny rather than my lands. In truth, I have none. Remember, Britain is my land. I shall be king of none of it.'

'Then we shall put it to him, Owain. His will shall be honoured. Here, my hand on it.'

They clasped hands firmly.

'Thank you for your generosity, lord. I acknowledge the great hurt I have done you.'

'Staying my hand was no act of kindness, Owain. It was not for me to judge.'

'Then we can be civil with one another?'

'Aye, as civil as I am able,' Tendubric growled.

***

I walked out of the feast. Owain was missing. By the door of his room I called his name, but there was no answer. Curious, I pushed the door ajar. The room was empty. I walked through the quiet villa to the stables. All were celebrating. Had Hengist wished to repeat his massacre, he would have found it easy tonight. Bran stood alert, despite the labours of the past few days. The stall beside his was empty; Cobyl had taken his master into the night. It was the first time that I felt the weight of Owain's destiny. How it separated him from his family and friends. Sighing with the distance it created between us, I turned. The hour was late, but I wanted to call in on Elen.

She was alone. Filan said sleep was the best medicine for her recovery, now she had cheated the reaper.

I paused by her bed. Her hair shone copper red across her pillow in the moonlight. The side of her face was still bandaged. Poultices protected against decay, so the wound might heal cleanly.

Her sound eye opened as I made to leave.

'Edern. Do the celebrations go well?' her husky voice asked.

'They miss your presence, lady. I thought to watch you sleep awhile. It's more joyous to me than drinking wine.'

'Your joy will be short lived when these bandages are off, Staff.' The womanliness she had sacrificed to be a warrior, seemed reborn.

'Many bear wounds, lady. My joy is that you live. It doesn't matter how you look.'

'You're a liar.'

Her voice trembled.

'There's more to us now than a gawping boy's lust,' I said. 'One scar changes nothing. I've loved you since I first saw you. I'll not leave you now'

'You won't find me desirable,' she persisted.

'You should have a snake as a device. You twist words to suit your mood. Of course you're desirable.'

'You'll change.'

I laughed. She was so transparent. 'Then you can call me Edern the fickle. Goodnight, my lady, sleep well.'

I retraced my steps to the door.

'Goodnight, Edern,' she whispered. 'Goodnight.'

***

459 AD - On the road to Dinas Ffynon

It was a hard two-day ride from Viroconium to Dinas Ffynon. Yet the stars still arched the sky when his nose twitched at the smell of woodsmoke. Cobyl whickered, flaring his nostrils at the scent. The woodsman's hut beckoned. An amber glow from the fire inside escaped through cracks into the starlit clearing. The oak's huge branches waved a gentle greeting as Cobyl halted.

She was placing fresh logs on the fire when he pushed open the door.

'You have won a great victory Arth-Ursus. Why do you not celebrate it?'

The question was brusque, yet her smile was inviting. She gestured for him to sit at the table. A black cooking pot was suspended over the flames. She spooned a rich broth into a plain bowl and set it before him, adding bread and a jug of ale. He slumped wearily to a low stool.

'Tendubric's was the real triumph. Hengist could have taken the whole realm.'

'Now Ambrosius governs, you have time to rebuild. Be thankful for it. Remember, your concern is not just politics. You now have the space to fulfil your true destiny.'

'You plague me with it, lady. Am I never to be free of it?' he asked. 'I came here because my kin celebrate. I feel distant from them. If I speak of my destiny, their eyes cloud. They think me crazed.'

She nodded, knowingly. He wondered how many times she had attended to one such as he. Her silence soothed him. She sat by the fireside, her pale complexion reddened by the flames.

'I will think on it, lady; never fear. If I do not, it will catch me unawares as Lailoken insisted. I have put it aside, too caught up in battle to dwell on it. Now is the time to see what can be done. I might start with my own following. Though they ride together, they bicker and taunt each other when they are idle. If I cannot unite them, what chance have I to fulfil my destiny? And then there is my son. I must face him while our swords are sheathed.'

His reward was a warm smile.

'Remember, I am here to guide you, Arth-Ursus. No doubt Lailoken would have urged you to begin with small challenges. There is the seed of some great oak in the acorn of your own band. That is good. Your son is a greater task.' Her smile waned.

'Your mortal being will be tested, Arth-Ursus. Those marked for destiny are flesh and blood, nonetheless. At such times, you must come to me. Your oath that you will.'

'More tests. What kind of tests?'

'All kinds that beset mortals, Arth-Ursus. Gwawl spoke to you of such matters. Though you steel yourself against the life of a common man, the burden will become heavy. At your most vulnerable, you will need me.'

He stopped eating, a piece of broth-dipped bread half way to his mouth.

'You would be my mistress, lady?' he asked.

She shook her head, her dark tresses reflecting shining umber in the fireglow.

'Much more than that, lord,' she smiled. 'You'll take some comfort from the pleasures of the bed, small though it is,' she nodded mischievously in the direction of the room's only other door.

He chewed the bread thoughtfully.

'Filan taught me that an oath was a powerful thing. He said there's power in names. Oaths shouldn't be declared to the nameless. How can I give you an oath when I don't know you?'

Her smile vanished. 'Your tutor was wise. I forget how much lore the druids know.'

'Why so reluctant, lady? Does your name carry so much power?'

'Your destiny is challenge enough, without complications from me.'

'Lailoken gave his name freely? He had power.'

She sighed. Silence engulfed them. The room was heavy with its presence.

'If you'll not swear an oath without knowing my name, I must give it. It is vital that you see me as a secure haven. If you are unsworn you'll not come when you need to.'

'You see the future? Lailoken and Ambrosius warned me against any who made such claims.'

The smile returned to her face.

'I am no seer, Arth-Ursus. It's a womanly knowledge I have, as deep as the land itself. Gwawl knows it too. A very human thing threatens you - your manliness. Only that prevents your success. I alone have the power to deal with it.'

'I know so little of my future. My tutors know me better than I know myself.'

'It is no more than the difference between a wise one and a novice. The wisdom of the elders comes with their years. I don't know how you will fulfil your destiny, but I can guide you in it.'

'So, then. My oath for your name, lady. I swear I shall seek you out in the future when I least wish to. Now tell me, to whom do I give this oath?'

'I have many names. The lady of the land; the white spirit of the forest. In your language, such translates as Gwynevhar,' she said.

'Gwynevhar,' he repeated.

'Then, Gwynevhar, you shall be my constant guide.'

'Your trials will be many, my lord. And they have just begun....'